KU-022-773

This novel is a work of fiction.
Names and characters are the
product of the author's imagination
and any resemblance to actual persons,
living or dead, is entirely coincidental.

For June and Peter Millership

Acknowledgements

Once again my sincere thanks to everyone at Random House for their continued support, especially my wonderful editor Georgina Hawtrey-Woore.

A big thank you to Caroline and everyone else at The Caroline Sheldon Literary Agency.

Acknowledgements

Chapter One

'Molly, Molly, where are you? I want you!' The plaintive cry that came from the back garden became a long-drawn-out wail and echoed through the house as eight-year-old Jodie Henderson searched everywhere for her sister.

'What do you want? I'm busy,' Molly replied. 'Mum needs me to help her get everything ready for this afternoon. Dad's coming home; you haven't forgotten; have you?'

'No, of course I haven't forgotten; that's what I'm scared about and why I need you,' Jodie wailed. 'I can't even remember what our dad looks like!'

As the whingeing cry turned into deep sobs Molly abandoned her dusting and polishing and went out into the garden to try and comfort her sister. A tall, thin twelve-year-old with bobbed nut-brown hair and turquoise blue eyes, Molly had an intelligent face with a generously curved mouth. She was thoughtful and kind; she could never bear to see her little sister upset.

Sitting down on the back doorstep she pulled Jodie on to her lap and gently stroked back the rather mousey, tousled straw-coloured hair from the small elfin face. Poor little mite, she thought compassionately, she'd gone short of so many things in her short life, no wonder she was so frail and nervous.

'Come on,' she said gently, 'tell Molly all about it; tell me what it is about Dad coming home that's worrying you.'

'I've told you. I can't remember him, not even what he looked like,' the little girl sobbed. 'Perhaps he won't love me or even remember me!' she added disconsolately.

'Of course he will,' Molly assured her gently, hugging her close. 'He's always loved you since the day you were born. He would never forget his little Jodie. You're very precious to him because you're the baby of the family.'

'I'm not a baby, I'm a big girl,' Jodie protested, pulling herself upright and hitting Molly on the arm.

'Then, in that case, you shouldn't be crying,' Molly told her, trying not to smile as she saw the indignant look on her sister's face. 'What do you think he's going to say if he arrives home and finds you with your face streaked with tears? He might believe you didn't want to see him and think how miserable that would make him feel.'

'I don't think I want him to come home,' Jodie snuffled. 'I like it as we are now; you, me, Mummy and Peter. We don't need

14

anyone else.'

'That's not a very kind thing to say, now is it? Our dad's been away at the war for four long years fighting to keep us all safe. He's had to live in a tent most of the time and he's had to suffer all sorts of hardships.'

'To keep us safe from what?' Jodie asked as she sniffed back a sob.

'From the enemy, of course. He's helped to stop the Germans coming here. Think how scary it would have been if they had managed to do that.'

'The only thing I'm frightened about is him coming home,' Jodie protested.

'He'll be home in time for your ninth birthday, just think of that!' Molly went on, ignoring her remark. 'You were only a very little girl when he went away so it's no wonder you can't remember very much about him.'

As she sat stroking Jodie's hair Molly inwardly sympathised with her sister. Although she was almost four years older than Jodie, she, too, could barely remember what their dad had been like when he'd gone into the army.

As far as she could recall he had been quite tall, broad and well built with thick black hair – the same as Peter had – and he had a craggy face and dark grey eyes. He'd always been dressed very smartly when he went to work, but at the weekends he wore grey flannels and a tweed jacket instead of his three-piece charcoal-grey suit.

She could remember he'd been fairly strict with her and Peter. He'd always been telling them to be polite and to mind their manners. He had always insisted that they put their toys away before they went up to bed. Shortly before he went into the army he had started making sure that Peter, who was a year and a half older than she was, cleaned his shoes every night.

On Saturdays he would take them to the park or down to the sea front at New Brighton for a walk. Sometimes it was just herself and Peter; at other times, their mum came as well and then she and Peter would push Jodie's pram while their parents walked along behind them.

On hot summer days he would sometimes buy them ice-cream cones and they'd all walk along the promenade licking them and seeing who could make theirs last the longest.

Ever since he'd been away Molly had dutifully sent him cards on his birthday and at Christmas. She always drew and coloured them in herself. She also wrote a letter to him once in a while. He'd never written back to her though, only sent his love and the occasional message in the letters he wrote to their mum and which she read out to them all.

For days now they'd been cleaning and polishing almost as if they were expecting royalty and she was sure that this was because their mother was as apprehensive as the rest of them were about him coming home.

For four years their mum had been the one in charge, coping with everything from running the house to budgeting the army allowance she received, and which had to keep them in food and clothes, pay the rent and all their expenses. There had been a lot of penny pinching and there had been very little left over to replace clothes or even boots and shoes as they outgrew them so hand-me-downs had become the order of the day.

Luckily her mum, Netta, was clever with her needle and she had cut down a lot of her own dresses to make clothes to fit Molly, and when she grew out of them, they were passed down to Jodie. Sheets were turned sides to middle when they became worn thin and the ragged edges were neatly trimmed off from towels when they started to fray and then they were either hemmed or neatened with blanket stitch so that they could still be used.

Most families whose breadwinner had gone off to war were in the same situation, reluctant to spend any of their allowance on anything other than food. So many things were in such short supply that prices had risen alarmingly, especially if they had to be bought from under the counter; yet often it was the only way to obtain them at all.

Ever since she had heard that their dad was back in England, and that they could expect him home quite soon, Molly's mother had been scrimping and saving and secreting away any foodstuffs that would keep so that she would be able to spoil him when he did arrive. It was a bit like the way they planned for Christmas, Molly thought, only this wasn't Christmas; it was April 1919.

The war had ended in November 1918, but like so many other soldiers, Bill Henderson had been kept in France to help with some of the clearing up that had to be done over there. When he'd arrived back in England there'd been further delays and although he was near enough to Liverpool for him to come home for a weekend he couldn't do so because they were confined to barracks.

Any day now, though, at long last he would be home for good; no longer a soldier but a civilian. He'd go back to his old job in the shipping office in Old Hall Street.

That would probably be almost as strange an experience for him as having him home was going to be for the rest of the family, Molly surmised. Still, he was lucky to have a job to go back to; many of the men who had returned from the army had discovered that their jobs had gone. They'd also found that getting a new one wasn't proving to be very easy so they had to stay on the dole which many of them thought was shameful.

While she'd been busy doing the cleaning her mother had been sorting out the clothes their dad had left behind when he'd gone into the army.

'I bet he can't wait to get back into his own clothes,' Netta sighed as she sponged and pressed the trousers of his dark grey suit and hung them up along with the jacket and waistcoat to air because they reeked of moth balls. 'He was always such a smart-looking man that he must be fed up with the sight of khaki,' she commented as she ironed his white cotton shirts with their detachable collars that he insisted must be starched so that they were stiff and shiny.

'Do you think his suit and the rest of his things will still fit him?' Molly asked.

'Of course they will,' Netta said briskly. 'He's a grown man, not a schoolboy who's still growing.'

'I know that, Mum, but after all this time he might be fatter or something.'

'Fatter?' Netta gave a hoot of laughter. 'He's been in the army, you ninny, not away on a holiday.'

'They have to give all the soldiers plenty of good food otherwise they won't be fit enough to fight,' Molly argued.

'They might feed the officers well, but not

the squaddies,' Netta said firmly. 'Anyway,' she added with a wry smile, 'these clothes will have to fit him whether he's fatter or thinner because we can't afford to buy new ones.'

'I wish we knew exactly when he would be home.'

'I've told you, any time now,' Netta told her impatiently.

'I know, but I wish we knew which day it was going to be. I hate the waiting. Every time there's a knock on the door I wonder if it is him.'

'He won't knock on the door, Molly! This is his home, he's not a visitor.'

Molly sighed. She'd never known her mother to be so tetchy. She seemed to be on edge too, the same as the rest of them. The sooner Dad arrived and they were all together again the better, she decided.

Bill Henderson sat on the edge of his bunk bed in Rawinstall Barracks. He'd been back in England for quite a while now, but like the rest of his company, even though he was a corporal, he'd been confined to barracks prior to being granted his discharge.

Tomorrow, with any luck, he thought, as he sorted his uniform into regulation piles and checked that everything was present and in good order, he would hand this lot in and be finished with the army for good. He couldn't wait to become a civilian once more and forget about all the horrors he'd experienced; all the mud and blood of the battlefield.

Tomorrow he would travel back to Liverpool, cross the Mersey to Wallasey, and be back with his family before the day was over.

It was four years, four long years, since he had seen them. It hadn't been an easy war for him, yet he was aware that in many ways he had been lucky because he had come through it more or less physically unscathed.

He had hated every minute of it. He'd disliked being shouted at and ordered around; he'd resented having his freedom curtailed; above all, he'd detested having to share his life with so many other men. He liked his own space, he didn't like people touching his possessions or helping themselves to his belongings.

He'd thought that once he had some stripes on his arm then life would be easier because then he would have some authority, but it hadn't made all that much difference. It had meant extra duties and responsibility and he'd still been shouted at by the sergeants and even by some of the officers.

He'd missed his wife and children but most of all he'd missed his home comforts. Even though it was rather small, their house in Derby Road was in a nice part of Wallasey. It was close to the central library and the park in Earlston Gardens. It was also within walking distance of the main shopping area in Liscard Village and there had been an excellent bus service to Seacombe to catch a boat over to Liverpool for work.

Until he'd been called up for the army he'd lived a well-ordered life. He'd had a responsible job in a shipping office; one that he'd grown to like. He'd worked there ever since he'd left school, and over the years he'd been promoted from office boy to senior clerk. If it hadn't been for the war, then in another few years, just as soon as old Dick Smart retired, he would have been promoted to take his place as Assistant Manager.

When that happened he'd planned to move from Derby Road to something a bit grander; a house which had a larger garden for the children.

Now, a big garden probably didn't matter quite so much as it had done then. Peter must be thirteen; Molly twelve and even little Jodie, who had still been in a pushchair when he'd been called up, would now be nearly nine.

He'd certainly see a difference in them, he thought as he packed away his cleaning kit. Probably see a difference in Netta as well. She'd be in her mid thirties now. He was thirty-eight. Another couple of years and he'd be forty and heading for middle-age. It didn't bear thinking about.

Four years of his life had gone by and his career was at a standstill, he reflected; what a waste it had been. Still, it was no good dwelling on that; the future was the thing. Next week, as soon as he was back at the office, he would be picking up the threads and showing them that he'd lost none of his skills or initiative and that he was more than ready for promotion.

He wondered how Netta had coped without him. She'd never been much of a letter writer, although he had to admit that she'd written regularly. She'd written every Sunday, although often he hadn't received her letters for weeks and then a whole bunch of them had turned up all at once. They were full of scraps of news about the kids and what they were doing at school, about all the shortages she had to cope with, and how much she was missing him.

On his birthday and at Christmas, Molly and Peter had sent him cards, usually ones they'd made themselves. Molly also wrote a letter to him now and again, but she didn't have a great deal to say either. Lately even hers had been short and uninteresting. It was almost as if they'd forgotten him.

Well, all that would soon right itself. He wasn't so concerned about Molly and Jodie, but he did wonder how Netta had coped with Peter. A boy of that age needed his dad to be around. Living in a house full of women he was probably either nagged to death or spoiled. He was bound to have lacked the sort of discipline as well as the masculine influence he would have had if his father had been at home.

Still, he'd soon sort that out and make a man of him. He'd seen too many weak-kneed specimens while he'd been in the army and knew how other men despised them. He intended to make sure that his son didn't fall into that category, he thought grimly.

He wondered what Peter intended to do when he left school next year. After the hardships he'd had to suffer, Bill didn't want a boy of his going into the army or navy. If Peter wasn't cut out for office work, then perhaps learning a trade would be the next best thing for him.

He would have liked to be a carpenter himself, he was fascinated by the feel of wood and what could be made from it, but his parents had thought that being a joiner or carpenter was too menial. They'd wanted their son to be a white collar worker which was why he'd ended up in a shipping office.

It had proved to be a fine job though and he'd enjoyed it and was looking forward to being back, earning good money again and supporting his family. Things must have been pretty tough for Netta trying to make do on his army pay.

The thought of being back home with his family, and above all with Netta, gave him a warm feeling of satisfaction. He'd missed them and welcomed the idea of being head of the household again.

Netta Henderson was well aware that her children were worried by the news that any day now their father would be coming home. He'd been away for four years, which was a long time in their young lives.

She was equally apprehensive. Before he'd gone away Bill had been the one in charge, and he'd expected the children to do as he said, but things had changed.

He'd always managed their finances. He'd given her a weekly sum for housekeeping, but he had paid all the other household bills. If she wanted anything, whether it was clothes or shoes, either for herself or for the children, then she only had to ask him for some money and tell him what she would be spending it on.

He hadn't given her any money for herself, but he was generous with the housekeeping allowance. Since he never checked up on how she spent it, she'd learnt to balance things so that she always had enough left over to buy herself the occasional magazine, lipstick or pair of stockings whenever she needed to.

If she wanted anything for the home, like

curtains, a rug for the fireside, or even new pots and pans for the kitchen, she found it was relatively easy to convince him that they were necessary.

In those days, she'd only smoked in the evenings or at weekends when Bill was there and she could help herself to his cigarettes. Occasionally she'd take a couple of extra cigarettes to have next day; sometimes he'd leave her a half packet saying he'd get some more on the way to work.

She had to admit Bill had always been very generous in so many ways. There had always been presents of lingerie and perfume for her birthday and at Christmas. He usually pretended that they were from the children and let them be the ones to give them to her. He'd always bought her major gifts like a new dress, or a coat, or even shoes and a matching handbag.

He liked to see her looking smart and well dressed so he was going to be shocked when he saw her now. She knew she looked down at heel and shabby in the patched and darned clothes she'd been reduced to wearing in recent months.

As she studied her reflection in her dressing-table mirror she wondered how he would react when they met up again after all this time. Four years was a long time and shortage of money as well as being unable to get hold of things in the shops had taken their toll on her appearance.

She sighed, her green eyes looked tired and drawn and her auburn hair, of which she'd been so proud, was dry and lifeless. For several years now she'd been washing it with ordinary soap instead of the special henna shampoo which she'd always used in the past and which had always left it looking bright and glossy.

She turned sideways and studied her figure. She still had plenty of curves even though food had been in short supply, but that was because she'd had to fill up on bread and potatoes, the same as the kids, or else go hungry.

Meat and eggs had been scarce and too expensive to buy on the black market even when they were available. Usually she had to make do with the cheaper cuts of meat and use plenty of vegetables to make them into scouse, broth or soup and then serve them up with chunks of stale bread.

However, things were slowly getting easier now, and the shops had more to offer, but she still only had enough money to buy the absolute basics.

Once Bill was back at work and bringing home a decent wage packet each week then that problem would be solved and it should make life easier for all of them, she thought hopefully.

Even so, she couldn't help wondering if he

might have changed. Living rough with a bunch of men, like he'd been doing for the past four years, was bound to have made a difference; possibly made him less considerate and patient than he had been.

Much as she was longing for him to be home again she couldn't help feeling a little nervous. He had been away such a long time that probably they were all going to need time to adjust. She wasn't the young submissive wife he'd left behind. These days she was used to standing on her own two feet, making her own decisions, and being the one in charge. She wasn't too sure how Bill was going to like that; at first they'd probably both find sharing their family obligations a little bit strange.

Chapter Two

From where she was lying naked on the double bed, Netta Henderson studied her husband's reflection in the full-length mirror of the wardrobe door as he rooted around for his clothes.

He didn't seem to have changed a great deal physically, except that he had lost some weight and what flesh there was on him was muscle, not flab. His hair was as dark and thick as ever, his grey eyes and his craggy features exactly as she remembered them.

His personality had certainly altered, she thought wryly. From the moment he'd come through the front door he'd been barking out orders as though he was still a corporal on duty in the army.

He'd barely been inside the house an hour before he'd told the children to run along to the park so that he could talk to their mother in peace, then he had ordered her upstairs on the pretext that he wanted to get changed out of his uniform and couldn't find his civvies.

The minute the bedroom door was closed he'd wasted no time in peeling off his uniform and ripping off her clothes. He was as lusty as ever and had barely uttered a word as he satisfied himself. She had forgotten how physical he could be, and how rough. Or was she just being over sensitive since it was so long since a man had made love to her? she asked herself.

She had been looking forward to feeling his arms around her and to being cuddled and petted first – or even afterwards – to hearing him say that he loved her and that he had been missing her as well as wanting her.

In the long lonely nights while he had been away she'd often been lonely and thought so much about their lovemaking. She had fantasised so often about his homecoming and dreamed of all the tender, seductive things he would say as they lay in bed together.

She had been faithful all the time he had been away, but that didn't mean she intended to go on being used simply to gratify his needs. Much as she loved him she felt that they had probably both changed and that now their marriage should be an equal partnership in lovemaking as well as in the way they organised their life together.

Had their abrupt coupling, without any warmth or tenderness on his part, been a warning that she was going to have to take a stand? she wondered uneasily. If she didn't she would once again be at his beck and call in more ways than one.

'It sounds as though the children are back, so get your clothes on and let's get downstairs. Tell Molly to make a pot of tea. There's probably a lot more you all have to tell me about what's been going on here in my absence,' he ordered.

'You go ahead, I'll be down in a few minutes,' Netta told him. Turning over on to her stomach she buried her head in the pillow to hide the frustration that she was feeling.

'I said now!' His voice was low and angry and the unexpected tone of his voice brought a spurt of tears to her eyes.

'Who the hell do you think you are talking

to?' she flared. 'I said I'd come down in a few minutes.'

'And I said that I wanted you to come down now, right away! Understand?'

Netta struggled to a sitting position, aware that he had the advantage of being fully dressed while she was still naked. 'Listen to me, Bill.' She pushed her hair back and faced him with as much dignity as she could muster. 'These days I don't take orders from you or anyone else. I stopped doing that when you went into the army. I've had to learn to stand on my own feet and as a result I'm used to being the one giving the orders around here, not taking them,' she told him firmly, her green eyes hard.

He'd never shown such anger towards her before and her eyes filled up with tears.

'Get dressed,' he snapped as he turned back to the mirror and concentrated on knotting his tie.

Afraid of causing a ruckus that would bring Molly running upstairs to see what was going on, Netta complied, but she was simmering with pent-up anger.

The children would be going to bed soon, and then she would confront Bill again and sort things out. She wasn't going to put up with this sort of attitude and the sooner she made that clear the better.

The rest of the evening didn't go at all well. As Bill pulled the big armchair up closer to the fire and settled himself into it, Jodie said innocently, 'You can't sit there, that's Mum's chair.'

'Well, it's mine now,' her father told her as he made himself more comfortable in it. Pulling a packet of cigarettes out of his pocket he lighted one.

'Come on, then, which of you is going to tell me what's been going on here all the time I've been away?' he questioned as he exhaled a cloud of smoke.

The three children looked at each other, each waiting for the other to speak, unsure exactly what he wanted them to tell him.

'I shall be leaving school at Christmas,' Peter announced.

'No you won't. You're not fourteen until next January,' his father stated.

'I know, but Mr Waters the headmaster said that as my birthday was only two days after the start of the new term I could leave at Christmas if I had a job to go to.'

Bill Henderson pulled thoughtfully on his cigarette. 'I see; so have you got a job to go to, then?' he demanded.

Colour flooded Peter's cheeks as he fiddled with a pencil and tried to avoid his father's eyes. 'Not yet I haven't, but I'm hoping I can find one before then.'

'Doing what?'

Peter looked uncertain. 'I ... I'm not sure,' he stammered, drumming the end of the

32

pencil on the table. 'I would like some sort of apprenticeship but it all depends on what there is when I start to look.'

'That's no way to plan your life,' his father sneered, stubbing out his cigarette angrily. 'You have to decide what you want to do and then look for a job, not the other way around.'

'I know that's what you should do, but there're not all that many jobs about and now with all you lot coming back there will be even fewer so I'll have to take whatever I can get.'

'Us lot coming back?' Bill Henderson scowled. 'What's that supposed to mean?' His voice rose louder. 'If we hadn't given up four years of our lives you wouldn't have the freedom to pick what sort of job you want to do. You'd be conscripted into the army; the Germans would have made sure of that,' he thundered.

Molly saw the tears glittering in Peter's eyes and tried to detract her father's attention. 'I'll be leaving school soon as well, Dad,' she said brightly.

'Don't interrupt me when I'm speaking. I'll talk to you when I've finished dealing with your brother. He's a boy, so his future is far more important than yours.'

All the pleasure Molly had tried to muster over her father's homecoming suddenly evaporated. She not only felt hurt and angry, but she could see that Jodie was becoming frightened by all the noisy exchanges.

'Mum, shall I take Jodie upstairs and help her get ready for bed?' she suggested, putting a comforting arm around her sister.

'Yes, luv, that might be a good idea,' Netta agreed, giving Molly a grateful smile. 'She does look tired. All this excitement seems to have worn her out. Give your dad a goodnight kiss, Jodie, I'll come up in a minute and tuck you in.'

'Stay right where you are,' Bill Henderson decreed as Jodie started to walk towards him. 'I'll say when you are going to bed. For the moment I want all three of you right here while I talk about what is going to happen in the future.'

No one spoke; all eyes became fixed on him apprehensively; fearful of what he was going to say next.

They'd looked forward to their dad's homecoming with a certain amount of trepidation, because they'd been so young when he'd gone away, but it was turning out to be far more frightening than any of them had imagined.

Their mother had told them stories about what a kind and loving dad he was. She often reminded them of how he had taken them out and played with them when they had been growing up, but at this moment none of them could imagine this hard-voiced, domin-

34

ating man ever doing anything like that.

They had grown used to the quiet voice of their mother telling them what to do and even the occasional nagging when they forgot to do the chores expected of them. They sensed that things were changing and that they would be very different now that their father was home again. They suspected that he wouldn't be anywhere near as easy going as their mum was.

Jodie started to snivel, clutching hold of Molly's hand and cuddling up against her as if for protection.

'You can stop that silly noise right away,' their father ordered, frowning at Jodie. 'Right, now sit down, all of you, and pay attention to what I'm going to say.'

He looked around the room with a critical eye as he waited for them to obey. He could see that it was clean and tidy and well cared for, like all the rest of the house, but it irked him that everything looked so shabby. The walls needed a fresh coat of distemper, the paintwork needed touching up. Surely Peter was old enough to have done jobs like that if Netta had told him to do so, he thought irritably.

'I have a feeling that you've done very much as you like while I've been away,' he commented severely. 'All that is going to change. For a start, you're all going to smarten yourselves up. Look at the state of your boots, Peter; when did you last clean them?'

'Last Saturday.'

'And you've not cleaned them since!'

'There's no shoe polish left and Mum said she couldn't afford to buy any more at the moment,' Peter muttered.

'Stop making such damned silly excuses,' his father exploded angrily.

'He's not making excuses; what he is saying is the truth,' Netta intervened quietly.

Bill held up his hand imperiously. 'I'm dealing with this,' he pronounced.

'No one is going to give you a job if you turn up with your shoes in that state,' he told Peter. 'From now on clean them every day, and you'll clean mine as well. That's only one of the jobs on the list of things I shall expect you to do.'

'I already clean all the shoes,' Peter told him. 'I do it every Saturday morning.'

'Once a week! That certainly won't do. No wonder you all look so scruffy. From now on, you do it every night before you go to bed. Understand?'

He waited for Peter to nod and mumble in agreement before he turned to Molly. 'Right! Now what about you? What chores are you responsible for doing?'

'I usually do the washing up every night, and I give Mum a hand with Jodie and take her to school. Mum comes and fetches her in the afternoon, though, because she comes out before I do,' Molly told him quickly.

'Washing up? You should be doing much more than that. Jodie is big enough to do that and she's old enough to get washed and undressed for bed without your help. You should be doing the ironing and mending as well as some of the cleaning.'

'Mum always does all those sorts of things while we are at school,' Molly told him.

'Your mother may have done them, but she won't be doing them any longer,' he corrected. 'From now on, the ironing and mending are your jobs and we'll decide what else later on. Remember, I expect my shirts and collars to be perfect – no creases, and pay attention to the cuffs; those should be wrinkle-free as well. Check that there are no missing buttons and that they are all sewn on securely as well. Understand?'

'I can't reach the sink and Mum says I'm not to touch the kettle when it is full of hot water,' Jodie piped up as he focused his attention on her.

'That's no excuse; we'll find a stool, or a box, for you to stand on until you've grown a bit taller,' her father told her. 'You can ask someone to pour the hot water out of the kettle into the washing-up bowl for you,' he added dismissively.

'Right, well, now you all know what is expected of you you can clear off to bed,' he

37

went on. 'In the morning, before you come down for breakfast, make sure you've made your bed and that you've left your bedroom neat and tidy. Anything that you leave lying around will be confiscated. Is that clear?'

Netta waited until the three children had gone upstairs before she turned on her husband, her face tense.

'What the hell do you think you are doing?' she demanded angrily. 'You've been home for barely half a day and already you are antagonising the children by treating them like slaves. They get all the discipline they need when they are at school. This is their home, Bill, not an army barracks.'

'Yes, and it looks a shambles,' he snapped. 'Everywhere looks shabby and run down, even the paintwork. From now on I want it to be spick and span at all times.'

Netta shook her head in dismay. 'What's happened to you, Bill? I'm not sure I know you any more.'

'I've learned how important discipline is,' he told her curtly, 'and I can see that it has been lacking here. I took a quick look at their bedrooms and they were like tips.'

'What utter rubbish. The children always hang their clothes up and make their beds; what more do you expect?'

'It's time that all three of them were taken in hand and made to toe the line,' he affirmed. 'You were always too soft with Peter

38

and Molly when they were little and now that they're older that's got to change. Jodie is spoiled, too. I've four more days at home before I'll be starting back at work, Netta, and in that time I intend to see that things are smartened up around here.'

'Really! Well, what if I don't want any of these changes to be made? I don't even approve of them, if it comes to that,' she added in a dangerously soft voice.

'We've never argued about domestic matters before and I don't intend to start now,' he told her dismissively. 'I'm the head of this family and what I say goes.'

'That may have been so in the past, Bill, but I've run things my way for the past four years, remember. We've had to go short of a great many things and if the place looks shabby it's because we've had to make do in order to get by. The one thing I've never skimped on has been showing the children love and affection. We've pulled together as a team and we've been happy, and I don't want that to change. You weren't regimented when you were a child, and neither was I, and I don't intend for our children to be treated in that way,' she told him defiantly.

For a long moment they stared at each other in silence. Netta was the first to speak.

'You go out and earn the money like you used to do, and leave me to run the home,' she told him quietly. 'It worked well enough before and it will again.'

He looked so angry that for a moment she thought he was going to start bullying her again so she quickly decided to change her tactics. She already suspected that if it came to an argument he would probably win because he could always remain so cool and logical at such times, whereas she became emotional.

Summoning up every ounce of courage she moved closer and, stretching up her hand, stroked his face gently. 'Come on, Bill, don't let's quarrel, not on your first night home.'

Impatiently, he brushed her hand aside and remained cold and unresponsive.

She took a deep breath, then kissed him on the brow. 'That's an order, soldier boy, not a request,' she said softly, her bright green eyes challenging.

Chapter Three

Bill Henderson was not a happy man. He had been looking forward to his release from the army ever since peace had been declared. As soon as he'd known the exact date of his discharge, he had been constantly visualising what sort of reception he would get when he arrived home.

Netta would be all dressed up for the occasion in her prettiest dress, her auburn hair shining, and she'd be so overjoyed to see him that she'd fling her arms round his neck and cover him with her lipstick kisses.

His three children would bound around him like playful puppies. He'd hug them, one by one, then he'd sit down with the littlest one, Jodie, on his knee and they'd hang on to every word he said.

The house would be exactly as he remembered it; newly painted and sparkling clean. Netta had always been a good housewife and proud of her home, and had made sure that it looked spick and span.

They'd all be so excited and pleased to see him that they wouldn't be able to do enough for him. Netta would brew a pot of tea and there'd be a plate of biscuits the moment he walked through the door. Even his slippers would be there ready for him by the side of his favourite armchair and they'd all be eager to wait on him hand and foot.

That's how he had imagined it would be, but it hadn't been like that at all. The three playful puppies had grown into a lanky, surly lad; a self-assured, almost grown-up daughter; and the baby of the family, little Jodie, a child who was now almost nine and had plenty to say for herself.

Netta was a faded version of the auburn-haired beauty who'd waved him off with tears clouding her bright green eyes. Instead of being as he remembered her, she now looked careworn and had drab, straggly hair. What was more, she was dressed in shabby, patched clothes and even had darns in her stockings.

Even more disturbing was the fact that she was no longer submissive, but appeared to be a self-opinionated tartar with a strong streak of independence. She seemed to have become a woman so used to dealing with things in her own way that she was obviously reluctant to let him resume his place as head of the household.

He'd put his foot down right away, of course, but instead of them all jumping to attention, like the men in his unit did when he barked out an order, they'd looked at him with resentment and the children had fear in their eyes.

He'd only intended to remind them of their places in the order of things, but since they had been so uncooperative he'd treated them in the same way as he handled unruly squaddies. He'd immediately laid down the law, made rules and ordered them to obey them.

It wasn't at all what he'd expected things to be like, but he knew when it was necessary to take a stand. It now remained to be seen how they reacted. He'd give them a reasonable time to adjust and then, if they weren't doing as he'd instructed, he'd take more stringent steps. He knew how to handle people; he'd had years of experience and he intended to make full use of it.

The first couple of days they were so slack that it took all his self-control not to scream at them. But he'd shouted at Netta, he thought ruefully. He regretted it the moment he saw the look on her face, but he had no intention of letting her know that. It would undermine his authority if he said that he was sorry.

She'd had a taste of what he could do, of what he was prepared to do, and he hoped it would not only teach her a lesson, but would also make her ensure that the children obeyed his orders as well.

As for them, Peter was so damn surly that he wanted to boot him up the backside. At least he wasn't snivelling all the time like young Jodie. She was such a frail-looking child that he didn't dare raise a hand to her. One slap and she'd be half dead!

The unknown factor was Molly. She seemed to be bright and intelligent. Although she didn't answer him back, or, for that matter, do anything at all to annoy him, it was the veiled look of disappointment in her turquoise eyes that infuriated him. It was all there, unspoken, but as clear as day that she didn't trust him. It left him feeling so bloody inadequate; and the worst of it was that he was pretty sure that she knew how he was feeling.

He'd arrived home late on the Thursday afternoon and so he resolved to give them a few more days before he really took them in hand; for the moment he had other things on his mind.

Returning to work had been another blow to his self-esteem. On Friday morning he'd telephoned his boss, Reginald Potter, to let him know that he was now at home and that he would be returning to work on the following Monday morning.

'Great to hear it, but there's no real hurry for you to come back to the office, you know, Bill. Enjoy some time with your family and get used to civilian life again; take the wife out and about, that sort of thing,' Reginald told him jokingly.

He wasn't having any of that; he'd been away from his job for four years, so what did he need to take another couple of weeks off for? All he wanted was to get back and pick up the threads of his former life.

On Monday morning he caught the ten past eight bus to Seacombe. He enjoyed being back into the rhythm of things. Walking up the floating roadway on to the *Royal Daffodil,* taking a couple of turns up on top deck before seeking the warm shelter of one of the saloons, and then joining the horde of people as they jostled to disembark when they reached Liverpool was almost like old times.

From the Pier Head it was only a brisk ten minutes' walk to Old Hall Street and he stepped out smartly, pleased to be arriving so promptly.

The reception he received from his colleagues was very mixed. Everybody shook hands with him, some slapped him on the back or made the usual fatuous remarks about being 'good to see you', and 'nice to have you back', but he was quite sure that not one of the buggers genuinely meant it.

As the day went on he had shock after shock: the entire general office had been moved round; his desk by the window had been taken over by someone else; and all the jobs for which he had been responsible had been divided up and shared out amongst the others. They'd devised a whole new system; a completely different way of running things, in fact. When he had questioned them about making so many changes he was told it was all to do with new shipping regulations or some nonsense.

Dick Smart was still there and he didn't look any older and seemed to have had a new lease of life. Dick was still the assistant manager, but in some strange way he had been moved sideways. Most of his previous responsibilities had been taken over by a young spindly-looking chap called Basil Perks who hadn't been fit enough to join the army. He'd had tuberculosis as a child and he looked as though a puff of wind would blow him away, but Dick claimed the man was a genius when it came to organisation.

Bill felt like a spare part for the first half-hour until they eventually found a desk for him to use. Even then he had to sit twiddling his thumbs for ages, waiting for them to allocate him some work, so that he had something to do. Then he was asked to fill out some custom forms and sort out some files and bring them up to date. That was the sort of work a junior did, not a man of his calibre.

Even the way they now processed things had been changed. It seemed that Basil Perks had instigated new methods of handling the accounts, making shortcuts that Bill most certainly didn't approve of or even like.

By midday he felt so brassed off that he went for a quick walk. He needed a chance not only to blow away the cobwebs, but also to have time on his own to weigh things up. He had an uncomfortable feeling that they were trying to push him out.

He'd discovered that this new chap who had more or less replaced him was a nephew of the boss's wife; which was probably one of the reasons why he had been moved into such a senior position and allowed to make so many changes. So where did that leave him? Bill wondered.

As he stood at the bar in a nearby pub, drinking a beer and smoking a cigarette, he was aware that involuntarily his hands were balling into fists at the very thought of what he would like to do to this upstart of a newcomer.

On his way back to the office he found himself wondering if he would have done better to have stayed on in the army rather than come back to so many disappointments: first, the changes in his family life and now here in the office as well; was this what he had fought for? Given his time over again and with hindsight, he'd have found some way of dodging the draft and staying home and keeping tight hold of his job.

But it was no good thinking like that, he told himself, the thing to do now was to change it all back to the way it had been before. He'd start by confronting Reginald Potter and demanding that he was reinstated as Senior Clerk.

When he arrived back at the office he found that Reginald Potter had already left for the day. Even more annoying was the information from Basil Perks that Mr Potter wouldn't be back in the office for at least two days.

The rest of the afternoon proved to be

even more frustrating than the morning had been. No one was interested in his opinions, he was given the most mundane jobs to do, and twice he was told he'd not done them properly.

By the time he joined the throng of people walking up the gangplank on to the *Royal Daffodil* for the six o'clock sailing back to Wallasey, he was inwardly seething.

The sly jibes and the affected surprise when he had questioned anything had irritated him. He suspected they were belittling him on purpose and he didn't intend to stand for it. Once Reginald Potter was back at his desk he'd ensure that he made this perfectly clear. He'd demand to be reinstated immediately in his old job or, better still, even be promoted to the position of Assistant Manager that he'd been promised would be his in due course.

In the meantime, Bill resolved, he'd concentrate on putting things at home in order. He might have to take insolence at work, but he certainly didn't have to stand for it from his family.

Once again he found himself thwarted.

The moment he entered the house, Netta called out to say that their meal was ready and that she wanted to dish up right away because Molly had to be at her typing class by seven o'clock.

The meal was scouse with treacle pudding

to follow. The scouse didn't have very much meat in it and when he pointed this out, Netta laughed.

'It's got twice as much as usual and most of that is on your plate,' she told him. 'You're not in the army now. Meat is a luxury; we're lucky if we can afford to buy it once a week and then it has to be the cheapest cut and usually has to make enough scouse to last for two or even three days.'

He ate his pudding without comment, but he could tell from the exclamations of delight from the children that they considered it to be a special treat. Netta shared it out very carefully as if to make sure that everyone had the same size portion. He would have liked a second helping but there wasn't a scrap left.

The minute she'd finished eating hers Molly pushed back her chair, kissed Netta, and said, 'I'll try to be home just after nine, Mum.'

'Hold on, young lady, you have to help clear this lot up first. Jodie can do the washing up, but I expect you and Peter to clear the table, help carry the dirty dishes through to the kitchen and, after Jodie's washed them, to dry them and put them away.'

'I know, but I can't do it tonight, Dad,' Molly explained. 'I'm going to night school. I'll be late if I don't leave right away.'

'Then you should have thought about that

49

and made sure that our meal was on the table earlier,' he told her.

'It was ready earlier, but we had to wait for you to come home, didn't we?' she pointed out quietly.

For a moment he wondered if Molly was deliberately being cheeky. Before he could reprimand her Netta intervened.

'She's right, Bill. Normally on a Monday we have our meal over long before now so that Molly can get to night school on time.' Turning to Molly she said, 'Hurry up then, run along or you'll miss the bus into Liscard and then you'll really be late.'

Bill felt nonplussed. He decided that for the moment it was probably best to say nothing. Then he became aware that while their discussion had been going on Peter had slunk quietly out of the room and he could hear him going upstairs.

Immediately, he shouted to him to come back down and clear the table. He bellowed so loud that Jodie burst into tears and even Netta looked taken aback.

'Let him go, Bill, he probably has home-work to do. I'll clear up here; it's what I usually do anyway. You go and sit by the fire and read your newspaper and I'll bring in a cup of tea for you,' she said, smiling patiently.

He was well aware that she was trying to restore peace, but he wasn't having his authority undermined. He was determined to establish that now he was home he was the one who gave the orders around the place and not his wife.

He sank back in his armchair by the fire, but even though he opened up his newspaper he couldn't concentrate on it. Instead he sat there brooding about what he was going to say to Netta when she brought in his tea.

When Jodie brought it instead of Netta he felt so annoyed that when he noticed that she had spilled some into the saucer it was the last straw and it took all his self-control not to clip her round the ear.

'Take it away and tell your mother to bring me in a fresh cup and to bring it herself this time,' he rasped. 'And for God's sake stop snivelling all the time, Jodie. I can't speak to you without you bursting into tears.'

'Perhaps if you spoke to her in a reasonable tone of voice, instead of bellowing as if you were on the barrack square, then she wouldn't be so frightened,' Netta told him as she handed him his tea.

He stared at her and scowled. 'Are you criticising me?'

'Commenting and offering a spot of advice, certainly not criticising; I wouldn't dare do that,' Netta said mildly. 'You've spent the last four years mixing with burly men; Jodie is only a little girl and she's easily frightened.'

'And whose fault is that? You're spoiling her like you've done with Peter and Molly. You allow them to do whatever they want instead of letting them know you're in charge.'

'They're good kids,' she told him earnestly. 'I'm trying to make sure they're independent and able to think for themselves. I don't order them to do things because I don't believe that is the right way to bring them up.'

'So you wait on them hand and foot, let them ride roughshod over you, and do nothing about it?'

'Of course not! It's not like that at all. If they are doing something I don't agree with, then I tell them so and we talk it over and I explain why I don't like them doing it.'

'And then they stop?'

'Usually, but not always, because sometimes after they've explained what is going on I can see they are acting in the right way.'

Bill laughed cynically. 'Good job you're not in charge of an army unit; they'd run rings round you. Discipline is the key; that and letting them know that you are the one in charge.'

'So that is what you are planning to do here now that you're home?'

He saw an angry glint come into her eyes and for a moment he felt unsure and wondered if he was handling this as well as he might.

He sipped his tea thoughtfully. He obviously wasn't going to find this as easy as he'd imagined. Netta was like a tiger with cubs when it came to the children so he'd have to plan his tactics as skilfully as an army manoeuvre.

Instead of taking the whole lot of them on together, he decided, he'd tackle them individually. It would take longer, but in the end he'd bring them all to heel. He lit a cigarette to help him concentrate on his strategy.

The right move might be to start with Molly, he felt. Break her spirit and make her obey his orders and that would show the others what was expected of them.

If he made sure that Netta understood that he intended to be obeyed and what would happen if Molly didn't conform, then she'd soon convert the others and bring them into line without him having to raise a finger.

It was for their own good, he thought smugly. They'd all thank him when they were older, surely Netta could see that.

Chapter Four

The rest of the week at Derby Road seemed to pass in a peaceful haze although all of them felt slightly apprehensive about what the future might bring.

Bill Henderson went off to his office each morning outwardly calm but inwardly seething. He had decided to do nothing until Friday and then face Reginald Potter with his ultimatum. He could see that his return had caused something of a hiatus but he had no intention of working there as a dogsbody, or under the thumb of a little upstart like Basil Perks.

Netta hoped that now that Bill was back at the office, and had an interest outside the home, he would leave them to continue as they had while he had been away.

Peter tried to ignore his father and avoid him as much as possible. He decided that life had been far easier while he had been away but he kept those thoughts to himself. He could see that young Jodie was scared stiff of their dad and he felt sorry for her. She was such a fragile-looking little thing and too sensitive for her own good when anyone criticised her or told her off.

Molly also felt apprehensive but she didn't know why. Several times she had caught her dad looking at her so speculatively that she felt uneasy. It was almost as if he was holding a grudge of some sort against her and she couldn't work out why that was.

He had seemed so annoyed because she had gone off on Monday night to her evening class. She would have thought that he would be pleased that she was studying shorthand and typing to try and better herself ready for when she left school. Perhaps he was worried in case she might start pestering him to get her a job in his office, but that was the last thing she wanted to do.

Molly couldn't understand why he was so moody and withdrawn. He criticised everything and didn't seem to show very much pleasure in being back at home. She had asked him one or two questions about his life in the army, but he'd said he didn't want to talk about it and more or less told her to shut up because talking about what had happened only gave him nightmares.

Her mother had told her afterwards not to mention it again. She had tried to talk to him about what had gone on in France and he had told her that it was all in the past and that he wanted to put it all out of his mind now that he was back home again.

'You'd better warn Peter, although I don't think he's likely to start up a conversation with his dad of his own free will,' Netta commented. She smiled sadly. 'I thought it would be great for the two of them to get together and that his dad would take an interest in the things Peter was doing, but it seems I was wrong. They avoid each other as much as possible.'

'Perhaps that's just as well,' Molly told her. 'Everything Peter says or does seems to be wrong. Peter doesn't like having his ears boxed, either, especially when it's in front of everyone. He'll be starting work soon so he doesn't enjoy being treated like a naughty schoolboy.'

'Yes.' Her mother frowned. 'Things aren't turning out at all like I had imagined they would,' she confided. 'Your dad has changed so much; he seems to have lost all his pleasure in everything, including his family. Even little Jodie seems to get on his nerves.'

'Well she has been rather difficult ever since he came home. I think she's disappointed. I don't know what she was expecting, because she says she can't really remember him before he went into the army. I think she thought she would be getting a lot of love and cuddles; instead, he seems to find fault with everything she does and she gets frightened whenever he raises his voice or even looks at her.'

'I know.' Netta frowned again. 'And I know that you are doing all you can to console her. Things will get better once he is more used to being at home. I don't think he's finding things very easy at work and that isn't helping. From what little he's told me someone has been brought in to do his job while he's been away and he doesn't like the way they're doing it.'

'Well, he wouldn't, would he! Nothing we do here at home is right,' Molly pointed out. 'He even criticises the food you give him even though you serve him the very best of it and a bigger portion than anyone else gets.'

'I think we'd better stop talking about him like this,' Netta told her firmly. 'He's your dad, remember, and he's had a hard time of it. I'm hoping that things will change for the better this weekend. I'm going to suggest that the two of us go out on Saturday night. You and Peter will be here to look after Jodie.'

Molly's face brightened. 'Where are you going?'

'Nowhere in particular. I thought I could get dressed up and your dad and me could perhaps go to the pub for a drink. We used to like going out on a Saturday night; it was one of the highlights of the week before Jodie was born and Granny and Granddad Henderson used to come and stay with us. It might help to cheer him up.'

'Do you good as well, Mum,' Molly told

her with a smile. 'You haven't been out anywhere like that for ages and ages, not since they died, in fact. Can I tell Peter? We'll play Snap or Snakes and Ladders with Jodie, which will be a treat for her as well.'

'Thanks, luv.' Netta gave her daughter a quick hug. 'I don't know how I would manage without you. Now shall we start getting the meal ready? I want it to be something special because this will be your dad's first pay day since he's come home so it ought to be a bit of a celebration.'

Bill Henderson was in a foul temper as he made his way towards the Pier Head to catch the boat back to Wallasey.

His knuckles were still sore and bruised from the thumping he'd given Basil Perks and although he felt no regrets at all about putting the cocky young upstart in his place he was devastated by the outcome of their brawl.

He had always thought that he and Reginald Potter had established a sound working partnership. True, Reginald had shares in the company, whereas he was merely an employee, but they were on first-name terms and had worked together for so many years that he considered him almost a friend.

Well, he certainly wasn't that, Bill reflected gloomily, not any more anyway. It proved that blood was thicker than water as his old mum had always said. Reginald had taken Basil Perks's side when it came to the fracas between them and Bill was quite sure it was only because Basil Perks was Reginald's wife's nephew.

Anyway, he didn't really care because he knew he could never have gone on working there. It was bad enough that Basil Perks had wormed himself into his chair while he'd been away and changed the way everything in the office was done, but when he discovered that he was being paid two pounds a week more than him, well that really was the end.

He hadn't minced his words; he'd told Reginald straight what he thought of such contemptible behaviour. He'd been shocked to the core when Reginald had said that if he didn't like it then he'd better look for something else.

That wasn't the sort of answer he'd wanted. He'd expected him to say that, given a week or so, everything would be sorted out. He'd be Senior Clerk again and in charge of everything or, better still, would be made Assistant Manager.

It had been a long hard week, but even so he shouldn't have told him exactly what he thought about him and his job. To make matters worse Basil Perks had walked into Reginald's private office at the precise moment he'd said it and the fatuous smirk on his pimply face had been the last straw.

He'd seen red; as his fist made contact he'd had a rush of adrenalin, almost the same as when they'd been ordered 'over the top' when he'd been out in France in the trenches.

Seeing Basil Perks drop to the floor like a stone had been a bit of a shock. He'd lain there so still that for a moment Bill felt a cold sweat trickling down the nape of his neck because he thought he'd killed him.

His heart had been going like a sledge-hammer as Reginald had pushed him to one side, dropped down on to his knees, hastily loosened Perks's bow tie and removed his horn-rimmed spectacles which were dangling from over one ear, and repeated his name louder and louder.

He'd breathed a sigh of relief when Perks had groaned and then opened his eyes and he knew that he would be all right.

There'd been a general how-do-you-do as other clerks from the general office rushed to help. Someone fetched a wet towel and somebody else supported Basil Perks and held a glass of water to his ashen lips and, at the same time, tried to stem the blood gushing out from his nose and oozing from his cut lip.

He'd stood there helpless, knowing they all regarded him as the villain, but he had nothing to say because he was damned if he was going to apologise. When he remained silent, Reginald Potter delivered the ultimate blow: instant dismissal.

'I've already handed you your pay packet for the work you've done here this week,' he said tersely, 'so you needn't come in again and don't expect a reference.'

And that had been it. As he'd collected his coat and bowler hat from the coat stand Bill had seen that they were all hanging about in the general office waiting to see what happened next so he'd shrugged on his coat and left without a word to any of them.

Instead of going for his boat he turned into the nearest pub, ordered himself a whisky, tossed it down in one gulp, and then ordered another. The fiery liquid brought him back to normality and as he slowly sipped the second one he realised that he was going to have to break the news to Netta that he was out of work.

What a wonderful start being back in civilian life was turning out to be. His home was shabby, his wife and kids seemed to be terrified of him and, as far as he was concerned, they were like strangers. He didn't know them any more. He remembered small happy children who'd climbed on his lap, put their arms round his neck and hung on his every word. Now, he thought gloomily, he'd got a son who was almost ready to go out to work and was so damn surly and uncommunicative that he might as well be a foreigner. He had two daughters, one who looked at him in a supercilious manner as if she resented and despised him, and the other who was such a whingeing cry baby that he daren't look at her let alone talk to her before she burst into tears.

He delved into his inside pocket and brought out a photograph of Netta that he'd carried with him all through the war. She'd been such a good-looking woman. Now she had turned into someone who only seemed to be interested in what she put on the table, not in making him happy the way a wife should. Half the time he felt as if she only suffered him in bed because she knew it was her duty to do so.

Bugger the lot of them, he thought as he downed a fourth tot of whisky and stumbled out of the pub. For two pins instead of going home he'd get on a train at Lime Street Station and set off into the unknown and leave them to sort themselves out.

Telling Netta he'd lost his job was only going to be the tip of the iceberg. They'd have to leave their house in Derby Road, the rent of that was well out of their reach if he was on the dole. And anyway, he wouldn't get any dole because he'd left his job of his own free will; leastways, that's what Reginald Potter would claim.

Netta couldn't believe her ears when Bill told her what had happened.

She could see that he was the worse for drink and she wondered if he had his story muddled.

'You've only been back at work a week, you haven't had time to settle back in,' she exclaimed weakly.

'Bloody well long enough for that little sod Basil Perks to get up my nose,' he snarled. 'Don't start lecturing me,' he warned as he pushed aside the plate of food she'd put on the table in front of him. 'You have no idea what goes on in the working world. All you have to deal with is a couple of kids who know that they have to do what you tell them.'

Netta said nothing as she finished dishing up and passed the children their plates. She'd made shepherd's pie and even added cheese to the topping to make it extra tasty. It had always been his favourite and seeing him push it to one side made her feel like crying.

The children were starving as it was almost an hour past their usual meal time and they, at least, tucked in with gusto. She tried to do the same but her mind was full of the news and what that was going to mean.

There was no longer any army allowance coming in and there would be no wage packet either and they had a pile of bills waiting to be paid.

Whatever else they went short of she couldn't deprive growing children of their food. Yet if they didn't pay the rent...

She closed her mind to the problem. There was no point in panicking, it might be best to wait until after the children were in bed and then find out how Bill intended to deal with the dilemma they were now in.

The moment they'd finished their meal Peter asked if it was all right for him to go out.

'Of course, luv, don't be late home, though.'

'Jodie is going to help me wash up,' Molly said quickly, 'and after that I'll read her a story before she goes to bed. I've got some shorthand homework to do so I'll stay up in my room afterwards and get on with it,' she added.

Netta smiled at her gratefully as she closed the kitchen door and went back into the living room to see what Bill had to say.

His solution left her shaking and open-mouthed in disbelief.

'You can't mean that,' she gasped. 'This is our home, we can't leave here. You haven't even tried to find another job yet. Maybe I can find something; working in a shop, helping at the school at dinner time, or something.'

'What sort of money are those piss-farting kinds of jobs going to bring in?' he said contemptuously.

'Well, not a lot. I know that, but if I could find a job in a shop, or perhaps a hairdresser's, it might help tide us over until you find something.'

'Oh yes! And where are you going to find a shop that is prepared to let you finish every afternoon in time to be here to look after young Jodie when she comes home from school?'

'Well, there is that.' She nodded worriedly, and then her face brightened. 'Perhaps I could get one of the other mums to bring her back from school and then Molly could look after her until I got home.'

'Don't talk so bloody daft. There're only about half a dozen shops in Liscard where you could get work and they all want young bright girls with no ties – and they've no trouble getting them, either.'

'I know there're not many, but at least I can try.'

'To get decent money you'd have to work in Liverpool and how the hell can you do that?'

'So what else are we going to do?'

'We're going to move from this house for a start. We'll find something at half the rent.'

Netta shook her head. 'We're happy here. It's been our home for so long that I don't want to move. The children are all settled in their schools. If we move out of the area, they'll have to go to different schools.'

'That won't hurt them, it will help to sharpen them up, to teach them a bit about life. What's more Peter and Molly can get part-time jobs.'

'If you don't think that I stand a chance of getting a job, then what makes you think they'll be able to?' she argued angrily.

'No, they won't find any on this side of the water, I agree with you there.'

'Well, I'm certainly not letting them go over to Liverpool at night or on a Saturday, if it comes to that. Think of what that would cost! They'd spend half their wages on bus and boat fares.'

'Not if they were already living in Liverpool.'

Netta stared at him, horrified. 'You want us to go and live over the other side?' she gasped.

'Why not? It's where the work is and it only costs half what it does to live here. You'll be able to buy meat and vegetables in the market rather than in posh shops where you're paying through the nose for everything.'

'No, Bill. I don't want to change all our lives like that. I've had to pinch and scrape for the past four years to try and get by on army allowance. I was looking forward to you bringing home a decent wage packet once more and for all of us to be able to have new boots and shoes as well as clothes. I'm sick and tired of making the girls' dresses out of my old ones, and struggling to be able to afford boots and clothes for Peter.'

'For Christ's sake, stop belly-aching, woman,' he laughed harshly. 'Let me tell you, I've had it a damn sight harder. You may think you've had it tough, but it's nothing to what's coming!'

Chapter Five

As Netta went upstairs to make sure that Jodie was in bed, kissed the overtired child goodnight and tucked her in, she wondered how on earth they were going to manage now that Bill had no job. She had only twenty-five shillings left in her purse and there was the rent to pay the next morning.

At least it meant that they had a roof over their head for the coming week, she told herself philosophically. But it also meant that there would be hardly anything at all left for food, and because it was the end of the week the larder was practically bare.

She'd been expecting a generous amount of housekeeping money from Bill, like she'd had before he went into the army, but he hadn't stumped up anything so far and, remembering how his breath had smelled of whisky when he had arrived home, she wondered how much he had wasted on booze.

She'd been looking forward to being able to afford a few extra luxuries when she went to the baker's, the butcher's and the greengrocer's. Now she couldn't even afford to buy their basic groceries because, with the mood he was in, she was afraid to even ask him for any money.

As she came out of the girls' bedroom, Netta noticed that Peter's door was already closed and she guessed that he had come in the back door and gone straight up to his bedroom in order to avoid his father's company.

For a moment she stood there on the landing, wondering whether to go in and speak to him or whether it was better to leave matters alone since it seemed pointless to do so. There was very little she could say to explain the turmoil that seemed to have erupted since his dad had come home.

'Would you like me to make you and Dad a cup of tea, Mum?' Molly asked, coming out of her bedroom and giving Netta an understanding smile.

'Thanks, luv.' Netta gave her daughter's arm a friendly squeeze. 'I'd love one.' Her head ached with the worry of it all and she felt full of foreboding about the future.

'Go and sit down in the living room, then, and I'll bring the tea in as soon as the kettle boils.'

Bill was asleep, sprawled in an armchair with his feet on the fender, snoring spasmodically in deep drunken gasps. Netta sat there quietly until Molly brought in their tea, mulling over what she was going to say to him.

'You've only brought in two cups,' Netta pointed out as Molly placed the tray on the side table.

'I know. I'm going to have an early night and that will give you and Dad a chance to finish sorting things out.' She gave a twisted smile as she nodded towards the recumbent figure and added softly, 'Good luck! I think you are going to need it.'

Netta gave the tea a couple of minutes to brew then she filled her own cup. She'd wake Bill before she poured his, she decided. He liked his tea very strong, so black that it was almost stewed.

He was still snoring when she'd finished drinking her tea and no amount of prodding or calling his name made any difference. She carried the tea things back out into the kitchen, left the tea in the pot, and covered it over with the teacosy to keep it warm, then she went back into the living room and tried again to wake him.

When it had no effect at all she went upstairs and collected a blanket from their bed, put it over him and decided to leave him there to sleep it off.

She hadn't expected to sleep with so much going on in her mind, but the moment she put her head down on the pillow she went into such a solid sleep that it was daylight before she woke up. She probably wouldn't have done so then but it was the sound of someone hammering on the front door that roused her.

Rubbing the sleep from her eyes she looked at the bedside clock and was shocked to see that it was gone nine o'clock. Hastily she scrambled out of bed. It would be the rent man. He always called early and usually she was up and they'd all had their breakfast, even on a Saturday morning.

She opened the window to call out to him that she would be down in a moment, but as she did so she realised that someone had already opened the door and that they were talking to him.

Thank goodness for that, she thought in relief as she quickly pulled on her skirt and blouse and ran a comb through her tousled hair to try and restore some order to it.

She was halfway down the stairs when she heard the commotion. At the same time the other bedroom doors opened. Peter and

Molly were both beside her on the landing, peering down at the scene in front of them in horror.

Bill, unshaven and in his shirt sleeves, was shouting and arguing with the rent man and, in the next second, his fist had caught the man full in the face and sent him crashing to the ground.

The hullabaloo had brought one of the neighbours round to see what was happening and as he looked at the prostrate figure lying on the doorstep he hastily moved back as if afraid he might be the next target for the flying fist.

As the rent man was helped to his feet he left everyone in no doubt that he was going to bring a case of assault against Bill and he warned Netta that she'd probably lose the tenancy of Derby Road. A small crowd gathered. Someone called the police and before Netta knew what was happening there was a bobby on the doorstep threatening to arrest Bill for what he had done. With so many witnesses she realised that there was no way of making peace.

The policeman made copious jottings in his notebook and before he left warned Bill that he would be hearing further from him and said that although he was not arresting him, Bill would have to appear in court sometime in the near future.

As soon as they could shut the front door

71

and be on their own, Netta sent the children back upstairs to their rooms and rounded on her husband. She was too angry for tears, but he was equally furious about what had taken place.

'How do you think we are ever going to face the neighbours after something like this? The whole street knows about it,' she said.

'Bugger the neighbours. Gawping bloody lot coming here and poking their nose into our affairs. Who gives a damn about what they say or think?'

'Well, I do for one,' she told him sharply. 'Think of the children when they have to face all their friends. By Monday morning it will be all round the school. I'd better put my hat and coat on and take the money down to the office in Liscard. With any luck I can be there before the rent man finishes his rounds and gets back and then they will have heard my side of the story first.'

'Rent money? What are you bloody well talking about? We're not paying that bugger another farthing,' he declared as he snatched the money from her. 'We're going to be out of here before the weekend is over. You can start packing now. I'm off across to Liverpool to find us a couple of rooms and to fix up for someone to collect our bits and pieces. What we can't take we'll sell or leave behind.'

Netta stared at him in disbelief. 'What's got into you, Bill? You've only been home a week and you're causing turmoil. I don't want to leave here and neither do the kids and I certainly don't want to live in Liverpool.'

'Well, that's where you're all going to live, so like it or lump it. What's more we're doing it right now so stop gabbing on about it and start packing.'

Without another word he strode out into the hall, took down his overcoat and trilby, and slammed out of the house.

Molly and Peter came rushing down the stairs the moment they heard the door close. It was obvious from the look on their faces that they had heard everything. They both began to protest about the idea of moving away from Wallasey, but Netta silenced them.

'I don't think we have much choice. If we don't pay the rent, we will definitely be turned out and, even if we do pay, they may still claim that we are undesirable tenants because of what has happened here today.'

Bill was back by mid-morning looking extremely pleased with himself. His mood had changed and he frowned darkly when he saw that none of them had made any attempt to pack up any of their belongings. Immediately he began dishing out orders as if they were a bunch of squaddies.

'Molly, make some tea. Peter, start dismantling the beds. You, young Jodie, start

73

folding up all the blankets and the rest of the bedding and wrap them in a sheet and then tie them up in bundles. Come on, get moving, I've got a chap coming round with a van at three o'clock and we want to be over in Liverpool, unpacked and settled in before bedtime.'

'For heaven's sake, Bill, calm down and talk sense,' Netta pleaded. 'We don't want to move away from here. Give me the rent money and I'll take it down to the office. If I go now I'll just manage to make it before they close at midday.'

'Don't you listen to a single word I say, woman?' he snapped, rounding on her with a thunderous look on his face. 'We're not staying here, and we are certainly not paying over any rent. I've made all the arrangements, so start packing! As well as clothes and all the other clobber, you'll need to take your pots and pans and anything else you can from the kitchen. Now move!'

'Do you still want that cup of tea making, Dad?' Molly called through from the kitchen.

'Of course we do. Cut up some sandwiches as well, you can eat them as you work. You can take the curtains down and roll them up in bundles, and don't forget the rugs from beside the beds as it's bare floorboards where we're going.'

'What do you want me to do now?' Peter

asked as he picked up one of the corned-beef sandwiches Molly had made and started eating it.

'Taking a break, are you?' Bill commented sarcastically. 'Get back to work and shift some more stuff. And keep an eye on young Jodie, or she'll be snivelling and crying and driving me mad.'

'Where is it in Liverpool we're going?' Netta asked.

'A street off Scotland Road.' He slurped a mouthful of tea. 'No point in me telling you its name, because you wouldn't know it.'

'Scotland Road? Isn't that down near the docks?' Peter questioned.

'It's the slums of Liverpool, we can't live there!' Netta said in a shocked voice.

'Mum's right,' Peter agreed. 'All the schools around there will be awful.'

'Well, that won't worry you, whacker, because you won't be going to school,' his father told him.

'What do you mean?'

'You'll be finding yourself a job and earning a bob or two to help out, so the nearer we are living to the docks the easier it will be for you to get some work.'

'Peter can't leave school until Christmas,' Netta reminded him.

'No one in Liverpool is going to know that; and anyway, he'll soon be fourteen.'

'The school board man will soon start

making enquiries if Peter doesn't go to school and then he'll be round knocking on the door to know why and we'll find ourselves in real trouble,' Netta pointed out worriedly.

'If they ever find us! I'm not telling anyone where we're going and if I find out that any of you have opened your gobs, then you'll be getting the hiding of your life. A long lanky drip like him will pass for fourteen, no trouble at all.'

'Do you mean we mustn't tell our friends that we're leaving Wallasey or where we're going to be living in Liverpool?' Molly gasped, her bright turquoise eyes wide with dismay.

'I've already told you, not a bloody word to anyone. We move out of here without any farewells or goodbyes to the neighbours or anyone else. We're not telling any of the buggers around here that we are going. What's more, none of you contact anyone over on this side once we cross the Mersey. Now is that understood?' he demanded, glaring at them all fiercely.

'What about my evening classes?' Molly persisted. 'Will I be able to come back over on Monday nights for those?'

'Forget about them. You'll be too busy finding yourself a job delivering newspapers as well as a Saturday job to earn a few extra bob to have time for any of that nonsense.'

'But—'

'From now on, girl, we're all going to have to pull our weight if we're going to survive. There's no army allowance or fat pay packet to keep you in comfort like before. Now, the whole lot of you, stop gabbing and put your backs into getting everything packed up and ready for the carrier when he arrives.'

By three o'clock all the belongings they were going to take were packed and most of them were stacked up in the middle of the floor in the living room.

'There won't be room for all this,' Bill admitted, 'but I'm planning on selling what we don't need in order to raise some money to tide us over until we all find work of some sort.'

Netta felt a lump in her throat as she looked at all her precious belongings. Even though they seemed to be much shabbier than when they were in their rightful places, they still meant a great deal to her.

Her head was whirling so much that she couldn't believe what was happening. She didn't dare to let herself think ahead to what was in store for them when they reached the other side of the Mersey.

Jodie was standing by the window, sucking her thumb and clutching her favourite doll. She looked so woebegone that Netta pulled the child into her arms, stroking her hair and hugging her close to try and comfort her.

A battered dark green van arrived almost at the same moment and as a scruffy-looking man in a khaki overall and a greasy grey cap jumped down from the cab Bill had the door open before he could knock on it.

The man opened the back door of the van and after a quick exchange about their plans he and Bill unloaded a pile of tea chests and brought them into the house.

'This is Fred,' Bill announced. 'He says he wants to be finished by six so get moving, the lot of you. Molly, you go and make us all a drink, and your mother and sister can pack all the china and stuff into these boxes. Make sure you wrap up anything that is likely to get broken in newspaper or clothes,' he reminded them.

'You can start carrying some of the other things out to the van, Peter. Leave Fred to stack them because he knows what he's doing. As soon as the tea chests are packed then I'll give you a lift with them. Understand?'

They loaded everything into the back of the van and Netta inwardly shuddered as she heard the sound of glass breaking when they dropped one of the tea chests.

'I'm going in the van with Fred,' Bill announced when they finally finished packing everything in and had even strapped some of the pieces of furniture on top of the van. 'I'm taking Peter with me to help us get the stuff unloaded.'

'What about us?' Molly demanded.

'You and your mother brush this place out and leave it tidy, then lock the front door and push the keys through the letter box. Don't go taking them down to the office for that rent bugger. Let him come looking for them when he realises we've gone. If he hasn't got a spare set, then he'll have to break in and that'll serve him damn well right,' he added with a bitter laugh.

He handed Netta a scrap of paper. 'This is the address; we'll see you and the girls there later.'

Netta looked at the piece of paper, frowning and shaking her head. 'Hold on, Bill. I don't know Liverpool and I've no idea where this place is.'

'Catch a bus to Seacombe and then get the boat over to Liverpool. You can get a tram from the Pier Head which will take you all the way to Scotland Road.'

'Yes, but what part of Scotland Road? I've never been there in my life but I've heard that it's a long road.'

'Then you'll have to ask someone. You've got a tongue in your head, haven't you?'

'Well yes, but it is going to take ages. I would sooner be there so that I can tell you where to put the stuff. Are you sure we can't squeeze into the van?'

'Not a chance.'

'Have you any idea how long it is going to take us to get there?' Netta prevaricated nervously.

'How the hell do I know! We'll probably have unpacked everything before you arrive. Better that way; we don't want you and the girls under our feet.'

'Are you quite sure we're doing the right thing in taking a decision of this sort, Bill?' Netta said anxiously. 'It's been such a terribly upsetting day, and so much has happened it's turned life upside down for all of us.'

'Yes, well, sudden emergencies call for drastic measures,' he blustered bombastically. 'You've had things too soft while I've been away.'

Netta looked around the bare rooms sadly. It was bad enough to be leaving the only home she'd known since they were first married, but it was even more alarming to be moving to one of the worst parts of Liverpool.

She felt scared stiff at the idea of having to find the place on her own and she was apprehensive about what sort of accommodation she was going to find when she did arrive there.

It was only a few days ago that she had been worried because their home looked shabby, but she had never dreamed that in under a week they would be moving out of it. All the plans she'd had for how she and Bill could brighten it up and improve it now seemed like some foolish dream.

As Netta watched the van with all their possessions, as well as her husband and son, pull away from the kerb, the future seemed to be so bleak and uncertain that for a moment she found herself wishing that she could turn the clock back and that Bill was still serving in the army.

She might have had to scrimp and scheme to make ends meet, but that was a thousand times better than the situation she now found herself in.

Chapter Six

It was late in the afternoon before Netta and the girls found the house in Mould Court. They'd walked past it twice because they couldn't believe it was the right address. It was not simply run down; it was absolutely squalid.

'It must be the right place because that's the van that collected our furniture and stuff,' Molly insisted, pointing to the ramshackle green vehicle that stood by the side of the pavement with its doors tied together with a length of rope.

Netta checked what was written on the crumpled scrap of paper in her hand again. It said Mould Court all right, so this must be the place. When she had first read the address she'd felt a shudder run through her and now that she was actually there she was shocked to see that it lived up to its name. The grim terraced houses were the drabbest, slummiest places she had ever seen in her life. Surely Bill wasn't expecting them to make their home here?

Molly was waiting for her to say or do something, and Jodie was sniffling as though she was on the verge of tears. Taking a sharp breath Netta gave Molly a little push. 'Go on, then, go and see if it is the right place.'

As Molly walked towards the cracked stone steps, Netta felt a frisson of fear and was tempted to call her back. Heaven alone knew what sort of people lived in such a dump. It wasn't fair to send her to face them. She should be the one knocking on that scarred door, she told herself, yet she did nothing.

She stared around her at the paper- and rubbish-strewn gutters, and at the mangy cats and stray dogs sniffing in the doorways; it was as if she was living in some dreadful nightmare.

As Jodie's sobs became louder Netta called out to Molly who was hesitating at the bottom of the steps, 'For goodness' sake, luv, hurry up and see if your dad is in there.'

She saw Molly stiffen, and then, squaring her shoulders, begin to go up the steps. Before she reached the door, however, someone came out carrying a chair and, to Netta's relief, she saw it was Peter.

Dragging Jodie by the hand she hurried over to him. 'Where are you taking that, Peter?' she asked as he moved towards the van with the chair.

'Fred's taking it somewhere,' he mumbled.

'Why? There's nothing wrong with it, is there? It hasn't got broken, has it?'

Peter shrugged. 'No, I don't think so. Fred's having it along with a lot of other stuff.'

'But it's my furniture! That chair belonged to my mother.'

He shrugged again. 'You'd better talk to Dad about it; I'm only doing what I've been told. Fred's taking some of the furniture instead of Dad paying him or something.'

'Wait right there, I'll soon sort this out,' Netta told him, her green eyes hard with anger.

'Here.' She thrust Jodie's hand into Molly's. 'You wait here as well and keep an eye on your sister while I find your dad and deal with this,' she stormed.

'Bill, where are you? Come here right this minute,' she called as she reached the front door.

It was Fred, not Bill, who answered her

83

angry command. 'What's up, missus?' he asked, pushing his greasy cap back from his brow and scratching his head.

'What's up? I'll tell you what's up! My son tells me that you're taking some of our furniture.'

'That's right. Your old man's given some of it to me in place of the money he owes me for carting this lot over from the other side. I reckon he's getting the best of the deal, though. Load of old tat and no mistake. It'll take me all my time to get shut of it.'

'Well, you needn't bother. I want it brought back right now.'

Fred gave a raucous laugh. 'What you want and what you get is two different things. Anyway, there's not much point in you keeping it because there isn't room for the clobber that's already in the place. I reckon the whole damn lot of you will have to sleep standing up. Can't swing a cat round in there.'

Netta ignored him. Stumbling on the cracked steps she pushed her way inside the house.

'It's the top floor, missus. Mind how you go because there's a bloody big hole in one of the stairs about halfway up.'

Fred was certainly right about that, Netta thought grimly. The handrail was also rickety and twice she nearly fell before she reached the two rooms at the top of the house which

Bill had rented as their new home.

As she stood in the doorway she felt so shocked that she couldn't speak. The two small rooms with their poky little windows and low ceilings were glorified attics; the sort of place where most people stored their junk.

She stared at the miscellaneous assortment of goods and chattels that had been piled into each room and for a moment tears blinded her. She found it hard to believe that the contents of the home she'd once been so proud of could look like so much rubbish.

Then, shoulders back, she faced her husband who was concentrating on lighting a cigarette and launched into an attack.

'You're not seriously thinking that we can live here, are you?' she said in a scornful voice.

'It's here or outside in the Court,' he told her, 'and that's a bloody sight damper than it is up here. Get young Molly to give you a hand to sort the beds out. That'll do for tonight. We'll see to the rest of it tomorrow.'

As he spoke he picked up his jacket and shrugged it on, pulled a scarf around his neck, then headed for the stairs.

'Where are you off to?'

'To the boozer. I promised Fred I'd buy him a pint when he'd finished unloading.'

'You can't leave me here in this ... in this

... in this hovel on my own,' Netta stormed, her green eyes hardening.

'You're not on your own. You've got the kids to help you. Make that lazy sod Peter do something for his keep.'

'Hold on, how can you afford to buy drinks when we need every penny to buy food?'

He winked and tapped his forefinger against his nose. 'Don't worry about it. I'll sort things out when I get back. Buying Fred a drink is cheaper than paying him for his time.'

'Just a minute!' Her voice became shrill with anger. 'Peter has just helped him to put some of our furniture back on his van; he said that was to pay for the moving.'

Bill shrugged. 'So it is! I need a gargle myself, though. Moving all that stuff's been thirsty work.'

'Yes, and I want my chairs and anything else you've given him to be brought back,' Netta told him angrily.

'Not a chance! The deal's been done. Anyway, where the hell would you put them? There isn't room as it is for all the stuff we've still got here.'

Bill was gone before she could reply. Netta looked around in despair. The two double beds had been put up, one in each room, and they filled the entire space. They had somewhere to sleep, but where were they

86

going to eat, or even sit? she wondered. Then she saw there was no bed for Peter, not unless he bunked in with the two girls, and that would never do.

'Oh, Mum! This place is horrible; it isn't really going to be our new home, is it?'

Netta looked up as Molly and Jodie came into the room and her heart contracted as she saw the disbelief on Molly's pretty face. Jodie said nothing; she sucked her thumb, clutched her doll, and clung on to Molly's skirt.

'Perhaps with Peter's help we can somehow manage to move the two beds into one room and then that will give us a separate room for living in.' Netta frowned.

It was hard work. Fortunately, although Molly and Jodie slept together, their bed was not a full-sized double bed but, even so, when they managed to get both of the beds into the larger of the two rooms they were practically touching.

'It means we're going to be sleeping in the same room as you and Dad,' Molly exclaimed in alarm.

'Don't worry about it, we'll fix up a curtain between the two beds to divide the room up,' her mother promised.

'What about Peter, where is he going to sleep?'

'His mattress will have to go into the living room and since we have only one armchair it looks as though we'll have to use it as something to sit on,' her mother told her.

By the time they'd made up the beds and stowed their clothes and as much of the other stuff as possible underneath them to give themselves room to walk around, Bill had returned. He handed Netta a large greasy bundle wrapped up in newspaper that smelled strongly of vinegar.

'Here, I've brought us all some fish and chips so dish it out before it gets cold.' From his coat pocket he pulled out a large bottle of sarsaparilla. 'This will help it go down.'

'I'd sooner have a cup of tea,' Netta told him.

'Well, you bloody well can't, not until tomorrow morning. I have to talk to the landlady first about when we can and can't use the kitchen so make the most of this.'

Living at Mould Court was a shock for all of them. Even a week later Netta still couldn't believe that this was to be their home for the foreseeable future. She longed to be back in Wallasey, in her neat little house in Derby Road which now seemed like a palace in comparison.

The long lonely war years when she'd thought herself hard done by now seemed like Utopia by comparison. Walking down to Liscard to do her shopping, or across the road to enjoy the flowers in Earlston

Gardens, or taking a bus to New Brighton and then walking along the sea front and enjoying the clean, bracing air, seemed like another world entirely.

The main thing which both saddened and infuriated her was that so many of her possessions were missing. It seemed that every day she couldn't find something she needed and it ranged from clothes to kitchen items. In addition she also found that most of her ornaments, pictures and other treasures were gone.

Looking back, she deeply regretted that instead of flying into a temper she had remained calm and insisted that Fred opened up the back of his van so that she'd been able to take a good look at what he was taking away with him. She'd been so incensed about him taking her chairs that she hadn't been thinking clearly. She now realised that they were only a part of a great many of her belongings which he had removed.

The money he got for them must have been divided up in some way between him and her husband, she mused, because although Bill still didn't have a job he had money in his pocket.

What saddened her most of all, though, was that Bill had insisted that there was no possibility of Peter continuing at school and that he must go and find a job.

'Get down to the docks, tell them you're

fourteen, and see what's on offer,' he'd ordered him on the Monday morning after they'd arrived in Mould Court.

'I don't want to work on boats or do anything of that sort,' Peter had said, scowling. 'I told you I wanted to get an apprenticeship in engineering. I've dreamed about it for years.'

'You'll do whatever brings in the money, whacker, and don't start giving me any lip about it. Clean your shoes, comb your hair and smarten yourself up. Pull your shoulders back; come on, try and look smart even if you aren't.'

When Peter had returned home late in the afternoon to report that he'd found no work at all down the docks, Bill had cuffed him round the ears and told him to get out and find himself a messenger boy's job or work in a factory.

It took Peter three days, but in the end he managed to get taken on at the nearby biscuit factory sweeping up the floors and acting as a gofer in the warehouse. He hated it, but Netta tried to console him by telling him to think of it as a temporary job and that he'd find something better soon.

Even Molly was told she would have to find some work. 'Get yourself a weekend job as well as something you can do after school,' Bill told her.

'Who's going to look after Jodie and bring

her home from school each afternoon if I have to dash off to do some stupid job?' Molly defended.

'She can bring herself home; she's old enough to cross the road on her own.'

'No she isn't,' Molly argued. 'Anyway, since you're the only one not working then you ought to go to the school and meet her each afternoon.'

'No bloody fear! If you think I am going to hang around the school gates jangling with a bunch of old biddies, you can think again,' her father sneered. 'Let her stand on her own two feet, like the rest of us are going to have to do. And as for me not working, let me tell you that there're no jobs going for men of my age and experience. We've fought for this bloody country for four years and now we're back home again no one wants to know about us. Those who have jobs to come back to are lucky buggers, let me remind you.'

'Well, you had a job to come—'

The rest of Molly's cheeky response was lost in the screech of pain she let out as her father's hand slapped her hard across the face.

'That will do,' he bellowed. 'I'm not standing for any lip from you or anyone else in this house.'

Netta wanted to protest, but she realised that with the mood Bill was in anything she

91

said or did would only make him even more irate. She knew that at the moment his nerves were on edge because, like her, he knew there were going to be bad times ahead for them all.

They had said nothing to the children, but the police had already traced them to Mould Court. Bill said it was all her fault that they'd managed to do this because one of the first things she had done was to take Molly and Jodie along to the nearby school in Hankin Street and enrol them. She'd had to tell the head teacher which school they'd attended before they moved to Liverpool and even give her previous address.

Bill was due to appear before the magistrates concerning the injuries he had inflicted on the rent man who was claiming that he'd suffered a broken jaw and dislocated shoulder. They were both pretty sure that when his case came up Bill would get a prison sentence. If that happened then Netta had no idea how she was going to manage for money. Her hopes of getting away from Mould Court within a few weeks would certainly come to nothing even though she hated every second she had to live there.

She had never endured such primitive conditions in her life. The two rooms were cramped, dismal and dirty. She'd done her best to spruce them up and make them comfortable, but with everything crammed in so tightly it was almost impossible to do anything more than the basic cleaning.

Being on the top floor meant that they had to carry all their rubbish down three flights of stairs and out through the back of the house to the yard outside. That was also where the lavatory was.

The kitchen, which she had to share with the people living in the rooms below them, was on the landing and there was only room for one person to be in it at a time. It was a dirty, smelly hole and if she left anything behind, whether it was food or a frying pan, then she found she had lost it. It vanished immediately and no one knew anything about it.

Water for washing themselves had to be carried up to their rooms from a tap out in the yard. At night they had no option but to use chamber pots and each morning these had to be emptied into a bucket and then carried downstairs and poured down the drain in the gutter outside.

Washing their clothes was another night-mare. It was a case of lighting a coal fire under the communal boiler that was out in the centre of the Court. After rinsing the clothes in an old tin bath they put them through the old wooden mangle that was also out there. Then they hung them to dry by stringing the larger items on a piece of rope that was suspended right across the

Court from one side to the other. Sometimes the clothes dried if there was a good wind or if the sun was shining. At other times they hung there limply, collecting all the smut from the nearby factory chimneys until it was difficult to know if they'd been washed or not.

The only other option was to take them to the public wash-house, but that cost money and was a luxury Netta knew she would not be able to afford very often.

When she went to see where the wash-house was and to find out what shops there were locally she was shocked by how dismal everything was compared to the bright clean shopping centre she'd been used to in Wallasey. The streets themselves were littered with old newspapers, tin cans, bottles and stray dogs sniffing around the doorways.

There seemed to be pubs on every corner and the sour smell of stale beer and tobacco came from them even though they weren't open. Apart from the corner shops which seemed to sell everything, there were butchers, greengrocers and bakers, but otherwise the shops were very different from what she was used to. There were several pawnbrokers and plenty of second-hand shops full of discarded household goods and old clothes, all at a fraction of the price they would be new.

Everything looked so shabby and grubby

that the thought of ever having to go in one of them and buy anything sent a shiver through Netta.

There seemed to be no parks or open spaces and she wondered where the children would be able to play. When, tentatively, she asked someone where the nearest park was they told her it was St John's Gardens and that it was up the end of Scotland Road not far from Paddy's Market.

She'd heard of Paddy's Market. It was the largest one in Liverpool and renowned for its second-hand clothes, but she'd not known where it was and, at the moment, she felt afraid to venture that far.

Chapter Seven

Bill Henderson's court case made a small paragraph on the inside page of the *Liverpool Evening Echo;* so small that Netta was sure no one, not even the children, had seen it. Nevertheless, she decided she had to tell Peter and Molly about what had happened and the fact that the reason their father was no longer at home was because he had been sent to prison.

'We don't tell anyone about this, remember,' she warned.

'So what do we say if someone asks us where he is?' Molly frowned.

'Say he's gone overseas. A lot of the men living around here go to sea, so let them think that's where he is.'

'They'll want to know the name of his boat and which country he's gone to,' Molly argued.

'Then you'll simply have to say you don't know. It's no one's business except ours where he is. I'm only telling you and Peter the truth because I feel you are old enough to understand.'

'And what about Jodie, what are you going to tell her?' Molly persisted.

'Nothing, nothing at all, and I'm pretty sure she won't ask,' Netta said firmly.

'She's bound to get questioned at school, so you'll have to tell her something,' Molly pointed out.

'Then we'll tell her that he's gone overseas and won't be back for a long time.'

'Exactly how long?' Peter asked.

'Well, your dad's got three years, but with time off for good behaviour he should be home again in about two years, I imagine,' Netta explained.

'Good behaviour! He wouldn't know what that was,' Peter muttered scornfully.

'That will do, Peter,' Netta told him sharply. She stood up and began smoothing out the clothes she'd washed in readiness for ironing them. 'We are not going to discuss it any more. He's going to be away for at least two years and until he does come home again we've got to pull together and earn enough money to support ourselves.

'You've already got a job at the biscuit factory and Molly can find herself a little job on Saturdays or delivering papers after school, or something of that sort,' she went on. 'I'll see if I can get a job in a shop or else cleaning. If I can't find any work of that sort, then I'll have to get a job in a factory. If we all pull together, we'll be able to manage,' she added as she spread one of their blankets on the table to make a pad to do the ironing on.

'It's not what either of us want to do, though,' Peter grumbled.

'Will we have to go on living here in this horrible place?' Molly asked, pulling a face as she looked round the shabby over-crowded room.

'We will for the present. I'll try to save a few bob each week, then, as soon as we have enough to afford to rent something better, we'll move. I promise you, we will,' she added as she saw the look of disbelief on both their faces.

In the weeks that followed, in many ways Netta found it a relief to be back to the old days of managing things on her own. Like the children she found it was so much easier without Bill there, yelling and cursing at them all.

They settled into an acceptable routine. The children helped without being asked to do so and Peter seemed to grow up overnight and assume many of the responsibilities which normally belonged to the man of the family.

Peter's job at the factory only lasted a few weeks so once more he tried his luck on the dockside. He went off each morning confident that he would get some work and he soon managed to convince one of the gangers that he could be relied on to work hard and not lark around and so was taken on.

Netta managed to find herself two office-cleaning jobs. They were in the same building in Old Hall Street where Bill had worked before he'd been sacked.

The hours suited her well enough. For one of them she had to be there at seven o'clock in the morning which meant that she had to leave Molly to make sure that Jodie had some breakfast and that she was properly dressed, before walking with her to school.

Netta's other job was at seven in the evening and the work usually took two hours, but Molly and Peter were both at home by then to look after Jodie.

The arrangement worked well; Netta was able to collect Jodie from school in the afternoon and that left Molly free to find herself a little job. She finally ended up delivering newspapers for Parsons, the newsagent on the corner of Mould Road and Scotland Road. It meant she had to go there straight from school, but she was home before it was time for Netta to leave for Old Hall Street to do her evening cleaning stint.

Molly also worked at the same news-agent's every Saturday. This fitted in quite well because Netta didn't work at all over the weekends so she was at home to look after Jodie. It also gave Netta a chance to make sure that they all had a decent cooked meal on both Saturday and Sunday even if she couldn't manage to do so during the week.

Between the three of them they were earning enough to be able to feed themselves and, if Netta budgeted carefully, to be able to buy second-hand shoes and clothes when they needed them from Paddy's Market which was quite nearby.

Try as hard as she could, though, Netta was unable to stretch their money to pay the rent on anything better than where they were living at the moment.

Netta was well aware that Peter and Molly hated everything about Mould Court as much as she did, and she knew from their remarks that the only good thing was that Bill wasn't there to make matters worse.

Jodie seemed to live in a world of her own and Netta wasn't sure about her feelings at all. As long as she had her thumb to suck and her doll clutched underneath her arm she seemed to be content enough.

When she tried to talk to her about school, and asked how she got along with the other children in her class, Jodie simply shrugged her skinny little shoulders and gave her mother a vague smile.

It worried Netta because Molly constantly complained about the treatment she received at school. Yet, as far as either of them could find out, Jodie was never teased or bullied. In fact, it seemed that the other children left her to play on her own and mostly took no notice of her at all.

Netta knew only too well though that neither she nor the children fitted into their surroundings. The other women living in the Court made that clear whenever she came into contact with them. They regarded her as stuck up because she never stopped to gossip with any of them; they laughed at her for the way she cleaned her windows and did so much washing. If she stood alongside any of them in the local shops they peered at her shopping and pulled a face.

'Don't your lot like fish and chips or scouse, then, missus?' one of the women asked her when she saw her buying a small bacon hock. 'What you going to do with that, then?' she guffawed when Netta made no reply.

'I'm going to boil it, of course,' Netta told her. 'Then I'll serve it hot with cabbage and potatoes and the next day use the broth to make a nourishing soup. The day after that we'll eat the rest of the meat cold with some cooked vegetables.'

'Bloody hell!' the woman exclaimed. 'Whatever next! I bet you're going to make omelettes or something else that's fancy out of those couple of eggs you've just bought instead of frying them up in a pan with a bit of fatty bacon and some black-pudding.'

Much as she hated getting involved with any of the local people that was the least of her worries. The thing she found so difficult to cope with was all of them living in just two rooms.

Molly and Peter had always been used to taking it in turns to have their bath in front of a roaring fire on a Friday night and then curling up with a mug of cocoa before going off to bed.

Now, there was only a poky little grate and no room to bring in a tin bath, even if they'd had one. Instead, it was a case of boiling up a kettleful of water and having a strip wash.

Peter was now too old for her to supervise him in such matters and she wasn't sure if he was keeping himself as clean as he should be.

Jodie didn't seem to mind being washed from head to toe whilst standing in a bowl, but Molly hated it and, like Peter, insisted on being on her own.

Even washing their clothes and trying to get them ironed was a problem, because it seemed to take for ever to heat up the flat iron on the tiny fire.

Netta sometimes felt that she never stopped washing and ironing. As soon as she had their clothes clean and mended they needed to wear them, and so she had to start all over again.

Each night before they went to bed she placed the rickety wooden clothes horse as close as possible to the dying embers of the fire, draped the clothes that she'd washed out by hand over it and hoped they would be dry by morning.

Once a month and always on her own, Netta went to visit Bill in prison. The two older children refused to go along with her and she decided against taking Jodie because she thought it might upset her too much.

Joining the long queue of people waiting outside Walton jail for the doors to be opened was utter torment for Netta. In her eyes they all appeared threatening. Some were haggard and down at heel; others were swaggering and brash or sly and evil looking. Often when the queue began to move forward she found herself being shoved or pushed to one side by aggressive women. Although she resented it she never retaliated because the women looked every bit as rough and frightening as the men in the queue.

She felt even more intimidated when she was actually inside the grim building. The screws, as Bill called them, watched their every movement and anything the visitors took in for the prisoners had to be handed over for inspection. Often it was kept back and visitors were told it would be handed over to the prisoners after they had left.

'Stuff a packet of fags down the front of your blouse and then smuggle them across to me when no one's looking,' Bill hissed when she turned up empty handed and explained the reason why. 'If you hand fags over to the screws then the buggers hang on to them and we never get them.'

Doing as he asked the next time she visited him scared her senseless. 'What happens if I'm caught?' she whispered nervously as she pushed a crumpled packet of Woodbines into his hand under the table.

'I'll be the one who gets punished, not you,' Bill growled.

Netta wasn't too sure about that. He had become such a liar and so resentful of any kind of authority that she didn't trust anything he said.

Each time she visited him he seemed to be more and more morose and increasingly

103

belligerent. So much so that she began to dread the thought of him coming home.

After her visits she would lie awake wondering if there was any way that they could get away from Mould Court before he was released. She dreamed about doing this and moving right away, to some place where he couldn't find them, but deep down she knew this was utterly impossible. For a start, she hadn't the money to make it possible, and, even if a miracle happened and she was able to afford to do so, he'd be bound to find them.

When Bill came home everything would be in a state of upheaval again. At the moment she had moved the two girls into the big double bed with her and Peter was sleeping in their bed. She'd put up a curtain between the two beds so that there was a degree of privacy. Once Bill was released then Peter would have to sleep in the living room again.

By pooling the money they all earned, apart from the sixpence a week she let Peter and Molly keep as pocket money, they managed well enough. As soon as Bill came home again she'd find it hard to make ends meet unless he found a job right away and she thought that was highly unlikely.

For one thing he now had a prison record and she couldn't see that there was any way in which he could disguise that fact. Prospective employers would want to know where he'd been working and if he lied they'd be bound to find out. Most of them wouldn't even bother to interview him unless he had references and his old firm certainly wouldn't provide those.

Once or twice when she went in to visit him she had tried to talk to him about their home life and all the things they'd enjoyed and what a loving family relationship they'd had but he merely shrugged and mumbled that it was all in the past.

Whenever she asked him what plans he had for the future, he refused to discuss it.

'Wait till I get out of this bloody place and then I'll think about what I'm going to do,' he told her. 'You and the kids are managing all right for money at the moment. Peter's working, Molly has a paper round and a Saturday job, so there's nothing to worry about, now is there?'

'Not at present, but when you come home it will be another mouth to feed and I'm only just managing to keep our heads above water as it is,' she explained.

'If I can't get a job, then you'll have to find yourself a proper job in an office or a factory instead of pottering about with those stupid cleaning jobs like you're doing now,' he told her.

Netta shook her head. 'How can I do that? Someone has to be there for Jodie when she comes home from school.'

'I'll be there, you daft bint!'

His voice was so loud and aggressive that the prison warder standing on guard by the door came over to see if she was all right, but when she smiled and nodded he went back to his place without saying anything.

'You know I always go and meet her at the school gates, Bill, and I can't see you doing that,' Netta said quietly.

'You're right on that score,' he agreed scornfully. 'It's time she brought herself home from school at her age.'

'If we were still living in Wallasey I'd let her, but there're so many rough kids in the streets round about...'

'She spends time in school with them, so why can't she walk home with them?' Bill interrupted. 'Wrapping her in cotton wool isn't doing her any good.'

'She's a funny little thing, so shy and dreamy. She looks as though a puff of wind would blow her away and some of the children who go to her school are so big and rough that if they decided to pick on her she wouldn't stand a chance,' Netta explained worriedly.

'What makes you think they'd pick on her? They leave her alone when she's in school, don't they?'

'I know, but the people in Mould Court don't like us; we don't fit in there, Bill.'

'No, you're a bloody Wallasey snob, that's

why. You always did think yourself better than anyone else and scousers won't stand for that.'

'Then why did you bring us over here to live?' she retorted angrily. 'Why couldn't we have stayed in Wallasey? We could have moved to Poulton or Seacombe, or even to one of the terraced roads up New Brighton if you wanted to pay less rent.'

'You know bloody well why we moved here. It was because I knew you wouldn't want to face any of the posh neighbours and friends you had in Wallasey after I lost my job and threw a punch at that bloody rent man.'

'Mould Court is a terrible place to live, Bill. It's crummy, infested with cockroaches as well as lice, and the walls are wringing wet half the time. It's going to be icy cold in winter and in summer so hot we won't be able to breathe.'

'It isn't exactly a picnic in here,' he sneered. 'You are able to walk out of the door whenever you want to. You can go to the park or down to the Pier Head and that's more than I can damn well do. What's more, there's no one telling you what you can or can't do, or making you jump through a hoop for no reason at all like the sadistic bastards in here are always doing.'

He stared at her balefully. 'Think yourself lucky and stop bleating at me about what hardships you have to suffer.'

Netta knew it was no good arguing with him. All she could do was hope that when Bill finally did come home he would realise how awful life was in Mould Court and do his best to get a decent job and get them out of there.

Chapter Eight

Molly Henderson knew she had never fitted into her class at school, not since the day she started, and now she felt numb with fear as she stood facing a hostile crowd.

They not only jeered and mocked her because her accent was different, but constantly fired questions at her about her father. They wanted to know where he was and refused to believe anything she told them in response.

'Working overseas,' May Fricker, a huge fat girl who was the class bully, sneered. 'You sure about that?' She tapped her fleshy nose with a grubby forefinger, 'I heard that he was in the Waldorf Astoria as a guest of His Majesty.'

'If he's got such an important high-falutin' job as you say he has then why are your lot living here in Mould Court instead of in that posh house back in Wallasey where you said you used to live?' someone else asked.

'What you going to do when you leave here, go to finishing school?' another girl taunted.

Molly pushed her hair back from her face and squared her slim shoulders as she fielded their remarks as best she could. She was determined not to let them see the fear that made her stomach churn every time they ganged up on her like this. She looked around for Jodie, hoping that her little sister would have the sense to keep clear of this jibing mob.

Molly was thankful that they rarely taunted Jodie; one shove from May Fricker and she'd be flat on the ground.

Molly had noticed that ever since they'd come to this school her sister didn't mix very much with any of the girls. At playtimes she leaned up against a wall, sucking her thumb and watching what the others were doing. Even if they invited her to join in she always shook her head and looked the other way. In the end they simply left her alone and ignored her.

For all that Jodie seemed to like school and enjoyed learning. Even at home she usually had her nose in a book or a comic and was oblivious to everything that was going on around her. When she was asked to help she did so in a listless way and with a dreamy look in her eyes. Whatever she was told to do was done in a half-hearted manner as if her mind was elsewhere.

Most of the time Molly found it was easier to do Jodie's chores herself than nag her into action. It annoyed her, though, because she had so little time to herself or to help her mother as much as she would have liked to do.

Every evening as soon as she came out of school, she had to go straight to the corner shop to do her paper round. And on Saturdays she worked all day in the shop standing behind the newspaper counter serving or, at other times, making the tea or running errands for the owner, Mr Parsons.

Sometimes she felt so tired and her feet ached so much in the badly fitted shoes she was wearing that she felt like crying, only she couldn't do that because it would upset her mum and she was finding things hard enough as it was.

She knew that part of the reason why her feet ached so much was because after school she not only did her own newspaper round but helped Brian Baldwin to deliver his newspapers as well. She'd started doing it when his arm was broken because he was worried in case Mr Parsons sacked him.

She'd felt it was the least she could do since his arm had been broken in a fight in the school yard when he'd been defending her. A crowd of their classmates had ganged up during morning break time and were taunting her, slapping her around and pulling her hair. He had come to her defence.

After that the two of them had become close friends and as a result their other classmates stopped their teasing and started to leave her alone as long as he was around.

Brian was a solid-looking boy with light ginger hair, pale blue eyes and freckles all over his cheeks and nose. His dad was a well-known bare-knuckle fighter and he'd taught Brian how to take care of himself. The rest of the boys at school knew this and when the fight was over their bloody noses and black eyes told their own story. Near the end of the fight, though, one of them had managed to trip Brian up and he'd fallen awkwardly and broken his arm.

Everyone had scarpered double quick, but Molly had stayed to help him up. When Miss Farmer, the headmistress, found out what had happened she said that Molly had better go in the ambulance to the Liverpool General Hospital with him and wait while they fixed his arm and then make sure that he got home safely.

'You didn't have to come with me or wait for me, you know,' Billy told her gruffly as they left the hospital.

'I know that and you didn't have to get into a fight because of me,' she retorted.

'My old man says you ought to help girls and old women if you see them in trouble.' He grinned.

'I thought your dad was a fighter,' Molly said in surprise.

'So he is, the best there is, but that don't mean he hits women,' Brian told her fiercely.

'I never said it did,' Molly said quickly. 'You won't get into trouble over breaking your arm, will you?' she asked anxiously.

Brian shrugged. 'Depends.'

'Depends on what? It wasn't your fault, and when you tell your mum what happened she'll be proud of you.'

'Not when she takes a look at my jacket! Look at it; it's all mucky with blood and it's torn.'

'Well, it's easy enough to put that right again,' Molly told him cheerfully.

Brian pulled a face. 'My mum hates sewing or mending and she's not very good at it, either. Dad's always going on about it because he says she just cobbles things together instead of doing them properly. She does it when she mends the holes in our socks and then they cause horrible blisters when you walk.'

Molly laughed. 'You'd better come home with me and let my mum do it, then.'

'I don't know,' Brian said doubtfully, as he studied it.

'Well, I do. Come on, we've got to walk because I've no money for a tram and I bet you haven't either.'

'If I did have some money then I wouldn't be wasting it on a tram; I'd buy something to eat. I'm so hungry my stomach thinks my throat's cut.'

'Come back to my place and I'll ask my mum if we can both have a jam butty,' Molly told him.

Although this cheered Brian up a good deal he still looked very worried.

'What's wrong now?' Molly asked. 'You look as though you think the sky's going to fall in.'

'I hope I don't get the sack from the news-agents when Mr Parsons spots that I've got my arm in a sling; you know what he's like!' he muttered gloomily as they walked along.

Molly looked concerned. For a moment she'd forgotten that Brian also delivered newspapers for Mr Parsons. 'Perhaps I can help you to deliver some of them,' she suggested practically.

'How can you?' Brian scowled. 'You've got your own round to do, haven't you?'

'I know that, but as soon as I've finished mine I could help you do yours. Or, better still, if you carried the papers then I could run and push them through the doors and we could do your round and mine between us and still be finished on time.'

Brian looked thoughtful. 'It's not a bad idea, but I'm not sure if I'd be able to carry your bundle of papers as well as mine, they'll weigh a ton.'

'We can try it,' she insisted. 'Let's see what my mum thinks of the idea. We can tell her while she's fixing your jacket.'

Brian's face suddenly lit up. 'I've got an idea. I can borrow the pram that my mam uses for my little sister. She'll understand if I explain everything. We'll pile the papers in that and I can pull the pram and you push the papers into the doors.'

Netta agreed that it was worth trying, but she told them they must explain their plan to Mr Parsons.

'It's only right to let him know, and then if you are a little late with any of the papers, he'll understand. If you don't, and someone tells him they've seen the pair of you with the newspapers in a pram he might think you're playing some silly prank.'

While Brian and Molly munched their way through their jam butties Netta not only mended his jacket but also sponged away the dirt and blood and then dried the damp patch by holding the sleeve in front of the fire.

'Gosh, it looks even better than it did before,' Molly told him with a grin.

'I can see that,' he said gratefully, 'thank you, Mrs Henderson, and for the nosh.'

'That's all right, Brian. The pair of you had better get a move on, though, or you'll be late getting to the shop,' Netta told them.

'And Mr Parsons will have our guts for garters before we've even had a chance to explain what has happened and how we're going to try and do the deliveries between us,' Brian agreed cheekily.

After that he and Molly had become staunch friends. They were relieved that Mr Parsons not only didn't mind that they were doing the deliveries together, but also that no one complained that their paper was late.

'We could go on doing our rounds together even after your arm is better if you want to,' Molly suggested.

'Yes, why not,' Brian agreed. 'I think it's better than doing it on our own.'

Molly couldn't have agreed with him more. It meant that she had no worries about someone from school accosting her and either shoving her over so that her newspapers went flying in all directions – as had happened once or twice when she'd been on her own – or trying to snatch some of the papers and run off with them so that she had to grab them back which meant they were often badly creased.

Brian kept her entertained with stories about the people and places where they delivered. He seemed to have such a fund of stories that she wasn't sure if they were all true or not. He had lived in and around the Scotland Road area all his life and he was equally fascinated by her accounts of the life she'd known in Wallasey before her family had moved to Mould Court.

'Is it true that your dad's in Walton jail because he thumped someone?' he asked casually a couple of weeks after they'd got to know each other well.

Molly hesitated, looking at him sideways, not at all sure whether to tell him the truth or not.

'I heard he was,' Brian went on conversationally. 'Nothing to worry about, half the men round here have done a stretch for something or the other.'

'Has your dad been in prison?'

'Of course he has! Bare-knuckle fighting is breaking the law and he's been caught more than once.'

Molly nodded understandingly. Somehow this made it all right for Brian to know about her own dad's prison sentence and, once she'd told him, she felt it made them closer than ever.

As the time drew nearer for her dad's release Molly found herself confiding in Brian about how worried it made her feel, and he seemed to understand.

'Being in prison is bound to change him, you've got to expect that,' he told her gravely.

'Yes, I'm sure you are right, but is it for the

better?' she asked doubtfully.

He grinned as he kicked at an empty cardboard box lying on the pavement. 'You taking the mickey? I meant that it makes them hard as nails.'

Molly shivered. 'He was bad-tempered and difficult to live with before he went to prison. Mum said it was being in the army that had made him so moody and quarrelsome.'

'Perhaps it won't make any difference to him, then,' Brian said hopefully.

'I can remember that when I was little I used to think he was the most wonderful dad in the world,' Molly sighed. 'He used to play games with me and my brother Peter, and when Jodie was only a baby he pushed the pram with her in it. When he came home again after the war he didn't seem to have time for any of us.'

'That's grown-ups for you,' Brian agreed, rattling a piece of stick he'd picked up against some railings. 'My dad is only interested in me and my brother because he can teach us to fight. He never takes a scrap of notice of my two sisters because they're only girls.'

'I didn't know you had any brothers and sisters,' Molly said in surprise. 'Which class are they in?'

'They all left school ages ago, before you moved here,' he told her as he aimed the stick over a high fence. 'They're older than me and all working except my littlest sister, and she's not old enough for school.'

'My brother Peter is working down on the docks,' Molly told him. 'He was working at the biscuit factory but he says he likes his new job much better because he never knows what he will be doing from one day to the next. He has to collect a number each morning and then stand around until someone calls it out and then tells him what he has to do that day.'

'That's a mug's game unless you're in with the head ganger,' Brian told her scornfully. 'He'll only be getting the filth jobs; the ones that no one else wants to do.'

'No,' Molly shook her head, 'it seems that the ganger has taken a shine to him and Peter says that the work is usually quite interesting.'

'He's lucky, then!'

'So what sort of jobs are the rest of your family doing?' Molly quizzed.

'Both of my sisters are in service and live in. My brother's at sea. He goes all over the world and when he comes home, which isn't very often, he tells me tales about the countries he's visited and some of the strange people he's seen.'

'Is that what you want to do when you leave school?' Molly asked, noticing the way his face had brightened when he talked

118

about his older brother.

'Perhaps. I haven't made my mind up yet.' He shrugged dismissively and started to whistle.

'You must have some idea what you want to do,' Molly persisted.

Brian pulled a face. 'In a way I'd like to go to sea, but I hate being on a boat. I feel sick even crossing over to New Brighton on a ferry boat. We once went over to Ireland to visit my gran and I was as sick as a dog the whole way. It was horrible; I still have nightmares about it.'

'That was probably because you were very young,' she told him. 'It might be different now that you are older.'

'Dunno. Anyway, there are lots of other jobs I quite fancy having a go at if I get the chance. Have you made your mind up about what you want to do?'

'Not yet. I was taking shorthand and typing lessons before we moved from Wallasey.'

'Well, make sure you don't become a skivvy,' Brian warned. 'Both my sisters hate it because they say you are expected to work from dawn to dusk. You have to be up and get the fires going and their breakfasts ready really early in the morning and they still expect you to be bright and smiling when you serve them a hot drink at ten o'clock at night. Some of the women can be really horrible to you if you do anything wrong or accidentally break something.'

'Why don't they leave, then?' Molly frowned. 'There must be plenty of jobs for girls in Liverpool.'

Brian shrugged. 'They didn't want to go into a factory and they get well fed and a bed all to themselves, so in a way they are better off than they were at home.'

As she made her way back to Mould Court after they'd parted Molly reflected on what tough lives everyone around Scotland Road seemed to have. Life had been so much easier for all the people she'd known in Wallasey. Perhaps that was why they were all so much nicer to each other, she thought philosophically.

Chapter Nine

As summer 1921 approached, every morning when she woke up Molly became increasingly worried about what sort of job she was going to do when she left school.

Brian Baldwin had left school at Christmas and was already working at a butcher's in Scotland Road. Molly missed his company when she did her round and as the time drew nearer for her to leave school she remembered what he had told her about his sisters and was determined that whatever happened she wasn't going to become a skivvy. There was no chance now of her ever being a shorthand typist and working with a group of other girls in a bright, friendly office as she'd once hoped. She'd even dreamed that she might meet a handsome young man there, fall in love, and perhaps even marry him.

She tried to look on the bright side; their home might be crowded and shabby, and Mould Court might be dank and dirty, but she still had the company of her mother, brother and sister. As long as they were all together and looking out for each other then their surroundings didn't matter so much.

Sometimes, before she fell asleep, she found herself wondering about what would happen when their dad came home again. She and Peter were dreading it. From what Brian had told her she was sure he would be more unbearable than ever after a spell in prison. She hadn't been to see him at all since he'd been in there; none of them had except her mother.

'It's not the sort of place I want any of you visiting,' Netta had said firmly.

Molly felt angry that they had been reduced to such squalid conditions because of her dad's rash behaviour, but most of all she felt sorry for her mum. She had been used to a nice warm home, good food and a far more comfortable life than she had now. Having to go out cleaning offices morning and night was something her mum had probably never dreamed she would ever have to do.

Molly admired the way she had faced up to it and that was one of the reasons she wanted to find herself a good job so that she could earn some more money to help out. There were so many things they were all forced to go short of including good food. Her mum did her best to provide them with nourishing meals, but by the end of the week she was always struggling to put something hot on the table for their evening meal.

As she finished her paper round a few days after her fourteenth birthday Molly knew that she ought to tell Mr Parsons that as soon as she could find herself a job he would have to find someone else to deliver the newspapers. She had put off doing so for as long as possible because she didn't want to find herself earning no money at all.

'I was wondering when you were going to tell me,' Mr Parsons pronounced. 'You've been waiting until you found yourself a proper job, have you?' he added rather sternly.

'No.' Molly shook her head vehemently. 'Not yet, I haven't, but I must start looking because the extra money is going to mean a

122

lot to my mum.'

Mr Parsons stopped pricing up some packets of cigarettes and ran a hand over his chin thoughtfully, staring at her as if seeing her for the first time. 'What sort of job are you after?'

'Shop work, I suppose. Before we moved here I'd started to learn shorthand and typing because I hoped to work in an office, but...' her voice trailed away.

Mr Parsons concentrated on what he was doing. There was such a long silence before Mr Parsons spoke again that Molly felt very uncomfortable and wondered if she ought to leave. When he did speak, she could hardly believe her ears.

'Well, if you haven't managed to find anything, then the best thing you can do is to start here. I'll expect you at eight o'clock sharp tomorrow morning.'

'You mean you want me to work in the shop full time?' Molly asked in an incredulous voice.

'Sweeping up, stacking the shelves, serving behind the counter and whatever else I might need you to do,' he said curtly. 'For the first week you might have to continue with your paper round, until I find someone else to do it.'

'That's wonderful! Thank you, Mr Parsons. Can ... can you tell me how much I will be paid?' she stuttered, her face flaming.

He frowned heavily, rubbing his hand over his chin again. 'Ten shillings a week to start with and if you're any good, I'll raise it by another half a crown.'

Molly could hardly get home fast enough to break the good news to her mother. Netta's face broke into a smile and they hugged and kissed each other and then began planning how they would spend the extra money that would be coming in.

'Peter needs some new boots and Jodie really ought to have some sandals to wear now that it is summer,' Molly pointed out.

'True, but what about you? You will need some proper clothes for work.'

'No, not really. I have to wear an overall, so it won't matter what I have on underneath it,' Molly told her.

Peter was equally delighted when they told him the news. 'Any chance that it means we can move somewhere a bit better than this place?' he asked hopefully.

'Well, not right away,' Netta said cautiously. 'I'll definitely put some of Molly's money away each week and perhaps by the time your dad comes home sometime next year we will be able to do so. That gives us quite a while to save up,' she added brightly.

Molly found that there was far more to learn than she had realised. Mr Parsons expected her to memorise the price for all the goods he stocked, not only the sweets and cigarettes she'd sometimes been allowed to serve on Saturdays.

'I know you are probably going to find it difficult to remember them at first so I've written out a list and you must keep it by the till. I don't want you calling out to me to ask the price every time you serve a customer.'

'Perhaps it would be easier if we stick labels on everything with the price on it,' Molly suggested.

'No, no, that wouldn't do at all.' He frowned. 'I wouldn't like it and neither would the customers. I suppose we could put the price on the edge of the shelf where they are stacked if you think that would help you. It might also help to remind you where everything must go when you unpack a new supply. Every item of stock has its allotted space and I don't want anything put in the wrong place, do you understand?'

Molly quickly discovered that making sure that everything was in its rightful place was of paramount importance in Mr Parsons's eyes and she did her very best to comply.

Furthermore, everything in packets or boxes had to be stacked with precise alignment; sweet jars also had to be lined up like an army of soldiers and with the labels all facing the right way; shelves had to be thoroughly cleaned once a week; and the floor swept at midday and again before they closed at night.

He issued Molly with two blue overalls and told her she must make sure they were always clean and that there were no creases in them and she must always look smart and tidy herself.

For the first week, because she also had to do her paper round, Molly felt so tired that all she wanted to do when she got home was eat her meal and go to bed. Gradually, however, she took it all in her stride and once she no longer had to deliver papers she started to go to the park with Jodie in the evenings as well as taking her out on Sundays.

She also had a new interest in her life, and his name was Steven Parsons. He was two years older than her, but because he went to a private school she had never met him before.

The first time she saw Steven he was picking up a chocolate bar from a display case on the shop counter and putting it into his pocket as he headed for the door. Because she didn't know who he was she grabbed him by the arm, accused him of shoplifting and refused to let him leave the shop.

Mr Parsons came rushing out of the stockroom to see what all the fuss was about and was astounded when he found his own son in an arm lock, being accused of thieving.

Molly was crestfallen when she realised what a mistake she had made, but Mr Parsons told her she had done the right thing and even Steven was grinning as she released his arm and he straightened his jacket and tie.

After that she and Steven had become quite good friends and he began to spend a few minutes down in the shop talking to her whenever his father was busy in the stockroom or upstairs in his office.

At first Molly felt rather shy of talking to him partly because of the mistake she had made, but mainly because she knew he went to a very posh school and she was afraid he would look down on her.

Steven, however, was very taken with the pretty new assistant with the nut-brown hair and intelligent face. He liked the thoughtful way she treated everything and the gleam of appreciation in her bright turquoise eyes when he said something clever.

The first time Steven asked her if she would like to go to the pictures with him Molly was so taken aback that she could only stare at him in wide-eyed silence.

When he repeated the question, she bit down on her lower lip and shrugged her shoulders.

'So what's that supposed to mean?' he asked with an amused smile.

'I'd love to, but I'm not sure that Mr Parsons would approve,' she said awkwardly.

Steven frowned. 'What has it got to do

with him?'

'Well, he is my boss and you are his son and I wouldn't want to lose my job because he didn't like us going out together,' she told him primly.

'Has he ever complained about me talking to you?'

'No,' she smiled nervously, 'but he is usually out of the shop when you do, so perhaps he doesn't know.'

'True!' Steven nodded. 'Perhaps it would be better for both of us if we keep it a secret. We'll meet outside the Rotunda, how about that?'

'Well, if you think it will be all right, then I'd love to come with you,' she agreed.

After that, going to the pictures with Steven on a Saturday night became a regular outing for Molly and one she looked forward to. Some of the pictures Steven wanted to see weren't quite what Molly would have chosen herself, but she never said anything and in most cases she found she enjoyed them, even though they were often rather on the serious side.

She was never sure if Mr Parsons knew that Steven was taking her out; if he did, he said nothing and Molly decided that she certainly wasn't going to say anything.

For the first few outings Steven was content to simply hold hands and give her a brief peck on the cheek when he said goodnight at the corner of Mould Court. Gradually, however, he became bolder and in the darkness of the cinema he sat with his arm around her shoulder and one evening he even tried to kiss her before the lights went up.

Molly wasn't too sure how to handle this. She hadn't made friends with any of the local girls and so there was no one she could ask. She certainly couldn't discuss it with her brother Peter because she knew he didn't particularly like Steven Parsons. They had only met twice, but Peter thought he was stuck up and arrogant.

'He makes sure that you know that his dad pays for him to go to a posh school, and that he gets ten bob pocket money every week. Just think of it, ten bob to spend as you like, no questions asked, and you don't have to lift a finger to earn it.'

'And all the chocolate bars he wants,' Molly added with a teasing grin, knowing how much Peter loved chocolate.

Although Steven never said anything disparaging about where she lived, Molly was very conscious of the difference in their circumstances. It was one of the reasons why she was determined not to let him overstep the mark with his advances. Peter was right, she reflected; Steven might have plenty of money to spend and, although she let him pay for her to go to the pictures, she had no intention of letting him think it gave him any special privileges.

Keeping him at arm's length became more and more difficult, however, especially when at Christmas he bought her a smart red leather handbag that she knew must have cost him several weeks' pocket money.

When he told her that he had also bought tickets to the Royal Court Theatre to see the pantomime, she felt so overwhelmed that she was almost on the point of declining.

It worried her so much that eventually she decided to confide in her mother even though she was afraid that Netta might tell her she was too young and try and discourage her from going out with Steven.

Netta listened to her in silence, looking more and more worried as Molly talked.

'You be careful, my luv,' Netta warned. 'I don't think that Mr Parsons will be too pleased if he gets to hear what's going on. Are you sure he doesn't know?'

'I don't think he does and that's what worries me.'

'He probably wouldn't like it if he did,' Netta agreed. 'You're quite sure you're not letting this Steven take any liberties with you?' Netta probed.

'I've told you, he puts his arm round me when we're in the pictures and there's the odd kiss or two, but always when the lights are down,' Molly admitted bashfully.

'What about when you are in the shop?'

'Heavens no! He just says "hello" or makes some remark about what I'm doing, or about something he's read in the paper. He knows his dad wouldn't approve if we just stood there chatting for very long when I should be working, and he never says anything that he would mind his dad, or anyone else, overhearing.'

'All of which means that his dad doesn't know how friendly you are with each other and he certainly isn't aware that Steven is seeing you outside working hours or that he's taking you out to the pictures,' Netta told her.

'No!' Molly sighed. 'I suppose you're right. Anyway,' she added brightly, 'once Christmas is over Steven is starting work in one of the shipping offices. He says it's a job with excellent prospects and that he will be earning a good salary.'

'Found for him by some friend of his father's, no doubt,' Netta said enviously.

'I don't know. You are probably right, though.'

'He most certainly won't be grubbing around on the dockside trying to catch the ganger's eye so that he gets a day's work like your brother has to do,' her mother sighed. 'In fact, it sounds like the sort of white-collar job I dreamed of our Peter having one day,' she added wistfully.

'Oh, Mam, don't take on so. I didn't mean to upset you. Dad will be home again soon and once he finds a proper job then everything will change for the better. We'll all be back on our feet in next to no time.'

'I hope so,' Netta agreed, using the edge of her pinafore to wipe away tears.

'Of course we will. Once we move away from here to somewhere decent, some place that's bright and clean, we'll all feel more optimistic. You won't have to go out to work any more and we'll all have a fresh start.'

'Let's hope you're right, luv, but I'm afraid it might be too late for you and Peter to be able to have the right training now to achieve the sort of future I wanted for you both.'

'Then we'll have to make sure that Jodie gets a better start in life and outshines us all,' Molly told her with a bright smile. 'She loves learning and she will do us proud, I know she will.'

'Well, it is certainly something to look forward to next year. With any luck 1922 will see a change in our fortune and life-style. There are times when I dream that I am back in Wallasey and that all that has happened to us over the past few years is nothing more than a nightmare.'

'When Dad comes home we will start all over again, and by next Christmas every-thing about living in Mould Court will

132

simply be a bad dream.'

Netta smiled and patted Molly's hand. 'Now, what about Steven Parsons? We still haven't decided what you ought to do about him.'

'Or what to do about accepting the expensive Christmas present he's bought me or his invitation to go to the pantomime with him.'

'It's probably the only Christmas present you are going to receive,' Netta said sadly. 'We're so hard up that I'm afraid this will be the worst Christmas we've ever known.'

'As long as we are all together and there are a few treats for Jodie, and perhaps a little present to make her happy, then Peter and I will understand,' Molly said brightly, giving her mother a quick hug.

Chapter Ten

Bill Henderson arrived home on a bitterly cold March day in 1922. The sky was leaden and there was a wild wind blowing in from the Mersey driving sleet and snow flurries ahead of it.

Netta let out a startled cry as he barged into the room.

'Heavens, Bill, you frightened the life out

of me. I thought it was someone breaking in.'

'Who the hell would want to break into this tip?' he snarled. 'What the devil are you doing in bed at this time of day? Huddled there you look like some old Mary Ellen. I thought for a minute that I was in the wrong bloody dump. Why the hell aren't you up and why haven't you got the fire going?'

'I can't afford the coal so I don't light it until the afternoon when the children come home,' she explained. 'After I've done the shopping and so on I wrap myself up in this old shawl to try and keep warm while I snatch a couple of hours' sleep. I have to be up at six in the morning to get to my cleaning job on time.'

'Well, get up and light it now and get me something to eat,' he ordered. 'I'm shrammed through to the bone,' he added, rubbing his hands together and shivering.

'I've only got a pan of scouse left over from yesterday and I'm going to reheat that for the kids when they come home tonight.'

'Then find me something else and be quick about it,' he muttered. 'And get this bloody fire going before I freeze to death.'

'It's all laid ready, all you have to do is put a match to it. You do that while I make a pot of tea.'

'Pot of tea! Hell's bells, haven't you got

anything stronger than that to offer me?'

'Of course I haven't; I can't afford to drink beer or stout, now can I?' Netta retorted.

'Well, give us one of your fags, then. I haven't had a smoke for days.'

'I haven't any of those, either.'

'Not a very warm welcome home, is it?' Bill Henderson snorted in disgust, as he reached for the box of matches on the narrow mantel shelf and put a light to the newspaper sticking out at the bottom of the grate.

The fire was slow to get going and smoke curled out into the room making them both cough.

'You never could lay a bloody fire,' he muttered.

'Well, now that you're home, you can do it,' Netta told him sharply. 'Hold a sheet of newspaper in front of it to help it draw. The chimney probably needs sweeping.'

There was a sudden short yelp of pain and a bright flash of flame as the newspaper Bill was holding up against the fireplace caught alight.

Netta rushed to help him, but before she could do so he had crushed it between his hands, putting out the flame but burning his hands in the process.

'Bloody silly idea!' he snarled.

Netta said nothing. It was the only reliable way she knew of making sure the fire got going and so far she'd never had any accidents. To tell Bill this would only enrage him further, so she reached for a dab of margarine and wiped it across one of his palms.

'Try smoothing that into your hand; it will take the sting away,' she told him.

Still muttering he did as she suggested, wincing with pain and cursing both her and the fire at the same time.

'Where's that cuppa you are supposed to be making?' he challenged.

'It's ready! Make yourself comfortable and I'll pass it to you.'

He slurped noisily from the cup before she could warn him that it was probably scalding hot and once again he was cursing and blaspheming. As he picked up the hunk of bread she'd put on a plate alongside his cup of tea, his anger flared anew.

'What the hell is this supposed to be? I don't want bread and dripping; haven't you any bloody cheese?'

'No, I haven't. I haven't bought cheese for weeks; it costs too much.'

'Then let's have some of that scouse you've got ready.' He peered at the cheap alarm clock balanced on the edge of the mantel shelf. 'By the time you've heated it up the kids should be home.'

'No they won't; I have to go and meet Jodie first. We don't have our meal until after six, because we wait for Molly to get home.'

'What the hell is she doing until then?

136

Running after boys or playing out some-where?'

'Neither. Molly is working at Parsons' the newsagents and she doesn't finish until six o'clock.'

'Parsons? Does he sell fags?' He held out his hand. 'Give us a tanner, then, and I'll stroll down there and get a packet and say hello to her at the same time.'

'I haven't got a tanner; in fact, I have no money at all – not even a couple of coppers. I don't get paid until Friday night and Molly doesn't get paid until Saturday evening.'

Bill raised his eyebrows in disbelief. Then his mouth twisted into a sour grin as he stood up and fastened his jacket. 'In that case I'll ask old Parsons to put it on the slate and to knock it out of Molly's money at the end of the week.'

Netta tried to protest, but Bill ignored her. Turning up the collar of his jacket he went out slamming the door so hard that it caused the smoke from the newly lit fire to billow out and fill the place with an acrid smell.

Netta sighed as she restored order in the room before she went to meet Jodie. Once more she coaxed the fire back into life, hoping that she could heat up the scouse over the top of it rather than having to do it on the gas ring. She hadn't even had a chance to tell Bill that she had to leave by half past six or that she wouldn't be home again from her cleaning job until after nine.

It worried her because it meant that she wouldn't be here to act as a buffer between Bill and the children when they met up again and she had an uneasy feeling that there might well be ructions between them all.

While Bill had been inside all three of them had been forced to adapt to their new surroundings and each of them in their own way now had a protective shell.

Going out to work had certainly made Peter much more grown up. Having to work alongside men twice or three times his age and to stand his ground when they tried to put on him, and having to accept their more mature judgement when it came to advice, had made him both shrewd and thoughtful. Whereas at one time he would have spoken out without thinking, he now considered what was being said very carefully before he replied.

Even so, she was worried about what Peter might say to his father. She knew he was still both bitter and resentful about the conditions they were being forced to endure because his father had been foolish enough to give way to his own feelings and to use his fists on the rent man.

Molly also harboured a grudge because she hated living in Mould Court, but she had accepted that they had no alternative and so she did her utmost to make the best of things. Doing a paper round when she'd still been at school had been only one of the ways she had shown her support. Netta was grateful that she was still so willing to help with Jodie even though she now worked full-time.

As these thoughts went through Netta's mind she wished that she could have warned Molly about what her father was intending to do. It was too late to stop him going into the shop for cigarettes today and Molly would be both annoyed and embarrassed if he asked Mr Parsons to deduct it from her wages.

Netta was also quite sure that Mr Parsons wouldn't like the idea either. He might even refuse to do so and if Bill became aggressive, then Mr Parsons might decide to sack Molly. There were always plenty of youngsters looking for work.

Perhaps, she decided, as she took off her print wrap-around pinafore and put on her outdoor coat, she should nip along there on her way to collect Jodie from school and see if Bill had caused any trouble for Molly.

She'd have to explain to Jodie that her father was home again to make sure that the little girl didn't say the wrong thing when she got home. If they got off on the wrong foot, then it would mean unpleasantness all round.

She moved the heavy iron saucepan that contained the remains of the previous night's meal more securely over the fire which was now burning brightly and gave the contents a vigorous stir. Then, setting the lid slightly tipped so that the steam could escape and there would be no fear of it bubbling over, she replaced the fireguard before she went out.

Netta hesitated after closing the door before turning the heavy iron key in the lock. If she locked the door then Bill wouldn't be able to get back in, and, with the mood he was in, she wouldn't put it past him if he lost his temper and broke the door down. With a sigh, she left it unlocked.

Bill's bad temper and aggression set the seal on his homecoming. Nothing any of them did was right. He was scornful about Peter's job, telling him that by this time he should have found something with more prospects. He ridiculed Molly working in a shop, was critical of Jodie because she was so waif-like and he scoffed at the idea of Netta cleaning offices.

'If they saw the state of this dump, they'd never have taken you on,' he told her. 'I've seen pigsties that looked better.'

Netta refused to let his goading affect her and whenever possible she intervened the moment he started on Peter. For the most

140

part he ignored Jodie, but Molly was a different matter. Molly refused to accept his criticism or ridicule. She immediately retaliated, usually giving him as good as she got. This not only infuriated him but also made him deride everything she did, or said, even more.

'For heaven's sake, shut your ears to his remarks; you only antagonise him when you answer him back and make him say things that are even more hurtful,' Netta told her.

'Maybe I do, but it is better than letting him walk all over me like the rest of you do. He's been home almost three weeks now and he still hasn't found a job. We are all working to keep him and he doesn't lift a finger to help around the place. In fact, he's run up a bill for so many packets of fags this week that I won't be bringing home any money at all on pay day.'

'I'm sorry about that, luv, but he doesn't mean any harm by it. I'm sure he's grateful to you for helping him out.'

'I doubt it! Anyway, we'll know when he comes in tonight.'

'What do you mean by that?' Netta frowned.

'I've told Mr Parsons not to let him have any more cigarettes unless he pays for them. I said he's not to charge them up against my wages.'

'You've done what!' Netta gasped in

141

horror, knowing how furious Bill would be when Mr Parsons told him there was no slate.

'I'm sorry, Mum, but I work hard and I don't see why Dad should spend every penny of my wages on smokes. In future, he'll have to learn to live without cigarettes unless he gets a job and pays for them with his own money.'

'I know you're right, Molly, but he'll be so mad with you that it might be better to give in.'

'Let him be mad. You know what they say – Sticks and stones can break my bones, hard words can hurt me never,' she quoted.

'It won't just be hard words, luv!' Netta warned her. 'If I was you, I'd make myself scarce before he gets home.'

'I'll have a job to do that in a place this size!' Molly grinned.

'I mean it, Molly. He'll be fighting mad and heaven alone knows what he will do.'

'Well, you keep out of his way, then, and leave it to me. I've told Peter what I intend to do so he'll back me up. You look after Jodie and stay out of it.'

Bill was in a dark, brooding mood when he came in. He ate his meal without a word, which worried Netta far more than if he had vented his spleen on them all.

When it was time for her to leave for her evening cleaning job she drew Molly to one

142

side and whispered, 'I don't like leaving you, luv, so be careful. If he turns nasty, grab hold of Jodie and come down to the offices where I'm cleaning. Do you understand?'

'Yes, but you don't need to worry. Peter will be here and he'll stick up for me.'

'If your dad's in a temper, then Peter won't stand a chance against him. Bill will simply beat him up and that's the last thing I want to happen.'

'I'll try and persuade Peter to come with us if there is any trouble,' Molly promised.

After her mother had gone Molly cleared away their dirty dishes and started to wash them up in the enamel bowl, while Jodie stood by her side drying them with the tea towel. Before she could finish Bill ordered her to make up the fire.

'I'll do it, Molly, you finish off the dishes,' Peter called out.

'I bloody well told your sister to do it. If I'd wanted you to make it up, then I'd have said so.' His father scowled.

'I was only trying to help,' Peter said quietly.

'Poking your nose into things that don't concern you, more likely,' Bill fumed.

Letting the plate she was washing slip back into the grey, greasy water Molly ran her hands down the sides of her pinafore to dry them and moved over to the grate. Bending down she began picking up knobs of coal and placing them on top of the glowing embers.

'Watch what you're doing, you silly bint,' Bill railed. 'You're smothering what bit of fire there is left. Next thing, you'll have put it out completely. Didn't your mother teach you anything?'

'Yes, to work hard and for all of us to pull together,' Peter said in a low voice.

'What did you say?' Bill's voice was unnaturally quiet and temper was smouldering in his eyes as they fixed on Peter.

'Is this better, Dad?' Molly said quickly as she removed some of the bigger lumps of coal and then gave the fire a gentle prod with the poker.

'Leave the bloody fire alone and get back to your dishes,' he ordered, snatching the poker from her and elbowing her out of the way as he savagely stabbed at the fire.

For a moment Molly thought that as he was venting his temper on the fire all was well, but the reluctance of the fire to respond seemed to stir him to fresh anger.

He stood back and, giving the grate and its contents a savage kick, turned to face Peter. 'You got any money?' he demanded.

Peter hesitated. 'Only my tram fare for work and enough to buy a mug of tea each day.'

'Hand it over.'

Peter hesitated a fraction too long.

'Now!' Bill said angrily and gave Peter a vicious cuff across the ears that brought tears to his eyes.

Biting down on his lower lip, Peter brought out the few coppers he had in his trouser pockets and held them out to his father.

Bill's eyes gleamed as he counted out the pennies and realised that there was enough for a packet of Woodbines and a half-pint of beer. Without a word to any of them he turned up the collar of his jacket, picked up his cap, and was gone.

'He'll have spent my tram fares and my tea money by the time he comes home,' Peter muttered angrily.

'I know. I'm sorry, it's my fault for telling Mr Parsons not to give him credit against my wages.'

'No, you did the right thing,' Peter assured her.

The moment Netta came in from work they explained what had happened.

'Could you make us all a cuppa, luv,' she said, smiling at Molly. 'With any luck we can have it in peace before he gets home again.'

'He won't be long and he can't get drunk because if he bought himself some cigarettes then he'd only have enough for a half-pint,' Peter reminded them.

'It depends on who he meets up with, doesn't it?' his mother pointed out.

145

Half an hour later they heard him lumbering up the stairs and they exchanged anxious looks. As he flung back the door and stood there looking at them all with a supercilious sneer on his face, Molly knew there was going to be trouble. What she wasn't certain about, as she placed a protective arm around little Jodie, was which of them was going to be the target for his temper.

'So, you're home again, are you?' he commented, speaking directly to Netta. 'What's all this business of you buggering off every evening and leaving the kids to see to themselves and clear up after you? Fine sort of mother you are!'

'I've been to work, Bill. I've been cleaning offices in Old Hall Street. You know all about it, I told you the first day you came home that I went out cleaning first thing in the morning and again in the evening,' she reminded him patiently.

'That's the yarn you spin to us. How the hell do I know you haven't been seeing another fella or been off down the boozer enjoying yourself?'

'You know neither of those things is true because I'm the one who brings money home at the end of the week to buy our food and keep a roof over our heads.'

He looked round their shabby room contemptuously. 'If this is the best you can do, then it's high time you found yourself a better-paying job,' he taunted.

'Oh no! Now you are home again you should be the one who's the wage-earner, just as you used to be,' Netta told him spiritedly.

The back-hander across her face almost floored Netta. The three children cried out in horror. Realising he had shocked them all, Bill turned and walked back out. No one said anything, no one called after him to stop.

Molly fetched a basin of warm water and tried to staunch the blood oozing out of her mother's mouth where her teeth had punctured the inside of her lower lip.

As Peter pulled on his jacket and made for the door, Netta held out a hand to stop him. 'Where do you think you're going?' she gasped.

'To find him and give him a hiding,' Peter growled.

Netta shook her head. 'No, son. You'd be the one who would get the hiding. He's only gone out to clear his head. He knows he's gone too far and he's gone for a walk to simmer down. The best thing you three can do is to get ready for bed and be asleep before he comes home. Peter, you sleep on the floor by the side of the girls' bed just for tonight.'

'And leave you to face him on your own!'

Peter exploded.

'I won't really be on my own, now will I? All three of you will be here if I need any help.'

'We weren't much good when he hit you just now, were we?' Peter said dejectedly.

'No, but that was because it was so unexpected. He's never hit me before in his life and I don't think he ever will again. By the look on his face this has brought your dad to his senses, so stop worrying and leave him to me.'

Chapter Eleven

Netta was right; when Bill Henderson returned much later that night he seemed to have sorted himself out and to have come to terms with his life and the situation they were in. He said very little as he accepted the mug of cocoa Netta made for him and as soon as he'd drunk it he said he was tired and ready for bed.

It was the start of a fairly peaceful interlude and not only Netta but all the children welcomed this. None of them said very much to him because they were still afraid of upsetting him and sending him into a rage.

Each day, dressed up in the one good suit he had kept, he went out looking for work, but because of his prison record no one was willing to employ him. He did, however, manage to pick up an assortment of odd jobs. These ranged from casual work clearing a building site, to helping to deliver coal, and, once, being a milkman for a week.

The rest of the time he helped Fred, the carrier who had brought their belongings from Wallasey. Whether or not Fred paid him for his services, none of them ever found out.

Bill never handed over any of his earnings to help towards the household expenses, but at least it meant that he had money in his pocket to pay for his beer and cigarettes.

Molly had received her promised pay rise from Mr Parsons and with what she was earning, together with her own wages and what Peter handed over each week, Netta found that by careful budgeting she was able to manage reasonably well.

Both Molly and Peter were annoyed that their dad didn't contribute anything at home and although they didn't voice their opinion aloud, they had quite a lot to say to each other about it when they were on their own.

'It's not fair on Mum,' Peter grumbled. 'She's still having to go out to work and I bet the money she put aside so that we could move has all gone by now.'

'It probably has, but it's not her fault. Anyway, as she says, it's better to say nothing and to keep the peace rather than have him shouting at us all.'

'I hate it here,' Peter muttered, 'and now he's back home I haven't even got a bed to sleep in.'

'At least you don't have to listen to him snoring every night,' Molly pointed out. 'Or his ranting and raving when he relives the battles he was in when he was over in France,' she added with a grimace.

Although they both laughed about it, neither of them were happy having to live in Mould Court, but because of Molly's friendship with Steven Parsons, she had another interest which helped to make her life bearable.

'Perhaps it's time that you found yourself a girlfriend,' she told Peter.

'Not much chance of me being able to do that on the spending money I get each week; I would never be able to afford to take her out,' he told Molly sullenly.

'Well, perhaps you are better off as you are.' She smiled consolingly. 'At least you've only yourself to please.'

'What's that supposed to mean? Are you having trouble with that Steven? If you are, then you have only to say the word and I'll punch his head in.' Peter glowered.

'And end up as a guest at the Waldorf Astoria like Dad did?' Molly grinned.

He shrugged. 'No, you're right; he's not really worth going that far for.'

Molly knew she should have seized the opportunity to speak up and tell Peter exactly how she felt about Steven, but instead she changed the subject.

When Steven had first started talking to her she'd been flattered but afraid that his father would object. Mr Parsons hadn't seemed to take any notice. She kept telling herself that it was probably because, in his eyes, Steven could do no wrong; or it could be because Steven rarely talked to her for very long if his father was around.

She was quite sure that Mr Parsons didn't know that Steven took her to the pictures and she wondered what his reaction would be if he knew they were kissing and cuddling.

She still marvelled that someone as handsome and well-off as Steven could be interested in her and she felt almost superstitious about it.

She sometimes felt that as long as she kept it a secret, then it would simply get better and better. But once she brought it out into the open and everyone knew about them going out together, then Steven might take fright and stop seeing her.

Although he still took her to the pictures once a week it was now on a Wednesday night. She was puzzled, and asked him why he had changed the night, because she much preferred to go out on Saturday nights.

'The crowd in the office where I am working all go out together on a Saturday night and when they invited me to go with them I agreed because I want to keep in with them,' he explained. 'You do understand, don't you?'

She'd said she did, although she didn't really. When she'd asked him if it was all young men or whether some of them brought their girlfriends along as well he'd said he didn't know. But, if they did go out as a mixed crowd, she couldn't understand why couldn't he take her as well.

She knew the answer, of course, even though she didn't want to admit it even to herself. They were all well dressed, came from good homes, were well educated, had similar jobs and shared many of the same interests, so he probably thought that she'd feel uncomfortable because she wouldn't fit in.

Their visit to the pictures, even though it was now on a Wednesday, was still the highlight of her week and something she looked forward to, and she always took great care to make sure that she looked her best.

Steven no longer seemed to mind what they saw at the pictures; all he wanted to do was kiss and cuddle once the lights went down. When his hands started roaming up under her jumper, or slid up her leg beneath her skirt, she didn't know what to say or do to stop him.

The minute the lights went up in the interval and the organ started playing, he was always sitting bolt upright again and didn't even have an arm around her shoulders. Usually he jumped up right away and went to look for the girl who walked up and down the aisle carrying a tray of crisps, chocolate bars and little tubs of ice cream. He always took so long doing this that usually the lights had gone down again by the time he came back.

She kept wondering why he acted like this when he was always telling her how much she meant to him. She was impatient for the day when he openly admitted that they were going out together and took her to meet his friends and his mother.

She found Saturday evenings were the worst times of all; her mind was always filled with doubts because she knew he was out with his office friends. The next time Jodie asked her if they could go for a walk and see what all the big shops looked like when they were lit up she'd take her, she decided, instead of staying home and moping.

They were walking along Church Street when she'd spotted Steven along with several other young men and girls coming in the other direction. A slim, fair-haired girl was clinging to his arm and laughing up at him. He was far too engrossed in the girl to notice Molly and Jodie, but the near encounter left Molly shaking.

The girl had been very pretty and had been dressed so attractively with an expensive fur wrap slung casually over one shoulder. She'd also been wearing the most enchanting hat Molly had ever seen. It had been a cloche style in a pastel blue shade with a wide, turned-back brim with very narrow edging of dark blue grosgrain, the same colour as the skirt she was wearing, and there had been an enormous bow in the same colour on one side.

As soon as they arrived home and she had made sure that Jodie had a hot drink and was safely tucked up in bed, Molly took the cardboard box in which she kept her best clothes – the ones she always wore when she went out with Steven – down from the top of the cupboard.

She took out the grey skirt and white blouse and held them up against her. They were very neat, but so drab that they did nothing, really to enhance her appearance. She certainly didn't look anywhere near as attractive as the girl she'd seen clinging to Steven's arm, she thought despondently, and wondered if she could ever hope to hold on to his interest and affection when she was faced with such competition?

If only she had the money to buy some new clothes, have her straight brown hair cut and shaped, or even buy a pretty new hat that would flatter her face.

With a feeling of despair, Molly carefully packed her precious best clothes back into the cardboard box to keep them safe, telling herself that she would try and think of some way of brightening them up before her next outing with Steven.

She'd worried about it for the rest of the weekend and even resolved that the right thing to do was to tell him that she'd seen him in Church Street the previous Saturday night and to ask who the girl had been.

She intended to say something to him on Monday, but she never had the chance. These days he didn't seem to arrive at the shop until after she'd left for home. Their long chats between her serving customers, or while she was stacking the shelves with new stock, were a thing of the past.

She tried to summon up the courage to talk to him about it, and when she next saw him on their night out she hesitated because she was afraid of what his answer might be. If they quarrelled, he might find someone else and she couldn't bear to think about that. She was so much in love with him that she knew that if he told her that she wasn't his only girlfriend it would break her heart.

It was silly to think like that, she told herself. After all, there had been several other chaps and girls with them, so the girl might have been someone he worked with; or the sister of one of the other chaps in their party.

She kept meaning to ask her mother's advice about what to do, but she knew Netta had so many other things to worry about that she kept putting it off. It didn't seem fair to burden her with what she might think was a silly problem.

Although all of them were still working, and both she and Peter were contributing more to the housekeeping than before, Molly knew that her mother was still finding it difficult to manage now that their dad was home. It was another mouth to feed, and he had a hearty appetite; Molly knew that her mother spent a lot of time looking for bargains to help make their money go as far as possible.

Molly sighed as once more her thoughts drifted back to Steven. It wasn't merely a silly problem, she told herself, because she truly was very much in love with him. If only she could find out what he felt about her.

She'd opened her heart to him, told him her worries and her dreams for the future. She had encouraged him in all the outrageous ideas he had regarding his future.

She had thought that since they had shared so many dreams it meant that they were as close as any two people could be.

She knew she was far too young to start thinking about getting married and having a home of her own and babies, but she couldn't stop herself. Steven was so tall and handsome and she really was crazily in love with him.

When they were together she was able to forget about the sordid surroundings of Mould Court and the way she and her family were being forced to live in two squalid rooms. Instead, she found herself picturing the sort of home she and Steven would have one day in the future.

It would be a lovely little house with a pretty garden and definitely be as far away from Scottie Road as possible. She would have liked it to be back in Wallasey, but if that wasn't possible, then possibly on the outskirts of Liverpool, where they were building smart new homes for newlyweds.

Above all, she wanted to get away from her father and his feckless ways and scary nightmares.

Sometimes she felt very guilty about feeling like this, but then she reminded herself about the way everything had changed. They had once been such a happy family but ever since their father had come home from the army he'd brought nothing but trouble and despair into all their lives.

Her father might have had it rough, seen some terrible sights and even been in danger, but they'd also had a hard time while he had been away and they'd had to put up with all kinds of shortages.

He'd returned a virtual stranger and, instead of things being all right again, everything had taken a turn for the worse and gone rapidly downhill.

In fact, the only bright spot in her life since they'd moved into Mould Court was her friendship with Steven and that was why she dreaded something might happen to spoil it for her.

From the very first day she had started work in his father's shop he had shown an interest in her. Their feelings for each other had grown so strong and become so much a part of her life that she was now quite sure that it really was love they felt for each other.

No one had ever dominated her thoughts the way Steven did; nor had she ever thought of herself as being in love with anyone else like she did with Steven.

Brian had been a very good friend and she would always be grateful for the way he had championed her at school and saved her from the bullying that was so rampant there. But she had never loved him like she did Steven, not even when because of her his arm had been broken.

Her feelings for Steven were different in every way from anything she'd ever felt for anyone else and that was why she was so positive that it must be true love and not merely a passing interest or infatuation.

All she wanted was reassurance from him that he had really deep feelings for her; feelings that transcended mere friendship. Then, no matter how long she had to wait, she would be confident that one day all her dreams about them spending their future together would come true.

She knew they were both very young and that he had only just started work, but she longed for him to make some sort of commitment. She didn't mean anything as grand as an engagement ring, but some small keepsake, perhaps a brooch or a bracelet that would be a symbol of how much he loved her.

Chapter Twelve

Bill Henderson felt very dissatisfied with his life. Deep down he knew that he had only himself to blame. Every step he had taken since he'd been discharged from the army seemed to be the wrong one. Not that he was prepared to admit that to his wife or to anyone else.

Getting sacked from his job had started it all. Looking back, he knew that his tactics had been all wrong. He should have weighed the situation up much more carefully and dealt with young Basil Perks in a more subtle manner.

The trouble was that he'd expected a hero's welcome when he'd turned up at the office, instead of which they'd treated him as if he was an encumbrance.

Throwing a punch at the rent man had been the next disaster and he blamed the army for that. He had been trained to think on his feet whenever a situation needed an immediate decision and he'd done just that. He'd retaliated without giving a thought to what the outcome of his hotheadedness might be.

Probably, even worse had been his hasty decision to skedaddle from Wallasey to Mould Court. At the time he had seen it as an attempt to evade the law if the rent man reported the incident, which he was pretty sure he would do.

He'd had no idea that it was quite such a slum. He'd thought himself damn lucky to find somewhere so quickly and had not stopped to look over it properly. After they'd arrived there and he'd seen what a hell hole it was he'd been furious and determined to move to something better and would have done so only the law had caught up with him and in next to no time he'd found himself in Walton jail.

Whoever had started calling it the Waldorf Astoria had a warped sense of humour, he thought wryly. It was worse than any army barracks he'd ever been in. So, too, was the treatment meted out to the inmates by the prison officers. He certainly never wanted to go back there if he could possibly avoid it.

He'd come out of the army leaner and meaner than when he went in, but he'd been reasonably fit and, apart from having his chest peppered with shrapnel when a hand grenade had exploded only a few yards away from him, he had come through the war more or less physically unscarred.

What it had done to his mind was another matter. He would never be able to forget some of the sights he'd seen or the things he'd had to endure. Sometimes, especially at night after he'd had one of his vivid nightmares, or if he was unable to sleep, keeping a stiff upper lip was impossible. Pushing it all to the back of his mind was easier in the daytime when there were other things to distract him and occupy his mind.

After his spell in Walton jail he'd ended up not only as thin as a scarecrow, but he'd also suffered physically. Both his nose and his ribs had been broken in various fights between the inmates. The ribs had healed and because they were out of sight no one was any the wiser about them, but his nose was another matter. It was now angled slightly sideways and, in his opinion, had ruined his appearance and made him look like a small-time villain.

He'd met all manner of men while he'd been in the army. He'd heard the life stories of a great many of them and had been astounded at all their different backgrounds. They had all been honest God-fearing types, however, and were not like the villains he'd encountered in jail. The minds of most of his fellow prisoners were so warped and twisted that it was obvious that they would never go straight, no matter what length of sentence they served. Even now, though, he often found that some of the things he'd learned while he'd been in the jail were affecting his outlook as well as his way of life.

Trying to get back on course again since he'd been released seemed to be almost impossible. He was no longer smartly dressed because while he'd been inside Netta had had to sell all his suits except the one he stood up in and that was now threadbare and didn't fit him as it should. His shoes had holes in them and the inner sole he'd made from an old scrap of lino rubbed his feet sore.

At every job he'd gone after they had

asked what he'd been doing since he'd been discharged from the army. He'd tried to cover things up, but it was useless. Every story he told was flawed and employers were astute enough to realise this. In the end he'd brazened it out and told the truth. As a result, because he admitted to his term in prison, he'd found that no one wanted to employ him.

Casual work was all very well, when it was possible to get any, but they only paid you washers. They knew that because of your background you had no option but to take it. So far, the pittance he had managed to earn honestly and the wheeling and dealing he'd done for Fred was only enough to keep him in fags and booze, and not a lot of either of those.

He knew Netta expected him to hand over some of it for housekeeping but there was no way that he was going to do that. Anyway, she was working and so were Molly and Peter, so it wasn't as though they were on the bread line and she was really desperate for his wages, he reasoned.

He couldn't understand why Netta didn't get herself a proper full-time job instead of messing around cleaning offices. Saying that she needed to be at home for when Jodie came in from school was just an excuse as far as he was concerned.

In his opinion, Jodie was big enough to

look after herself and to be doing a damn sight more around the place than she did. In fact, it might be all to the good if Netta pampered her less. She was a mardy little thing, thin and puny, and half the time she seemed to live in a world of her own.

Whenever he asked her to do something she stared back at him as if she didn't understand what he was on about. Her look was so vacant that he could see she wasn't deliberately being stubborn, but it irked him nevertheless. So far he'd controlled himself and never raised a hand to her, but he wasn't sure that he was going to be able to restrain himself for ever.

Giving Netta a back-hander had been a big mistake and one he'd never forgive himself for, even though he wasn't prepared to openly admit it. He was fully aware that she'd been mortified when she first saw Mould Court and realised he was expecting her to live there. He could see that she'd done her best to make a go of things while he'd been inside, but the place was still overcrowded and they were all living on top of each other; he knew that she was desperate to get out of there. So was he, if it came to that. It wasn't a good address when he had to tell potential employers where he lived.

Hitting Netta across the face had sobered him up more than any shouting match between them would have done. He'd never hit a woman before in his life and he'd been shocked to the core when he realised what he'd done.

Since then he'd tried to come to terms with things, but the money he earned was really pitiful and their rooms were so depressing that he had to get out at nights. He was used to being in men's company and he needed the consolation of fags and a couple of beers to make up for all the other disappointments he had to contend with in his life.

He'd never meant to risk his precious few bob on gambling and, so far, he'd kept the fact that he gambled from Netta, but one win and he'd been hooked. The trouble was, of course, that the wins were few and far between and in no way made up for the losses. It was money down the drain without a shadow of doubt, but there was also the thrill when he managed to turn a measly couple of bob into a quid or more.

It had been Fred the carrier who had introduced him to gambling. Fred was addicted; he couldn't help himself. He'd bet on absolutely anything; from how long it was going to take a fly to creep up to the top of the windscreen of his battered old van to how many cockroaches or spiders they were going to disturb when they moved some furniture out of a room.

The trouble was that it was Fred who invariably won, especially when it was on the dogs or horses. He knew an awful lot about racing and he talked endlessly about form and pedigree; he seemed to know all about the riders and trainers and how important they were.

Betting was how most of the money Bill earned from helping Fred ended up back in Fred's pocket and not in his. Fred blinded him with science and it always turned out to be to Fred's advantage, Bill thought ruefully.

It was one of the reasons why at this very moment he didn't have enough coppers in his pocket to buy even a single cigarette, he thought dolefully as he made his way towards Mould Court.

His kids had more money to spend than he had, he thought bitterly as he neared Parsons's newsagent's. He'd thought he was doing all right when he'd first come home and old Parsons had agreed to let him have a packet of fags whenever he wanted them and to take the money for them out of young Molly's wages; only, of course, the miserable little bint had put a stop to that.

He stopped outside the shop and peered in past the jars of striped humbugs, cinder-toffee, liquorice sticks and acid drops. He could see Molly behind the counter in her blue overall. There were no customers in there at all and she was busy opening up some boxes of cigarettes and checking that the number of packets inside was correct.

The sight of them increased his craving for a smoke and he wondered what sort of mood she was in. If he went in and asked her nicely, would she let him have a packet of Woodbines if he promised to give her the money for them in a couple of days' time, as soon as he'd managed to earn some? It was worth a try, he told himself.

As he opened the door and stepped inside Molly looked up quickly and he noticed how her polite, welcoming smile quickly turned into a frown, but he ignored it.

'Hello, luv, can I have a packet of Woodbines?'

He saw the way she stiffened, then she reached behind her, took down one of the green packs of five and, clearing a space, put it down on the counter. 'Tuppence, please,' she stated, keeping her hand on the packet.

Her action inflamed Bill. It was almost as if she doubted whether or not he was going to pay for the blooming things, he thought angrily.

'I've changed my mind, I think I'll have Lucky Strike instead,' he told her.

'We don't stock those and anyway, you always smoke Woodbines. Two pennies, please.'

He shook his head. 'No, I don't want

Woodbines. I only smoke them because they're the cheapest fags there are, but they give me a sore mouth. I think I'll give Kensitas a try for a change. You do stock those? I can see you do because you're unpacking them,' he added before she could answer.

'Very well.' Biting her lip in annoyance Molly turned to replace the Woodbines back on the shelf and at the same time reached down a shiny white packet of Kensitas. 'They do cost a lot more, you know,' she warned as she put them down on the counter.

He pretended to look surprised. 'Perhaps it had better be the Woodbines, then,' he sighed.

As she turned back to get them Bill snatched up the packet of Kensitas and slipped it into his pocket.

It wasn't the cleverest bit of stealing he'd ever done, but he thought he had fooled her because there were so many other packets of that brand already piled up on the counter. What he hadn't realised was that Mr Parsons himself was in the back of the shop and was watching all that was going on. When he suddenly put in an appearance and laid a firm restraining hand on Bill's forearm, Bill almost jumped out of his skin.

He tried to bluster his way out of the predicament he found himself in. 'Molly will be paying for them out of her wages, won't you, luv?' he said quickly as she turned round and stared at them both in bewilderment.

'I don't think so,' Mr Parsons said grimly. 'As I think you very well know, she has already told me that I am not to let you have anything that has to be charged against her wages.'

Bill tried to laugh. 'That was only a silly misunderstanding. Of course she doesn't mind, do you, luv?'

Before Molly could gather her wits together, Mr Parsons shook his head firmly. 'You stole that packet of Kensitas, Mr Henderson, and there is nothing for it but to report what has taken place to the police and that is what I intend to do.'

Bill blustered, then pleaded that it was all a misunderstanding; he tried every way possible to persuade Mr Parsons to change his mind, but to no avail.

'Molly, go and fetch a constable, there's bound to be one in Scotland Road,' Mr Parsons ordered.

The colour drained from Molly's face. 'I'm sorry, Mr Parsons, I can't do that,' she exclaimed aghast. 'I'll pay for them; I can't help to have my own dad arrested.'

Quivering with anger because his authority was being undermined, Mr Parsons drew himself up to his full five feet eight, his eyes bulging and his face puce.

'Right, you two, I've had enough of this stupid farce,' he declared furiously.

169

'So what are you proposing to do now, take the price of these cigarettes out of Molly's wages, or do you want me to give them back?' Bill asked.

'I'll have them back,' Mr Parsons told him in a deadly cold voice, 'because there won't be any money for Molly at the end of the week, Mr Henderson. As a result of your action your daughter is no longer working here.'

Turning to Molly he ordered her sharply, 'Remove your overall and get your coat. I want both of you out of my shop immediately and I forbid you to ever set foot in here again.'

Molly stared at him in horror, tears clouding her eyes. 'Whatever are you saying? You can't possibly mean that you're sacking me, Mr Parsons! I've done nothing at all wrong, so why should I lose my job like this?'

Percy Parsons stood with his arms folded across his rotund chest in an authoritative manner. 'I'm not mincing words with either of you because my mind is made up,' he told them in a resolute voice. 'Unless you leave my premises this instant, I shall hand the pair of you over to the police and have you arrested on a charge of conniving and stealing,' he added grimly.

Chapter Thirteen

Molly couldn't believe what had happened. With tears streaming down her face she ran out of the shop, her coat open, her hair flying, her hat in her hand as she turned into Mould Court.

She heard her father's ponderous footsteps behind her, heard him calling out her name, but she was too upset to take any notice. It was all his fault. She'd loved working there. She'd liked and respected Mr Parsons and been proud that he trusted her and gave her more and more responsibility. She'd been elated when he'd given her a pay rise and had vowed to herself that she'd work so hard that one day he'd raise her wages even more.

Now, all chance of that happening had gone and all for the sake of a packet of cigarettes. She'd see even less of Steven as well. He didn't come into the shop all that often these days and even when he did he was quite formal when he spoke to her, but a smile and a few words from him could lift her spirits and set her heart pounding. She'd never be able to forgive her dad for this, she thought resentfully.

The minute she reached home she sought

the solace and the comfort of her mother's arms as she related what had happened.

Netta listened to her outburst in growing dismay. She knew Bill had inflicted nothing but trouble on their heads since the day he'd been discharged from the army, but to have ruined everything for Molly like this over a packet of fags was beyond belief. What could he have been thinking of? If Parsons had called the police, then Bill would have been straight back in jail without a doubt.

'So what are you going to do now, luv, go and look for another job?'

Molly looked at her wide-eyed. 'I don't know, Mum. I haven't thought that far ahead.' Her face hardened. 'Under the circumstances, I don't suppose I can expect Mr Parsons to give me a reference,' she said dispiritedly.

'Probably not,' Netta agreed. 'Anyway, everyone up and down Scottie Road will know all about what has happened before the day is out so no one locally is likely to take you on. The best thing you can do is try somewhere where you're not known, or go for a different kind of job altogether.'

'Like what?' Molly frowned.

'Factory work, something of that sort, I suppose,' Netta said reluctantly.

They stared at each other in dismay. Both of them knew that would be a last resort and, although neither of them voiced it aloud,

172

they also knew that they couldn't afford for Molly to be out of work for very long. As it was, wherever she found work they wouldn't be paying her until the end of the week after she started and by then things would be so tight at home that they'd definitely be on the bread line.

Netta and Molly talked endlessly about what her future prospects might be. When Peter arrived home he listened with growing anger to her account of what had happened.

'Where is he now?' he demanded.

'I don't know.' Molly shrugged. 'He left Parsons' shop the same time as I did and he was walking home behind me, but he hasn't turned up.'

'No, I bet he hasn't; he's too afraid to face the rest of us. He's probably in a boozer somewhere spinning a yarn about how hard done by he is to a bunch of thickheads in the hope that they'll buy him a drink.'

'Perhaps he's gone to look for a proper job,' Netta suggested. 'He must be aware of how much losing Molly's wages is going to affect us.'

'I very much doubt it! He hasn't found one in all the time he's been out of the slammer so he's hardly likely to do so now,' Peter said scathingly.

'Don't worry, Mum, I'll go and look for something else, first thing tomorrow,' Molly said quickly. 'I'm sure I can find a job of some sort, so don't worry about it.'

Molly's optimism was in vain. Although she spent the whole day going from shop to shop and even to a couple of factories, she had no luck at all.

Footsore and dejected she returned home in time to be there to take care of Jodie when her mother went off to do her evening cleaning job.

'Your dad's still not turned up, then?' Netta said worriedly as she pulled on her coat and rolled her working pinny and dusters up in a bundle to tuck under her arm. 'I hope Peter is home soon because it worries me to leave Jodie on her own and you're going out tonight, aren't you?'

'I'm not sure.' Molly frowned.

'Well, it's Wednesday night and you always go to the pictures with Steven on a Wednesday night...' Netta's voice trailed away and there was a look of consternation on her face. 'Don't tell me that Steven has broken off with you because of what happened.'

'No – no, Mum, of course he hasn't. With all that's been going on I don't feel like going to the pictures. I suppose I should, though, because I don't think Steven would like to be stood up,' she added with a smile. 'It's just that I hate having to tell him what's happened; I feel I am letting him down.'

As she prepared a meal for herself, Peter and Jodie, Molly wondered if what had happened at the shop the day before was going to cause any problems between her and Steven. If he loves me half as much as I love him, then he'll understand it wasn't my fault, she reassured herself.

An hour later Molly was full of trepidation as she left Mould Street and headed for their usual meeting place. She was so on edge that although there was a crowd waiting outside the Rotunda she couldn't focus on them individually enough to see if Steven was there waiting.

When someone caught her by the arm she swung round in alarm, her heart thundering. She let out a long sigh of relief when she found that it was Steven.

'Hey, hey, what's the matter? You look as though you've seen a ghost,' he laughed.

'I have in a way,' she gulped.

He frowned, looking bewildered, and waited for her to explain. When she told him about what had happened at the shop and how his father had dismissed her on the spot, he looked very taken aback.

'That's pretty hard on you,' he admitted, 'but knowing my dad I don't think he will back down.'

'I know, that's the problem, and I imagine it's a waste of time asking him for a reference.'

'Probably,' Steven agreed. 'Aren't you going to find it pretty hard to get a new job without one, though?'

'Of course I am!' She smiled wryly. 'I've been trying all day and the first thing they want to know is why I left my last job. Their second question is do I have a reference. Even the factory jobs I went after wanted a reference of some kind.'

'Most employers do,' Steven assured her. 'So what are you going to do?'

'Keep on trying, I suppose. My mum is worried sick about it. She relies on my wages.'

'So your dad's still not working?'

Molly shook her head. 'It's the same story; he hasn't any references and when they ask what he's been doing since he came out of the army, well, that's it. He says that he always tries to avoid answering because once he tells them the truth then that's the end of the interview.'

Steven nodded. 'I can understand that. Never mind,' he added, giving her arm a squeeze, 'let's go and enjoy the pictures and we can talk about it again afterwards. Who knows, I might be able to think of something by then.'

Inside the cinema, sitting with Steven's arm around her, Molly felt safe and almost happy. She pushed all her worries to one side and moved closer to Steven and let herself be transported to the make-believe world on the silver screen.

Steven was disconcerted that his father had acted so severely, but he also knew that in no way would he retract what he'd done. 'Would you mind doing some other sort of job, Molly?' he asked as they strolled back towards Scotland Road.

'No, not really. I'll try anything, as long as I get paid a decent wage.'

'Have you considered housework?'

She looked at him puzzled. 'I hadn't thought of doing anything like that,' she admitted. 'Why? Do you know where there's a job of that sort going?'

Steven pursed his lips thoughtfully. 'Not really,' he admitted, 'but there might be one.'

'Either there is or there isn't,' Molly rejoined, wondering if he was teasing her.

'Well, our maid is leaving quite soon, so I thought I could ask my mother if she would consider taking you on as a replacement,' he said cautiously.

Molly was silent as she considered what that would entail if she went to work at his home.

'Well, what do you think? Are you interested?' Steven questioned. 'I know it's not the sort of work you want to do but it need only be temporary until you find something more suitable.'

Molly still hesitated. She knew how to clean and polish, but she had never done a job of that sort and she wasn't sure that she would be able to do the work to Mrs Parsons's standards. Also, she wondered what Mr Parsons would say about it. If he didn't want her working for him in his shop, then she was quite sure he wouldn't want her working in his home either.

As they walked along Steven listened to her arguments in silence. He could see the reasoning behind them, but he still thought it was worth a try.

'I'm sure my mother will be concerned when she hears what has happened and will agree that you have been treated rather unfairly to be sacked because of a crime committed by your father.'

'It wasn't really a crime,' Molly defended quickly.

'Oh yes it was; he'd already taken them and slipped them into his pocket,' Steven pointed out.

'I know that, but he didn't consider it to be stealing,' she added weakly. 'He really did think that I wouldn't mind if he charged the cigarettes up against my wages.'

'Well, whether he did or didn't, it doesn't make any difference to the fact that you were dismissed unfairly because you did nothing wrong,' Steven stated, squeezing her hand and giving her a quick peck on the cheek, 'and I'm pretty sure that my mother will agree with me about that.'

'So you really think she would give me a job, do you?' Molly said, her hopes rising.

'I don't know for sure, but I think it's worth a try.'

'And what happens when your father finds out, do I get the sack again?' Molly asked worriedly. 'He's bound to find out because I will have to go through the shop to go upstairs.'

'He won't interfere. They have a mutual understanding. She doesn't interfere in what he does in the shop and he doesn't interfere with what she does at home. And by the way, we don't live over the shop.'

Molly stared at him in surprise. 'I thought you did. You used to come down the stairs into the shop every morning as you were leaving for school.'

Steven shook his head. 'No, we don't live over the shop,' he reiterated. 'I used to travel with my dad each morning, but since he opens the shop up very early I used to spend some time upstairs in his office, finishing off my homework or reading, until it was time to go to school.'

Molly's face brightened. 'Really! So is that why I rarely see you these days, since you started work, I mean?'

'I would have thought you'd have managed to work that out long before now. Upstairs, apart from Dad's office, the place is used for storage.'

Molly bit her lip as she heard the scorn in his voice. 'I didn't know that because I've never been upstairs.' She smiled. 'It has always been out of bounds, even your Dad's office, and I thought that was because you lived up there.'

'So what about this job? Are you prepared to do housework or not?' Steven asked, returning to their discussion. 'Give it a try. You can always leave if you don't like it,' he urged when she still hesitated.

'All right, then, if you are sure that the fact that your father sacked me won't make any difference.'

'I told you, I'll explain the whole thing to my mother, leave it to me. I need to know, though, whether you are willing to do work of that sort before I mention it to her. I don't want to persuade her to give you a job and then find you turn it down simply because you think it is too menial to be helping to clean someone else's house.'

'I wouldn't dream of doing that,' she assured him. 'What's worrying me is whether I will be able to do things the way she likes them done, but I'll certainly do my best.'

'That's all that can be expected of anyone, to do their best,' he told her solemnly. 'She'll soon show you how she wants things done. Leave it with me. Meet me tomorrow night and with any luck I'll have an answer for you.'

Molly still felt doubtful about whether or not she was doing the right thing, but she was comforted that Steven was taking so much trouble on her behalf. She didn't even know where the Parsons family lived or what sort of house they had. She really had thought that, like most of the other shop-keepers in and around Scotland Road, they lived over the premises.

When she got home she was surprised to find that her mother was still up. 'I waited to let you know that your dad is back,' Netta told her. 'He's asked me to tell you that he is sorry about what has happened.'

'Not half as sorry as I am,' Molly told her. 'Anyway, why ask you to tell me, why can't he do it himself?'

'He will tomorrow, luv,' her mother promised. 'He was dog tired, he's not been to bed since it happened; he's been sleeping in doorways because he was too upset to come home.'

'I wouldn't believe such a hard-luck story as that, if I was you,' Molly said cuttingly. 'He's looking for sympathy.'

'I think he's telling the truth. He really did look quite ill. He was dirty, unshaven and starving hungry so I made him have a good all-over wash and change into some clean clothes while I was heating up some of yes-terday's scouse.'

'Lucky old Dad! You always forgive him

and you only ever see his good points, don't you?' Molly sighed.

'Even though he's changed I still love him and always will,' Netta said quietly. 'He looked a different man when he'd finished eating,' she went on, 'but he was so tired he could hardly keep his eyes open so I packed him off to bed. I thought we could have a cuppa together when you got in, that's if you are not too tired after your evening out.'

'I'm glad you did wait up,' Molly told her. 'There's something I need to talk to you about.'

Her mother shared her doubts when Molly told her about Steven's suggestion.

'It's a big commitment, luv,' Netta said thoughtfully as she sipped her tea. 'You've never met the woman. Where do they live?'

'I don't know. I was so taken aback at Steven's suggestion that I didn't even think to ask him. All I do know is that they don't live over the shop.'

'It might be a big rambling place and difficult to keep clean. What's more, she could be a right tartar to work for, you know; as fussy and pernickety as hell.'

'So could the boss if I went to work in a factory.'

'Yes, I suppose that's true enough,' Netta agreed. 'Cleaning is not easy though, luv. I find that doing the offices night and morning wears me out.'

'Yes, but then you have to come home and start all over again. You still have to shop, clean, cook and all the rest of it for us lot,' Molly reminded her.

'Yes, that's true. Well, luv, there's no harm in giving it a try. If you don't like it, then you can always pack it in and look for something else.'

'If I did that she wouldn't give me a reference, though, would she?' Molly pointed out.

Netta picked up the poker and stirred the dying embers of the fire back into life then banked it up with wedges of newspaper which had been soaked in water before piling lumps of coal on top of them.

'No, that's true enough,' she admitted as she turned down the gaslight, leaving only a glimmer so that Peter could see when he came in, 'but you'd be no worse off than you are at the moment because you haven't got one now.'

Chapter Fourteen

Molly was relieved when Steven had said that his mother was willing to consider employing her and that he had explained everything to his mother himself.

'I'll take you and show you where the house is and then you will know where to go tomorrow. She wants to see you at half past ten. Can you manage that?'

'Of course I can, I'm not doing anything else, am I?' she said with a wry smile.

'Well, make sure you are there on time because she's a stickler for punctuality.'

'Don't worry, I will be,' she assured him. 'Tell me the address and I can find it.'

'No,' he insisted, 'I'll take you there myself and explain which bus you have to catch after you get off the ferry.'

'So where is it that you live that's so difficult to find?' she asked, her curiosity aroused. 'Is it somewhere in Birkenhead?'

'No, I live in Wallasey.'

She stared at him in astonishment. 'You've never said so. Why didn't you tell me that when I told you that I used to live over there?'

Steven shrugged. 'It didn't seem to be important. You don't live there now.'

'Why on earth didn't you go to a school in Wallasey? There are plenty of them there.'

'Because they both wanted me to go to one over here that they considered to be better. For heaven's sake, Molly, why all this probing? What does it matter?'

'It doesn't matter in the slightest,' she told him stiffly. 'It's just that discovering you live in Wallasey has taken me by surprise. It also

184

accounts for the fact that ever since you started work I hardly ever saw you in the shop.'

'Of course you didn't. Once I was working they agreed I was old enough to look after myself. My uncle owns the shipping company where I'm working so if I had an accident or something and didn't turn up on time he would be on the phone to my mother straight away to find out where I was.'

Their conversation went round and round in her head next morning as she crossed over on the *Royal Daffodil* and then boarded a bus at Seacombe to take her to Warren Drive.

Uppermost in her mind as she approached the fine red-brick house was Steven's warning, 'Look, I think it is best if you don't let on that we occasionally see each other in the evenings.'

When she'd asked him why he didn't want his mother to know, he'd been annoyed. 'Because she fusses about me and so does my father, as you can probably gather from the arrangements they always made to see I didn't come to any harm on my way to school.'

'You're not at school now, though,' she reminded him, 'so surely what you do in the evenings is your own affair.'

'Not really, not while I am living at home,

and I'm not likely to be able to afford a place of my own for at least another six or seven years.'

'So where do your parents think you are when you take me out?' she persisted.

'Out with my friends, of course,' he told her evasively. 'Most of them live over our way and my parents have known them for years so they are both quite happy about it.'

'I see,' Molly said, but inside her stomach had been churning. It was exactly as she had thought; Steven hadn't told his parents how well he knew her and she suspected it was because he knew they wouldn't want him going out with someone who lived in a place like Mould Court and who had a family like hers...

She felt hurt, but there didn't seem to be any point in saying anything. If she took him to task about it then she would probably lose not only him but her chance of a job as well.

Molly paused at the huge iron gates. The red-brick house at the end of the gravel drive looked even more imposing in the morning light. She couldn't help being impressed; she'd never visited a house like it in her life and she'd certainly never been inside one that was anywhere half as grand.

Steven had told her to go to the tradesman's entrance and the resentment flared up anew as she walked past the imposing oak door with its highly polished knocker and bell pull and made her way to the side of the house.

Steven had taken her as far as the gate the previous night, to make sure she knew which house it was, and she'd spent half the night thinking about what it was going to be like inside.

Now she was more concerned about what sort of person Mrs Parsons would be. Mr Parsons and Steven were not a bit alike. Mr Parsons was rotund and had a florid face; his small, calculating eyes missed nothing that went on in his shop, as both she and her dad knew to her cost.

He was very brisk and businesslike, and sharp when it came to buying and selling, especially with the commercial travellers who called at the shop. He certainly had his own ideas about display, which centred on the methodical rather than what was eye-catching.

Steven was handsome, there was really no other word to describe him, she decided. With his thick, dark, brushed-back hair, smooth tanned skin, strong face and winning smile, he was as great a heart-throb as any film star.

It never ceased to amaze her that he was interested in her and enjoyed her company so much when he took her out. She could even forgive him for going out with his friends on a Saturday night as long as he took her out during the week.

The woman who opened the door to her looked as if she were about thirty, and she was heavily pregnant, so Molly knew why she was being considered as a replacement.

'Hello, I'm Sally, and I take it you are Molly Henderson,' the woman greeted her as she invited her inside and led her into a big spacious kitchen. 'Wait here, Molly, and I'll tell them you've arrived and see if Mrs Summers, the housekeeper, wants to speak to you first before Mrs Parsons interviews you.'

Left on her own Molly looked round the huge room in awe. It was almost as large as the two rooms where she and her family lived, ate and slept put together.

A window looked out on to the gravel drive at the side of the house and there was a massive cooking range with various pots and pans standing on it. Judging from the savoury smell that permeated the room a meal was being prepared.

Molly looked at the line of cupboards along one wall and wondered what was in them. At the far end of the room was a Welsh dresser with matching cups, saucers, plates and serving dishes displayed on it.

Dominating the room was a large table, the top of which was scrubbed white. There was a high-backed wooden armchair at the head of it and two smaller wooden chairs at each side.

As she stood there nervously listening to the ponderous tick of the large clock fixed on the wall above the window, she could hardly breathe she was so nervous.

She gave a gulp of relief when Sally re-appeared. 'Madam herself will see you now in the morning room. Are you ready? Come along, I'll show you the way.'

The room was adjacent to the kitchen, but the picture window overlooked a stretch of lawn at the back of the house and the June sun was streaming in, making it bright and welcoming. A slim, dark-haired woman who was standing looking out of the window turned to face them as Sally opened the door.

Mrs Parsons was as trim and graceful as her husband was rotund. Her eyes were a vivid blue, so similar to Steven's that for a moment Molly found her breath catching in her throat because it was almost as if she was looking at Steven.

'Come in, Molly, come and sit down and let us have a little chat,' she invited in a low, cultured voice. 'My son has explained that you were working for my husband so there is no need for you to tell me anything about that. I am far more interested in knowing how much you know about domestic work.'

'Not – not very much, I'm afraid,' Molly stammered. 'I've helped my mum do things, of course, but – but not in a house as big as this. We used to live in Derby Road,' she added quickly in an effort to make it quite clear that she hadn't always lived in Liverpool's Scotland Road area.

'Yes, so I understand.' Mrs Parsons nodded. 'My son has also told me about the misfortunes your father has encountered since he left the army.'

'Things have not worked out as he expected them to,' Molly explained. She felt flustered because she wasn't sure how much Steven might have told his mother and she didn't want to run the risk of jeopardising her chances of working there by saying either the wrong thing or more than was necessary.

'Well, as long as you are a good, willing worker I don't mind too much that you have no experience of this sort of work,' Mrs Parsons told her. 'In fact, I think I prefer it because it means that right from the start you will be doing things the way I like to have them done.' She smiled sweetly. 'So now, all we have to do is to decide when you are going to start working here.'

Molly's face brightened. 'You mean I've got the job!' she gasped delightedly.

'Well, let's say I'm prepared to give you a trial and see how you get on. Sally won't be leaving for another two weeks so she will be here to guide you as well as Mrs Summers who is my housekeeper. They will make sure you know the general routine and also where everything is kept.'

'Thank you! Thank you, Mrs Parsons. I am sure I will give every satisfaction,' Molly assured her.

'Well, we'll soon find out, won't we? Now, when are you free to start?'

'As soon as you wish. I could even come tomorrow, if you wanted me to.'

'Yes, very well. The sooner the better, I suppose, in case Sally has to leave early. Her baby is not due for about a month, but you can never be too sure about these things,' she added vaguely.

'What time do you want me to be here tomorrow morning, Mrs Parsons?'

'Eight o'clock, and I expect you to be punctual.'

Molly was so eager to cooperate that she was about to agree, but then she remembered that her mother went out cleaning first thing each morning and that it was left to her to make sure that Jodie got ready for school and didn't sit reading or day-dreaming.

Before she could explain all this to Mrs Parsons she saw her frown. 'You do have to come over from Liverpool, so I suppose we will have to allow for that. Shall we say nine o'clock, then, for the moment and see how

191

things go?'

'Yes, that will be fine,' Molly agreed.

It was going to mean that Jodie would have to take herself to school, but it really was high time she managed to do that without anyone supervising her, Molly thought.

'Right,' Mrs Parsons stood up, 'now is there anything else you need to know?'

Molly looked uneasy. The one thing they hadn't discussed and which was more important to her than anything else was the matter of her wages. She was anxious to know not only how much she was to receive but also when would she be paid, only she didn't know how to ask the question diplomatically.

'What have I forgotten?' Mrs Parsons probed when she saw her hesitation.

Molly's throat felt dry and her palms damp. 'You ... you haven't said what my wages will be.'

'Oh, we must settle that, of course. How much were you being paid when you started at the shop?'

'Ten shillings a week to start with, but I got a half a crown rise after I'd been there a few weeks.'

'Ten shillings. I see.' Mrs Parsons looked thoughtful. 'The shop was within walking distance of your home, wasn't it?'

Molly nodded. 'Yes, only a few minutes away.'

'Hmm.' Mrs Parsons paused and seemed to be considering the matter. 'You will have to pay bus and boat fares each day so I suppose I ought to pay you a little bit more to cover those. Right, then, shall we say that for the first month your wages will be ten shillings and that in addition I will give you travelling money separately. Will that be all right?'

Molly nodded, thankful that she wasn't going to be as much out of pocket as she had feared she might be.

'You won't have to work on a Sunday but I shall expect you here on a Saturday.'

'Yes; yes, of course.'

'You needn't work all day on Saturday, perhaps until about three o'clock. Once you've washed up after our lunch and cleared everything away you will be free to go. Right?'

'Yes, thank you,' Molly murmured. It was going to be a long week, but at least she would be finishing early on a Saturday, she reflected. The money was better than she had expected and she had nothing else to go to so really she had no option but to accept the terms she was being offered.

'Right, we seem to have dealt with everything. Here's five shillings which will more than cover your fares for coming here today and for the rest of the week. You will be paid on Friday night for the work you do this week and then on Friday each week after that if I decide to keep you on. And, as I have already said, each week I will give you the money for your fares separately.'

'Thank you, Mrs Parsons.'

'Report to Mrs Summers, my house-keeper, tomorrow morning, and she will provide you with a uniform.'

'Uniform?'

'While you are at work you will be expected to wear an overall which I will provide for you, and which you will wear in the mornings when you are doing housework. You will be responsible for making sure it is always clean and that you look presentable. At twelve o'clock you will change into a black dress and a white apron ready to answer the door to visitors and serve at table when I am entertaining. All these items will be kept here and you will change into your own clothes to go home.'

Molly went home in a daze. She still hadn't seen over the house, and didn't know how many rooms there were, or how much work she was going to be expected to do. From the outside it looked as though there might be four or even five bedrooms as well as a dining room and drawing room. Would she be working on her own and expected to keep them all clean? she wondered. If so, it was going to be an awful lot of hard work.

She still had to meet Mrs Summers and

she wondered what she would be like since it seemed she was going to be the one she had to take orders from in future.

As she crossed back over the Mersey her head was in a whirl. She couldn't believe what a wonderful house it was and couldn't wait to see the rest of it, especially Steven's room. Perhaps one day she'd even be invited to stay there, once Steven spoke up and told his parents that she was his girlfriend, she thought with an inward smile.

Chapter Fifteen

Working for Mrs Parsons wasn't anywhere near as arduous as Molly had feared it might be. What Mrs Parsons hadn't told her was that as well as Mrs Summers, who seemed to run things like clockwork as well as doing all the cooking and baking, a daily woman came in each morning to do the heavy cleaning and another woman came in twice a week to do the washing.

Mrs Summers was stout, middle-aged, with grey hair in a fat bun in the nape of her neck and sharp grey eyes. Beneath her strict appearance she was kindly and caring as well as being something of a martinet.

Molly found that her duties each morning

consisted of tidying the rooms in readiness for the daily woman to clean and then doing the dusting. There were a great many valuable objects in every room in the house and Sally pointed out that they were much too fragile for the daily woman to look after.

Molly had never seen a house like it. It was far grander than she had imagined. Downstairs, as well as the kitchen which had a large walk-in pantry opening off it, and the breakfast room which she had already seen, there was an oak-panelled dining room, a very large ornate drawing room, and a smallish library which was also used as a study.

The dining room was furnished with heavy dark mahogany furniture. There was a huge extending table, a massive sideboard with a carved-frame mirrored over-mantel. There were two matching highly polished glass-fronted cabinets; one which was filled with expensive-looking china while the other was slightly smaller and held exquisite ornaments.

The drawing room was very grand with three matching armchairs and two couches upholstered in red plush and facing each other on either side of the marble fireplace. There was also a chaise-longue positioned under the huge picture window so that anyone lying on it could look out over the Mersey to the Welsh hills which were a misty blue in the far distance.

The study was dominated by a huge walnut desk. Three of the walls were lined from floor to ceiling with books, some with handsome tooled-leather covers.

Upstairs there were five bedrooms and a family bathroom with a huge gleaming white porcelain bath, and a matching fluted washbasin and lavatory.

The large front bedroom had a huge canopied bed, with figured walnut bedside tables on each side. These matched the two massive wardrobes, dressing table and tallboy. On either side of the bed were two enormous cream sheepskin rugs.

Her heart gave a flutter and she felt the hot blood rush to her cheeks when Sally took her into a large room at the rear of the house, which had its own small bathroom, and looked out on to the back garden, and told her that it was Mr Steven's room.

The largest of the remaining bedrooms was used by Mrs Summers as a bed-sitting room and the remaining two bedrooms were guest rooms.

There was also a big attic which was used as a place to store things. The cellars beneath the kitchen were divided into a laundry room and a place to keep various items of household equipment which were only used occasionally.

Molly found it hard to take it all in. Surely three people didn't need all this room to live in, she thought in amazement.

Her next thought was far more practical; how on earth did they afford to live like this on the takings of a small newsagent and tobacconists in the slums of Liverpool?

'Lovely place, isn't it?' Sally said proudly. 'I'm going to miss being here, I can tell you. Bit different to my two-bedroom house in Poulton, I can tell you.'

'Yes, it is lovely,' Molly agreed. 'Not a bit like the shop Mr Parsons has in Liverpool.'

'Oh that,' Sally sniffed. 'That's more of a hobby with him than a real business. Mrs Parsons is the one with the money. This house was part of her inheritance from her parents when they died. He doesn't really have to work at all, but you know what men are like. He doesn't want to be a kept man; he wants to be captain of his own little empire.'

'I can understand that,' Molly said thoughtfully, 'but why pick a place like Scotland Road to have a shop? Why not have one over here or in New Brighton?'

'Don't ask me,' Sally shrugged in a disinterested way, 'I work for Mrs Parsons and as long as she treats me well and pays me regularly I don't want to know about their private affairs.'

Even though she was still curious, Molly accepted the rebuff and said no more. There were plenty of other things for them to

198

discuss, and learning how Mrs Parsons liked to have things done was what was important at the moment.

From what Sally told her, Mrs Parsons had plenty of rules and preferences. They ranged from which day each room was turned out right down to the methods employed. Her precious china and other ornaments had to be handled with the greatest of care and must always be put back exactly where they had been positioned before. Slipshod work was simply not tolerated.

'She has very sharp eyes and she notices even if they are only half an inch out,' Sally told her.

'Some of them look so fragile I shall be afraid to pick them up,' Molly murmured.

'Yes, I know what you mean. I'm a bit of a butter-fingers myself but I've been lucky, I've never dropped one, or even chipped one, if it comes to that, and I've worked here almost four years.'

In every room there was something of importance or some rule that had to be remembered and by the end of the first couple of days Molly's head was in a complete muddle as she tried to remember everything Sally had listed.

'Mrs Parsons always does the flowers herself, but she expects you to top the vases and containers up with water each day. Whatever you do you must be careful not to disturb the arrangement. There's a special long-spouted indoor watering can that I use. Remember, though, to always carry a cloth with you because sometimes it can drip and unless you mop it up right away even a single spot will leave a mark and she will be bound to notice it.'

Another of her jobs would be making the beds each morning. 'You need to do that the minute you get here so that any feathers you make when you turn the beds over will be cleared away by Maggie, the daily woman. She usually starts by doing the grates and polishing the doorsteps and things like that so you will have plenty of time. After she's swept the carpet and polished the surrounds then you go back in and dust the furniture and make sure everything is back in place.'

As well as her household duties, Molly found that when Mrs Parsons had guests for luncheon or afternoon tea she was expected to lay the table and then to change into her black dress and white frilly apron ready to open the door and later to help serve the food.

'She has luncheon parties twice or even three times a week,' Sally explained. 'Usually they are ladies and they arrive at about twelve-thirty and are gone again by four o'clock. After they've eaten they like to have coffee served in the drawing room. Remember, you must always address her as

"Madam" when there's company.'

Molly was working at the Parsons's house for almost ten days before Sally's labour pains began. Mrs Summers insisted that Sally must sit down immediately and not move a muscle.

'Molly, you make Sally a cup of tea while I go and tell Mrs Parsons what is happening.'

Before Sally could drink it Mrs Parsons came hurrying into the kitchen to say that she had sent for a taxicab.

Molly was thankful that she was fully knowledgeable about what her job entailed. She had settled in well to her new way of life and no longer felt nervous about asking either Mrs Summers or Mrs Parsons if there was something she was not sure about.

Coming over on the boat every morning certainly brushed the cobwebs away, especially when there was a fresh breeze invading every nook and cranny of the ferry boat. If the weather was calm she often took an invigorating walk on the top deck as they crossed to the other side so that by the time she reached Seacombe she felt as if she had entered another world.

There was only one problem as far as she was concerned and that was her friendship with Steven. She thoroughly enjoyed cleaning his room, even though he left it in a terrible mess each morning. She had learned so much more about him from seeing the books he enjoyed reading, almost reverently dusting the guitar he played and tidying up everything else in his room.

She had studied the pictures he had on his walls with interest; there were lots of cricket and football groups and he was prominent in all of them. There were also more recent pictures of what appeared to be an office outing and her heart beat faster and she felt a flush of jealousy as she recognised the girl she had once seen him with amongst the group in the photograph.

One day she hoped there would be a picture of her amongst his treasures, or even better still one of them both together. Deep down she suspected that wouldn't be for a very long time. He was constantly warning her that whatever happened she must never mention to his mother that he sometimes took her to the pictures. His explanation was that his mother simply wouldn't understand.

'She's always inviting friends to dinner who have daughters about the same age as me in the hope that I will strike up a friendship with them and it makes her annoyed when I never do. If she knew it was because I was seeing you then she would be furious,' he explained. 'Not only would you lose your job, but I'd get a severe talking to. I'm used to that, but I wouldn't like to think you'd been given your marching orders simply because we are friends. Anyway,' he went on quickly when she frowned, 'it's much more romantic if we keep it a secret between ourselves.'

She'd agreed, of course. She couldn't afford not to do so and in some ways she liked the idea that it was their secret. Steven had assured her he wasn't interested in the girls his mother invited to the house, or even the ones who accompanied him and his crowd of friends when he went out with them on Saturday nights. He'd even said that his feelings for her really were very special and that she meant a great deal to him, which was why he wanted it to be their secret.

Even so she wasn't too sure that his feelings were the same as hers were for him. In her case she knew it really was love and she longed for him to say that he felt the same way about her. If he openly told her he didn't have those sorts of feelings for her then she would be heartbroken.

Sometimes he seemed almost offhand and uncomfortable when they were in the same room and someone else was present and she couldn't help feeling hurt when he treated her almost like a stranger.

She never discussed it with him, but she felt that his family wouldn't regard her as an employed servant if he told his parents how he felt about her.

The only time when her position didn't seem to matter was when they were at the pictures. The moment the lights went down he became the ardent boyfriend she had lost her heart to. His arm was around her within seconds, and no matter how absorbing or exciting the action on the screen might be it always seemed to fade into insignificance for both of them.

All her worries that he felt self-conscious about being in her company vanished as he caressed her or pulled her closer so that the warmth of his body filled her with a passionate longing that they could really be on their own; somewhere private, and not in the back row of the cinema.

When his lips sought hers she willingly returned his kisses, her interest in what was happening on the silver screen completely obliterated as she indulged in her own fantasies.

The moment the lights went up he was immediately cool and formal towards her and dashed off to get their refreshments. Although she welcomed whatever he fetched back for them, the fact that he always delayed doing so until the lights once more dimmed annoyed her because she had the niggling suspicion that he did it deliberately so that no one would see them together.

He laughed at her when she mentioned this, but once or twice she saw him stop to talk to people. They were obviously colleagues from work or friends from Wallasey, and never once did he mention anything to her about them when he returned to his seat. Nor did he ever introduce her to any of them.

Whenever he did see someone in the cinema that he knew then she was very aware that he always decided to leave immediately the picture ended and before the lights went up and everyone stood while the National Anthem was played. Again she suspected that if they stayed, someone might see them together and that was something that Steven most definitely didn't want to happen.

Fortunately, he was rarely in the house at Warren Drive at the same time as she was. He'd left before she arrived in the morning and she'd left for home before he arrived back in the evening, even when he came straight home after work.

The only time when they did occasionally meet there was on a Saturday when he slept late and then she was always on tenterhooks waiting for him to make an appearance.

When he did, he merely nodded at her as if she was more or less a stranger. This always brought the blood rushing to her face and when he realised this, Steven made a point of not even nodding to her if his mother was close by.

Mrs Summers noticed. When he was late getting up Steven would come into the kitchen to ask her to fix him some breakfast and although she pretended to scowl and always scolded him and said it was putting her out when she was working her fingers to the bone, she always did.

It was obvious that she had a soft spot for him and when she saw the effect he had on Molly she was quick to tell her, 'Now don't go breaking your heart over that one because he won't even give you a second glance. He's got a string of girlfriends as long as my arm. Regular heartbreaker, he is. He's had girls running after him ever since he was a nipper.'

'No one special, then,' Molly probed.

'Oh, I don't know about that. Mrs Parsons has some very rich friends and several of them have some very pretty daughters. Playing the field, is Master Steven. He'll get caught one of these days, though, you mark my words,' she chuckled.

'So he has someone in mind?'

'He likes variety, but his mother is very ambitious and she'll make sure that he picks the right one to pop the question to, you mark my words.'

Molly said nothing but it left her with a heavy heart. Somehow she thought that Mrs Summers was probably correct, even though Steven stoutly denied the fact when, teasingly, she told him what had been said.

'No one tells me what I can or cannot do,' he boasted. 'Why should I be interested in anyone else when I have a secret romance

206

with the loveliest girl on Merseyside?'

Molly felt flattered; she wanted to believe him, but in her heart of hearts she knew that once Mrs Parsons made her mind up about something she rarely changed her mind.

Even so, she found that Mrs Parsons was a very considerate employer. She always insisted that Molly had a scone or a piece of cake when she had her mid-morning break and provided her with a substantial meal at lunch time. Often when there were leftovers after they'd been entertaining she told Molly to wrap them up and take them home with her.

Sometimes it was a huge lump of cooked ham, or some beef; at other times half of a cake that she said would otherwise go stale if kept until the next day. Netta found them a godsend because they brought something appetising into their stodgy daily fare, especially towards the end of the week when her housekeeping was at its lowest ebb.

Bill Henderson would scowl and mutter, 'Does that bloody woman think we are beggars, tossing us her bloody crumbs?' Nevertheless, he was always the first to welcome the tasty meal Netta would make from the meat and always cut the biggest wedge from the cake for himself.

Chapter Sixteen

It was a bitterly cold December day but Molly was so hot working in the kitchen helping Mrs Summers with all the extra baking that had to be done for Christmas that she had rolled up her sleeves and undone the button at the top of her white overall.

Mrs Summers had just opened the oven door to lift out the second batch of mince pies she had made that morning when there was a timid tap on the back door.

Frowning in annoyance and at the same time pushing a straggle of hair from her face that had escaped from her bun she looked across at Molly, 'Now who on earth can that be?'

'I don't know, shall I answer it?'

'Your hands are all covered in flour so I'd better do it,' Mrs Summers grumbled. 'A time waster or someone begging, you mark my words,' she muttered as she made her way to the door.

'Yes? And what is it you want? If you've come begging, then there's nothing here for you so run along and remember to shut the gate as you go out.'

'Please, missus, I-I'm not begging. I want

to see my sister.'

Molly's heart did an uncomfortable jump as she recognised Jodie's thin, whining voice. Brushing as much flour as she could from her hands and then quickly wiping them on a damp cloth, she rushed over to the door.

'It's all right, Mrs Summers. It's my little sister.'

As she spoke she looked at Jodie in horror. No wonder Mrs Summers had thought that she was begging. Her dress was hanging unevenly under her shabby brown coat, one of her grey socks was down around her ankles and there was a big hole in the toe of one of her black shoes. She had a navy-blue woollen hat pulled down low on her forehead and her thin, straggly hair hung round her face in uncombed knots.

'Jodie,' she pulled the child into her arms and gave her a reassuring hug, 'what on earth are you doing here? You shouldn't have come all this way on your own! However did you find the house?'

'Dad brought me across and he's waiting for us down the road,' Jodie snuffled.

As she came into the kitchen she shivered as she encountered the sudden warmth and she rubbed her coat sleeve across her nose which had started to run.

Molly quickly brought out her own handkerchief and handed it to her, hoping Mrs Summers hadn't seen what she'd done. In the pristine clean kitchen and with both her and Mrs Summers wearing white overalls, Jodie really did look extremely dirty and disreputable. Molly repressed a shudder.

'What do you mean, Jodie, when you say he's waiting for us?' Molly asked.

'He wants you to come home and see to Mum because he doesn't know what to do.'

'What do you mean? Whatever's happened, has she had an accident of some sort?'

'No.' Jodie shook her head, rubbing the handkerchief across her face. 'It's not an accident. It's her chest,' she sobbed, 'she's got bronky something or the other.'

Molly frowned. Her mother had been suffering from a heavy cold for over a week but she hadn't seemed any worse when she had left home that morning.

'Has Dad called the doctor?'

'Yes,' Jodie sniffed loudly. 'He says it might get worse and turn to something called monia. She can't breathe very well and that's why Dad says you must come home because he doesn't know what to do,' Jodie said breathlessly.

'You mean your mother might have pneumonia,' Mrs Summers intervened.

Jodie bit down on her lower lip and nodded, her eyes filling with tears, her hand reaching out to clutch at Molly for reassurance.

210

'And your father expects Molly to come home right away to look after her?'

Molly was already taking off her overall. 'I'll have to go,' she explained. 'My mother's not been well for the last couple of weeks, but she's insisted on carrying on as normal. It must be serious for them to come for me, Mrs Summers.'

'That's as maybe, but we're up to our eyes here, my girl. You can't go sloping off to look after your family every time one of them gets a cold.'

'It's not like that, though, is it? Pneumonia is very serious. I'm sure Madam will understand if I explain it all to her.'

'Well, she's not at home so that means I am the one who will have to give you permission.'

Molly held her breath. She didn't want to start a row with Mrs Summers but she felt her duty to her own mother came first and no matter what Mrs Summers might say she was determined to go back to Liverpool with Jodie.

Mrs Summers gave her a long, stern stare, and then sighed deeply. 'I can see you've already made up your mind. Well, go and get your coat, then. Try and arrange for someone else to look after her, though, because you are needed here. There are no end of parties and dinners planned between now and Christmas. In fact, Mrs Parsons was

211

only saying to me yesterday that she intended to ask you if you could work longer hours for the next few weeks.'

She was still speaking as Molly went out of the door and into the next room to get her outdoor clothes. She'd already put her coat on and was pulling on her hat when she heard the rumpus coming from the kitchen. As she dashed back to find out what was happening she was in time to see Jodie splutter and choke as Mrs Summers slapped her hard across the face.

'What on earth is happening? Whatever do you think you are doing?' Molly gasped.

'This thieving little varmint has just pinched one of my freshly made mince pies,' Mrs Summers exclaimed in an outraged voice. 'Pinched it the minute my back was turned and rammed it into her mouth as if she was starving.'

'I'm sorry but she probably is starving and she's certainly very cold and hungry,' Molly apologised.

'That's no excuse for stealing! Why couldn't she ask if she wanted one?'

'She was probably afraid to do so; she is very shy.' Molly turned to her sister who was crying, partly with fright and partly from pain. 'Tell Mrs Summers you are sorry and that you know it was a naughty thing to do,' she told her.

Mrs Summers was not so easily appeased.

'Saying sorry won't do. Those mince pies were for a special occasion and now I'm going to be one short and I can't make another batch because I've used up all the mincemeat. Anyway, it was stealing and one thing I can't abide is a thief. She looks like a little guttersnipe and, so it seems, that's exactly what she is. Go on, get out of my kitchen and take her with you. Make sure that she never comes here ever again.'

Grabbing the sobbing Jodie by the hand, Molly made a hasty retreat. She could understand why Mrs Summers felt as she did, because she hated anything at all going wrong in her kitchen but nevertheless there was no need to slap Jodie across the face.

Their father was waiting for them at the corner and Molly was glad he hadn't come to the door with Jodie. Her sister might look dirty and uncared for but he looked even worse. He was hollow-cheeked and un-shaven and she had never seen him looking so dishevelled. He looked more like a down-at-heel tramp than the smart soldier who had returned from the war, or the well-dressed businessman he'd once been, she thought sadly.

'What the devil is she snivelling about now?' he greeted them irritably.

As Molly felt Jodie clutch more tightly to her hand she tried to cover up for her. 'You know how shy she is, Dad, and Mrs

Summers the housekeeper is a bit formidable.'

He grunted but said no more and as they hurried to the bus stop in Warren Drive he remained silent. Once they reached Seacombe and were on the boat he began telling her how bad her mother was and how worried he was about her.

'Surely you haven't left her on her own?' Molly murmured anxiously.

'Of course I have, what else could I bloody well do?' He nodded in Jodie's direction. 'That one's afraid of her own shadow so I couldn't let her come over here on her own and she's so bloody useless that there was no point in leaving her there. If your mum had one of her gasping or choking attacks that one would have just stood there and screamed or started crying. Your mother is really ill, Molly, and I don't know what to do. With any luck she's been asleep all the time we've been out.'

Molly hoped so as well. When they finally reached Mould Court she was the first one to Netta's bedside and was utterly shocked by the state she found her mother in.

Netta hadn't been at all well the previous evening and Molly knew she had been coughing and struggling for breath when she'd left home that morning. Now, in a matter of hours, she had lost all her colour; her breathing was strained and noisy and she looked as frail as a little old lady of seventy.

'What did the doctor tell you to do?' she asked, turning to her father who was still taking off his coat.

'He said something about a poultice but I didn't know what he was on about. He left a prescription. I took it to the chemist but I haven't picked it up yet.'

'Then you'd better put your coat back on and get it as quickly as you can,' Molly told him sharply.

'Give over, I want a cuppa and something to eat first, I'm famished after going all the way over to Wallasey. I thought the least you'd do would be to call us into the house and give us a brew and a bite. They can spare it; look at all the stuff they throw out that you bring home.'

'I'll make you some tea while you go for the medicine,' Molly told him. 'She'll get better a lot more quickly if you fetch it now and I give her a dose right away.'

She turned back to the bed, straightened the crumpled pillows, and smoothed the sheets.

'Fetch the face flannel,' she told Jodie and when her sister brought it to her, she wiped the sweat from her mother's face and forehead.

'Is she going to be all right, Molly?' Jodie asked in a frightened whisper.

215

'Yes, of course she is. We'll soon make her better. Now you go and take your coat off and put the kettle on ready to make us all a cup of tea. Can you do that?'

As she turned back to attend to her mother she saw Jodie hesitate uncertainly. This was no time to pamper her, it was high time Jodie did more to help, Molly decided, and now was as good a time as any for her to start.

For the rest of the day Netta appeared to get worse. Her fever increased, she was burning hot, and Molly spent all her time bathing her face and neck and moistening her dry, cracked lips with tiny dabs of cold water.

By late evening, the fever was at crisis point. Netta, drenched in sweat, was tossing and turning, her mind was rambling and her breathing became so laboured that it seemed as if every gasp would be her last one.

After Peter had helped to get their meal ready and then cleared away afterwards, Molly suggested to her father that he should try and get some sleep since he claimed he was worn out.

'You can't sleep with Mum, so you and Peter have our bed for tonight.' He didn't need any persuading and within minutes he was snoring noisily.

She made up the mattress for Jodie in the living room and told Peter he'd be sharing with his dad. Peter wasn't too keen on the idea and said he would sit up and help her to nurse their mum, but Molly insisted that he needed his sleep if he was going to be fit to go to work next day.

Left alone, Molly sat by her mother's bedside, alternately holding her hand or bathing her face and forehead until finally she was breathing more quietly and her forehead was no longer burning hot.

Then she went very still, almost as if she was sinking into a coma, but whether it was a deep sleep or unconsciousness Molly wasn't at all sure.

Molly stayed by her bedside, scared that it might mean that her mother was near her end. She was far too tired and too frightened to cry. She sat there in a numb vacuum, simply holding her mother's hand and from the occasional twitch or jerk consoled herself that her mother was still alive.

How long she sat there like that, waiting to see what happened next, Molly was not sure because she knew that from time to time her own eyelids drooped and she suspected that she dozed for several minutes or possibly even longer, but suddenly she was fully awake. It was still dark outside, her father was still snoring, but there was no other sound whatsoever.

Fearfully she looked at her mother. Netta's breath was no longer rasping and in the flickering candlelight her face looked more relaxed. Molly fought back the panic that surged inside her own head and forced herself to pick up her mother's hand which was lying limply on top of the covers. It was still warm. She was sure that the bedclothes were lifting slightly, as though her mother was breathing normally. Molly couldn't believe it because otherwise she was as still as a waxen figure.

She stretched out a hand and touched her mother's brow. It was cool but no longer damp and clammy. As she held her own breath, still afraid that she might be wrong, her mother's lips parted with a faint sigh and then she moved as if trying to make herself more comfortable in bed.

Molly fretted, wanting her to open her eyes or speak so that she could be absolutely sure she was going to be all right, but inwardly she knew that the crisis had passed and that her mother had taken a turn for the better.

She wondered if she ought to waken her father and tell him the good news, but she decided that there was really nothing to gain from doing so. He would only be annoyed at being disturbed.

Her mother was still going to need careful nursing for at least another week but the worst was over. Pulling a blanket around her own shoulders Molly made herself as comfortable as she could in the chair and within minutes was sound asleep.

It was two days before Molly felt confident about leaving her mother in her father's care and returning to work.

'She still needs to be looked after, you know,' she told her father. 'You'll have to do the shopping and everything else for a few more days. She must rest; make sure that she either stays in bed or sits by the fire. Don't let her go doing anything at all, certainly not ironing or anything strenuous. Do you understand?'

'I hear what you're saying,' he muttered. 'I'm not a complete idiot, you know.'

'I know you're not, but I'm not sure that you realise how very ill she has been or how weak she is. She's been living on soup and stuff like that for days and so she's as weak as a kitten. She needs plenty of kindness as well as attention,' she added with a disarming smile.

'Then perhaps you should stay home; you'd be better at that than me,' he suggested.

'I would, gladly, if you had a full-time job and you were bringing home enough money to keep us.'

'You think I'm a bloody failure, don't you, girl?' he said bitterly.

'No, not exactly a failure, but I do think you've taken the easy way out since you came home from the army and that you don't try hard enough to get back into the swing of things.'

'You want to listen to yourself, Molly! With all your bloody lecturing, anyone would think you were a bloody schoolmarm,' he laughed.

'I might have been one if you hadn't made me cut short my schooling and brought us over here to live in this dump,' she said wryly.

'No good thinking about all that now,' he scowled. 'You'd best get off back to your grand house and precious job in Wallasey first thing tomorrow and leave me to manage things here.'

'Well, mind you do. Mum has never properly got over having to give up our nice little home over there and move to this place. It broke her heart and I think it's because of that she's become so run down and that is why she's ended up ill like this.'

'That'll do!' Bill muttered. 'I've heard enough. What with your preaching, your brother's surliness and young Jodie's whingeing and whining, it's enough to drive a man to drink.'

'That might sound like a good excuse to go to the pub, but don't think for one minute you can get away with it,' Molly warned him. 'If I find you've been going boozing during the day and left Mum here on her own—'

'You'll what? Cut along and leave me to run things. I know only too well how ill she's

220

been and it's made me realise that I've got to get us out of this dump. Don't worry, as soon as she is well enough to be left on her own I'm making a fresh start,' he promised.

'It's Christmas in three days' time,' Molly sighed. She laid a hand on his arm. 'Once that is over and we are into the New Year, will you try and get a proper job, Dad, please!'

He bent and kissed the top of her head, 'I promise I will, luv. 1923 is going to be a different sort of year for all of us, and that's a promise.'

Chapter Seventeen

As she left the *Royal Daffodil* at Seacombe and boarded a bus to take her to Warren Drive, Molly felt a surge of relief. It was as if she was once again stepping from the dismal surroundings of her own home into the background she had come to enjoy.

It was bitterly cold and she was shivering by the time she walked down the gravel drive and around to the back of the house.

'Oh, it's you back at last, is it?' Mrs Summers commented as she opened the door. 'Madam wants to see you the minute you arrive. You'd better wait in the passageway while I tell her that you're here and find out where she wants to see you.'

Molly was too taken aback to say anything. It was not at all the sort of reception she had been expecting. She'd left a note at Mr Parsons's shop to let them know what was happening and she'd thought that Mrs Summers would enquire after her mother and welcome her back because it was another pair of hands to help out over the Christmas festivities. Then she remembered the incident with Jodie taking one of the mince pies and her heart sank. She hoped that Mrs Summers wasn't still holding a grudge about that. Surely she hadn't reported the incident to Mrs Parsons!

The moment she walked into the breakfast room Molly's suspicions were confirmed. Mrs Parsons's greeting was extremely curt and her manner distant.

'I'm afraid, Molly, that we have decided you are no longer suitable so you will have to leave.' She held out a small envelope. 'Here is your pay to date.'

Molly made no attempt to take the envelope. She stood there stiff and numb until anger brought the words bubbling out. 'Is this about what my little sister did when she came to say how ill my mother was?' she asked.

Mrs Parsons frowned. 'Yes, Molly. To some degree, it is to do with that.'

'Jodie apologised to Mrs Summers,' Molly

said quickly. 'Poor little thing, she was so cold and hungry that she was overcome by the smell of Mrs Summers's cooking. The temptation was just too great for her. She knows what she did was wrong and she was so sorry about it, but once she'd taken a bite of the mince pie it was too late to do anything. And she did tell Mrs Summers that she was very sorry,' Molly repeated.

'I know all that; nevertheless, it was stealing and that is something I will not tolerate.'

'I do understand and I have told her she must never come here again. It was an emergency. My mother was so ill they thought she was dying. She's still very ill. By rights I should have stayed to look after her, but I thought it would be inconveniencing you with Christmas almost here and everything.'

'The mince pie incident is indeed very regrettable, Molly, but it is not the only matter about which I am concerned. I have been informed that you have been seen talking to Steven, my son, away from this house, outside a picture house in Liverpool, in fact, and that simply cannot be permitted.'

'Talking to Steven!' Angry colour rushed to Molly's cheeks. 'I've been talking to Steven for years. Ever since I started working at Mr Parsons's shop. In fact–'

Mrs Parsons held up her hand to silence Molly. 'I don't wish you to tell me all the sordid details. My informant has already told me far more than I wished to hear. I would have liked to believe it was misinformation, but I can see from your demeanour that this is not the case.'

'So what is wrong with me talking to Steven?'

'Everything. Absolutely everything! I'm a fair woman and you seem to me to be a nice, sensible girl, Molly, so surely you can see that Steven isn't really interested in you and certainly not ready to have a steady girlfriend.'

'No, you are quite wrong,' Molly defended. 'We've been going out together for ages and we're very fond–' she hesitated then squared her shoulders and blurted out, 'we are in love with each other.'

Mrs Parsons's eyes hardened and her manner changed. She'd been expecting Molly to accept what she'd told her. Now her voice became very authoritative.

'Mr Parsons and I have discussed this at length and we are in complete agreement in telling you that you are not on any account to speak to him again. You will not have the chance to do so here in future, but we also mean that you shouldn't speak to him in Liverpool or anywhere else.'

'Surely it is up to Steven to decide whether or not he wants to speak to me?'

Mrs Parsons's mouth tightened. 'Then it

is all the more important that you make it quite clear to him that you do not want to have anything further to do with him. Now is that understood?'

'No!' Molly shook her head angrily, her eyes glittering. 'Steven has been my boyfriend for a long time, so why should I suddenly stop seeing him and cut him dead just because you've asked me to do so?'

'Because I have *told* you to do so,' Mrs Parsons repeated coldly. 'I've met girls before looking for a rich husband and I know he probably seems a good catch for a girl like you, but I have no intention of letting him get mixed up with a family like yours. If you refuse to do as I am asking then I shall report your young sister to the authorities,' she threatened. 'Mrs Summers will confirm that she was stealing. At her age, and with your family's reputation, she will probably be put in a home of some kind and your father will probably be fined. If he is unable to pay then he might well find himself back in prison again.'

The colour drained from Molly's cheeks and there was hatred in her eyes as she stared back at her employer. 'You wouldn't! That would be so wicked. You couldn't do a thing like that,' she challenged.

'I most certainly could, and I will unless you do as I am asking,' Mrs Parsons said firmly. 'Sever all contact with Steven immediately and promise me that you will have no further dealings with him in the future.'

'If I do that, then can I keep my job?' Molly asked.

'No, you most definitely cannot! I want you off the premises immediately. I feel that you are a bad influence and that you come from a disreputable family.'

Molly stood there for a moment in stunned silence. Her head was pounding as she thought of all that had been said and weighed up all the consequences. She was losing her job no matter what she did but did she really have to stop seeing Steven? Would either Mr or Mrs Parsons know if they still went on meeting in Liverpool? She could still let him take her to the pictures.

As if reading her mind, Mrs Parsons said sternly, 'We shall be taking Steven to task about this matter as well. He will also be warned that in future he is to have nothing more to do with you. Now, is that understood?'

'He won't take any notice; he loves me and I love him.'

'He'll listen to us,' Mrs Parsons told her confidently. 'He realises what it will mean if he doesn't. As our only child he wouldn't want to be cut off without a penny,' she added dramatically.

'What do you intend to tell him?'

Mrs Parsons's lips tightened into a hard

line. 'That is really none of your concern. We shall explain matters to him and we know he will adhere to our decision.'

'You can't be sure about that until you ask him,' Molly argued stubbornly. 'We've been friends for a long time, ages before I came here to work. He'll believe my side of the story.'

'And we both know why you lost your job at the shop and had to come here to work,' Mrs Parsons reminded her.

'That wasn't my fault,' Molly retorted.

'I have nothing more to say. There are other far more pressing matters waiting for my attention,' Mrs Parsons said dismissively. 'Take your money and leave, Miss Henderson.'

Angrily, Molly snatched the envelope that Mrs Parsons once again held out to her. There was obviously not going to be any reprieve so she might as well take what was due to her, she decided. Heaven knows, now that neither she nor her mother would be working, they were going to need every penny they could get to tide them over the coming weeks. Her only hope now was that her father would do as he had promised about finding work and that he'd do it right away and not wait until Christmas was over.

Feeling as bleak as the weather, Molly waited until she was on the ferry boat before she opened the envelope. It contained the exact amount due to her, not a penny more.

'Miserable old cow,' she muttered as she tucked it away in her coat pocket. The Christmas bonus she'd been promised, money that she had been counting on to buy a last-minute present for Jodie and some extra treats for them all on Christmas day, hadn't been included.

All for the sake of one measly mince pie, she told herself angrily. In her heart she knew that wasn't the sole reason for her dismissal. She wondered who had tittle-tattled about seeing her with Steven, perhaps even said that they went to the pictures once a week. She suspected it might be Mrs Summers, but she wasn't sure because she rarely went out at night. Whoever it was they had certainly ruined everything for her, she thought despondently.

She wondered what Steven's reaction would be when his parents told him he wasn't to see her again. She suspected that despite him constantly telling her how much she meant to him he would do what they asked and that was what hurt the most.

Common sense told her that Mrs Parsons didn't like the idea of them seeing each other because she came from a different level of society to them. His father might only be a shopkeeper but Mrs Summers had said that Mrs Parsons came from a well-to-do family. Steven had already mentioned that his mother was always inviting the daughters of her rich friends in the hope that he would take an interest in them. He'd also told her that it was his mother's brother who owned the shipping company where he worked.

He'd probably agree to do as they asked because she was sure she wasn't the only girl in his life. She had seen him out with other girls, she reminded herself miserably, and although he'd said they had been part of a crowd from the office she had sometimes suspected that it wasn't true.

By the time she reached Mould Court, Molly's mind was made up. She wasn't going to chase after Steven but she would turn up outside the Rotunda on Wednesday night as usual and see if he was there or not.

When she explained to her father what had happened and why she had come straight back home he wanted to go back over to Wallasey and have it out with Mrs Parsons.

'What good will that do? She doesn't have to employ me.'

'Maybe not. She doesn't have to call your sister a bloody thief, either,' he ranted.

'Jodie did help herself to a mince pie,' she reminded him.

'So what! One bloody mince pie. There were probably so many on the table that if the old woman hadn't seen our Jodie pick it up and stick it in her gob, she'd probably never have missed it.'

She was on the point of telling him that he had started it all by pinching cigarettes from Mr Parsons's shop, but she knew that would only enrage him even more, so she said nothing. Nor did she tell him that she had been told to have nothing more to do with Steven; she didn't know if he was aware that Steven took her to the pictures or not, and it was safer not to tell him. The mood her father was in, she was afraid that he might even go and threaten Steven and that would make matters even worse.

'Never mind,' she said brightly, 'perhaps it is all for the best. Mum still needs looking after and you said that as soon as Christmas was over you wanted to make a fresh start, so at least I will be here to take care of her while you look for work.

Bill Henderson scowled and looked away, muttering something she couldn't catch. Molly was pretty sure that his promise had been nothing more than hot air and one that he'd had no intention of carrying out. Losing her job had put him on the spot which might be a good thing, she thought hopefully.

It was not a very joyful Christmas for any of the Hendersons because money was so tight. Molly bought a chicken in St John's

Market late on Christmas Eve when they were almost giving them away, knowing that they would be unfit to eat if they kept them until the holiday was over.

Cooking their Christmas dinner presented problems because the people they shared the poky little kitchen with also wanted to cook theirs at the same time. In the end their meal was delayed until almost five o'clock. By then they were all so hungry that they attacked what Molly put on the table with gusto and all of them claimed to have enjoyed it.

She had insisted that there must be a present for Jodie and she had bought her a jigsaw puzzle which had a lovely country scene on it and which kept Jodie happy and occupied throughout the day.

In the week that followed Molly gave most of her attention to her mother, making her nourishing broth from the remains of the chicken and tempting her with little snacks in an attempt to build up her strength and get her back to full health.

She also took over her mother's office cleaning. At first there had been some doubts at the offices about taking her on. When she explained how ill her mother was and that it might be several weeks before she would be well enough to return to work, then the managers at both offices agreed that it would be just as convenient to let her do the cleaning as it would be to find someone else.

The knowledge that both her cleaning jobs were safe and waiting for her when she was fit enough to do them again seemed to set Netta's mind at rest and do her almost as much good as the tempting meals Molly provided for her.

The moment Christmas was over and Peter was also back at work, Molly reminded her father of his promise to look for a job. To her surprise he agreed with her. She washed and ironed his best shirt, sponged his one good suit, brushed his overcoat and trilby hat, and even pressed his tie so that he looked smartly turned out.

'Off you go, then, and don't come back until you have found something,' she told him with an encouraging smile.

She said nothing to her mother but she waited with bated breath for his return. She felt sure that if he did manage to get a job, then it would improve his spirits and really would be the turning point they all needed.

It took Bill Henderson several days and each night when he returned home he was so despondent that Molly was afraid he was going to give up and sink back into his apathetic mood.

Then, out of the blue, he struck lucky and was taken on as a gatekeeper at one of the warehouses on the dockside. It wasn't the sort of job he wanted or was used to doing, but it was one he claimed he could do with his eyes shut.

She grinned. 'Well, don't let them catch you with your eyes shut during working hours.'

It meant another change in their routine. Although Netta was now up and about she still wasn't fit enough to go to work, so they agreed that Molly would carry on doing her office cleaning jobs for a while longer.

'With your dad's money coming in we'll be able to manage fine,' Netta explained. 'I'll be able to make sure that Jodie gets a proper breakfast and be here when she gets home from school.'

'Yes, Mum, but it's high time that Jodie was able to take care of herself; she's even old enough to have a Saturday job.'

'I know you're right, luv, but she's still such a frail little thing that I can't help worrying about her.'

'Once you are completely better we'll start planning to move somewhere else. We should be able to do so now that Dad has a job and Peter will be getting a pay rise soon. Once you feel fit enough to do your office cleaning again I'll be able to find a full-time job. 1923 is going to be a new start, Mum, and it's going to be better than anything we've ever known.'

Chapter Eighteen

Molly was very surprised at how enthusiastic her father was about his new job. He insisted that he must look smart and that his shirts, especially the collars, were properly ironed. He brushed his jacket and made sure he had a clean white handkerchief before he left each morning.

'There's a lot more to being a gatekeeper than people realise,' he told her at the end of his first week. 'People think it is just a matter of sitting in that little box watching the traffic pass by and nodding to people or directing them where to go once they get inside the factory yard.'

'Really!' She looked at him with raised eyebrows, her turquoise eyes full of curiosity. 'Go on, then, tell me all about what you have to do there.'

'Well, for a start, I have to make a note of everything and everybody that passes in or out of the factory yard, whether they are on foot, in a horse and cart, or in a van, lorry or whatever.'

'You mean the person who is driving the vehicle and his mate, if he has one.'

'That's right. And I have to note down

their time of arrival and departure and so on.'

'What about the workmen as they arrive and leave?'

'No, they have to punch the time clock. Their records are quite different and nothing to do with me.'

'So do you have to enter all these details down in a book or something?' She frowned.

'Yes, I have to log them all in and it's important to keep an accurate account of everything. There are columns to denote their time of arrival and the time they leave. I also have to record details of whatever it is that they are bringing in or taking away. If they are bringing stuff in, then there's a separate docket to be filled in and that goes to the warehouse for checking.'

'And what about if they are leaving the factory yard?'

'If they are leaving with a load of goods, then they have to hand me a docket from the warehouse and I have to enter the reference number of that in my log,' he explained. 'Oh, and I have to check that what they have on the lorry tallies exactly with what is listed on the docket to make sure they've not pinched anything,' he added.

'It sounds a very responsible job,' Molly agreed, 'are you happy doing it?'

'Nothing to it. Don't forget that when I was over in France in the army I was looking

235

after a platoon of men and making sure that none of the buggers were hiding anything, especially those who worked in the stores. Pilfering was rampant, so I know exactly how to do this job efficiently.'

'Well that's good, Dad. Mum will be pleased when you tell her all about it.'

'I doubt it. Like the rest of you, she'll be far more interested in the size of the pay packet I bring home each week than in how I earn it,' he guffawed.

Nevertheless, when they were eating their meal that night he told the rest of them all about his job. He even ended up having a man-to-man talk with Peter about what working down at the docks involved and sharing anecdotes with him.

Molly listened in silence, pleased that for once they were getting on so well and delighted that they now had something in common to chat about. The atmosphere was no longer so tense and it boded well for the future, she thought hopefully.

The fact that Bill was working at last was obviously a great relief to Netta. At the end of his first full working week, even though it was a bitterly cold, frosty night, she agreed to go with him for a drink when he asked her.

'Do you think you should go out, Mum?' Molly said worriedly. 'It's freezing outside.'

'I'll wrap up warm, luv, and we are only

going to the Brewery Vaults just along the road.'

'It'll be ever so smoky in there,' Molly warned. 'That won't do your chest any good.'

'I'll only be in there for about an hour, not long enough to do me any harm,' Netta reassured her.

'I'm only thinking about you, Mum,' Molly told her. 'You have been almost at death's door, you know.'

'Please don't start fussing, Molly, and spoiling it all for me. I'm really looking forward to the chance of going out with your dad because it's something we haven't done since he came home from the army. You don't mind staying in to look after Jodie, do you? You weren't planning to go out with that Steven, were you?'

'No; no, I hadn't made any plans to go out,' Molly told her with a catch in her voice.

Going out with Steven was a thing of the past. The first Wednesday after she'd been sacked by Mrs Parsons, despite the warning that she wasn't to have anything else to do with Steven, she had gone to the Rotunda as usual because there was a film showing that she knew they both wanted to see. She had been on tenterhooks wondering whether or not he would obey his parents.

He was there, looking very smart in his dark blue suit, crisp white shirt and blue and grey tie as he stood on the steps outside. He was smoking a cigarette and looking up and down the street so expectantly that it had set her heart thudding. Before she reached him, though, the pretty blonde girl she'd seen him with once before came tripping down the street and made a beeline for him.

She'd felt a lump rising in her throat as she watched him pull her into his arm. This was the girl he'd said didn't mean a thing to him and yet he was greeting her as if he knew her very well indeed. She was unable to take her eyes off them as she saw the girl tilt her face back and Steven bend his own head down and their lips met in a long, passionate kiss.

She felt a stab of jealousy; he hadn't even contacted her. She might be heartbroken over what had happened, but judging by what she had witnessed, Steven certainly wasn't giving it another thought. He was getting on with his life, Molly thought bitterly; he'd probably been two-timing her all along.

The fact that she had skimped that evening on the cleaning job she was still doing on behalf of her mother, in order to rush home and get changed and come to meet him, made her realise what an idiot she'd been to trust him.

As she made her way home she realised that since it was the same girl she'd seen him with before it must mean that it really was all over between herself and Steven.

From then on her mind was buzzing with questions. She wondered how serious he was about this new girl or whether he was leading her a dance as well. She wondered if the girl came from the sort of background that Mrs Parsons would approve of and whether or not Steven had taken her home to meet his parents.

Perhaps he didn't need to do that. It was possible that even though she was obviously working somewhere in Liverpool she was one of the desirable girls that his mother was in the habit of inviting to dine with them.

The only person who seemed to notice that she was no longer going to the pictures on a Wednesday evening was Peter. 'You and that smart-arse broken up then?' he asked the following Wednesday when she made no effort to get ready to go out.

'If you mean Steven, then the answer is yes, we have split up and I'm not seeing him any more.'

'Found himself a fresh bint, has he?'

'Peter!'

'Come on,' he grinned, 'comb your hair and I'll take you out and buy you a lemonade shandy.'

Although she knew her brother had never liked Steven, nevertheless, as they sat in a quiet corner of The Vaults, she found herself confiding in Peter about what had happened.

'I thought there must be more to it than Jodie nicking a cake,' he said triumphantly. 'That was just their excuse to make you break it off with Steven.'

'Do you really think so?' Molly looked surprised. 'She did steal the mince pie,' she reminded him.

'So what?' He took a drink of his beer. 'It was a pity she did it because it gave old Ma Parsons an excuse to get rid of you and, at the same time, find a way to stop you seeing her precious son.'

Molly was silent for a minute, thinking about what he had said.

'You don't think that she would have taken any action over Jodie?' she asked thoughtfully.

'Of course not! Think how heartless it would have made her look; it was Christmas, and she grudged a starving kid a mince pie. Her sort gives them out hand over fist to the carol singers.'

'Jodie wasn't singing carols, though,' Molly chuckled and took another sip of her shandy.

'No, I know that, but you can see what I'm getting at. She wouldn't want people to think what a miserly old bitch she was. Anyway, I shouldn't fret about it; you're far better off without him.'

'Maybe, but don't forget it also meant that I lost my job again, didn't it?'

'Some good has come out of it, though.' He grinned. 'Dad's working, and he seems to like what he's doing so he's paying his way the same as the rest of us and you're keeping Mum's job open for her,' Peter pointed out. 'Once she's strong enough to take over again, and that should be any day now if she's well enough to go to the boozer, then you can get another job.'

'Maybe, but I'm going to find it difficult getting work of any sort without a reference.'

'Mm, you have a point there,' Peter agreed. 'You don't want to be a skivvy at other people's beck and call; you're too good for that. Perhaps you'd better carry on with the office cleaning and let Mum be the one to get a new job.'

Although she laughed at the idea, Molly kept thinking that it might be sensible to do as he suggested. If only she'd obtained a qualification to work as a shorthand typist as she'd dreamed of doing, she thought longingly.

Both the offices accepted her as a stand-in and seemed to be completely satisfied with her work. If she found some more cleaning jobs for other times in the day, then she was sure they would be willing to vouch for her. What was more, they would probably also be willing to give her mother a reference if Netta asked them for one.

The possibilities of Peter's suggestion and

the fact that they would then all be working and earning money made her feel more optimistic. She decided to talk it over with her mother as soon as she had the chance to do so.

Netta quite liked the idea. Her good long rest had restored not only her strength but her confidence as well.

'I was getting a bit fed up with cleaning offices,' she confided. 'If you're sure you're happy to go on working there, then I'll have a look around and see what else there is.'

'I don't really have much choice if I haven't any references or qualifications,' Molly said despondently.

'Don't be like that, luv. If you are only working mornings and evenings, then it means you'll have the rest of the day free so perhaps you could start studying again.'

Molly shook her head. 'I think I would need to get some extra work. Cleaning those offices for a couple of hours each day is not bringing in very much money, is it, Mum?'

'No, but remember, I'll be working. You could help out here with the cooking and cleaning.'

Molly promised to think about what her mother had suggested, but she wasn't completely sure that it was the sort of arrangement she wanted to go along with. Yet her mother seemed to be very keen on the idea, more enthusiastic than she had seen her for a very long time. It was as if her illness had transformed her into a different person and Molly felt she didn't want to say or do anything to send her back into the depressed state she had been in before.

'If I get a full-time job, I'll probably be too tired to do very much when I get in at night,' Netta went on. 'We could make sure you had Wednesday night free to go out with Steven.'

'That won't be necessary, Mum, I don't see him any more.'

'Oh, Molly!' Netta looked crestfallen. 'I had no idea, you never said a word. Was it because of what happened with Jodie?'

'Peter knew. I didn't think it was worth mentioning to you when you were unwell,' Molly said evasively. 'So what sort of job were you thinking of looking for, Mum?' she asked, hoping to divert her mother from asking any more questions.

'I don't know, luv, but at this moment I feel ready to tackle anything that comes my way. Seeing your dad so happy and interested in what he's doing has bucked me up no end. When we went for a drink the other evening he was even talking about trying to get some money together so that we can move away from Mould Court to somewhere better.'

'That would be wonderful, but don't get your hopes up too soon,' Molly warned her.

'Well, it might be possible if we all pull together and save hard. If I can manage to get a decent job we should be able to do it, given time,' Netta said optimistically, her face lighting up. 'Getting away from this miserable dump is what we all want to do, now isn't it?'

'Oh yes, there's nothing I'd like better, and I'll do whatever you feel is best to make that possible,' Molly agreed as she hugged her mother enthusiastically.

'What is more,' she added, 'I am sure that when we talk to Peter he will say exactly the same. He's hated living here right from the moment we arrived.'

'Good, then let's sit down, have a cuppa and see what we can plan to do,' Netta told her.

'We're all living on top of one another, that's the problem. None of us has any privacy or the chance to be on our own. It wouldn't be so bad if there was another bedroom. Or even to have a proper kitchen; one that was large enough to eat our meals in,' Molly said.

'A kitchen that we didn't have to share with another family would be nice,' Netta sighed. 'I find this business of having to wait until they are not using it, especially when we're in a hurry to get to work, makes everything so difficult.'

'It probably wouldn't matter so much if

we liked the people we have to share with, but that family are really horrible. They always leave the place in such a mess,' Molly agreed.

'Or if they were people we could trust! Not being able to leave things in the cupboards and know that they'll still be there next time I want to use them again is what really annoys me,' Netta complained. 'They even take my saucepan out of the cupboard and use it without even asking permission.'

'And leave it lying there dirty,' Molly added, wrinkling her nose in disgust.

'It's all so different to our lovely little house in Wallasey,' Netta sighed. 'I'll never feel really happy or settled on this side of the Mersey. Still, we can't turn the clock back. All we can do is hope that there is something better just round the corner.'

'Well, you know what they say, Mum, when you reach bottom you can only go up again.' Molly grinned.

'That's true, so I think the best thing we can do is to have a cuppa and see what sort of plans we can make for the future.'

'Yes, let's really try and make 1923 the year when we all get back on our feet again,' Molly agreed.

Chapter Nineteen

All Molly's hopes that 1923 was going to be a great year for all of them, and that it would see them moving away from Mould Court, were quickly shattered.

In spite of Molly's warnings that the smoky atmosphere wasn't going to be good for her, Netta had insisted on taking a job as a barmaid at the Dryden Arms in Great Homer Street. She'd barely settled in to working there when tragedy struck. Molly had just returned home from her morning office cleaning stint and was having a cup of tea with her mother before Netta went off to work when there was a loud hammering on their door and the sound of a man's voice calling out Netta's name.

'Who on earth can that be?' Molly frowned.

'You'd better open the door and find out,' Netta laughed. 'I haven't got time, I want to get ready and I need to leave in a few minutes. Jim Bowler, the landlord, is a real clock watcher and has plenty to say if anyone is a second late.'

From the way he was dressed in hard-wearing trousers, heavy dark jacket, muffler, grey cap and boots with steel toecaps, the man who was standing there was obviously a docker. Molly felt a shiver of fear as she saw the grim expression on his face.

'Does Mrs Netta Henderson live here, Missy?' he asked, pulling off his cap and rolling it nervously in his hands.

'Yes she does, and I'm her daughter, Molly. How can I help you?'

He looked uncomfortable and coughed and swallowed before he said gruffly, 'It's about Bill Henderson ... your dad. He's been badly hurt. They've carted him off to hospital. Your mother or someone ought to be there with him.'

Netta overheard what was being said and came rushing to the door. 'What's happened? How has Bill been hurt? What sort of accident?'

The words came tumbling out as Netta grabbed hold of the man by the sleeve. She was so overcome and upset that she was almost shaking him as she anxiously pressed him for more details about what had happened.

'That's all I can tell you, Missus,' he said as he unrolled his cap, rammed it on his head and began to retreat backwards, eager to get away.

'Hold on, you haven't told us which hospital he's in,' Molly said quickly.

'They've taken him to the Infirmary, of course.'

Molly and her mother looked at each other in consternation. Before they could ask for any further details the man had gone. Molly called out to him to wait and was about to run after him, but Netta grabbed her arm and pulled her back.

'Why waste time on that silly fool? We'd better put our coats on and get to the Infirmary as fast as we can and then we can find out for ourselves how badly hurt your dad is.'

Molly felt as if they were in some horrible nightmare as they made their way across Liverpool, changing from one tram to another, neither of them too sure how to find the Infirmary.

'We don't even know what sort of an accident Dad has had,' she mused. 'That man was in such a hurry that he didn't stop to even tell us that much.'

'He mightn't have known; that's probably why he wanted to get away so quickly. He was only a messenger. He mightn't have even been there when it happened.'

'He must have had some idea. Surely he would have known if Dad had been knocked down, or if something had fallen on him. Dad must have been hurt pretty badly for them to send him to the Infirmary,' Molly said worriedly.

'Well, we'll be able to find out for ourselves once we get there,' Netta told her. 'I should have popped into the pub and let them know that I was going to be late,' she added. 'I'll be in Jim Bowler's black books and I can't afford to lose my job, not if your dad is going to be laid up.'

'Well, by the sound of things, if he is hurt enough to be taken straight to hospital, then he is bound to be off work for a while. It's such a pity that something like this has happened because he seemed to be really enjoying his new job.'

'Yes, you're right.' Netta smiled. 'I was beginning to think that at long last we were managing to sort out all our problems. Nothing seems to have gone right for us since the day your dad came home from the army.'

When they arrived at the hospital no one seemed to have heard of Bill Henderson and for one, fleeting moment Molly wondered if they had been sent on a wild-goose chase.

'Surely no one would do a terrible thing like that,' her mother exclaimed when Molly voiced her thoughts.

A few minutes later and Bill's details were traced, Netta and Molly were asked to go into a side room where a middle-aged sister, in a navy-blue dress and a crackling starched white apron and headdress, came to explain the delay.

'The reason there was difficulty tracing Mr Henderson was because he was already dead when he was brought into the hospital and his body was taken straight to the mortuary,' she explained in an apologetic voice.

The news stunned both Netta and Molly and it was several minutes before either of them could understand what she was telling them.

'Dead when they brought him in,' Netta murmured in a puzzled voice. 'That can't be right?'

'Do you know what happened? What sort of accident he had?' Molly asked.

'As I understand it, he was knocked down by a lorry,' the sister told her.

'Do you mean in the street or on the dockside where he worked?' Molly persisted.

The sister shook her head. 'I'm afraid I have no other details at the moment, but the police will be here in a few minutes and they should be able to give you more information.'

'The police? Whatever have they got to do with it?' Netta asked in alarm.

'All fatal accidents have to be reported to the police,' the sister told her. 'Now I want you to wait in here until they arrive. Try not to worry. I will ask a nurse to bring you both a cup of tea.'

Before either of them could reply or even thank her she had gone. Left alone, Molly and Netta looked at each other in utter despair and disbelief.

'I should have asked to see him,' Netta murmured. 'They may have made a mistake; it mightn't be Bill after all. How could he be knocked down by a lorry when he spends all day in that little wooden office? He doesn't go out into the yard or the roadway; he talks to people out of that window.'

'Well, he must move out of there sometimes,' Molly reasoned. 'Unless it happened in the street before he got to work. Perhaps he was crossing the road and didn't see the lorry coming. It's always mad busy with trams and lorries around the Pier Head.'

'Nonsense! Your dad was always very careful about such things as crossing the road.'

'Well,' Molly sighed, 'I'm sure the police will be able to tell us, they said they'll be here soon.'

The tea was hot, sweet and reviving. They were still drinking it when the police arrived. There were two of them; one of them was a sergeant, and he wasted no time in getting straight to the point.

'Which one of you is going to identify the body?' he asked, looking directly at Netta.

'I will. He's my husband,' Netta agreed. 'That is, if it is him, and you haven't made a mistake,' she added hopefully. 'I think you may have done,' she added lamely.

There had been no mistake. The body in the hospital mortuary was that of Bill Henderson. Molly stood beside her mother,

251

holding her hand and trying to stop the convulsive shudders that kept going through her own body.

She had never seen anyone dead before and she couldn't believe that the figure lying there on the hospital slab really was dead. It was her father; she had no doubt about that, but although he was motionless he looked as if he was asleep. There was no sign of suffering on his face, no trace of any injuries, even though they insisted he had been involved in an accident.

As the white-coated attendant pulled the green sheet back over his recumbent form Molly nudged her mother and propelled her towards the door where the two policemen were waiting. Their faces were solemn as, in respectful silence, they accompanied Molly and her mother back to the waiting room.

Once inside the room the sergeant tapped his leg with his baton, almost as if calling for attention.

'That is your husband, Mrs Henderson? You are quite sure about that?'

Netta could only nod; she was far too upset and dazed to speak.

'Yes, it is my dad,' Molly confirmed in a shaky voice.

The sergeant nodded towards the constable and waited until he had made a note of this in his pad before proceeding.

'And your home address?'

When Netta didn't give him an answer Molly told them that it was Mould Court.

'What happened, what sort of accident did he have?' Netta demanded, suddenly alert and angry.

'He was knocked down by a lorry that was leaving the yard where he was employed.'

'I don't understand! How could he have been knocked down by a lorry when he was inside his little wooden box?'

The sergeant cleared his throat. 'From the information we have been given, Mr Henderson was trying to apprehend the lorry as it was leaving the factory yard,' he explained.

'What are you saying?' Netta stared at him in disbelief. 'They just carried on driving? Is that what happened?'

'The facts are not completely clear as yet,' the sergeant explained. 'From what we've been told, they had goods on the lorry that shouldn't have been there. When your husband endeavoured to stop him the driver panicked and tried to drive off and that was when Mr Henderson was knocked down.'

'You mean he drove the lorry over him without stopping?'

'No, no. We understand that the lorry hit him and as he fell he hit his head against a stone pillar.'

'Surely you don't die from simply hitting your head,' Netta said with a puzzled frown. She stood up and made for the door. 'I'm sure there's been a mistake,' she pronounced. 'I'm going back in there; I want to make sure that he really is dead.'

'There is no mistake, Mrs Henderson,' the sergeant assured her, placing a restraining hand on her arm.

Netta shook herself free. 'You're all saying he's dead when I know perfectly well that he's not.' Her voice rose hysterically. 'Why are you doing that? I'm going to take him home; he'll be as right as rain in a few days, I know he will.'

Molly jumped up in alarm. Her mother had such a wild look on her face and her eyes were staring. She looked so out of control that Molly was frightened.

Quickly the sergeant moved between Netta and the door to stop her leaving the room. 'You can't go back into the mortuary, Mrs Henderson. I'm afraid that what we told you is correct and that your husband is dead, you saw that for yourself,' he went on. He hesitated when he saw the look on Netta's face. 'Now, come and sit down, there are still a few more questions I have to ask you.'

Although his voice was very firm and calm it had no effect whatsoever on Netta. She fought him like a wild cat to try and get out of the room.

At a signal from the sergeant the constable put away his notebook and left the room. A few minutes later he returned with the sister and a nurse. When they were unable to calm Netta with firm but comforting words the nurse was instructed to give her an injection.

'It's only a sedative, my dear,' the sister told Molly when she saw that she was watching them wide eyed.

'Your mother is suffering from shock at the moment, that is all,' she went on. 'We have given her an injection and now we're going to put her into bed in a side ward for a little while. She will have a good deep sleep and when she wakens she will be feeling rested and much better.

'Now, are you all right? Is there anyone else in your family who can be with you?'

Molly shook her head. 'My brother Peter won't be home from work until six o'clock.'

'Well, it is almost three o'clock now so probably by the time you get home he will be there and he can come back here with you to help you take your mother home.'

'Almost three o'clock!' Molly clapped a hand to her mouth. 'Oh no, I must get back right away. My little sister will be out of school at four o'clock and she'll be scared stiff if she finds there's no one there when she gets home.'

'You'd better go, then, but you must come back again later to collect your mother,' the sister reminded her.

Molly nodded. 'Can you tell me which tram I have to catch?' she asked. 'I've never been here before and I'm not too sure about how to get home.'

'The constable will go with you,' the sergeant intervened.

'I only need him to come as far as the tram stop to tell me which one to catch,' Molly said quickly.

She was concerned about what the other occupants in Mould Court would think if she turned up escorted by a policeman. Although it bothered her she realised there was not going to be anything she could do about it if they insisted on coming home with her. What was more important was that she got back before Jodie got out of school.

Molly felt depressed by the thought that she was going to have to break the news to Jodie and Peter, but there was no way out of it. Her mother was now in such a deep sleep that she very much doubted if she would be in any fit state to tell them herself when she woke up.

She took a deep breath. The sooner Peter arrived home and she could explain to him what had happened the better. He'd help her to deal with everything. There would be the funeral to arrange as well as comforting and supporting their mother and Jodie. All of them would have to pull together if they were going to get through the next few weeks.

It wasn't going to be easy for any of them.

What was more, it meant the end of their hopes of getting away from Mould Court.

She could forget all about that. She would have to find a proper job herself because they were going to need every penny they could earn and she wasn't sure if her mother would be in a fit state to work for quite a while.

The funeral was going to put them in debt for months to come, even if all three of them were working, she thought worriedly. Her mother would insist that their dad was given a decent funeral, even though they couldn't really afford it.

The policeman had said something about having to appear in court, but everything was so confused in her mind that Molly found she couldn't think that far ahead.

It was all so frightening. It seemed so unfair that at the very moment when her dad had found his feet again, when he not only had a job but was enjoying it and they were all looking forward to the chance of moving out of Mould Court, it should end in such a terrible tragedy.

Chapter Twenty

As she prepared their evening meal, Molly decided she ought to tell Peter about what had happened first so she was relieved that Jodie didn't ask why their parents weren't there.

She waited until they had finished eating and then told Jodie that she could read her comic if she wanted to as Peter was going to help with the washing-up.

Before Peter could protest she whispered to him, 'There's something important that I have to tell you.'

Once the two of them were in the tiny kitchen on the turn of the stairs she told him all about the accident and how their mum had reacted.

'So as soon as we have finished doing the dishes do we have to go and collect Mum from the Infirmary?'

'Yes, I think perhaps we should both go, don't you? By the way, from what the policeman said, it seems that when the accident happened Dad was trying to stop the lorry because there were things on it that shouldn't have been there,' she added.

'You mean the driver was trying to steal

some goods from Bennett's and Dad was hit by the lorry when he tried to stop him?' Peter asked in disbelief.

'It sounds like it. He took his job very seriously,' she reminded her brother. 'Remember how he told us every detail about it when he first started there? He was really conscientious, it seems. The policeman said that the boss at Bennett's told him that Dad was one of the best gatekeepers they'd ever had.'

'Then why did the policeman warn you that there would be a court case? Was he talking about the thieving or the accident?' Peter asked, looking perplexed.

'Well, about both, really, I suppose. The one led to the other, didn't it?' Molly frowned. 'The fellow driving that lorry is going to be in serious trouble on both counts, I imagine. He'll probably end up with a long spell inside.'

'I suppose so, but he deserves it.'

'It won't bring Dad back though, will it?' Molly sighed.

It was a comment that Molly was going to repeat a great many times over the next few days. What seemed to be so unfair was that it was only in the last couple of months that Bill Henderson had turned over a new leaf, pulled himself together, and had not only found a job but had been determined to improve things for his family.

To their great relief, the funeral costs were undertaken by Bennett's, and in addition they also gave Netta a generous sum to compensate for her loss.

'Does that mean we are finally going to be able to move away from here?' Molly exclaimed in relief.

'No, it's not nearly enough for that,' her mother said ruefully. 'Although his firm paid for the funeral we had to buy our own black clothes and that's made a hole in the sum already.'

'You will put what's left away, though, and save it towards finding somewhere better to live,' Molly persisted.

'Of course, luv. I'll try not to touch another penny piece of it, but we will probably find it hard going on the pittance we're all earning. Even when it is all put together it barely covers the rent and food and so on. You know how we have to scrimp,' she sighed.

'I'll get some more office cleaning, or a better job altogether and that will help,' Molly promised.

'What about Jodie, though? If you work full-time it will mean she comes home to an empty house and she's such a dreamer that I don't like the idea of her doing that, not while we are living here in this horrible place.'

'Mum, I keep telling you, Jodie is old enough to stand on her own two feet. I was doing a paper round when I was not much older than she is.'

'Yes, but you were so much more responsible when you were her age. Jodie lives in a world of her own. She's hardly said a word about her dad dying and she didn't shed a single tear, not even at his funeral. It's almost as though she doesn't take any notice of what is going on around her.'

'She's never going to be grown-up, as you put it, if you go on treating her like a baby all her life,' Molly said crossly. 'Let's start by telling her that there won't be anyone at home at night when she comes in from school. Try it for a week and see how she gets on.'

'I'll be at home in the late afternoon,' Netta agreed. 'I don't need to go to the pub until five o'clock.'

'Yes, but you still mightn't be here. If I get a full-time job then you will have to do the shopping in between your midday stint at the pub and when you go back again.'

Jodie accepted the new arrangement without a word. Coming home to an empty house didn't seem to bother her at all. If there was no one else in, then she simply sat and read. After her mother went off to work she buried her nose again in whatever it was she was reading until either Molly or Peter came in and told her what they wanted her to do to help.

'It looks as though you're right, Molly; she doesn't seem to be at all worried about being on her own,' Netta admitted.

'Good! Well, now I shall start looking for a full-time job.'

Finding work other than cleaning seemed to be impossible because of her lack of experience. Memories of the unpleasant happenings at the Parsons's home made her averse to becoming a servant again, but it seemed that it was the only sort of work she was considered qualified enough to do.

When she talked about it to Peter, he suggested that it might be better if she was working at a lodging house or hotel instead of in someone's home.

At first the idea didn't appeal to her at all, but the more she thought about it the more she realised that it might be a good idea. Although she would only be able to supply references as an office cleaner, the fact that she had worked as a domestic would stand her in good stead.

She scanned the *Liverpool Evening Echo* every night for almost two weeks, applying for jobs that ranged from waiting at table to working in the kitchens. Each time she went along for an interview she was told that there was someone else with more experience who was considered to be more suitable.

She was on the point of giving up when she replied to an advertisement for a chambermaid's job at the Brunswick Hotel on the corner of Tithebarn Street and Brunswick Street. To her surprise she was told she could start the following week.

The hours were long, but the work wasn't anywhere near as arduous as cleaning offices had been, and the money more than she'd ever earned before. Once she was into the routine, Molly found she enjoyed the company of the other men and women who worked there.

The housekeeper, who was in charge of all the maids, was a quietly spoken middle-aged woman called Mrs Roberts who had a keen eye for detail and abhorred any form of skimping.

Molly found that her instructions were clear and precise, and that she treated everybody very fairly. Each chambermaid was responsible for an entire corridor of bedrooms and was expected to work without constant supervision.

Most of the guests only stayed for one or two nights. Usually they had either arrived by boat and were spending only one night in Liverpool before taking a train to some other part of the country, or had arrived by train and had to wait until the next day before they could board their boat out of Liverpool.

There were some regulars; mainly commercial travellers or shipping representatives paying regular periodic visits to other agents in and around the docks. Molly soon recognised them and knew when they liked things done in their room without having to ask.

After working completely on her own in an empty office block mornings and evenings Molly found she liked the bustle of the busy atmosphere at the Brunswick. She enjoyed the constant change of faces and personalities.

She discovered that some guests left their rooms in good order; others left them in complete chaos. When they arrived she tried to decide which sort of guest they were going to be, but more often than not she found she was wrong.

Jodie was still so quiet and withdrawn that Molly sometimes worried about her. When she wasn't working she tried to find time to take Jodie out, either to St John's Gardens, or to look round the shops in Church Street; occasionally, when she could afford it, she took her to the pictures.

When Molly again suggested that Jodie should find herself a little job, Netta finally agreed to think about it.

'She could deliver newspapers after school like I did,' Molly persisted, 'but make sure she doesn't ask at Mr Parsons's shop on the corner,' she warned.

'He probably wouldn't remember her after all this time.' Netta smiled tolerantly.

'Don't you believe it! What's more, even

though he wouldn't give her a job, he'd also make sure that he told all the other news-agents not to employ her either.'

'Well, it's not likely to happen, is it?' her mother said resignedly. 'I can't see anyone trusting Jodie to deliver anything, because she's such a dreamer. Most of the time she's living in that world of her own.'

'She's nowhere near as bad as she was,' Molly defended, 'and at school she's usually top of any test they are given, apparently. She still loves learning, so some good must come from the fact that she's always reading.'

Jodie was the least of Molly's problems. Like Peter, she was far more concerned about her mother and the sort of life she was leading, though neither of them knew how to tell her, or even talk to her about it.

After their dad had died they had been pleased that instead of moping their mother had gone straight back to work at the Dry-den Arms almost as if nothing had hap-pened.

'I can't let Jim Bowler down, not after he has been so good about everything,' she ex-plained. 'I was off three days without a word to him and yet he kept my job open for me.'

'He probably knew about Dad's accident almost as quickly as we did,' Molly pointed out. 'A lot of dockers go in there and they would have told him the news.'

'Even so, he was very understanding. What's more, he's also said that if I'd like to work some additional hours, then he will pay me extra money and I'm more than happy about that because I'll feel I'm doing my bit.'

'Doing her bit', as Netta put it, involved working until closing time each evening. What worried both Molly and Peter about this was that more often than not, by the time she got home, she had usually had far too much to drink.

'You've got to accept a drink when one of the punters offers to buy you one, or else they get offended,' Netta told Molly.

'Tell them to put one behind the bar for you and that you'll have it later on. I'm only mentioning it because Jodie doesn't see very much of you. You're still asleep in bed in the morning when she goes off to school and you're off out to work almost the minute she comes home in the afternoon.'

'You were the one who said she was able to look after herself and who told me to stop mollycoddling her so don't try and put all the blame on me,' Netta said huffily.

From then on, although the situation worried her a great deal, Molly kept her own counsel, except for the occasional discussion with Peter. He agreed with her that their mother was drinking far too much, but like Molly he could see no way of stopping her from doing it.

'We could ask Jim Bowler to have a word with her,' Molly suggested.

Peter shook his head. 'No,' he said firmly, 'that wouldn't be right. She would hate our interfering like that and it might only make her drink more. I think she is doing it to forget Dad and what happened to him.'

'I know, but I think she is also drinking at home. I found a gin bottle in amongst her clothes when I was collecting them up to do the washing. I also noticed that there was a half-empty bottle of vodka tucked away in one of the cupboards. We're never going to manage to save up enough money to get out of this dreadful place if she is squandering money on booze,' Molly added crossly.

'Hell! You don't think she's spending the money that Bennett's gave her on drink, do you? She promised to save that so that we could get away from here,' Peter exclaimed.

'I'm not sure. I don't know what she's done with it. She promised to put it away somewhere safe and I've looked everywhere, but I can't find it.'

'When we came home after the funeral she put the money in a blue tin box,' Peter told her.

'Yes, but where's that box now? I've searched for it high and low and we've only got two rooms, so there are not all that many places for her to hide it.'

'Do you know how much was in there?'

Molly shook her head. 'Not really. I know she bought us new black clothes to go to the funeral out of it.'

'Yes, and she bought herself a new hat and some gloves when she had to appear in court.'

'I know, but they didn't cost very much because she bought them from a second-hand stall in Paddy's Market.'

'So what's happened to the rest?' Peter demanded.

'I don't know. Surely she wouldn't spend it on drink; not all of it, anyway!'

'Well, she isn't spending all that much on food; we still seem to live on scouse most of the week and more often than not it's jam in the butties I take to work.'

'That's because Mum is always trying to economise,' Molly pointed out.

Peter shook his head, a puzzled look on his face. 'She's never mentioned that money since the time we all sat down and talked and made plans right after the funeral.'

'No, you're right,' Molly agreed.

'I tell you what, when we hand over our pay packets at the end of this week we'll ask her about it.'

'I'm not sure she'll like us doing that, Peter,' Molly said thoughtfully.

'You think she may refuse to tell us?'

'Possibly. I also think she may get pretty

upset and feel we don't trust her.'

'It's our money and it's our future we are all saving up for, so it's time we all took an interest in it and talked about it openly.'

'Well, if you put it like that, then I suppose you're right,' Molly admitted.

'Look, if she's boozing our money away instead of saving it then I may as well spend mine on some new shirts and trousers,' Peter stated. 'The ones I'm wearing are so thread-bare that they're dropping to pieces and I've got holes in my boots. Young Jodie looks like a scarecrow and I bet it's months since you bought yourself any new clothes, now isn't it?'

Chapter Twenty-one

There was no opportunity that weekend for either Molly or Peter to discuss anything with their mother because Netta didn't come home until they were all asleep on Friday night.

They were used to her being late, but when it came to half past eleven and she still wasn't home, Molly became worried. Jodie was already in bed and fast asleep, but she and Peter felt on edge, positive that there was something wrong.

'She's probably still in the bar jangling to some of the punters,' Peter said grumpily.

'Not this late, surely. Do you think you ought to walk down and see if she is all right?'

'What you really mean is that you think she might be too sozzled to walk home on her own?'

'No, not really,' Molly said hesitantly. 'She's never got that drunk before now, has she? If you don't want to go, then I will. I can't settle until she's back.'

'I'll go.' Scowling, he put on his boots, stood up and reached for his coat. 'I feel pretty daft going out looking for my mum and I don't think she will be very pleased about it either.'

'She'll be tickled pink that you care so much about her,' Molly teased.

It seemed ages before he returned and when he did, he was on his own and looking rather worried.

'Where's Mum? Wasn't she at the Dryden Arms?'

'I shouldn't think so!' he said crossly. 'The entire place was in complete darkness, obviously everyone had gone home ages ago and I didn't think that Jim Bowler would want me banging on his door since it's gone midnight and he's probably in bed.'

'Well, I wonder where she is then?' Molly frowned.

'According to some old geezer who was hanging around at the top of a nearby jigger, she went off with a fella, but he didn't know who he was. A smart-looking, young-ish chap, was how he described him. Mind you, to someone of his age, anyone under sixty would probably be considered young.'

'I don't believe it,' Molly gasped. 'She wouldn't go off with a strange man; it's only a couple of months since Dad died.'

'Well, that's what the old boy told me and he seemed pretty certain about it being her,' Peter told her, yawning noisily. 'I'm off to get some shut-eye. I've no idea who he was or where they can have gone at this time of night, and I'm certainly not waiting up any longer to find out. You can, if you like.'

Molly felt a sense of panic, so she made herself a cup of tea to try and calm herself. What was happening to them? she pondered. Nothing had worked out since the day her dad had come home from the army, but she had been hoping that now, with both herself and Peter as well as their mother working, they would be able to turn their lives around.

She couldn't believe that her mother would take up with another man, at least not yet. There was something so unaccept-able about the idea that she didn't even want to think about it.

She'd been so pleased when her dad had

kept his promise to make a fresh start in 1923 and that he and her mum had seemed to become close to each other once again. She'd really thought that it meant that he had finally adjusted to being home and that they really were turning their lives around.

Molly realised that her mum wasn't all that old and that when she took the trouble to smarten herself up she was still quite attractive. Lately, she had certainly been making sure that she looked her best when she went to work, but she thought that the reason she was taking pride in her appearance was because she'd been told it was expected of her as a barmaid.

Molly quite understood that looking smart and chatting up the punters was all part of the job. It didn't mean singling one of them out for special attention, though, and going off on a jaunt with him after closing time without letting any of her family know where she was.

Molly waited until almost one in the morning then, as there was still no sign of her mother, she crept into bed beside Jodie and once she was under the bedclothes her eyelids drooped and she was asleep before she knew it.

When she woke the next morning, Molly knew there was something troubling her, but she couldn't think what it was. Then, when she saw that her mum was in the bed lying on the other side of Jodie, she remembered her vigil of the previous night.

Peter was already up and had made a pot of tea when she went into the living room. He looked at her questioningly.

'Yes, she's home,' Molly told him. 'She's still sound asleep. Have you any idea what time she came in? It must have been very late because I waited up until almost one o'clock.'

Peter shook his head. 'She must have been very quiet because I didn't hear a thing.'

When Netta finally woke up she offered no details about where she had been, she simply said that she'd been with a friend which made Molly both annoyed and concerned.

'Next time you're planning to be so late could you let us know you won't be home at your usual time?' Molly told her. 'I sat up half the night waiting for you and worrying in case something had happened to you. I even persuaded Peter to walk down to the Dryden Arms about midnight to see if he could find out where you were.'

'Bigger fool you. I'm a grown woman, I don't have to ask permission from my kids before I go out and have a bit of fun,' Netta responded sharply.

'I was worried about you and so was Peter. What would you say if one of us stayed out all night without saying a word to you?'

'To start with, I'd tan your hide the minute you got home, but then you are only kids. I'm grown up and I don't answer to you or anyone else.'

Peter looked so angry that Molly was afraid of what he might be going to say as he faced his mother. Nevertheless, she was determined to back him up.

'Molly's right, Mum, we were worried in case you'd had an accident or something. We know you can do as you like but to save us worrying—'

'I've already told you,' Netta cut him short, 'I don't intend reporting to you like some school kid. If I'm not home by eleven, then you can take it that I won't be coming home until very much later and get yourselves to bed and don't wait up for me. All I do when I get home is turn in, so whether you're awake or in bed asleep it makes no difference to me.'

There was a strained atmosphere for several days. Peter thought she was being selfish; Molly felt uneasy that her mother was behaving so irresponsibly.

As she watched her tarting herself up each night and noticed that she had bought several new and rather revealing blouses, she wondered who the man was.

She couldn't bring herself to go into the Dryden Arms to see if she could find out so she tried to persuade Peter to go again.

274

'Not on your life. If I saw some fellow getting fresh with her, I'd knock his block off and that would upset her and get me thrown out of the pub or arrested.'

'I know how you feel, but if this chap is as young as you were told, then he is very unsuitable and we might be able to talk her out of seeing him any more.'

'You're talking absolute twaddle, Molly,' Peter said scathingly. 'She's already told us the rules; she can do as she likes, but we have to do whatever she says.'

'I don't think she meant it quite like that.'

'Oh yes she did, and I bet you any money you like that Dad is turning in his grave.'

'I wonder if this chap she is seeing is someone from around here or whether he's a sailor,' Molly mused.

'What the hell does it matter who he is? It doesn't make it right, and you know it.'

'True, and that's probably why she won't talk about it. She's probably ashamed of what she's doing.'

'Don't talk daft. If she was ashamed of what she's doing, then she'd stop. No one is making her go out with this fellow, whoever he is, now are they?'

'She's probably feeling lonely,' Molly sighed. 'She must be missing Dad terribly. Remember, they were getting on so well again and he'd started taking her out.'

'How can she be lonely when there are

three of us here?'

'Yes, I know that, but in her eyes we are still only kids. She probably feels she needs another grown-up, someone who sees things her way.'

'Oh for God's sake, Molly, stop making excuses for her. I think she's a heartless bitch.'

'Peter! That's a terrible thing to say about your own mother,' Molly gasped.

'Well,' he looked slightly shamefaced, 'she isn't really acting like a mother, now is she? It is all right for us, we are older, but Jodie needs her mother still. She's not setting any of us a good example; I think she's behaving more like some dockside Judy.'

After that they didn't talk about it. Peter ignored his mother as far as possible and Molly was acutely aware of the tension whenever they were both at home.

The only person who seemed to be unaware that anything was wrong was Jodie. She had taken to coming in from school to an empty house quite happily. She foraged around for something to eat and then curled up with a book until Molly or someone came home.

For a couple of weeks things seemed to settle down to the old routine. Netta arrived home from the pub well before eleven o'clock and there were no questions asked.

The following week, however, the problem repeated itself. On the Friday night, when

276

their mother still hadn't turned up at eleven o'clock, Molly once more became angry.

Peter went off to bed shortly before midnight but Molly stayed up until the early hours of the morning, listening for every sound, willing her mother to come home.

Finally, cold and tired, she crept into bed beside Jodie, hoping that when she woke up the next morning her mother would also be there in bed with them.

Her hopes, however, were dashed and she struggled to push all the uneasy premonitions about what might have happened from her mind.

'She didn't come home at all, then?' Peter asked as he spread margarine on a slice of bread and covered it with jam.

Molly shook her head.

'So where the hell did she go this time?' he demanded, a bewildered look on his young face.

'I've no idea but if she isn't back when you finish at midday, then before you go off out for the afternoon you'd better go along to the Dryden Arms and see if she has been in to work,' she told Peter. 'If she hasn't, ask Jim Bowler if he has any idea where she could be.'

'If she hasn't turned up for work, then I would think she has lost her job and he'll be so mad at her because she's left him short-handed on a Saturday, the busiest day of the week, that he won't want to talk about it to me.'

'You don't know that. Anyway,' she gave a forced smile, 'with a bit of luck she'll be there and will spend the afternoon tucked up in bed sleeping off her hangover. It might be an idea to pop in here and check with Jodie whether she's back before you go to the Dryden Arms looking for her.'

'If she is here and in bed asleep, what do I do then? Do I wake her up or go and make excuses to Jim Bowler for her, and say she is ill or something?' he asked sourly.

Her mother's behaviour wasn't the only thing on Molly's mind as she set off for the Brunswick Hotel the next morning. The previous evening, shortly before she left for home, she was positive that she had seen Steven Parsons going into one of the rooms on her landing; and he hadn't been on his own.

The girl with him had been tall, slim and very pretty with copper-coloured hair. She'd been wearing high heels and silk stockings and a pale blue coat trimmed with fur around the collar and cuffs, and a matching cloche hat. They'd been holding hands and the girl was giggling. Neither of them appeared to have any luggage.

She'd tried to put the incident out of her mind and then, when that was impossible, she had told herself that she'd been imagining that it was Steven. Of course it wasn't; it was just someone who looked like him.

Although it had been several months since she'd last seen him he was still very much in her thoughts. When she had been dismissed by his mother she had hoped that he would come after her, and assured her that it was all a mistake.

After she'd seen him at the Rotunda with that girl she had tried to harden her heart against him. She realised that he was a flirt and a heartbreaker. Even so, how could he have been so insensitive as to arrange to meet someone else at the same time and at the same meeting place?

She wondered if he had done it deliberately. Had he suspected that she would turn up there again and had it been his way of telling her that it was all over between them? She felt anger rising up inside her as she felt sure that had been the reason.

Since then, because of her father's death, her mind had been so full of other things that she had managed to put her feelings for Steven to one side. Now, sure that she had seen him at the Brunswick and seeing him accompanied by a girl had stirred up all her old feelings and brought them rushing back.

She'd even checked the hotel register before she'd left for home, but, as she'd expected, his name wasn't on it. She gave a rueful smile as she saw that the room in question was occupied by a Mr and Mrs Brown.

That didn't mean anything, of course, she reminded herself. She'd quickly discovered that a lot of people booked in under a false name if they were having an illicit liaison, and she had been astonished by how many people did so.

As she arrived at the Brunswick to commence her day's work she felt a sense of unease, wondering what she should say, or do, if it was him. There was always the chance that if he was still there they might bump into each other.

Although it was very unlikely that they would, she told herself, because, if it was Steven, then he would probably have already left for work. In fact, he might even have gone back home to Wallasey the evening before in order to make sure that his parents wouldn't have any idea of what he was up to.

As she started on her cleaning routine she deliberately left the room she knew that he and the girl had been occupying until the very last. When she finally had to go in there she could feel her heart thumping and she would have liked to turn tail. It was only the thought of having to explain her action to Mrs Roberts if she did such an irresponsible thing that made her get on with it. She knocked very loudly on the door, not once, but twice, before she summoned up the courage to walk in.

The room was empty but, as she moved towards the double bed and saw how badly crumpled it was, her pulse raced. Gritting her teeth she began to remove the sheets and pillow cases then held her breath as a man's handkerchief fell on to the carpet.

As she picked it up and saw the letter 'S' embroidered in one corner she felt more convinced than ever that it had been Steven who had been using the room and she wondered why he had to use this particular hotel when there were so many others in Liverpool.

Chapter Twenty-two

As spring 1923 became summer, Molly worried more and more about her mother's behaviour. She tried to ignore the snide remarks that were made by some of the women in Mould Court whenever she was within earshot, but they filled her with shame.

She didn't like hearing her own mother described either as a Judy or a floosie; or the ribald laughter that followed. It seemed to get right inside her head and to go on echoing long after she had passed the women by.

She presumed that they had been told by their husbands, who probably frequented the Dryden Arms, of the way her mother was carrying on with one sailor or punter after another and she couldn't help wondering what was said to Jodie about it. She was sure her sister's classmates must hear their own parents talking about it; they were old enough to snigger amongst themselves and she wondered what Jodie felt because, although she was quiet and reserved, she was much less of a day-dreamer these days and would hear what they were saying.

She waited for Jodie to complain, or even to skive off school rather than face them, but Jodie never said a word. She continued to remain calm and aloof. Despite this, much to Molly's relief, Jodie was becoming extremely helpful and Molly was now able to rely on her to do the shopping each day after she came home from school.

Peter, on the other hand, was becoming increasingly aggressive. He still didn't have a girlfriend because he claimed he didn't have the time or the money.

'I feel as if I'm not getting anywhere,' he grumbled. 'I'll never earn decent money because I haven't got a trade and it's too late now for me to become an apprentice.'

'We're both in the same boat,' she pointed out. 'Being a chambermaid is still the same as being a skivvy.'

'The only one who seems to enjoy going to work is Mum,' he muttered. 'That's if you can call what she does work.'

'Oh come on, she works hard behind that bar and she does a midday stint as well as an evening one.'

'Yeah, and she does plenty of overtime as well, by the sound of it. There are even fellows down on the docks who know all about her and the way she carries on.'

'I know, but what can we do? I have tried talking to her about the way she's behaving these days. I've warned her that she's a bad example for Jodie and what the women in Mould Court are saying about her, but all she does is either laugh or tell me to mind my own business.'

Peter nodded gloomily. 'She seems to be getting worse rather than better. I'm surprised she hasn't been picked up by the police before now.'

'Don't say that!' Molly gasped. 'That would be terrible and really give the women around here something to gossip about. I find it bad enough as it is having to face up to them and listen to all their taunts and jibes.'

'Perhaps you should try ignoring their remarks. They probably only do it because they can see how much it upsets you.'

After that Molly decided that perhaps it was better not to discuss the matter with

Peter since it only seemed to make him bitter and discontent and to increase the tension between him and their mother.

Although she was disillusioned by her mother's behaviour she decided to ignore it. Instead she concentrated on her job at the Brunswick, although even there she had to try and close her mind to some of the things that were going on.

She was very much aware that Steven was now a regular visitor there and that each time he booked into a room it was with a different girl. Fortunately, even though the room was usually in the corridor where she worked, so far they had not encountered each other. She wondered what his reaction would be if he ever found out that she was the chambermaid who cleaned his room after he'd left.

At home and at the weekends when she wasn't working Molly spent more and more time with Jodie who was gradually coming out of her shell.

She had started taking a pride in her appearance, Molly noticed, as well as showing more interest in what was happening around her. Her hair was no longer tousled and mousey but brushed until it shone and framed her elfin face in pretty waves. She was meticulously neat and everything she wore was spotlessly clean. She never had a drooping hemline or even a button missing.

Her blue eyes, which had once seemed to be either unfocused or distrustful, were now bright and alert and Molly found she had become very good company.

It was late July when once again their lives were turned topsy-turvy by another accident. Molly was having her ten-minute mid-afternoon break when she was told that there was a young girl in the hotel foyer asking for her.

Mystified, she went to see who it was and was shocked to find Jodie there looking white-faced and frightened.

'What's wrong, what's happened?'

'There's been an accident,' Jodie gulped. 'It's Mum, and they've taken her to the Royal Infirmary.'

Molly felt herself freeze. The Royal Infirmary ... an accident ... again! She didn't want to believe it.

As she put her arms around her sister she realised they were both shaking, so she made a huge effort to pull herself together and to take control of things.

'How do you know this?'

'A man came to the school. He said Mr Bowler had sent him to let me know.'

Molly tried to control her own rapid breathing. 'Do you know what happened? Is she badly hurt?'

Jodie shrugged. 'I don't know. He said something about her being in a fight.'

'A fight!' Molly breathed more easily. 'I thought she'd been knocked down or something. Who was she fighting with, for heaven's sake?'

Jodie shook her head. 'I don't know, that was all he said, and then he was gone. I asked if I could come and tell you...' Her voice trailed away as she choked with suppressed tears.

'Did he say where this fight happened? Was it at the Dryden Arms?'

Jodie bit her lower lip. 'I don't know. I'm so sorry, Molly, I didn't even ask.'

'Well, it doesn't matter, luv. We'll find out soon enough,' Molly told her. 'Wait here for a couple of minutes while I go and explain that I will have to take some time off. Now stop crying; everything is going to be all right, you'll see.'

When she returned about ten minutes later, Molly was relieved to see that Jodie had stopped crying, but she still looked very forlorn and unhappy.

'Come along, let's be on our way to the Royal Infirmary and find out exactly how bad things are. At least I know how to get there this time.'

Jodie remained subdued and withdrawn until they reached Prospect Place and then once again the tears began to stream down her face.

'Stop that,' Molly chided. 'Think how it

will upset Mum if you're crying when you go in to see her.'

Jodie shook her head, then gulped and scrubbed at her face with the handkerchief Molly gave her.

'That's my girl,' Molly whispered. 'Come on; let's find out which ward she's in and if they will let us see her.'

Ten minutes later they were taken along to the ward Netta was in and it was only Molly's warning look that stopped Jodie from bursting into tears again when they reached her bedside, because they were both so shocked at their mother's appearance.

Netta's eyes were both black and swollen and there was a deep gash on the bridge of her nose. Her lips were swollen to twice their normal size. One of her arms was in a sling and her other hand and wrist were heavily bandaged.

She tried to speak as Molly bent over her but her lips were too badly swollen for her to form any words. As Molly gently touched her mother's forehead with her lips, Netta flinched with pain.

Realising that it was no good asking her what had happened, Molly left Jodie by her mother's bedside while she went to ask one of the staff if they could give her any details.

'As far as we know she was involved in a fight with another woman who was also brought in at the same time and has similar injuries. She has been put in a different ward for her own safety,' the sister told Molly frostily.

'Do you know where this happened?' Molly asked.

'We were told that they were involved in a drunken brawl in some pub or the other off Scotland Road,' the sister said disapprovingly. 'I've never seen injuries like it. They must have been fighting like animals to do so much damage to each other.'

'Does my mother have to stay in, or can we take her home?' Molly questioned.

'She'll have to stay in overnight because we need to monitor her progress. She might have internal injuries from the blows they exchanged. The best thing you can do is to come back tomorrow and see how she is. By then she may be able to tell you herself about what happened,' she added ominously.

Peter was hopping mad when they reached home and told him what had happened. He was very reluctant to do as Molly asked and go to the Dryden Arms to see if he could find out what the fight had been about.

'You ought to go, Peter, if only to let Jim Bowler know how she is doing and to tell him that they are keeping her in overnight. If it did happen in his pub and one of his customers was involved then he must be worried stiff.'

When he returned an hour later Peter looked so grim and angry that Molly was almost afraid to ask him what Jim Bowler had been able to tell him.

'Isn't it time you were in bed, Jodie? Go on,' he added irritably, 'I want to talk to Molly on her own.'

'If it is about what happened to Mum, then I think Jodie should hear what you have to say,' Molly told him. 'You can bet your life she'll be told all about it when she goes to school tomorrow, so she may as well hear the truth and not a garbled version.'

'Well, she isn't going to like what I have to tell you,' Peter warned them.

Molly and Jodie listened in disbelief as Peter related what had happened that morning.

'This woman, Mrs Bandar, came in and asked for a glass of stout and as Mum was passing it to her the woman grabbed Mum by the hair and dragged her clean over the counter. Mum was winded, but she lammed into Mrs Bandar and the two of them used their fists and their feet to knock the hell out of each other. Mrs Bandar twisted Mum's arm back so hard that someone said the crack sounded like a gun going off. Then Mum slammed Mrs Bandar against the counter and it seems that's when the other woman's arm was broken.

'By now both of them were so covered in

blood that no one was sure how badly hurt they were. Two of the punters managed to separate them and someone went for a scuffer. Then they sent for an ambulance and both of them were carted off to the Royal Infirmary. You've been there to see her, so you know the rest.'

'Whatever were they fighting about, for heaven's sake?' Molly frowned.

Peter looked at Jodie and hesitated.

'Oh go on, she's thirteen, she's not a kid. Living round here you soon get to know all about the seedier side of life,' Molly told him bitterly.

'Well, it seems Mum has been carrying on with this woman's husband. That's who she's been with when the pub closes and she's been staying out all hours,' he said, avoiding their eyes. 'Alan Bandar is a regular at the Dryden Arms and he and Mum have got matey; too much so, by the sound of it. His missus got to hear that he was carrying on with Mum and decided to take matters into her own hands.'

'What happens now, will the police be involved?' Molly asked worriedly.

'Jim Bowler said he had already made a statement. It seems he had no option since it happened on his premises and the police were called to help sort things out. It's a question now of waiting to see if Mrs Bandar is going to sue Mum, or if Mum decides she wants to sue her, I suppose.'

'Well, there's not much point in Mum doing that now, is there? She hasn't a leg to stand on because she's the guilty party,' Molly pointed out.

'That's true,' Peter agreed. 'I suppose it's more than likely that this Mrs Bandar will take Mum to court; that's unless her husband can manage to talk her out of it. I don't expect he will want it to be blown up into a full-scale court case with headlines in all the newspapers.'

'No, and I shouldn't imagine he will be having anything to do with Mum any more, either,' Molly said grimly.

'Jim Bowler has banned him from the Dryden Arms. He wouldn't say what he intended to do about Mum and her job, though. Some of the punters were taking her side, but others in there were saying she has been asking for trouble the way she dresses and carries on.'

Chapter Twenty-three

Netta was kept in hospital for three days. When Molly and Peter brought her home her face was still bruised and she was still in a fighting mood and vowing vengeance on

291

Flo Bandar.

'Stop talking so much claptrap,' Peter told her. 'You were the one who was in the wrong; you were carrying on with her old man behind her back.'

'The pair of them have been at logger-heads for years; time and time again he's told me she's a right cow and what a miserable life he has living with her.'

'Well, he was hardly going to tell you any-thing good about her, was he? Not when he was cheating with you behind her back,' Peter pointed out.

'Why did you have to do something like this, Mum?' Molly murmured sadly. 'It's not like you. You've always had such high prin-ciples. What about all our plans to get out of Mould Court and move somewhere more respectable and start afresh? You promised us. We were all saving towards that.' Her face paled. 'Mum, you haven't been spen-ding our precious savings on drink, have you?' she asked anxiously.

'For God's sake stop preaching at me, Molly,' Netta muttered grumpily.

Molly sighed. She could guess what the answer was and she knew Peter would be angry; he had gone without so many things in order to make sure that he could help add something to their savings each week and he was going to be furious when he discovered that it had been squandered on drink.

Molly's main concern at the moment was how they were going to nurse her mother while she was still unable to do everything for herself, and also to make sure that Netta stopped drinking. She could give her a wash and make her breakfast before she went to work, but that would mean waking her mother very early because she had to be at the Brunswick by seven-thirty in the morning. She couldn't manage to come home during the day, which meant that Netta was going to be left on her own until evening.

The obvious answer was that Jodie would have to take care of her. The school holidays were about to start so that could be the answer, she decided. She had been talking to Jodie about finding herself a job, but she had no idea what she wanted to do and so far she hadn't found anything so if she was willing to look after their mother, that seemed to be the perfect solution all round.

Molly was a little worried at first about whether Jodie was capable of doing so, but she surprised them all. She was so calm and unflustered that she made the perfect nurse and she was impervious to Netta's moans and groans. Jodie even found time either late morning or early afternoon to do the shopping while her mother was asleep.

It was over three weeks before Netta was fit to return to work. Molly suspected that she was enjoying all the attention she was getting from Jodie and would probably have spun it out even longer but for the fact that Jim Bowler sent a message to say he couldn't keep her job open for much longer. Was she coming back to work or not?

From that moment Netta's recovery seemed to be almost instantaneous. Whatever happened she didn't want to lose her job. She made the effort to be back at work by the following Thursday in time for the weekend rush, even though her arm was still in a sling.

'I'll manage; I'll be able to use my hand to steady the tray when I'm carrying drinks over to the tables and it's strong enough to hold a glass when I'm pulling a pint,' she assured them all.

Since there was only a week of the school holidays left there was now no question of Jodie finding herself a job, so once more she indulged in her favourite pastime of curling up with a book as soon as she'd completed the list of chores Molly left for her to do.

'I wonder what trouble the old girl will be in next?' Peter said cynically.

'I should think after what has happened she will behave herself.' Molly smiled.

'I doubt it,' he said disparagingly, 'although I imagine she'll steer well clear of both the Bandars. That Flo Bandar can certainly pack a punch.'

'From what I've heard she didn't come

out of it all that well,' Molly reminded him. 'She also had a broken arm and some cracked ribs.'

'Yes, that's true!' Peter laughed.

'I'm surprised Mum has the nerve to go back to the Dryden Arms. I would have thought she would never want to see inside a pub ever again and I'm equally surprised that Jim Bowler wants to have her back working there.'

'Of course he does! That fracas boosted his trade. Men from the docks who never go in the pub all made a point of going there for a pint just to hear what happened first-hand from the regulars. When that lot hear she's coming back to work, they'll all be flocking to the Dryden Arms to see how she is after the affray. She'll be a star attraction.'

Molly looked worried. 'That means she'll be plied with free drinks and will be arriving home sozzled again.'

'More than likely,' Peter agreed. 'There's not a lot either of us can do about it. It's all so hopeless that I sometimes feel like packing my bag and clearing off; it's probably the only way of getting away from this place.'

'The only way we'll get away from here is by pulling together,' Molly told him.

Peter shook his head and sighed. 'You'd better have a chat with Mum and ask her not to get into any more fights,' he suggested.

'I don't think she would take any notice,' Molly said, her face clouding. 'She'd only tell me to mind my own business like she did before.'

As they feared, once Netta went back to work she started drinking heavily. The first weekend she was only slightly tipsy, but the following Saturday night she arrived home so drunk that she collapsed the moment she got in and Molly and Jodie had a struggle to get her on to the bed.

Molly was so annoyed that once they did manage to do so, she was prepared to take Peter's advice and leave her there and ignore the fact that she kept being sick. Jodie was more sympathetic. She insisted on bathing her mother's face and sat by the bed, ready with a bowl each time Netta heaved or felt she was going to be sick again.

By the next day Netta was fully recovered and even promised that she wouldn't binge on booze ever again. They smiled and agreed it would be a good idea, but all of them were pretty sure that it was a promise she wouldn't keep.

'Do you think you can manage here without me for a few days?' Molly queried. 'There's a crisis at the Brunswick because of a staff shortage and they've asked me if I can help out by working nights for a couple of weeks.'

'Of course I can. Don't worry about it.'

But Molly did worry. It was the first time she'd left Jodie to look after things completely on her own and she wondered if she was giving her more responsibility than she could handle.

'Jodie will be leaving school soon, so of course she can cope. Stop making such a fuss about them both,' Peter told her dismissively when she explained things to him. 'I'll be here in the evenings.'

'I won't be home during the day, though, except for a couple of hours' break around midday. They want me to sleep there. It's only for a couple of weeks until things get sorted out. One of the night staff has left without giving any notice and it takes a little time to find a suitable replacement.'

'You mean they're expecting you to do nights as well as your day shift?' Peter asked in surprise.

'It's not as bad as it sounds. I'll only be on call in case anyone needs anything, so I will be able to doze.'

Molly had been so full of her own problems at home that she no longer looked out for Steven.

On her first night on duty when she was summoned to one of the bedrooms, it never entered her head that it would be him and the shock of seeing him there wearing only pyjama bottoms when she walked into the room made her gasp.

Before she could utter a word, however, her attention was drawn to a deep moaning sound that was coming from the bed where a young blonde girl was doubled over in agony.

'We need some help, either a doctor or an ambulance right away,' he gabbled. 'My ... my wife is in terrible pain.'

'Have you any idea what is wrong?' Molly asked, avoiding his eyes and not sure if he had recognised her or not.

'If I knew that, then I wouldn't need medical help,' he snapped scathingly. 'Do something ... immediately.'

'Of course!'

Molly hurried out to the reception desk and asked the night porter to send for an ambulance.

'Any idea what's wrong?' he asked as he picked up the receiver and gave the operator the hospital number.

'Not really. She's writhing in pain so it could be a stomach upset or it might be something much more serious like appendicitis.'

He nodded and turned to speak into the phone again. 'They're on their way,' he told her as he replaced the receiver. 'You'd better get back there and tell them that and stay there until the ambulance arrives.'

'I don't have to go to the hospital with her,

do I?' Molly frowned anxiously.

He shrugged. 'No, I wouldn't think that will be necessary. Her bloke can take care of all that. Once she's off the premises she's not our responsibility any more.'

The blonde was curled up in a ball, alternately crying and screaming with pain. Steven muttered a terse 'Thank you' when she told him the ambulance was on its way.

'Has she a coat she can put on?' Molly queried.

'We'll take one of your blankets,' he stated curtly. As he began to pull it off the bed the girl moaned in agony as he rather clumsily moved her to one side.

Molly felt helpless and she was relieved when, a few minutes later, the ambulance men came into the room and took over.

'We won't need that, sir,' the man told Steven as he pulled the blanket off the girl and dropped it back on to the bed. 'We'll use our own, if you don't mind.'

Steven muttered in annoyance, but then stood back, leaving them free to strap the girl on to the stretcher they had brought with them while he turned his back on them and hurriedly got dressed, pulling his suit on over his pyjamas.

'Right then, sir, we're ready to go so are you coming in the ambulance with us?'

Steven hesitated for a moment, and then shook his head. 'No, don't wait for me; I'll follow on as soon as I've finished getting dressed,' he mumbled.

'I'll pack up anything you have left behind and you can collect it all later,' Molly told him.

'That won't be necessary,' he stated, avoiding Molly's eyes, 'I am taking everything with me and I will settle up my bill as I leave.' He delved into his trouser pocket and Molly heard the chink of coins. For one embarrassing moment she was afraid he was going to give her a tip.

It was three days before she had any news of the young girl although she asked the night porter several times.

'That young Mrs Brown, you know, the one who was taken ill and we had to send for an ambulance for, the one you keep asking about, well I heard today that she died,' he told her one day.

'Died!' Molly stared at him in disbelief.

'She had a miscarriage, it seems. Don't know all the details but she passed out on the way to the hospital and she never came round again.'

'That's terrible!'

'Yes, a dreadful thing to happen to a young couple like that, don't you agree?' He stared at her enquiringly as if waiting for her to say more and aware of how stunned she was by the news.

Molly nodded. She wanted to move away.

She needed to be on her own to think about what had happened, but she felt rooted to the spot she was so upset by the news.

'Funny, the way he was determined to settle his bill before he left,' the porter went on garrulously. 'Most young husbands would have been more concerned about the welfare of their missus. With a name like Brown I did wonder if they were properly married. We do get young couples coming in who aren't, you know. I can usually spot them a mile off because they're nervous and on edge when they sign in. Now he wasn't a bit like that, but I thought she seemed to be a bit tense. And then there was the matter of him being so prompt at paying, almost as if he didn't want the bill sent to him at home later on...'

Molly pulled herself together and walked away, leaving him still puzzling over the strangeness of the young couple. She knew they weren't married and understood why Steven had been in such a rush to pay and to take all his belongings with him, but she had no intention of confiding all this to the night porter.

It had been a shock seeing Steven, but to discover that the girl he was with was not only dead, but that she had also been pregnant, made her realise what a near escape she herself had probably had.

The realisation scared Molly so much that

the prospects of what could have happened invaded her dreams that night. She woke up in the small hours of the morning, drenched in sweat from her nightmare and then found she was unable to get back to sleep.

When later, the next evening on her way to work, she found Steven waiting for her near the Brunswick Hotel, she felt she was in a living nightmare and decided that the wisest course was to ignore him, even though she was sure he was waiting for her.

'Molly.' He reached out and grabbed at her arm as she tried to hurry past him.

She shook him off, intending to walk on, but Steven was determined he was going to talk to her. This time he pulled her to a stop and turned her round to face him.

'Listen to me,' he hissed, his handsome face dark with anger. 'About what happened the other night.' He paused and drew his breath in sharply.

'I've already heard that the girl you were with had a miscarriage and that she is dead,' she told him coldly.

The colour drained from his face, leaving him looking pasty and frightened. 'Who told you that? You surely don't believe it?' he blustered.

'The management were informed by the hospital.' She faced him boldly. 'You didn't even go to the hospital with her, did you? Was it your baby, Steven?'

He was about to deny it, then realised the futility of doing so and shrugged dismissively.

'What happened is none of your business, so if you're thinking of telling my mother, or anyone else, that I was in any way involved then forget about it. If I hear that you have mentioned my name in connection with what happened to anyone at all, then believe me I'll take action against you.'

'You will?' She looked at him contemptuously. 'And what sort of action would that be?'

'Keep your mouth shut, Molly, and forget all about it or you'll be finding out,' he warned.

'Is that why you're waiting here for me, Mr Brown?' she taunted.

She could see anger smouldering in his blue eyes, but her own fear of him had gone. She saw him for what he was; a weak, selfish young man who had no compassion or conscience about what had happened and whose only interest was to save his own skin.

'Remember what I've said; if you're asked for any information about me you know nothing. If you say anything or let on that you know me then you'll be in deep trouble.'

'Nothing compared to the trouble you'll be in if I do.'

'I've warned you, Molly!'

When he saw that his threats were having

no effect he changed his approach. 'Come on, Molly, for old times' sake. You can't have forgotten the good times we had together or the way I tried to help you. I even persuaded my mother to give you a job after my father sacked you from his shop. It wasn't my fault that you lost your job again!'

'I'm not saying it was, but you used me, Steven. You knew that I was in love with you and you let me think you felt the same way about me.'

'I never made any promises,' he reminded her. 'I took you out and gave you a good time and you enjoyed yourself.'

'What about that poor girl?' she asked, her eyes filling with tears. 'Does her family know about what has been going on? That she was expecting your baby, and that that's why she died?'

'That's none of your damn business,' he told her, his anger flaring up again.

They stood facing each other like two sparring partners sizing each other up, and then Molly pulled away. 'I'll be late for work if I stay talking any longer,' she told him dismissively.

'Can I count on you to say nothing?' he called after her.

She didn't bother to answer. She hurried away, indignant that he even thought she would squeal on him even though she knew that it was her duty to do so.

She despised him for his callous attitude, yet in one way she knew she was no better than he was. She should report what she knew and see that he was punished and that justice was done, but she also realised that it would be her word against his and knew that Steven could be very plausible.

Above all, she felt deeply sorry for the girl who'd died and the sorrow and heartache it would bring to her family.

Chapter Twenty-four

Molly's concern over Steven was hurriedly pushed to the back of her mind by the things that were happening back at Mould Court.

At first Jodie had said nothing, not wanting to worry Molly and confident that she could deal with the problem on her own. But when she found that her mother simply laughed at her whenever she tried to protest about her bringing men home she realised she'd have to tell Molly.

It was something Netta had started doing almost immediately she discovered that Molly was having to stay at the Brunswick overnight. She knew that Peter would be in bed and asleep when she came home because he had to be out very early in the morning, so she was confident that he wouldn't be aware of what was going on.

Molly felt outraged when Jodie told her what was happening. 'Haven't you mentioned it to Peter?' she asked.

'No.' Jodie shook her head. 'I was afraid to do so because he gets so angry,' she said hesitantly. 'I knew he and Mum would have a terrible row if I told him, so I thought it was best to let you know first of all.'

'Yes, you did the right thing,' Molly assured her, giving her a quick hug. 'Now, tell me a bit more about what has been going on. How long do they stay?'

Jodie shrugged. 'All night usually.'

'All night!' Molly's voice rose in exasperation. 'Are you saying what I think you are, Jodie?'

'What do you mean?' Jodie twisted her handkerchief nervously in her hands and avoided Molly's eyes.

'Are you saying that she takes them to bed?'

'Yes!'

It was barely a whisper, but the single word spoke volumes. Molly stared at her sister in disbelief.

'You sleep with Mum, though,' she said hesitantly. 'You don't mean...' her voice trailed away; she was unable to complete her question for fear of what the answer might be.

'I sleep under the table in the living room; where Peter used to sleep when Dad was at home.'

'Surely Peter must have noticed and wondered why you were doing that?'

'I told him that I'd had a row with Mum and wanted to be on my own,' Jodie mumbled, the colour rushing to her face.

'And he's never noticed that there was someone else in bed with Mum?' Molly asked hesitantly.

Jodie shook her head. 'I don't think so. Peter is always asleep when they get home. Most of the time he is still half asleep when he leaves for work in the morning,' she added with a feeble smile.

Molly felt bewildered. She stared at Jodie, shaking her head and trying to make sense of the situation. She found it hard to believe that her mother could act so irresponsibly, yet she knew that if Jodie was telling her the truth, and she was quite sure that she was, then something had to be done about it and she must take action very quickly.

'Look, Jodie, you say nothing to Mum or to Peter,' she told her sister. 'I won't be working nights any more, I'll be home tonight and I'll talk to her and sort it all out, so you don't need to worry about it any more.'

Her mother had already left for work when Molly arrived home that evening, but

Peter was still there and he was getting washed and ready to go out. Quickly she explained the situation to him. As she saw the look of incredulity on his face it was obvious that Jodie was telling the truth when she said he knew nothing at all about what was going on.

'You mean she's been doing this right under my nose and I've never cottoned on?' he exploded.

'It certainly looks like it, and it has to be stopped,' Molly said determinedly.

'Definitely. Right now! You and Jodie shouldn't have to put up with this sort of thing. I wish I was earning enough to get you out of here,' he sighed, 'but I can't even afford to take a girl out myself.'

His face was red and angry. 'How the hell could I have let it happen? The trouble is that up until now I've left everything for you to do and I've taken it for granted that everything was all right. It's going to be different from now on. Wait until she comes in through that door tonight and then heaven help her and any man who comes back here with her.'

'Hold on, let's be reasonable. We don't want to start any trouble or have a fight on our hands,' Molly warned.

'Reasonable! That's hardly something you can be with her these days. I sometimes think that she must be round the bend. What on earth is she thinking about? I would have thought that ending up in hospital after the barney she had with Flo Bandar would have taught her a lesson, but it seems she's behaving worse than ever.'

Netta didn't take at all kindly to the fact that they were all waiting up for her when she arrived home shortly before midnight. The burly, balding man with her also looked taken aback at having to face all three of them. Both he and Netta had had far too much to drink and they were in an aggressive mood.

'What's this then, a welcoming party?' Netta guffawed as they came into the room. 'Or have you come to say hello and that you're back home again with us, Molly?' she hiccuped.

'We want to talk to you,' Peter told her. 'On your own,' he added ominously.

'If you've anything to say, then you can say it in front of Sid,' she told him huffily.

'I think it might be best if you left right now, whacker,' Peter glowered, ignoring his mother's comment.

'Sid's going nowhere, except to bed with me after we've had a nightcap,' Netta told them. 'You may as well know that Sid's moving in with us.'

Molly and Peter exchanged bewildered glances. They were so completely taken aback by the turn of events that they were uncertain how to handle the situation. They

309

had foreseen a row of some sort, but this was not at all what they'd expected.

'Don't talk bloody rubbish,' Peter exploded. 'He can't move in here, there's barely room for us lot. You can't swing a cat round in this place as it is.'

'We've only one bedroom, Mum, so it's ... it's impossible because we wouldn't want to share it with a complete stranger,' Molly pointed out.

'Sid's no stranger; we've been knocking around together for quite a while and we are going to shack up together from now on, so the lot of you can like it or lump it.'

'But Mum, we've only got one bedroom,' Molly repeated in a shocked voice.

'I bloody well know that, but it is divided down the middle with a curtain,' Netta said balefully. 'You and Jodie can use the bed on one side and me and Sid will have the other one. As for you,' she said, looking at Peter, 'you can go back to sleeping under the table in the living room, like you've always done, and if you don't like doing that then you know what to do, don't you?' Netta told him waspishly. 'You can bugger off.'

There was a stunned silence. Peter and Molly knew they were defeated and that it was useless to argue with her.

'Now, if we've all had our say, then Sid and me are going to bed,' Netta told them smugly. 'You lot can do what the hell you like,' she added in a challenging voice.

Molly could see that Peter was incensed, but she was also aware that Sid was twice the size and weight of her brother. She was pretty certain that if it came to a fight, Peter would be the loser and that it would end by him being badly hurt.

'Come on, Jodie, it looks as if it is our bedtime as well,' she said, putting an arm around her sister's shoulder. 'I'll bring out a pillow and a blanket for you, Peter.'

Peter looked so angry that she thought there was going to be a scene. Then, to her relief, he nodded and without a word began to move the chairs so that he could make himself comfortable on the floor under the table.

Molly felt embarrassed by the way they were accepting the situation, but she didn't know what else they could do. She would try talking to her mother before she went off to work the next morning, but she didn't think that there was very much hope of persuading her to change her mind.

She couldn't help thinking how surprised as well as smug Sid had looked when her mother had said that he was moving in with them. It seemed to be as big a shock to him as it was to them.

Molly wondered who he was and what he did for a living, and if he was married.

Judging from the size of his beer belly and

the state he'd been in when he'd come in with Netta, there was no doubt where they had met. With his fat, round face he could be any age from thirty to in his mid-fifties. The only thing to be said in his favour was that he looked reasonably clean and tidy in his grey flannels, tweed jacket and blue and white striped shirt.

Unable to sleep, Molly was tempted to go back into the living room and see if she could talk things over with Peter. It would be best if the two of them could decide what to do without involving Jodie.

She waited for ages, until deep guttural snores from the other side of the curtain proclaimed that her mother and Sid were asleep. Jodie was already curled into a ball beside her so she cautiously moved away from her and out of the bed.

She wasn't sure if Peter was awake, but the minute she crept into the living room he spoke her name. Like her, he found that the situation they were in was preventing him from sleeping.

'Fancy a chat?'

He nodded and crawled out from under the table.

'What are we going to do about it?' Molly asked.

'I should have thumped him the minute he came through the door,' Peter muttered regretfully.

'I'm glad you didn't.' Molly shuddered. 'He looks like a prize fighter. If you had gone for him, then you'd probably be in the Infirmary now, being stitched up.'

'How can she do something like this?'

'I don't understand it either,' Molly sighed. 'She seems to have gone completely off the rails since Dad died; she's so different from the mum we used to know. It's almost as if it has done something to her mind,' she murmured, picking up the poker and stirring the fire back to life.

'It wouldn't be so bad if we knew something about this Sid. Does he live around here? Will his wife be coming to claim him back like Flo Bandar did her old man, or is he a complete stranger?' Molly said worriedly.

'He must be a stranger or he'd know what sort of woman our mum is,' Peter said bitterly.

'He obviously drinks at the Dryden Arms. Can you ask around at work tomorrow, Peter, and see if any of your mates who go there can tell you anything about him?'

'If you want me to, but it still doesn't solve the problem about him moving in with us.'

'I know that. We're going to have to put up with him living here until Mum tires of him and kicks him out. Even so, it would be good to know something about his background. We don't want the police around here looking for him, now do we?' she added as she carefully placed a couple of lumps of coal on top of the glowing embers.

'Have you asked Jodie if he's been coming here in the daytime when we're both at work?'

Molly shook her head. 'I haven't had a chance. Now I'm back I'll have more opportunity to see what's going on.'

Although Molly and Peter talked for almost an hour they still hadn't resolved how they were going to deal with the situation.

'I must get some sleep,' Peter yawned as he crawled back under the table to his makeshift bed.

'Leave it with me. As I said, I'll be here tomorrow when they get up in the morning and I'll see if I can find anything out. Mum might have been taking a stand last night because she could see how annoyed we were. She mightn't have meant it when she said he was moving in here; well, not permanently, anyway.'

Molly found next morning that Netta did mean it and Sid left her in no doubt that he was in full agreement with the arrangement. He even began throwing his weight around, not only telling her what he wanted for his breakfast but how he liked it cooked.

'I hope you're going to turn up the money to pay for this,' she told him as she slapped a plate of fried bread, bacon and egg on the table in front of him.

'You watch your lip, Molly,' her mother intervened before Sid could answer.

'Look, Mum, we can rarely afford to eat this sort of breakfast and since I give up most of my wages to help pay for things here I don't want to see it wasted.'

'Oh, it won't be wasted!' Sid gave a hearty laugh and rubbed his ponderous stomach in appreciation. 'I like good food.'

'Yes, that's easy to see,' Molly agreed sarcastically. 'So where have you been getting it from up until now?'

'You trying to find out a bit about me?' he asked, his green eyes glinting with amusement.

'It might be interesting. At the moment I don't even know your full name.'

'Sidney. Sidney Cook. My friends call me Sid. I'm not sure yet if that includes you!'

Molly flushed at his insulting tone, but said nothing.

Sid belched loudly. 'Well, is there anything else you want to ask me?' he demanded as he ran the remains of his fried bread around his plate.

Molly bit her lip. She knew she was taking a big risk, but she wanted to know all she could about him, and if she didn't ask now, she might never find out the truth.

'Is that it, then?' He pushed his empty plate away and took a noisy slurp of tea.

'No. I have plenty of questions, but I wonder whether I will get straight answers if I bother to ask them.'

'You'll get them, all right. Fire away, then, I haven't got all day to waste.'

'Are you from around here?'

'Born and bred in Keysham Court which is off Scottie Road.'

'Why aren't you living there now?'

'Because I've moved in here.' He belched again. 'What's your next question?'

Molly bit her lip; she suspected that he was mocking her, but she made one last attempt. 'Where do you work?'

'Here and there; wherever the job takes me. I'm one of these new-fangled electricians. I go wherever the work is. I do the job, get paid for it, and then spend the money while I'm hanging around waiting for the next one.'

Molly looked at him in disbelief.

'Satisfied?' He tilted his chair back and pulled a packet of Woodbines out of his pocket and lighted one.

'So you haven't really got a proper job?' Molly probed.

'It's skilled work; not many men are as qualified as I am and the money's good,' he told her as he exhaled a cloud of blue smoke in her direction, making her cough.

'What else? Do you want me to strip off so that you can check the rest of my credentials?' He laughed coarsely as he saw her stiffen and her face turn a dull red with embarrassment.

'Shouldn't you be at work?' he questioned when she remained silent and began stacking up the dirty dishes.

'I should, but I thought it was important that we had a proper chat if you are definitely thinking of moving in here,' she told him.

'Is that so?' His eyes narrowed. 'Well, we've had one. If you have any other questions you want answering, then you'd better hurry up and spit them out. There are other things I have to do.'

'Like going out round the docks to see if anyone needs your expert services?'

'No, I don't need to do that. I have such a good reputation that people come looking for me.'

'Does that include your wife?'

His face hardened. 'Has anyone ever told you that you've got an evil mind and a gob on you that's too big for your own good?' he said nastily. 'In fact, you're so bloody sharp that it's a wonder you don't cut yourself.'

'You were the one who invited questions. I can't help but be curious about you. Not many men reach your age without being married.'

'Cynical for a young bint, aren't you?

What's up? Having trouble getting a bloke of your own?'

'We're discussing your background, not mine,' Molly told him icily.

'And I've given you all the answers I intend to give you,' Sid snarled. 'Let's get this straight. Your mother has asked me to move in with her so that's what I'm intending to do. I'll shack up with her for as long as I like and I won't stand any lip from either you or that brother of yours. Young Jodie has more sense than to interfere and if you have any nous, then you'll take a leaf out of her book.'

'Wait on you hand and foot and say nothing? You'd like that, wouldn't you?' Molly jibed.

Sid gave a self-satisfied smirk. 'It's only what I expect.'

'And I expect you to treat my mother properly and leave the rest of us alone,' she told him hotly. 'What's more, I'm going to make sure that you pay something towards the housekeeping each week.'

'Well, if that's the end of the lecture, then I'm about to escort your mother to the Dryden Arms so that she can pull me the very first pint of the day.' He advanced towards her, his hands reaching for her shoulders. 'Do I get a kiss?'

'Don't you dare touch me!' Molly warned as she stepped back out of reach, her eyes blazing with anger. 'Not now or ever, do you understand? And that goes for my sister as well!'

Chapter Twenty-five

Sidney Cook coming to live with Netta caused ructions at Mould Court not only with the rest of her family but also with the other occupants in the crowded tenement.

Peter was very disgruntled about it and took an instant dislike to Sid. Molly had already crossed swords with him and had decided that she neither liked nor trusted him. Jodie more or less ignored him and carried on as though he wasn't there. If he asked her to do something, she did it automatically but never smiled at him or even spoke to him unless she was unable to avoid doing so and then it was usually a stilted 'yes' or 'no'.

Their objections to him moving in were echoed by most of the other people sharing the house, but Netta took no notice of what they said. As far as she was concerned, since she paid her rent regularly and on time she couldn't be evicted, no matter what she did. She turned a deaf ear to their comments about her behaviour, telling them it was none of their business if she had friends staying with her.

It was impossible, though, for Netta to ignore the antagonism that existed between Sid and Molly or their protracted fiery arguments. Sid seemed to take a special delight in goading her and she retaliated with such bitterness that even Jodie looked puzzled and asked if everything was all right between the two of them.

'Molly doesn't like me, I'm afraid,' Sid laughed. 'She likes to be boss and to tell everyone what they've got to do. Look at the way she orders all of you around.'

'I don't order anybody around; Jodie is more than willing to help when I ask her, which is more than I can say for some people,' Molly told him as she put a cup of tea in front of him.

'If there is anything you want me to do you have only to say so,' Sid told her mildly as he helped himself to sugar.

'Then try pulling your weight the same as the rest of us do,' Molly told him caustically.

'In what way do you want me to do that?' he asked, raising one eyebrow super-ciliously. 'I put more ackers into the kitty than you and your brother put together.'

'And take more out,' she retorted sharply. 'You eat twice as much as any of us and you never lift a finger when it comes to shopping for it, cooking it or cleaning up afterwards.'

'That's women's work,' he told her dismissively, pushing his empty cup aside. 'Men earn and women spend.'

Molly glared at him. 'Women do all the work while men sit around doing nothing and expecting to be waited on. My mum works all hours and yet you still expect her to wait on you hand and foot.'

'Your mum wait on me?' He laughed. 'Not her. As for working all hours, well that's her choice. She enjoys prancing around in the Dryden Arms showing off her legs and exchanging banter with all the punters.'

'I don't suppose you like the fact that she's so high spirited and popular, do you!'

Sid shrugged. 'It doesn't bother me.' He gave a self-satisfied smile. 'Most of the regulars are jealous of me because they know that when it comes to going home time I'm the one whose arm the flirty old cow will be taking and who will be sharing her bed.'

'Don't you dare talk about my mother like that,' Molly flared. 'If that's the way you think about her, then why have you moved in here with her?'

Sid gave her a supercilious smile. 'You'd better ask her that. She was the one who invited me. Probably because she can't resist me.' He stretched and gave an exaggerated sigh. 'Women all seem to feel the same way about me.'

'I don't think so,' Molly told him cuttingly.

'I think you are the most hateful man I've ever known.'

'Well, that's either because you've not known very many men or else it's because you fancy me for yourself and you're jealous of your mother.'

'Jealous, because of you! I've never heard anything so ridiculous in my life,' Molly told him in a withering tone.

Sid's eyes narrowed. 'Watch your tongue. Don't try and get all hoity-toity with me. I can make life a misery for you and your sister and brother if I choose, so you'd better remember that.'

'You already do!' she flared. 'None of us likes you,' she added vehemently.

'Except your mother,' he said softly. 'She believes everything I tell her so watch your step. You want to remember that I can turn her against you if I want to.'

From then on it was open warfare between the two of them. Sid found fault with everything Molly did. He contradicted everything she said. He ignored any request she made, whether it was to move his feet so that she could get by, to passing the milk across the table.

If she asked him to give her mother a message, he always forgot to do so. He made trouble between her and Jodie and tried to do the same between her and Peter.

Peter didn't like or trust him either and so

he ignored his comments completely.

Netta was so enamoured by Sid that she didn't even seem to notice what was going on. If Molly ever said anything detrimental about Sid, she immediately took his side. If Molly ignored something that Sid asked her to do, then Netta was up in arms.

Molly was sure that Sid was making a fool of her mother, but realised that she was so infatuated with him she couldn't see it, or at least she didn't want to.

Most nights Netta and Sid didn't arrive home until well after eleven o'clock and when they did, they'd both had far too much to drink. This meant that they were either in a quarrelsome mood or were so maudlin with each other that Molly felt physically sick to see the way they were carrying on.

Usually she tried to be in bed before they came in and she made sure that Jodie was always in bed and asleep. Peter came home so very much later that it was almost as if he was trying to wait until after his mother and Sid were out of the living room so that when he came in he could go straight to bed.

Peter seemed to be very moody and un-settled and the close companionship she'd once shared with him seemed to have gone. It was as if he had some deep, dark secret that he wasn't prepared to share with her.

Molly wondered if he had a girlfriend at

last, but whenever she questioned him about it he laughed it off in such a scornful way that she wasn't sure if he had one or not.

The only person who seemed to be unaffected by Sid's presence was Jodie. Once more she had become deeply absorbed in her school work and reading and even though Sid constantly ridiculed her about it she took no notice.

Molly had other things to worry about as well. Several times there had been policemen at the Brunswick asking questions in their attempt to find out more about the young girl who had died.

Molly was sure that they suspected she knew more than she was telling them and wondered if any of the other staff thought the same. She didn't see how they could since she had never spoken to Steven when he had been visiting the hotel.

She had spoken to him since on several occasions, though, because he had waylaid her on her way home. Each time he had been checking to make sure she had said nothing about him knowing the girl or telling anyone that he had been the man with her at the hotel that night.

It was possible, Molly realised, that someone from the Brunswick may have seen her talking to him in the street and recognised them both. She was being neurotic, she told herself. Even so, she worried about it constantly.

She was afraid that if it ever did come to light that she knew Steven Parsons had been involved, and that she had withheld the fact, then she would be in trouble. Losing her job at the Brunswick would be the least of her problems if this happened, she kept reminding herself. There was even the chance that she might end up in prison for withholding evidence.

She was so worried about this happening that in the end she confided in Peter.

'You must be mad putting yourself at risk because of him,' he said in a deprecating voice. 'I've warned you about him for years and told you how selfish and self-centred he was.'

'I know you have, but he was taking me out to the pictures every week and I really thought he was in love with me,' Molly sighed. 'Also, he did help me when I lost my job at his dad's shop,' she pointed out defensively.

'Yes, he got you a job as a skivvy for his mother. That shows how much he thought of you.'

'I couldn't get anything else; I didn't have a reference,' she reminded him.

'Old Parsons was wrong not to give you one; it wasn't your fault, now was it? Dad was the one stealing from his shop.'

Molly shrugged. 'Dad probably wouldn't have been in the shop if I hadn't been working there and he certainly wouldn't have asked for credit.'

'What happened shouldn't have made any difference to how Steven felt about you if he loved you.'

'It didn't at first; he still went on seeing me and taking me to the pictures.'

'Yes, meeting you on the sly and making sure that his dad never saw you together; and after you went to work at his home over in Wallasey he made sure that his mum didn't know that he was taking you out. Once they knew, you got your marching orders pretty quick.'

Molly shook her head in protest.

'Oh yes you did,' Peter insisted. 'Look what happened when Jodie pinched that mince pie. His mother dictated that you stop seeing her precious son or she'd tell the police about what Jodie had done.'

Molly bit her lip and remained silent, knowing that Peter was right and that it was pointless arguing with him.

'If I was in your shoes I would have told the police everything. Not only about him being at the hotel that night with the girl who died, but also about how often he was there and that it was with different girls each time. I'd have dropped the bugger right in it. It's still not too late for you to do so.'

Molly gave it a lot of thought and the next time she saw Steven she plucked up the courage to issue him with an ultimatum.

'If you don't stop waylaying me, then someone from the Brunswick is going to see us together and recognise you and tell the police that we're in cahoots. If that happens, then I shall tell the police all I know; even about you being there with other girls as well.'

'Don't threaten me,' Steven said resentfully, 'I don't like it.'

'Then leave me alone.'

'You don't really mean that, I can see by your face. If right now I asked you to come to the pictures with me, you'd jump at the chance.'

'No.' She shook her head. 'Not any more, Steven. Those days are long gone, I have realised what a two-timer you are and I never want to see you again; is that clear?'

He looked taken aback, but then he laughed. 'Are you after money or something?'

Molly's hand made sharp contact with his face before she could stop herself.

With an oath, Steven clapped his hand to his cheek which was a vivid red. 'You little wildcat!' His eyes gleamed. 'You do still care about me,' he smirked.

'The only thing I care about is that you keep away from me in the future. If you come near me once more, then I shall go straight to the police. Understand?'

Molly was still shaking when she reached home. Sid took one look at her and knew something was wrong and immediately took advantage of the fact. 'Have they found you out at long last and given you the sack?' he taunted. 'They certainly haven't promoted you because you look like something the cat dragged in.'

Molly was so near to tears that she couldn't answer. Pushing her way past him she headed for the kitchen so that she could make herself a cup of tea.

Sid followed her and stood in the doorway, trapping her into the tiny space.

'Come on, tell me what's wrong. There's certainly something up.' He advanced a couple of steps, pressing her up against the shelves. He grabbed hold of her with one hand and pulled her towards him then he placed his other hand under her chin, holding it in a savage grip as he raised her face.

Molly tried to twist away from him but he ignored her struggles as his mouth covered hers.

Unable to get free she stamped down hard on his foot, making him yelp with pain. As his grip on her shoulder slackened she punched him as hard as she could in the stomach and felt a shock of satisfaction as she heard him draw in his breath sharply as he doubled over in agony.

'Don't you ever touch me again, do you understand, or I'll have the police on you,' she told him furiously. This was her second unpleasant encounter within an hour and she felt sickened by what was happening to her.

First there'd been Steven, and now Sid. She seemed to be a prey to men who were callous and unsavoury, she thought, and felt filled with self-loathing. She gasped with relief as she heard Sid stumbling down the stairs and guessed that he had gone to the Dryden Arms to seek solace and a drink from her mother.

Molly wondered if she should tell her mother about what had happened in case he approached Jodie, but since Netta always took Sid's side she determined it was probably a waste of time. If her mother did say anything to him, he'd either deny it or give her a garbled version of what had happened. In any case, she was pretty sure it wouldn't be the truth.

Chapter Twenty-six

Finding Jodie waiting for her when she came out of the Brunswick a few days later, looking upset, with her eyes red-rimmed as if she'd been crying, set Molly's heart racing.

'What's happened now?' she asked as her sister came running up to her.

Jodie took her hand and clung on to it almost as if she was afraid to tell her.

Molly felt irritated; Jodie was thirteen, yet there were times when she still behaved like a ten-year-old. 'Come on, what's happened? Have you broken something, lost something, or...?'

'It's Peter,' Jodie interrupted.

'Peter? What's happened to him? He's not had an accident, has he?' she asked in alarm.

Jodie shook her head, tears trickling down her face. 'No, not exactly.'

'So what's wrong with him?' Molly persisted, glancing sharply at her sister.

'He's gone!' Jodie gulped.

'What on earth do you mean by that? Where's he gone?' Molly asked impatiently.

'I don't know where. All his things are

gone as well and he's left a note.'

'Go on, what does it say?' Molly demanded, trying to keep her voice calm. She put an arm around Jodie who was shaking, and her own mind clouded as it filled with dread.

'I don't know,' Jodie faltered. She fished around in her coat pocket and then brought out a grubby-looking envelope and held it out to her sister.

Molly took it and turned it over. It was sealed, and on one side he'd printed her name.

Feeling almost too terrified to open it she propelled Jodie out of the way of people passing before she slit the envelope open and pulled out the sheet of lined paper from inside. For a moment the words danced before her eyes, a jumble of scrawl that had no meaning whatsoever.

'What does he say, Molly?'

Her sister's urgent whisper cleared her mind. She focused on the piece of paper in her hand and the words seared themselves into her mind:

Molly, I can't stand the way things are at Mould Court any more. I've been thinking about doing this for quite a while. I'm off to sea. I've signed on and the boat is going to South America. Not sure when I will be back. Take care of yourself and of little Jodie. Sorry to be doing this to you, but it's never going to work out and I can't stand it any longer.

Molly read the words through twice.

Jodie tugged at her arm anxiously. 'What does he say?'

Molly took a deep breath, determined to stay calm. 'Peter's decided to go to sea.'

Jodie stared at her, speechless for a moment. 'Do you mean that he's left us?' she whispered, her eyes filling with more tears.

'Don't worry; he'll be back, luv,' Molly assured her.

'When? Does he say when he'll be coming back?'

Molly shook her head. 'Not an exact date. I don't think he knows yet,' she added, trying to soften the blow.

'Why not? Where's he going to be, then?' Jodie sniffled.

'He's gone to sea; to South America.'

Jodie's face clouded. 'All that way! He'll be gone for months and months, perhaps years,' she said forlornly.

'Well, never mind, you've still got me,' Molly told her as she hugged her. 'Peter's always wanted to go to sea, now hasn't he? We all knew that he would go someday.'

They walked back to Mould Court with their arms around each other, absorbed in their own thoughts.

Molly couldn't imagine life without Peter.

He had never had a great deal to say for himself, but he had always been there; a pillar of strength when she needed someone to confide in. He'd always supported her, and given her good advice.

She wished now that she had told him about the way Sid had molested her the other night. If she had, then probably he wouldn't have left, she thought despondently.

That was nonsense, she told herself. This wasn't a spur-of-the-moment sort of decision; he must have been planning it for ages. It would have taken months to find a ship that was looking for new crew. You didn't simply walk up to the Captain and say, 'I want to go to sea', especially when you had no experience. You had to find the right ship, assure them that you would be useful to them, and probably produce references, Molly reasoned.

The thought that he had been planning it and that he hadn't confided in her saddened her. Then common sense told her that if he had done, she would have tried to talk him out of it and he was no doubt aware of that.

'Did Peter leave a note for Mum, Jodie?' she asked as they turned into Mould Court.

'No, there was only that one for you. He probably thought it best to let you tell her. She's bound to be upset.'

Jodie was right. At first Netta refused to believe that Peter could do such a thing.

Then she blamed Molly, saying that she must have known what he intended doing so why hadn't she said something to try and talk him out of it.

The only person who seemed to be pleased by the news was Sid. He was well aware that Molly had relied on Peter, for moral support if nothing else, and now he had gone she would be far more vulnerable and that suited him very well indeed. He was determined to teach her a lesson, one which she wouldn't forget in a hurry, for the way she had treated him.

For the next few weeks Molly missed Peter so much that she felt as if the bottom had fallen out of her life. They'd never in the whole of their lives been apart before. He'd always been there in the background, but until now she had never realised what an important part he played in her everyday life.

Peter had listened to her, whether it was a question of doing something she asked, or listening to her problems. She had been able to talk to him about anything. She valued his opinion because his judgement was usually so sound that she never doubted the advice he gave her and she took it for granted that she could rely on him at all times.

Sid moving into their lives had affected them all but now she realised that it had upset Peter far more than she had realised.

She knew that he'd resented Sid, but she had been so concerned about her own problems that she hadn't appreciated just how much Peter hated the intrusion.

Peter was gone, she thought resentfully, but Sid was still there. He would be a constant reminder that she could have done more to help Peter, to share his worries and disillusionment.

She went down to the docks, not once but several times, and asked what ships had sailed for South America in an effort to find out what boat he was on. It was useless. No one remembered him from her description; no one had heard the name Peter Henderson. This puzzled her so much that she came to the conclusion that he had given a false name because he didn't want to be traced and she felt that this meant she really had failed him.

She made up her mind that from now on she'd make sure that she took more notice of Jodie and that nothing like this ever happened between them.

Jodie had suffered as much as herself and Peter had done. Supposing it had been Jodie instead of Peter who had taken it into her head to run away? Molly shuddered to even think about it. At least Peter was old enough to look after himself. One day he would come back to them, she told herself optimistically. When he did come home again she hoped that all this could be put behind them and forgotten, and that once more they could be a united family.

She felt sure that by that time Sid would have gone from their lives for ever and that perhaps her mother would have reverted back to the loving person they had known as children. She did her utmost to convince herself that it was a dream worth holding on to.

Netta refused to accept that Peter had gone to sea. She read the note he had left behind then screwed it into a ball and threw it towards the fire. It fell short and Molly quickly retrieved it. With tears in her eyes she smoothed it out and then folded it up carefully and slipped it into her pocket.

'He's playing a joke on us,' Netta declared. 'He's gone off somewhere on a binge and he'll be back home again in a week or so, you'll see. He's written that stupid note because he doesn't want us worrying.'

'I don't think so, Mum. Peter isn't like that. He never does anything reckless; you know that.'

'Well, he has this time. Silly young fool. When he does come home, I'll give him a piece of my mind, worrying the life out of me like this. Don't you agree, Sid?'

Sid was not to be drawn into the argument. He had never liked Peter, he felt he was far too quiet. He hated people like that because he could never fathom them out. Peter had been a surly young sod as far as he was concerned, but he wouldn't say that in front of Netta because he didn't want to upset her. He never trusted a chap who didn't drink and he'd only seen Peter in the Dryden Arms about twice the whole time he'd been living with them.

He didn't blame him for clearing off, but whether or not he'd gone to South America he didn't know, or for that matter care. He knew one thing, however, and that was that if *he'd* had to sleep on the floor every night then he'd have cleared off long before this.

Jodie missed Peter. Next to Molly she thought of Peter as being the best person in her life. He never shouted at her or criticised her, and he slipped her the odd penny from time to time without even asking her to do anything to earn it. He brought her home books and she always looked forward to getting those. There wouldn't be any more now, or even the odd few pennies to buy them.

The other thing that worried Jodie was that if Peter could decide to leave home without a word to any of them, then one day Molly might do the same because she hated Sid even more than Peter had done, she thought worriedly.

Sid constantly teased and taunted Molly; he ridiculed her and made her life so miserable that Jodie knew it took her sister all her time not to hit out at him. He'd never done that to Peter. In fact, he'd rarely spoken to him. Sid had ignored him in much the same way as he ignored her.

She preferred it that way and so had Peter, and yet he'd left home. So what must Molly be feeling when she was the brunt of Sid's nastiness all the time?

It frightened her to think about what might happen in the future. She wanted to talk to Molly about it and have her sister reassure her that she would never run off and leave her, but she was too afraid to do so. Yet Molly was the only person she could confide in about how worried she was because, these days, her mother never seemed to have any time for her.

Jodie hated Sid. She didn't like the way he looked at her, or the way he stroked her hair or ran his hand down her back from her shoulders right the way down to her bum.

She hated the way he watched her. Sometimes when he was lying back in the chair with his eyes closed she knew he wasn't really asleep but watching whatever she was doing. That was why she hated having to strip off and have a wash when he was at home, because she knew he was watching everything she was doing and it sent creepy shivers through her.

It was the last thing she thought about

when Molly tucked her up in bed at night and the first thing that came into her mind when she opened her eyes in the morning. Intuitively, she reached out to make sure Molly was still there in bed beside her, always fearful that she might not be; that like Peter she'd decided to leave home and there would be only a note to tell her that she had gone.

She'd hated it when Molly had worked nights at the Brunswick. She'd only done so for a couple of weeks but Jodie had missed her all the same. It had alerted her to what it would be like if Molly ever did decide to leave home.

Chapter Twenty-seven

The kitten followed Molly all the way home from the Pier Head. It was small, black as night except for a white patch on its chest that looked like a badge, and it was half starved and very bedraggled. Jodie spotted it and took to it immediately. She picked it up and cuddled it and after that there was no question in her mind of chasing it away, even though her mother warned her that it was probably full of fleas.

Sid hated the kitten. The first time he

picked it up it spit, hissed and scratched his hand. He dropped it with an oath, threatened to wring its neck, and lifted his foot to kick it out of the room, only Jodie forestalled him.

Dashing forward she screamed at him, picked up the squalling bundle of matted fur, and held it close to her chest. It was the first time he had ever seen her in such a fury and he listened in open-mouthed astonishment as she threatened what she would do to him if he ever hurt the kitten.

From then on it was Jodie's constant companion. It waited at the top of the cracked steps of the house in Mould Court until she came home and then followed at her heels while she did her chores. Afterwards, it would curl up in her lap, purring contentedly, while she sat reading.

Molly was pleased that she had something that brought her so much happiness; its devotion to Jodie intrigued her. The kitten was so friendly, however, that she realised it must have been someone else's pet and although she hated having to do it, she kept reminding Jodie that they ought to try and find out if anyone had lost it.

'If they have, they will never think of looking for it here,' Jodie told her. 'It followed you all the way from the docks, remember. I think Peter sent it. It was probably a ship's cat or else lived in one of the warehouses down on the docks.'

'Well, if it is a stray, then I suppose it will be all right to keep it,' Molly agreed.

Sid didn't agree. 'Waste of bloody money feeding that damn moggy,' he grumbled when he saw Jodie putting down a saucer of milk for it. 'One of these days it will take it into its mind to wander off again, so you may as well wring the damn thing's neck now, or else kick it out in the street and let it find somewhere else to live.'

'That's a cruel thing to say,' Jodie told him furiously. As it grew, the cat's fur had become gleaming and glossy, and she now stroked it lovingly from between its ears to the tip of its tail and smiled with delight as it arched its back in pleasure.

Netta refused to be drawn into the argument. She neither liked nor disliked the animal. The cat was as wary of her as it was of Sid; in fact, the only one apart from Jodie it tolerated touching it was Molly. When now and again she stroked it, or put down some of the leftovers when she was clearing up after a meal, it would either purr or rub around her ankles.

Jodie called it Pedro. 'It's the Spanish for Peter,' she explained to Molly.

For some unexplained reason this infuriated Sid even more. He was determined to get rid of the cat and Jodie was equally resolved on keeping it. His continual interference over the cat was the only thing that really made Jodie lose her temper.

'You should have been a bloody cat yourself,' he told her, 'you hiss and spit like one.'

'Then leave me alone and don't touch Pedro,' she told him.

When he was sober, Sid always kept his own counsel. He would aim a sly kick at Pedro if the cat came within his reach, but apart from that he ignored both it and Jodie. He still taunted Molly whenever he had the opportunity to do so, but he never attempted it when Netta was within earshot.

Somehow he had found out about her friendship with Steven Parsons and constantly made nasty jibes, insinuating that she was meeting him at the Brunswick.

'If you are anything like your mother, you're probably still seeing him on the sly,' he guffawed. 'Hot stuff, your old dear, and I bet you'll be a chip off the old block,' he leered. 'Is that why you took to staying there all night?'

When Molly assured him that she'd been working he smirked knowingly and refused to believe her.

'I was doing some extra duties because they were short staffed,' she explained.

Sid gave a deep belly laugh. 'Extra duties? That's a fancy name for it.' He slid an arm around her waist. 'How about doing some extra duties for me, eh?'

She pushed him away angrily.

'You make me sick,' she told him, a disdainful look in her eyes. 'I've told you before that if you dare touch me I'll thump you. I made you yelp once and I'll do it again,' she threatened.

Sid laughed contemptuously. 'Don't try it; I could overpower you with one hand tied behind my back.' His hand shot out and grabbed hold of her hair, savagely twisting her head backwards so that she had no alternative but to look up into his unshaven face. 'Do you understand?'

Her scream of protest was smothered as his mouth came down over hers in a wet, slobbering kiss that made her stomach heave and bile rise in her throat.

Hate boiled up inside her as she fought him off, scratching her nails down the side of his face so hard that she drew blood and he bellowed with pain.

'Spiteful little cat,' he snarled as he pulled back, almost throwing her to the ground in his savage effort to push her away.

'You're as bad as that little bitch of a sister of yours; you're wildcats, the pair of you. No wonder that bloody animal likes you both. You're birds of a feather.'

When he repeated his version of this down at the Dryden Arms as he tried to explain away the vivid long red scratches that were all down one side of his face, it brought a roar of laughter from the crowd around the bar.

'Had one too many, haven't you, Sid, talking about them being catty and then comparing them to birds!'

Sid didn't see the joke and was about to aim a punch when Netta intervened.

'Bugger off home if you're going to make a scene,' she hissed. 'If I lose my job, we'll all be going hungry. You haven't worked for weeks, you lazy bastard; you're doing less and less, and sponging off me all the time. If you start causing ructions here, you'll get both of us thrown out.'

Angrily he stormed out, cursing her and vowing retaliation against both Molly and Jodie who were the cause of this rumpus, he told himself.

The incident festered in his mind for days. Netta upbraiding him like she'd done in front of everyone rankled; he had expected her to take his side as usual. Molly's disdainful attitude and Jodie's paranoia over the cat built up so much resentment in his mind that he could think of nothing else.

He had to admit things weren't going as smoothly between him and Netta as they'd done at first; he was pretty sure that she blamed him for Peter's disappearance.

He knew they needed the money, but she seemed to spend far too much of her time at the Dryden Arms. And so did he. He was well aware that most days he was there when they opened at midday and that he was still propping the bar up when they closed again at two in the afternoon. He was back there again before six in the evening and he was still there to walk Netta home when she finished around eleven o'clock at night. By then he was so well oiled that he didn't know if he was coming or going. Netta was either dog-tired or on cloud nine because some fella or the other had been chatting her up.

He knew she was popular; he accepted that. In the beginning it had been something of a challenge because he had won her from under the noses of half a dozen other men.

She'd been different then, he told himself. She was still good-looking, but she was becoming more raddled by the day as she downed glass after glass of gin or vodka and slapped on more and more make-up to try and make herself look better.

One of the reasons he hung around in the Dryden Arms so much, instead of getting down the docks and asking around to see who had any electrical work that needed doing, was that he didn't trust Netta. He'd found her ready and willing with her favours when he'd first met up with her and what she'd do once she'd do again if it suited her, he told himself. He had no intention of being the laughing stock of the pub because he was being cuckolded.

As long as she was behind the bar, he didn't need very much money for his booze. Occasionally, he would make a show of buying a round, but only when Jim Bowler himself was behind the bar. At other times, he relied on Netta to keep his glass topped up.

He was happy enough downing beer and chatting to whoever was in the bar. He and Netta had a couple of hours at home to themselves in the middle of the day, and with Molly at work and Jodie at school, they made the most of it. They were settling into a routine, though, and it was becoming monotonous. He wondered if perhaps it was time for him to move on.

The good times, he reflected, were outweighed by the irritations. Mostly these were caused by Molly who treated him like something out of the gutter.

He was pretty sure that both of the girls had resented him ever since he had first put a foot over the threshold. He'd planned to get somewhere with Molly but he was beginning to think now that he never would.

The only one he seemed to have any power over these days was Jodie, he thought sourly. He was pretty certain that she was still afraid of him even though she had stood up to him over the cat. Perhaps tormenting her might be a good way to retaliate and it would certainly upset Molly.

He thought about it for several days as he drank himself into a hazy stupor. He couldn't taunt her like he had Molly because there was nothing to tease her about. Jodie went to school, she came home, did whatever jobs her mam had told her to do, and then sat and nursed the cat and read a book.

Watching the way the cat responded to her petting gave him an idea. He'd try a different approach from the one that he'd used with Molly. No more teasing or taunting, he decided. He'd even befriend the cat; well, for as long as it suited him to do so, but he would get even with the whole family and show Netta and her girls he wasn't one to be trifled with or ridiculed.

The cat was wilier than Jodie. It seemed to know that he wasn't to be trusted. Although Pedro was tempted by the titbits of meat he saved, when Sid offered them to him, he sniffed at them then quickly retreated as if he suspected a trap.

Jodie seemed pleasantly surprised by his change of attitude and even began to encourage Pedro to accept them.

'Drop them on the floor, Sid, then Pedro will eat them,' she suggested.

It took several days of persuasion before Pedro was sufficiently confident to do so.

After that the cat began sitting beside Sid's chair, waiting expectantly for scraps. A week later and it would even allow Sid to stroke it.

Sid felt a sense of victory the day the cat jumped up on to his lap, curled up into a ball, and then went to sleep. He'd tamed it, and now he was confident that he could tame young Jodie in much the same way.

He studied her covertly. She was no longer a scrawny little runt but a thirteen-year-old who was fast developing into a woman. Given time, she was going to be a beauty, he decided. Her face-framing chin-length hair was no longer tousled, but well brushed and it gleamed with a mixture of brownish gold shades. Her face had lost its pinched look and filled out so that, with her big blue eyes, she was almost pretty.

She was still a dreamer and when she wasn't reading she would sit lost in a world of her own, stroking Pedro and humming to herself. Sid was aware, though, that she still ignored him unless he spoke to her and even then she would often smile vaguely as if she wasn't really listening to what he had to say.

When he did manage to get her to talk to him her voice was surprisingly soft and pleasant after the rasping voices he usually heard when he was in the pub. She wasn't prickly like Molly, she wasn't provocative like Netta. What he liked, too, was the fact that she listened to what he had to say without interrupting him or shouting him down all the time.

Sid intended to string Jodie along, lull her into trusting him, and then turn the tables on her. In what way he hadn't yet decided. It would have to be something to do with the cat, he mused, since that was what she focused all her love and affection on.

If he killed her cat, especially if he did it in front of her, then she'd be so heartbroken that it would upset Molly so that would be retaliating against both of them.

The longer he left it, though, the more reluctant he found he was becoming about doing it. Jodie was so vulnerable, so different from the sort of girls who lived around the Scottie Road area. She was like a beautiful flower in the midst of a cartload of old weeds, he mused as he watched her curled up in a chair nursing Pedro.

Even as he thought it he laughed at his own stupidity. He was out for revenge on Molly, he reminded himself. He wanted to make her pay for all the insults and scorn she'd treated him to ever since the first day he'd moved in with them.

It was a pity that Jodie had to be used like this, but he wasn't backing down now. He wasn't too sure what Netta's reaction was going to be, but he didn't even care about that either. The more drink he had inside him the more determined he was to carry out his plan. No young bint was going to treat him like dirt the way Molly did and get away with it, he vowed.

He kept wavering about what he would do, depending on whether he was sober or under the influence of drink. The more booze he consumed the more devious he became about the kind of revenge he would carry out.

Netta was constantly commenting on his changeable moods and asking him what was on his mind.

'Has something upset you, or are you planning to do a robbery?' she asked in an irritable voice.

'Don't talk so bloody daft. I'm not a god-damn thief like your old man. I'm as honest as the day is long and I always have been,' he said angrily.

'Well, there's something wrong; you're even muttering in your sleep,' she told him.

That was when he knew he couldn't put it off any longer. He despised himself for his hesitation when he'd always prided himself on being a man of action.

The very next time Molly said or did anything that made his hackles rise he'd act, he resolved. He wasn't going to take any more lip from her.

Chapter Twenty-eight

A week later, when Molly arrived home from work, she found Jodie in tears because Pedro was missing.

'I've looked everywhere for him; he hasn't even eaten the food I put down for him before I went to school,' she wailed.

'Did you ask Mum if she's seen him? He may be curled up somewhere asleep; somewhere you haven't looked.'

'Of course I did. She said she hadn't seen him since she came back from the pub.'

'What about Sid? Have you asked him?'

'No.' Jodie rubbed the tears from her eyes with the back of her hand. 'He's been out all day and isn't home yet. Mum says she thinks that he's gone down the docks to see if anyone wants him to do any work for them.'

'Have you asked any of the other people living here and around Mould Court?'

'Of course I have.' Jodie sniffed and then starting to cry again. 'That was the first thing I did when I couldn't find him. I thought he might have gone into someone else's place and found a warm corner somewhere.'

'Well, don't worry too much, luv, he'll

come back again when he's hungry. Cats have a habit of wandering off, but they always come home again if you give them time.'

Jodie wasn't convinced. When it came to bedtime she was distraught because Pedro hadn't turned up. Molly tried to comfort her but without success. She insisted on staying up until her mother and Sid came home from the pub so that she could ask him if he had seen Pedro before he'd gone out that morning.

'Of course I haven't seen your bloody cat,' he said balefully. 'I haven't been here all day.'

'I wondered if he was here when you left this morning.'

'He might have been. I don't remember.' He yawned and belched loudly. 'I've had a skinful, so I'm off to bed and that's where you should be at this time of night.'

'He'll probably be back home in the morning,' her mother told her. 'Now scram, get off to bed, and stop making so much fuss about the damn thing.'

Pedro was not back in the morning and his saucer of food was still untouched when Jodie came in from school later in the day. Netta tried to take her mind off it by giving her some money to go and buy some sweets, but even that failed to cheer Jodie up.

The search for Pedro went on diligently for over a week and then Molly told Jodie very firmly that she must stop worrying and forget about him.

'He's probably found a new home. Remember before he came to us he was living somewhere else, so he obviously likes to move to different places from time to time.'

Jodie remained inconsolable. Nothing Molly or Netta said made any difference. Sid remained mute. He left early each morning saying he had work to do down at the docks and sometimes went straight to the Dryden Arms when he finished in the late afternoon, so the two girls saw very little of him.

Saturday was the first time he encountered Jodie and fully realised how desperately upset she was. Molly had gone to work, and Netta was doing her midday stint when he finally got up and went to find something to eat. Jodie was curled up in an armchair but she was crying not reading and when she looked up at him her face was so streaked with tears and her eyes so full of utter misery that he had to look away.

Hard hearted as he was, he found himself telling her to stop worrying about the cat. 'That's what moggies are like,' he said gruffly. 'Dogs, now, they stick by their master, but cats are only interested in getting their next meal and finding a warm spot where they can curl up and sleep.'

'Pedro wasn't like that,' Jodie sobbed. 'Pedro was my friend, my only friend. With

Peter gone and now Pedro disappearing I'm so lonely because I have no one to love.'

'You've got Molly and your mum,' Sid told her.

'They're both out working all the time, so they've got no time for me,' she snuffled. 'I've no one who loves me.'

'Come on, I care about you! You can talk to me,' he added, lifting her out of the armchair and then sitting down in it himself and attempting to pull her on to his knee.

Jodie stiffened and pulled back. She looked so frightened that Sid was afraid she was going to start screaming. He tried to think of some way to stop that happening. He didn't want to walk away, but he felt almost as scared as she seemed to be. He pulled himself out of the chair and went to find the bottle of whisky he'd bought that morning, which was still in his jacket pocket.

As he unscrewed the cap and took a long swig to steady his own nerves he had a brainwave. Whisky would be too strong for Jodie, but Netta always kept a bottle of vodka hidden away in their bedroom. A slurp of that in some orange juice might be the answer.

It took him a couple of minutes to get the taste to his liking, and then he carried it back into the living room and held it out to Jodie. 'Here, kiddo, have a drink; it'll make you feel better.'

Surprised, she took the glass from him and

smiled weakly before taking a long drink.

'Now, tell me, what have you been doing all week while I've been working?' he prompted as he settled back in the armchair.

'Nothing except looking everywhere for Pedro,' she told him mournfully as she took another mouthful of the orange drink.

Sid waited until the glass was empty, then took it from her and refilled it, putting in rather more vodka than before. He waited until she'd drunk half of it, then held out a hand and pulled her close.

For a moment she seemed reluctant to comply, as she remembered the dreadful things he'd said he'd do to Pedro, then, with a shuddering sigh, she relaxed. Sid had probably only been joking, she told herself. Anyway, he seemed to be the only one now who understood how upset she was over Pedro's disappearance.

Sid only intended it to be a fatherly cuddle, but the sensation of her firm warm body with its budding curves stirred his senses. He rested his face against the top of her head and took a deep breath, trying to control his feelings.

As she snuggled in closer to him he felt a tug of emotion. As she closed her eyes, as if going to sleep, he knew he should push her away, walk out of the room, until he felt calm. But he was so confused and mesmerised by the unforgivable thoughts running through his head, that he went on nursing her on his lap, holding her closer than was good for either of them.

He lost all sense of place or time as, rhythmically, he stroked her nubile body. He found himself becoming increasingly aroused as his hands roamed ever more intimately over the bare tender flesh of her arms and legs.

When the door suddenly opened and Netta walked in and stood there for a moment gaping at the pair of them as if she couldn't believe her eyes, he was so startled that he froze.

'What the hell's going on here?' she demanded, her eyes blazing and her voice rising.

Sid struggled to sit up straight and push Jodie from his lap. 'Just given her a nip of vodka in some orange and now I'm giving her a cuddle because she's so upset about her cat going missing,' he explained lamely.

He felt momentarily uneasy as he saw the mixture of disbelief and animosity in Netta's unflinching stare.

'Get off his lap this minute, Jodie! You're not a little kid any more; you're far too big for that sort of behaviour. Go into the other room at once,' she ordered in an icy voice.

'But...' Jodie yawned and looked up bewildered.

'Now!'

Netta's shrill voice cut through the air like a whip and Jodie fled. The moment she was out of the room Netta turned on Sid like a wildcat.

'I know you're a two-timing bastard, but one thing I will not stand for is you touching either of my girls, so you can pack your bags and get out.'

'Calm yourself, I told you I was only trying to comfort her because she was upset,' he retaliated angrily.

'Your hands were all over her. If I hadn't walked in at that moment God knows what else you would have tried.'

'You're a dirty-minded old bitch,' he snarled. 'You think everybody carries on like you do. I've seen you at the Dryden Arms flaunting yourself, chatting up all the old buggers who go in there.'

'How I behave when I'm there is because that's what's expected; I'm supposed to keep the punters happy. You know damn well, though, that I wouldn't let any of them even walk me home. You, though, you pick on a young girl who is so innocent that she doesn't realise what a lecherous sod you can be or what your intentions are.'

'I've been living here for months now. Have I ever harmed either of your girls?'

'How the hell do I know whether you've done so or not? You are such a crafty old dog, you'd probably bribe them or threaten them with dire retribution if they said a word about it to me. From the way you were holding young Jodie that's not the first time you've had your hand up underneath her dress...'

'You foul-mouthed, evil-minded bitch!'

Sid was so angered by Netta's accusation that he was out of his chair and had grabbed her by the shoulders and begun shaking her before she could answer.

Netta flung his hands off and, white with rage, laid into him, pummelling him with her fists with vengeful determination. Her fist met his nose in a vicious hammer blow and as blood spurted down his face, and he twisted out of her reach, her foot went out and caught him hard on one shin.

Sid felt sick to his stomach as monstrous bolts of pain assailed him. In a daze he heard Netta again screech at him to get out of the place immediately.

He was too shaken by her onslaught to argue. Retreating like a beaten dog he went into the bedroom. Jodie looked at him in silent horror as he mopped the blood from his face with one hand and rooted for his belongings with the other.

Netta stood in the doorway, angry and threatening, watching him like a hawk, silently defying him to speak to Jodie.

'Get back into the living room, Jodie,' she ordered.

Jodie hesitated for a brief second, looking from one to the other of them, still rather befuddled.

'Go and put the kettle on,' Netta said in a more moderate tone, 'I could do with a cup of tea.'

By the time Jodie had made the tea Sid had gone.

When Molly came home Netta took her to one side and explained what had happened and about the vodka. Jodie listened in dismay. She vaguely remembered that she'd had a lovely drink and that she'd been sitting on Sid's lap and that her mother had been angry and told Sid to go; now she felt so embarrassed by the whole incident that she hoped he would stay away for ever.

That night Netta was later than ever coming home and when she did, she was so drunk that she fell across the bed with all her clothes on, even her shoes.

Molly was worried both about her mother and Jodie. Every night since Netta had censured Sid about his behaviour towards Jodie and thrown him out of the house, she had come back well after midnight and she'd been so drunk that she was incapable of undressing herself.

When she'd tried to reason with her, Netta had told her to shut up and mind her own business and not to interfere with the way she ran her life.

Jodie was also a problem. She had reverted once more into being moody and withdrawn. She still spent hours looking for the missing cat and often cried herself to sleep at night.

When Molly suggested she might like to have another cat to replace Pedro Jodie had burst into tears and hit out at her, she was so angry about the idea.

Whenever she was free Molly took Jodie out, but she was listless and completely disinterested in whether they went shopping or to the park. Unless they saw a black cat, which immediately brought squeals of excitement which quickly turned to gulping sobs when she realised that it wasn't Pedro.

Neither of them ever mentioned Sid, or talked about when he had been living there with them. It was almost as if he had never existed. Molly dreaded that, in time, her mother would bring some other strange man home, but so far it hadn't happened and Molly hoped she never would again.

Molly still hoped that Peter would come home and wished she knew which boat he was on so that she had some way of getting in touch with him.

For the first few weeks after he'd left home Molly hoped that they would hear from him so that they would know that he was all right. Even if he didn't want to tell them where he was it would have been comforting to at least get a card from him.

She knew he had resented Sid being there from the moment he'd arrived and understood that he probably wanted to make a new life for himself and, in many ways, she didn't blame him at all. Living in Mould Court had been such a come down for all of them after growing up in Wallasey.

To some extent Molly could understand her mother's unhappiness because she was quite sure that she must be missing Sid. She could remember how lonely and neglected she'd felt when she'd first broken off with Steven. It had been almost as if the bottom had dropped out of her world.

It was no doubt why her mother had once more resorted to drowning her misery by drinking. What she did between the time the Dryden Arms closed and when she arrived home at one or two in the morning Molly wasn't sure.

Time was a healer and had helped her to put her feelings for Steven into perspective, and she hoped that it would do the same for her mother, Molly reasoned.

Steven had broken her heart when she'd realised that to him she'd been just another conquest, but she didn't think it had been like that for her mother and Sid. Bringing him back home, though, and expecting them to let him take their dad's place in their lives, had been a big mistake.

She wondered if it had really been concern for Jodie's welfare that had sparked such a terrible row between them, or whether it had been jealousy that he had eyes for someone else that had enraged her mother so much.

It was impossible to turn the clock back, but she worried about what lay ahead of them. Moving away from Mould Court seemed to be more impossible than ever with only her wage and her mother's to scrape by on, yet it was the only goal to aim for if they were ever to become a loving, united family again.

Chapter Twenty-nine

Gossip and rumours about Netta's behaviour were rife in Mould Court and ricocheted from there to the Dryden Arms as well as up and down Scotland Road.

The way she carried on with the regulars in the Dryden Arms, and the state she was in when she went home at night, was already standard gossip. Now the company she kept after closing hours and what transpired between them was fuelling fresh scandal.

A dark dreary day at the beginning of

November brought matters to a climax. It had been heavily overcast all day, but by four o'clock when Jodie came home from school it was almost dark.

As she let herself in she could hear what sounded to her ears like a drunken brawl, and when she looked into the bedroom it was to find her mother cavorting with a heavily built good-looking young man in his mid-twenties. When they looked up and saw Jodie standing in the doorway watching them, the man gave a drunken howl of delight, before reaching out and grabbing at her, dragging her on to the bed alongside them and trying his best to remove her blouse and skirt.

Jodie struggled wildly to free herself from his clutches. Netta fought the young man, pinning him down underneath her, leaving Jodie free to make her escape.

Terrified and shaking Jodie fled back to the living room. There was no light and she had no money for the gas meter so she groped around in the semi-darkness trying to find the bottle of vodka she knew her mother had hidden away in a cupboard by the fireplace.

Ever since Sid had given her a drink of orange and vodka, one that had soothed her when she'd been feeling upset, she'd tried several times to make it for herself from one of the bottles kept hidden around the place.

363

At first, because there was no orange with it, she hadn't liked it, but the after effects were so wonderful that she developed a craving for it. After what had just happened she felt desperate for a drink now. Even though there wasn't any orange to mix with it she could still drink it straight from the bottle like she'd done so many times before.

For a while she lay curled up in the armchair, clutching the bottle and alternately sobbing and taking a deep swig from it. She stayed there until her head began to reel and her stomach started heaving so badly that she knew that at any moment she was going to be violently sick.

Struggling out of the armchair she reached for one of the paper spills that were kept on the mantelpiece to try and get a light so that she could see what she was doing.

She felt so light-headed that it took her three attempts to stick the spill into the glowing heart of the fire. Once she saw it had caught she groped around for the stub of candle that stood on a saucer in the middle of the table.

Her hand was shaking so much, and she felt so dizzy, that she found it difficult to focus long enough to connect the flaming spill with the wick of the candle. Before she managed to do so the spill had burned right down to her fingers.

With a sharp cry she dropped the burning

fragment and it fell on to an old newspaper which caught alight immediately. Befuddled, she desperately beat at it with her bare hands in an attempt to put it out, but this only seemed to make it burn more fiercely and in no time at all it was flaring up and there were tongues of flame spreading everywhere and even setting light to the curtains.

Within minutes the whole room was blazing. Jodie shrieked; she yelled out to her mother and the man she was with to come and help, but both of them were too engrossed in what they were doing to take any notice.

As she tried to beat out the flames the pain in her hands was so intense that she found herself gasping for breath. Realising after a few minutes how futile it was to try and staunch the blaze on her own she fled out into Mould Court, shouting for help.

The flames and smoke seemed to follow her. People living in the other rooms in the house and in the adjoining houses all began to hurry out into the open air; some shouting, others screaming. Someone sent for the fire brigade; others tried to calm Jodie, wrapping her in an old coat and arguing amongst themselves whether she ought to be taken to hospital or not.

Molly arrived home in the midst of all the kerfuffle. So many people tried all at once to tell her what was going on that she was unable to comprehend what had happened.

In the midst of the hullabaloo the fire engine arrived and the crowd were forced to move back so that the firemen could unroll their hoses, connect up to the nearest hydrant, and take steps to try and extinguish the blaze.

It was only when that happened that Jodie told Molly that their mother and a chap she'd never seen before were both still inside the burning building.

Leaving Jodie in the care of one of the neighbours, Molly dived under the cordon that they'd erected to keep people back and grabbed hold of a fireman who was struggling desperately with a long length of hosepipe.

At first he shook himself free of her clutching hand. Then as she shouted at him again and again he stopped to listen. His face became concerned when she told him about her mother and a man being in the building and he called out to a senior officer who assured her that they'd do whatever was necessary to rescue them.

It was a tense fifteen minutes before they finally brought Netta out. An ambulance had already been sent for to take Jodie to hospital so that the burns on her hands and arms could be treated. It pulled up at the same time as they carried Netta out from the house. She was badly burned and unconscious and so she was stretchered straight into it along with Jodie.

Molly went with them. Realising that there was nothing she could do to help her mother, she sat cradling Jodie who was sobbing uncontrollably.

Netta was already dead by the time the ambulance reached the hospital. Jodie had to be taken to a special unit so that the terrible burns on her hands and arms could be dealt with, but they refused to let Molly go with her.

Instead, she was required to answer a string of questions about what had happened and how the fire had started. Over and over again she told them that she hadn't been there.

'If you let me talk to my sister, then I may be able to help you,' she kept telling them.

'That's not possible. She's under sedation. The best thing you can do is to go and get some rest yourself and come back tomorrow about midday. By then she may be well enough to talk to you.'

Even though she begged to be allowed to stay, or at least to see Jodie before she left the hospital, they were adamant and firmly refused to let her do so.

Shocked and concerned, Molly returned to Mould Court. The fire had now been put out, but the firemen were still dampening down the smouldering building to make sure that it didn't flare up again.

A crowd of people were still gathered outside the house. Many of them were the other families who lived there and who were now homeless, just as she was, and who were waiting to see if they were going to be allowed to go back in to collect some of their belongings.

The moment they saw Molly they swarmed round her asking one question after another; about her mother, Jodie, how the fire had started, and giving her no chance to answer.

Confused, she shook her head, telling them she had no news at all then pushed her way through them to go and thank the fireman she'd spoken to first, and who had brought her mother out of the blazing inferno.

'Hello, Molly, how are they both?'

His face was blackened by smoke and he looked so exhausted that for a moment, even though he smiled at her in a friendly way, she had no idea who he was. She assumed that he must have heard her name mentioned by some of the people still crowded together outside the house.

'I'm afraid my mother died before we reached the hospital,' she said sadly.

'What about Jodie?'

'My sister is being treated for her burns, but they say they have had to sedate her and they wouldn't let me see her.'

'Oh, I am sorry, especially about your mother!' There was real concern in his voice and on his grime-stained face.

'I am as well, especially when you risked your own life bringing her out.'

'I would have done that in any case, because it's my job,' he said sombrely. 'You don't remember me, do you, Molly?'

'Remember you?' She frowned. 'Only that you were the one who went in to bring my mother out.'

'I mean before that; when we were both at school.'

Molly stared at him puzzled. Then, as he pushed his helmet back and she saw his light ginger hair, her face cleared. 'It's Brian,' she exclaimed in surprise. 'Brian Baldwin! However long is it since I last saw you?'

'Quite a while.' He smiled. 'We were still at school and delivering newspapers for old Parsons from the shop on the corner and now we are both grown up.'

'That's right! You broke your leg and we did our paper rounds together.'

'I broke my arm not my leg.' He grinned. 'We took the papers in my little sister's pushchair. It just shows how you've forgotten all about me,' he added teasingly.

'Leg, arm, what does it matter?' she laughed. 'I remember it as clearly as if it was yesterday. You were always very kind to me and stuck up for me at school when the others bullied me.'

'I can see we have plenty to talk over, but

this isn't the time or the place. Perhaps we can meet for a chat sometime.'

'I'd like that.' Molly smiled. 'I want to get back to the hospital, now, of course. I think I ought to be there when Jodie wakes up ... and thank you for all you did today, as well as in the past.'

As she moved away Brian called after her, 'You do know you won't be able to stay here, have you anywhere else to go?'

'I'll be all right,' she assured him. 'I work at the Brunswick so I will be able to stay there for the present.'

He nodded and then turned his attention back to stowing away the equipment they had been using to extinguish the fire.

Jodie was still sedated when Molly returned to the hospital. She was lying on her back; both her hands and arms were heavily bandaged and were lying outside the covers so that she looked more like a puppet than a living girl.

As she stood there looking down at her, Molly wondered whether it had been her mother or Jodie who had set fire to the place. Jodie had been so dazed and disorientated that Molly wondered if she had been drinking.

She suspected that it was possible because ever since the day Sid had given her a drink of orange that had vodka in it she'd often found Jodie searching for the bottles Netta brought home and kept hidden amongst her clothes, under the bed and in all sorts of strange places. She'd done her best to stop Jodie drinking the stuff, but she suspected that she sometimes did when there was no one else in the house.

Jodie had mentioned that there had been a youngish man there with her mother and she wanted to ask her who he was and what had happened to him after the fire had started.

'I thought I told you that it was no good coming back again until tomorrow?'

The sharp voice of the ward sister startled Molly.

'Yes, I know, but I am very worried about my sister and I felt I had to come back and see how she was,' Molly explained apologetically.

'There will be no change whatsoever until tomorrow. Now please go home.'

Knowing she had no alternative but to do as she'd been asked, Molly took one last look at Jodie before leaving the ward. She was fearful about what state Jodie would be in when she woke up.

The memory of her little sister lying there looking like some strange puppet haunted her. She hoped she wouldn't say anything that might incriminate her in any way and lead them to suspect that she was the one responsible for what had happened.

Back at the Brunswick, Molly had the painful task of explaining to Charles Wardle, the manager, what had happened and of answering the hundred and one questions that he and the rest of the staff asked her.

'If you need time off, then you can have it,' Charles Wardle told her. 'If there is any other way we can help, you have only to ask.'

'Thank you, Mr Wardle, I am very grateful,' Molly told him. 'There is one big problem, however; I have nowhere to live. Would it be possible for me to use one of the staff bedrooms until I have the time to make some other arrangements?'

'Of course, that is no problem.'

'I probably won't have time to look for anywhere else for at least a week,' she pointed out quickly. 'You see, there will be my mother's funeral to arrange and I have to visit my sister every day whilst she is in hospital.'

'I quite understand, Molly. Now don't worry about a thing and remember that you can have as much time off as you need,' he reassured her.

It wasn't until next day that she realised that she had not only lost her mother in the fire, but she had also lost all her possessions, including every item of clothing she had, and that all she owned was what she was standing up in.

In desperation she had to once more ask Mr Wardle for help, this time to see if he could see his way to letting her have an advance on her wages.

Before going to the hospital the next morning she made her way to St John's Market to buy the very cheapest second-hand clothes she could find.

As she counted out the money in her purse Molly realised that Jodie hadn't anything to wear either, but she decided she wouldn't buy her anything until she absolutely had to.

She felt overwhelmed by all that had happened that day. It had been strange meeting up with Brian Baldwin again and finding that he was still her friend, and she looked forward to seeing him in the future.

What lay ahead of her was what was important at the moment. There was not only the funeral to arrange but also the job of finding somewhere to live, and Jodie was going to need weeks of nursing. How on earth was she going to be able to do that and keep her job on at the same time?

Chapter Thirty

When Molly visited the hospital the next day she found that Jodie was still lying stiff and straight, both her heavily bandaged hands and arms on top of the bedclothes, exactly as she had been when she'd left her. She was awake, but she refused to open her eyes, or to respond in any way.

As she sat by her sister's bedside, gently holding one of her badly injured hands, Molly was dismayed to find that Jodie refused to talk to her.

Sister Pickford, who was in charge of the ward, was extremely concerned in case the shock of what had happened had temporarily rendered her unable to do so.

'Has your sister ever suffered from fits?' she asked Molly.

'No, never,' Molly told her. 'Why do you ask?'

Sister Pickford frowned. 'She has spasms of trembling and shaking and we are unsure what is causing them.'

Molly bit her lip, wondering whether she ought to tell Sister Pickford about Jodie's drinking in case they gave her the wrong treatment or medicine.

Sister Pickford noticed her hesitation. 'Look, if there is something you should be telling me, then please do so. Are you sure that she isn't on any sort of medication? Are there certain things she mustn't eat or drink?' Sister Pickford probed.

Sister Pickford's voice was no longer soft and cajoling but very firm and authoritative.

'Jodie drinks.'

'She drinks!' Sister Pickford sounded

shocked. 'She is still only a child, a school-girl.' She frowned. 'What sort of drinking are you talking about?'

'It's not her fault,' Molly went on hurriedly. 'A friend of Mum's started her off doing it.'

'You mean the occasional glass of wine or cider when you have a party, do you?'

Molly shook her head. 'Not wine, vodka. She drinks vodka. He gave it to her one day and now she drinks it straight from the bottle, almost like it was pop or lemonade. Sometimes she drinks more than she should and doesn't know what's going on around her.'

'And you say it was a friend of your mother's? Why ever did your mother allow it?'

'She didn't know. I think she probably suspected when she found that there wasn't as much vodka left in the bottle as she thought should be there. Mum used to have bottles of the stuff hidden away all over the place but Jodie was always able to find them.'

'I find this is very hard to believe. And you say it was a man who started her off doing this. Do you know why?'

Blood rushed to Molly's face. 'I think so,' she muttered, 'but I'd rather not talk about it.'

Sister Pickford shook her head from side to side. 'I can imagine, whether you tell me or not,' she said sternly. 'Why on earth didn't you report it to the police?'

'Because that would have meant my little sister might have been taken away, and perhaps put into a home or borstal.'

'It certainly would have meant that she was taken into care and if that had happened then this terrible tragedy might have been avoided. Your mother might still be alive.'

Sister Pickford had voiced aloud what had been in Molly's mind ever since the accident had happened. She didn't want Jodie blamed for what had happened. Their mother might be dead, but Jodie still had her life ahead of her.

'I'm sure the police and the fire service will get to the bottom of it,' Sister Pickford said crisply. 'Have they questioned you yet?'

'They know I wasn't there when it happened,' Molly said quickly.

Sister Pickford pursed her lips. 'To get back to your sister,' she said sternly, 'now that you've explained the underlying cause of your sister's attacks, at least we will be able to make sure she has the right sort of treatment. She will certainly not be getting any alcohol while she is in here. These tremors she is experiencing are probably withdrawal symptoms.'

'Will it affect her recovery?'

'It certainly won't help matters. If she is

used to indulging in vodka, then not being able to do so is going to affect her feeling of wellbeing and there are bound to be unpleasant side effects.'

'You won't report her though, will you?'

'This is a hospital, not a police station. I shall leave you to deal with that side of things,' Sister Pickford said primly.

'Thank you. I am very grateful,' Molly told her. 'It was never her fault, so it wouldn't be fair for her to be punished.'

Molly's mind was in turmoil as she left the hospital. She wasn't sure that she should have told Sister Pickford about Jodie's drinking. It would go down on her report sheet and although Sister Pickford might keep her word and say nothing, what about the doctor when he did his rounds and read the report? He might very well take it upon himself to speak to the authorities.

Even if he didn't do it right away it was possible that if Jodie was slow in making a full recovery, then he might consider it was his duty to do so. Yet if she'd said nothing, then they wouldn't know how to treat Jodie and if they gave her all the wrong medicines then she might never recover, Molly told herself worriedly.

Sid was the real culprit and he should be punished for what he had done. Her mother had been right to throw him out but it had been too late; by then Jodie had already discovered the comfort she could obtain from drinking vodka and had become addicted.

She had no idea where Sid was now or how to go about finding him, so what good would it do if she did go to the police and tell them what had been going on?

It was bad enough losing her mother and finding herself homeless, but now this was an added burden and it was one she had no idea how to handle. If only there was some-one she could talk to, someone who would tell her what was the right thing to do, she thought longingly. There was no one in Mould Court whom she counted as a friend; she no longer thought of Steven as a friend, and she couldn't bring herself to confide in any of the people at the Brunswick about such a matter.

She would do nothing for the moment, she resolved. There was her mother's funeral to face. Perhaps after that was over she would be able to think more clearly. At the moment everything was one wild jumble inside her head. She had to find money for the funeral and she had to find somewhere to live.

She didn't even know how to start organ-ising the funeral. Sister Pickford had said that she would have to go to the police station to find out when the body would be released and had said something about a coroner having to give permission for her mother to be buried because she hadn't died from natural causes.

She was so engrossed in the thoughts churning around inside her head that she didn't notice the man standing on the corner near the Brunswick. She had almost passed him when he spoke her name, and she swung round in surprise.

'Molly, are you all right? Is Jodie worse? You were miles away and you look really upset.'

For a moment she stared blankly at the solid young man in the smart grey suit with no idea as to who he was. Then she recognised the light red hair and freckled face. 'Brian! What are you doing here?' she gasped.

'I came to find out if you were all right and the chap on the reception desk said you had gone to the hospital to see your sister. He said that you would be back before too long, so I thought I'd wait around for a while in the hope of seeing you.'

'Oh Brian!' Suddenly all her endeavour to keep a stiff upper lip collapsed completely. Tears streamed down her face and she was shaking.

'Hey, hey, this isn't like you,' Brian told her. He took her by the arm and led her down a side street away from the curious stares of passers-by.

'Come on, there's a café not far from here. What you need is a cup of tea and while you

379

are drinking it you can tell me all about what has been happening.'

It wasn't until the pot of tea and a toasted teacake were on the table in front of her that Molly realised how famished she was. She couldn't remember when she had last eaten or what it had been.

While she tucked in, enjoying every mouthful, Brian was the one who did all the talking. He told her of the jobs he'd had after he'd left school and how eventually, the moment he was old enough to do so, he had joined the Fire Service.

'I've only been a fireman for a year, but I've finished my training, and I'm enjoying every minute of it,' he enthused. 'This was the first really big fire I've attended. Usually it is warehouses or the rubbish behind the lock-up shops that we get called out to, not a full-scale house fire.'

'And yet you were the one who dashed inside,' Molly said in awe.

'Well, I thought someone might be trapped inside there, but I had no idea it was your mother,' he said awkwardly, the colour rushing to his face.

'Brian!' Tears filled Molly's eyes and she stretched out a hand to grasp his and squeeze it. 'It's lovely to be back in touch again. I've often wondered what happened to you.'

'I've never forgotten you,' he said bashfully.

Molly stared at him wide-eyed. 'Really?'

Brian looked uneasy. 'I've seen you about from time to time, but I thought you were still going out with Steven Parsons so there didn't seem to be much point in trying to stay friends. I didn't think you'd have any time for me.'

It was Molly's turn to look disconcerted. 'We only went to the pictures together now and again, that was all. We stopped seeing each other ages ago.'

Brian nodded. 'I thought I hadn't seen him around. I know you can't do so at the moment because of the fire and Jodie being in hospital and so on,' Brian rushed on, 'but perhaps when you have more time you'd like to come to the pictures with me.'

'Yes, I'd like to do that. At the moment, though, as you say, I have far too many things that I have to see to. There's my mother's funeral to arrange and I don't know how to go about doing that, I don't even know how to find out how much it is going to cost. Do you think if I asked they would let me pay for it bit by bit?'

'I don't know, but I wouldn't have thought that was possible.' His light blue eyes were full of concern. 'Look, Molly, perhaps I can help you. I could find all that out for you. I know people who would be able to tell me. If I came and met you tomorrow with all the answers, would that help?'

'It most certainly would, that's if you can spare the time,' she said gratefully.

'Right, well, I know most of the details because they were taken down after the fire. Shall I meet you tomorrow and let you know how I have got on?'

'Of course. I shall be going to the hospital to see Jodie about the same time as I did today.'

'Right, then I'll be waiting for you outside the hospital at four o'clock.'

'You are not taking time off work to do this for me I hope?' Molly frowned anxiously.

'No! I work shifts; we all do in the Fire Service. Now, if it was next week, then I wouldn't be able to meet you. I'm on nights at the moment and that means I must go any minute now or I will be late,' he added, looking at his watch.

As he summoned the waitress to ask for their bill, Molly opened her purse, hoping she had enough to pay for her share, but he gently stopped her. 'My treat!' he told her.

'I'll see you tomorrow. I'll be outside the hospital at four o'clock,' he assured her as they parted.

As she made her way back to the Brunswick, Molly found that it was hard to believe that the handsome-looking young man she'd been talking to was the same scruffy schoolboy who'd championed her when she'd first arrived in Mould Court. True, he still had the same light red hair, a rash of freckles across his nose and cheeks, and the same friendly blue eyes that she remembered so well but now he had so much self-assurance as well.

It felt good to have Brian back as a friend. She'd never forget how he'd defended her once against a mob of schoolmates; she'd appreciated what he had done then and she was grateful to him now for his offer to help her.

Chapter Thirty-one

Molly and Brian and a few customers from the Dryden Arms attended the funeral service when Netta was buried a week later. None of the neighbours from Mould Court came to the service or the burial, and Jodie was still too ill to leave hospital, so Molly felt very relieved when Brian insisted on being there with her.

Afterwards, when he took her to a quiet restaurant for a meal, she confided in him the reason why Jodie was making such a slow recovery. He listened in silence as she told him all about her father being killed and about the way Sidney Cook had come into their lives and how he had tempted

383

Jodie with drink.

'This is unbelievable; she's only thirteen!'

'She'll be fourteen in a few weeks' time.'

'Even so, she shouldn't be drinking. Where is this Sid now? Was he at home when the fire started?'

'He and Mum had a terrible row months ago because she came home and found both of them had been drinking; Jodie was on his lap and he was fondling her.'

'Poor kid! No wonder she is in such a state, and then the fire on top of everything.'

'Yes, I know.' Molly pushed aside her plate and rubbed her eyes, trying to quell her tears. 'I feel so guilty for not realising what was going on; I feel I've let her down badly.'

'Don't get upset. It will work out all right. Do they know all about Jodie at the hospital?'

'Yes,' Molly nodded, 'I thought I had better tell them; only about her drinking, of course.'

'Perhaps you should have told them the whole story,' Brian said thoughtfully. 'If she can talk about it, or if someone discusses it with her and explains she has done nothing wrong, then she may feel a whole lot better about everything.'

Molly looked at him in surprise. 'Do you really think so?'

He nodded. 'It may be why she isn't getting any better. She mightn't want to.'

'What do you mean?'

'She may feel so unhappy about it all that she doesn't want to have to face the world again. She may feel safe whilst she is lying there in a hospital bed, with people looking after her, protecting her from any un-pleasantness.'

'I never thought of that,' Molly said slowly. 'I suppose you could be right.'

'Going back to the day of the fire,' Brian said in a puzzled voice, 'if this Sid wasn't there when it happened, then who was the chap who ran from the house as we pulled up? We all noticed him because he was only half dressed and he belted away from Mould Court as if the devil himself was on his heels.'

'I don't know,' Molly admitted. 'Jodie did mention that there had been someone there with Mum, but she had no idea who he was. Probably someone my mum had picked up in the Dryden Arms.'

Brian grimaced. 'Yes, I've heard about some of her antics,' he said, his voice a mix-ture of contempt and compassion. 'She had quite a reputation!'

'Only since Dad died; it was her way of coping with things,' Molly said sadly.

Brian nodded understandingly. 'It must have been hard on you, though.'

'Things weren't too bad until she brought Sidney Cook home. I think she thought we'd let him take our dad's place, but it was out of the question. My brother Peter couldn't stand him and in the end he ran away to sea and we've never heard from him since,' she said sadly.

'Anyway, things went wrong long before that, even before we moved to Mould Court,' she said with a deep sigh.

Brian said nothing, just sat there holding her hand, silently supporting her and waiting patiently for her to continue if she wanted to do so.

Molly found it was such a relief to talk to someone about all her problems that after a moment she started telling him about what her dad had been like when they were growing up, the problems he'd had to face after he'd been demobbed and how these had led to them leaving Wallasey.

Brian nodded or murmured from time to time as she continued her story, neither condemning nor commenting. When she'd finished she felt as if a load had been lifted from her shoulders. Her mind was clear of the misty muddle that had built up inside it over the past few years. Things which had troubled her and which she had never been able to understand she found she could suddenly see with an overwhelming clarity.

Although Brian said very little his very presence gave her strength. As she saw the compassion in his blue eyes, felt the pressure of his hand, warm and firm as he held her own, she felt safe and happy.

She said very little about Steven Parsons; it was a part of her life she didn't want to dwell on. Brian knew she had dated him, but he looked astonished when she said she had gone to work as a skivvy at the Parsons's home and she felt she had to briefly explain how that had come about.

'Tell me,' she smiled, 'what has been happening to you since I last saw you? I've been so wrapped up in my own problems the only thing I've asked you is how you came to be in the Fire Service.'

Brian shrugged non-committally.

'Come on,' Molly urged. 'I really do want to know.'

'Well, after I left school I went to work down at the butcher's, but I didn't like it there; it was better than going on the dole.'

'You didn't stay there very long?'

'No!' Brian shook his head. 'My dad worked down at the docks as a stevedore and so I went to work down there as well. I hadn't been there long when he met with an accident; he fell down a ship's hold and broke his neck.' Brian's voice caught in his throat and for a moment he couldn't go on. 'He died instantaneously.'

'Oh, Brian, that's dreadful. I am so sorry.'

'The worst of it was I couldn't face the docks after that. Every time I went to work I seemed to see him everywhere. I'd go dashing into a warehouse after him only to find when the bloke turned that it wasn't my dad. What scared me was that more often than not the chap was nothing at all like him.'

'So you joined the Fire Service?'

'No, it wasn't that easy. I was too young. I filled in doing all sorts of odd jobs, anything that would bring in some money. My mum was ill; she never got over Dad's death and she died a year after him.'

'What about your little sister? What has happened to her?'

'My eldest sister is looking after her. She's married with kids of her own and lives in Rochdale so she took her up there to live with them.'

'So you are completely on your own?'

Brian nodded.

'So where are you living now?' Molly frowned. 'Are you in lodgings somewhere?'

'No, I kept my mum's place on. I couldn't face selling everything up; it was too much of a wrench at the time. Believe it or not, I found I liked living there on my own and looking after myself. I've even learned how to cook. Nothing very fancy, mind you, but I haven't ruined anything yet.' He grinned.

'You've not had it easy either,' Molly commiserated. 'It's odd how some people sail through life with no worries or problems and others seem to get one thing after another going wrong.'

'Most of my problems are over for the moment,' Brian assured her. 'You've still got some ahead of you. Don't forget Jodie is going to need a lot of looking after when she comes out of hospital.'

'Yes, I know,' Molly agreed. 'Now that the funeral is over, I must start looking for a room for us. I'm still staying in a staff room at the Brunswick but I don't think they will allow me to have Jodie staying there with me.'

Brian looked thoughtful. He started to speak then stopped and fiddled with the cutlery on the table. Avoiding Molly's eyes, he said in a rush, almost as though he was afraid to voice his thoughts aloud, 'Why don't you both come and stay at my place? There's a spare bedroom and I'm out of the house a lot because of working shifts, so you would be able to do more or less as you liked there.'

'Brian, that's awfully kind of you, but you've just said that you like living on your own,' Molly protested.

'I do, but I wouldn't mind you two being there,' he said sheepishly, his colour rising.

'I really am grateful, Brian. Perhaps you should think it over, though. I wouldn't want to accept and then for you to find out that you'd made a terrible mistake.'

'I've given it plenty of thought,' he assured

her. 'You don't have to make up your mind right this minute, if you would rather think it over. I won't mention it again, but the offer is there if you don't manage to find anything better by the time they send Jodie home.'

Molly didn't know what to say. It was such an unexpected offer, and even though it was the perfect solution, she didn't want to take advantage of his generosity.

When he summoned the waitress and asked for their bill she knew she ought to make a decision. She not only knew him, but liked him and knew she could trust him; it would be nice to be living in a friendly atmosphere.

As she pulled on her black gloves and stood up to leave, she reached out and touched his arm. 'Brian, thank you for all you've done for me today and I would very much like to accept your offer of somewhere to live if you really mean it and if you don't think it would spoil things for you.'

She felt a sudden glow of happiness as she saw the way his face lighted up. It was a funny way to repay him for all the help he had given her ever since the day of the fire, but it seemed to be what he wanted. She would do everything possible to make sure that the arrangement did work, she resolved.

'Would you like to come and see my place right now?' he suggested.

'Yes, I certainly would, if that's convenient,' she agreed enthusiastically.

Although she knew he had lived close by, she still couldn't remember exactly where his house was. The only thing she could recall from the days when she had been there with him was that they had a huge ginger cat and that when she had tried to stroke it, it had hissed at her. Brian had grabbed hold of it and put it outside because he had said that he knew it was going to scratch her.

Brian didn't want to sleep. He lay in bed, comfortable, warm and relaxed, going over in his mind the events of the day.

The funeral had been a pathetic affair with so few people attending. Molly had borne up well, but he could see she was devastated.

The meal afterwards and their long talk had seemed to help to restore her. Even so, she had still looked pale and tense. Black didn't suit her and the ill-fitting coat and the black cloche hat which he suspected came from a second-hand stall at the market drained every vestige of colour from her face.

He knew he had taken a bit of a risk suggesting that she should move into his place, but somehow it had seemed to be the appropriate moment even though he was aware that it might be playing on her vulnerability to do so.

She'd seemed so uncertain when he first mentioned the idea that he was sure she was going to turn it down flat, even though she had nowhere else to go. He smiled to himself; Molly was not only fiercely independent but also very resourceful, and no doubt if he hadn't come up with the suggestion of moving into his place then she would have found somewhere else before Jodie came out of hospital.

As it was, she'd accepted and that was something he was very pleased about. He'd always liked her when they were at school and did their paper rounds together. Meeting up with her again reminded him of what good friends they'd been.

He'd seen her around many times since then, of course, and he'd been tempted to go and speak to her and see if she remembered him, but she'd usually been with her younger sister so he'd not done so.

Another reason why he'd kept his distance was that he'd also seen her at the Rotunda a few times with Steven Parsons. He knew Molly was sweet on him and because of that he felt he stood no chance. Steven was a couple of years older, good looking, better spoken, and, most important of all, he had money. Even as a schoolboy he'd been able to take her to the pictures once a week and Brian had felt that if she was still going out with Steven, then she wouldn't want to be friends with him.

Showing her over his house had been so rewarding after all the hours of hard work he'd put into transforming it from the muddled, over-furnished, cluttered place that it had been when his mother was alive to the clean, neat and tidy place it was now.

When he'd opened the front door he'd had a moment's concern in case she found it too Spartan, too masculine, but she hadn't. She'd liked the plain walls and the clean, uncluttered look.

He'd explained to her that one of his reasons for keeping it so simple was because it made it easier to keep clean and, in his estimation, it made it more peaceful.

'When you move in, you can make any changes you like, of course,' he'd assured her. 'I don't mind if you cover every inch of the walls with pictures, pile cushions up mountains high on the couch and the arm-chairs, or fill every nook and cranny with ornaments and knick-knacks, as long as you feel comfortable.'

He'd had his dreams, of course, but after his dad died things had started going wrong at home and his days, and for that matter his nights as well, were taken up helping his mother when he wasn't at work. After hand-ing over most of his pay packet to help run the house he never had more than a few coppers left in his pocket, barely enough to buy a mug of tea each day. After his mother had died, he'd decided to start a new life; that's when he'd joined the Fire Service.

Strange that it should have been because he was now a fireman, that he and Molly had been brought together again; he couldn't help wondering if it was Fate playing a hand.

Chapter Thirty-two

It was another ten days before they allowed Molly to bring Jodie home from hospital. She looked so weak and fragile that Molly was sure she would never have managed to get her to Hankin Street if Brian hadn't been there with her. Once again she felt heavily indebted, as well as grateful, for the way he helped her.

Ever since she had accepted his offer for her and Jodie to move into his home she had been filled with a mixture of relief that she had found somewhere so nice and safe for them both. She was also glad that she could afford to pay rent so that there was no embarrassment about accepting such a favour.

It was obvious that he took a great pride in his home; the furniture was comfortable and pleasing to the eye and everywhere was well cared for and spotlessly clean.

Even though it was only a stone's throw away from Mould Court it was so completely different from the two cramped, overcrowded rooms she and her family had occupied there that it was like moving into a different world. It took her back to her childhood days in Wallasey before their luck had changed and everything had started to go wrong.

It was hard to believe that, being on his own, he had made such a tremendous effort to make such a transformation and wondered if there was an unhappy romance in his past that he wasn't mentioning. Even though he kept telling her she could make any change she wished she knew there was nothing at all she wanted to alter. In her eyes it was all absolutely perfect and she hoped Jodie was going to like it as much as she did.

When not visiting Jodie at the hospital she had been working overtime at the Brunswick to earn some extra money to buy clothes for her.

Once again she had resorted to the second-hand stalls at Paddy's Market, carefully selecting items which she thought Jodie would like. Seeing her dressed, she knew she should have bought them several sizes smaller. Jodie had never been very robust but now she had lost so much weight that they simply hung on her, making her look more waif-like than ever.

When she remarked on this to Brian he had only smiled. 'A couple of weeks at home and Jodie will look a different person altogether,' he assured her.

She hoped he was right but at the moment Jodie seemed to be so dispirited and so tired out by the journey from the hospital, that Molly had her doubts.

Exhausted though she was Jodie looked round in surprise as they went into Brian's house. When Molly had first told her that this was where they would be living she had seemed quite upset at the idea.

'Well, we can't go back to Mould Court, it's still in ruins after the fire,' Molly explained.

'I don't want to ever live there again,' Jodie shuddered, 'but when you kept talking about our new home, I thought we were going back to Wallasey.'

'I'm afraid that is out of the question,' Molly sighed. 'Perhaps one day, when you're working, then, if we save hard, we might be able to do so,' Molly promised, 'but we're living in Brian's house for the moment and it is lovely here, ever so much nicer than Mould Court.'

As Brian helped Jodie into the living room and settled her in an armchair by the side of the fire, Molly's hand flew to her mouth to stop her calling out a warning as he shooed

Rusty, the enormous ginger cat, out of it.

She expected the cat to hiss and snarl as it did whenever she went near it, but, to her surprise, it merely stood on the hearth rug, arching its back and stretching. It stayed there, perfectly still, watching as Brian settled Jodie in the chair and spread a rug over her knees to make sure she was warm enough.

Then, to both Molly and Brian's amazement, the cat leapt up on to Jodie's lap, turned round and round a couple of times, kneading the blanket with its feet, then settled down, purring loudly as Jodie stroked it.

'I've never seen him do that the whole time we've had him,' Brian said in surprise.

'He only ever hisses at me,' Molly agreed.

'He's lovely,' Jodie told them. 'He really wants me to live here so he's going to be my special friend from now on.' She smiled happily as the cat looked up at her, half closing its green eyes as if in full agreement with what she had said.

From that moment all the doubts Molly had harboured about whether she was doing the right thing about coming there to live vanished. Jodie was delighted about having the cat for company and so contented with her surroundings that she seemed completely at home.

Molly had been wondering how she was

going to manage to carry on working and look after Jodie, but even that problem was solved quite easily.

By organising her times at the Brunswick around Brian's shifts at the fire station, there were very few occasions when Jodie had to be left on her own. Even when it did happen, Jodie had Rusty for company and so she was perfectly happy to either lie in bed, or sit in the armchair, with the cat beside her.

As the cold, drab days of winter were gradually left behind Molly was pleased to see that Jodie had not only regained her strength but was also maturing into a sensible, thoughtful girl.

She had missed so much schooling that Molly agreed she could stay on past her fourteenth birthday in order to catch up. Jodie still hadn't made her mind up what she wanted to do when she did leave, but Molly told her there was no hurry.

Her own job at the Brunswick was going extremely well; she had been promoted and was now in charge of the entire floor, so she was supervising the chambermaids instead of having to do the work herself. As a result she found she was not working nearly as hard as she had done as a chambermaid and yet she was earning more money.

Right from the start she had insisted on

going fifty-fifty on all the bills at Hankin Street. It was so well furnished and equipped with everything from bed linen to cleaning materials that her weekly bills were very reasonable.

Brian often bought things for the home without telling her and insisted on paying for special treats for all of them out of his own wages. As a result, Molly found that she had more money in her purse at the end of the week than she had ever had in her life before.

She was able to buy clothes for herself and Jodie to replace the ones they had lost in the fire, but she also made sure that she saved some of her wages each week. The years of desperate poverty had left their mark and she wanted the security of having some money put away in case they ever needed it in the future.

With Jodie back to full health and starting to enjoy life again she felt that at last she was able to put the unfortunate episode over Jodie's drinking from her mind.

The only time she had tried to discuss it, Jodie had looked at her blankly as if she didn't know what she was on about. Molly wondered if this was Jodie's way of shutting it all out and eliminating her unpleasant memories, so she didn't pursue the subject. If Jodie preferred to regard it all as part of being ill in hospital, then, as far as she was concerned, that was the best solution.

Sometimes she wasn't even sure if her sister remembered very much about the fire, how it had started, or that their mother had died as a result, and Molly didn't think there was very much point in stirring it all up again in Jodie's mind.

She was so content with her new life that she didn't want to start looking for trouble. Living in Brian's house was so enjoyable; he was a great companion, and, more and more, she found she was enjoying his company as they shared a cup of tea together and talked over what they'd been doing.

She couldn't help thinking how different he was from all the other men she'd known, and wondering why a nice chap like him was still single.

When Brian suggested that the three of them should take advantage of the lovely summer weather and have some days out together, Molly was hesitant at first. She felt that he was already doing so much for them. But Jodie looked so excited by the idea that, in the end, she hadn't the heart to refuse.

'It will do us all good,' Brian enthused. 'It will help to put the colour back into Jodie's cheeks and give her eyes a rest from all the swotting she is doing.'

Molly found she enjoyed these outings, not only because it was good to see Jodie so happy, but also because Brian was such good company and always so considerate.

She was growing more and more fond of him and sometimes she secretly wished that she and Brian could go out on their own occasionally.

Brian Baldwin kept wondering how long the idyllic situation of having Molly living at Hankin Street could go on. There was such an incredible aura of happiness and contentment between them that he was enjoying every moment, even with Jodie living there as well. It was as if they were one happy family.

The only thing that irked him was having to halve all the bills with her; he hated taking money from her, even though they had agreed right from the start that sharing all the costs was the way things should be. Not a day passed when he didn't rack his brains to try and find a way to overcome this, but he was aware how sensitive she could be and how fiercely independent she was, so he had to be careful not to overstep the mark.

His reward, he kept reminding himself, was knowing that Molly was safe and sound. Not only was she living under his roof, but he was also able to see her and talk to her every day.

He knew he should be satisfied with this, but he still wasn't completely content. His feelings for Molly had grown even stronger; in fact, if anything, they were deeper and more pronounced than ever and it took him all his time to keep them under control. He wanted to be the one who was the centre of her universe; the one who mattered to her more than anyone else.

He wished he'd had the nerve to ask her out years ago; as long ago as when he'd first left school and started earning enough money to do so. The trouble was he had always felt that he didn't stand a chance when she had Steven Parsons dancing attendance on her.

He was pretty sure that Molly was no longer seeing Steven, and he wondered what had happened to cause the break-up between them. Had Molly finished with him, or had it simply fizzled out? Or had Steven's parents put a stop to it because of the terrible reputation Molly's mother had?

He wondered if Jodie knew and even thought of asking her, but he couldn't bring himself to do so because somehow it seemed underhand to be talking about Molly behind her back. The only thing he could do, he decided, was be patient and hope that in time Molly herself would confide in him.

Living under the same roof, even taking her and Jodie on the occasional outing, was rewarding, but it was also frustrating. He wanted so much more; he longed for the opportunity to go out with Molly on their own. He wanted to take her somewhere special and let the whole world see them together. Now that Jodie was so much better, and her hands and arms had healed and she showed no interest whatsoever in drink, he could see no reason why they couldn't do that.

He was sure that if they could have some time completely alone he'd be able to discover how she really felt about him and perhaps even ask her the all-important question that would seal their future. It wasn't easy to do so because of the hours she worked and him being on shifts. He needed to be with her on her own, not just over a cup of tea or an ordinary meal; he wanted to make an occasion of it.

Finding the right opportunity was all important and, day in and day out, he racked his brains to try and decide when that should be. There had to be a special reason, preferably some occasion that would stand out in their memories for evermore.

The answer came to him like a bolt of lightning and he couldn't understand why he hadn't thought of it before. He could do it on her eighteenth birthday. What could be better or more appropriate?

He could visualise it all in his mind's eye. He'd book a table for the three of them at a restaurant. They'd wear their best clothes to make it a special occasion. He'd order her favourite foods and a bottle of wine. She'd think that this was his birthday present for her, but afterwards, when they were all feeling relaxed, he'd raise his glass in a special toast to her and then produce a ring and propose to her.

Would she accept? There was a tiny whisper of doubt in his mind but he refused to listen to it. She wouldn't turn him down, he told himself. She liked him, she was caring and affectionate towards him, and she liked living in his house. She and Jodie had been there for over six months and they hadn't had a single disagreement, so why on earth should she reject his proposal?

Since it would be Molly's birthday, he'd have to invite Jodie along as well and take her into his confidence about the arrangements for their meal out in case she and Molly were already planning to do something different.

Even the ring was going to be a surprise. He spent a long time debating what it should be like; he knew she wouldn't want anything flashy or too ostentatious.

He kept looking at her hands as she passed things to him; her fingers were so slender that he eventually decided there was really only one sort of engagement ring that would be right for her. A gold band with a single stone; a diamond solitaire.

Chapter Thirty-three

It was quite the hottest July on record. Every window in the Brunswick was wide open, but the air was still oppressive. Everyone felt listless. The maids Molly was responsible for looked exhausted as they cleaned the rooms and changed the bed linen. Everybody seemed to be complaining about trivial things that under normal circumstances they would have barely noticed.

Many of the guests were coming back to their rooms in the middle of the day for a nap because they found it so hot outside and then they complained because it was hardly any cooler in their room than it was in the street. Although the maids didn't like it they became used to finding guests lying on their freshly made beds from mid-morning onwards which often prevented them from completing the cleaning of the room.

Molly sympathised with them, knowing how annoying it could be. Fortunately, even though she was much younger than most of the girls, she seemed to have the knack of keeping them happy. Nevertheless, she seemed to spend half her day either placating staff or apologising to guests because they had been disturbed.

'The chap in Number Twenty-nine is very annoyed because I went in without knocking and he was lying on the bed undressed. Now he's demanding to see "whoever is in charge" because he was lying on his bed and he says I invaded his privacy,' Melinda, one of the maids, complained to Molly.

'Don't worry about it; I'll explain things to him,' Molly told her. 'Is he young or elderly?' she asked as she straightened her black dress and smoothed down her hair.

'Youngish. Dark hair. Full of himself. I think I've seen him here several times before; not always in the same room, and he usually has a girl with him. Not the same one each time, mind,' she giggled.

'That will do, Melinda,' Molly said reprovingly. 'You carry on doing the other rooms you are responsible for cleaning and leave Number Twenty-nine until later.'

Although the door was slightly open, Molly decided to take no chances of offending further so she knocked and waited until a man's voice called 'come in' before entering.

As Melinda had said, he was sprawled on the bed and even though the white cotton sheet was covering him, it was quite obvious that he was at least partially undressed.

Before she had a chance to speak he had sprung out of bed and, for one terrifying

406

moment, she thought he was going to attack her. Instead, he brushed her to one side, headed for the door, locked it, and removed the key.

Molly's eyes widened in shock as the man turned around and she saw that it was Steven Parsons. With an insolent grin he dropped the sheet he'd been grasping with one hand and stood there, completely naked, waiting for her to say something.

'I understand you are complaining about one of the maids invading your privacy,' Molly said in as calm a voice as she could muster, keeping her gaze fixed on his face.

'Is that the best sort of greeting you can give me?' he said in a teasing voice. 'Surely you haven't forgotten me, Molly?'

'No, and I hope you haven't forgotten you agreed to stay out of my life,' she told him coldly.

'I don't bear grudges; I am prepared to be friends,' he told her in an amused voice.

'You may not bear grudges, but you certainly don't honour your promises,' she told him scathingly.

Steven shrugged nonchalantly as he advanced towards her. Grabbing hold of her shoulders he made to pull her into his arms but Molly twisted away out of his reach.

'You're not playing hard to get, are you,' he laughed, 'because it won't work. You're a prisoner; the door's locked, so you can't escape, and I'm in no hurry. I've got all day.'

'Well, I haven't. My day is very busy and if I don't put in an appearance within the next ten minutes then the maid who asked me to come and see you will report my absence to the Manager.'

'You mean that tarty little bitch who walked in on me without even bothering to knock?'

'That's right. She reported the incident to me and that is why I am here.'

'You surely haven't come to tell me off over that? She was the one at fault,' he pointed out.

'I am fully aware of that and I came to apologise on her behalf,' Molly told him stiffly.

'Go on then, apologise. I'm waiting,' he insisted.

'I hardly think it is necessary,' she said quietly. 'If I had known who the occupant of the room was, then I wouldn't have taken the trouble to come at all.'

'But you did and now I have you trapped here so what are you going to do now?' he parried.

'For heaven's sake, Steven, grow up! Stop acting in this stupid way. Unlock the door and let me get on with my work; we'll say no more about any of it and in future remember your promise to keep out of my way and leave me alone.'

'That's what you'd like, but it is not what I intend to do,' he retorted.

Before Molly knew what was happening, he had grabbed at her again, and forced her down on to the bed. With one hand he pinned her arms above her head and rammed his other hand over her mouth to stop her screaming for help.

His eyes narrowed as he studied her. 'You have a choice,' he said softly. 'You can submit willingly or I'll force you to do what I want. Which is it to be?'

Desperately Molly tried to twist her head free but Steven only held her down more firmly.

For all his fine education and money he was no better than Sid, she thought bitterly.

Realising that he was far stronger than her and that she stood no chance if she antagonised him, she forced herself to go limp to signify that she was ready to capitulate and do whatever he asked.

'If you promise not to call out, then I'll remove my hand from your mouth. All you have to do is blink twice for yes.'

Obediently she did as he asked.

With a triumphant smile he cautiously raised his hand but held it poised above her face ready to slam back down again if she didn't comply with his request.

He waited a moment but then when she made no sound he nodded with satisfaction.

'Glad to see you've come to your senses,' he smirked.

As she tried to free her hands he tightened his hold on them, twisting them so savagely that she winced with pain. 'Not so fast,' he warned. 'I haven't finished with you yet!'

Molly tried to control the waves of panic rising inside her. 'If you don't let me go immediately, then—' she paused as he raised his hand threateningly.

'Go on!' He smiled sardonically. 'Finish what you were going to say, or are you afraid to do so?'

'You can put your hand down,' Molly said quietly. 'I said I wouldn't scream and I don't break my word. I was going to remind you that if you keep me here any longer then someone will come looking for me because they know I am here.'

'So you said,' he mocked, 'but I thought you were the one in charge of this floor.'

'Come on, Steven, be reasonable. She didn't burst in on you, as you put it. She had no idea that you were in here, she was simply doing her job and came in to clean your room. You upset her by speaking so sharply to her.'

Steven shrugged impatiently. 'We're wasting time discussing such stupid trivialities. Come on, Molly, you must know perfectly well what I want.'

Before Molly could answer he had caught

hold of the neck of her black dress and there was a tearing sound as savagely he ripped it away from her throat. Buttons flew as the fastenings came undone and her dress was opened from throat to waist and torn halfway down the front of the skirt.

Terrified as she saw the look in his eyes and realising what his intentions were, she wondered whether to fight or submit. She managed to smile weakly. 'I'm not a mind reader,' she prevaricated, trying to divert his attention.

'Even you must know what the answer is,' he said scathingly. 'I've dreamed of this for so long that I don't intend backing down now, so let's get on with it,' he muttered as he began fumbling with her underclothes, pulling and tearing at them in a frenzy of desire.

She shuddered as she felt his hand making contact with her flesh, exploring every inch of her exposed body. He seemed to be stroking, pinching, squeezing and probing as if he was committing every curve, every bone, to mind.

He was lying across her, making it difficult for her to breathe and she found it was impossible to wriggle away from him. The feel of his hot clammy flesh covering her body was so repugnant that it sickened her and made her all the more determined to get free.

Her ears were full of the sound of him grunting with pleasure as he continued to stroke, lick and bite every inch of her body. There was no tenderness, only lustful, tormenting degradation that she found utterly intolerable.

She felt angry and appalled that he could treat her like this. As she felt his mouth on her breasts she gave a violent jerk of rejection.

Steven seemed oblivious to her feelings or the resistance she was struggling to make. Panting like an animal he remained focused on gratifying his own desires.

All the time he was muttering under his breath, but what he was saying she couldn't make out. She wondered if he was drunk but there was no smell of liquor on his breath. Surely no one in their right mind could treat a woman in this terrible fashion.

Making a renewed effort, Molly managed to push free of his weight. She draw in a deep breath, trying to quell the nausea she could feel rising up into her throat, filling her mouth with acrid bitterness. There had been a time when she'd dreamed about them making love for the very first time and she had imagined it as being a tender, sublime moment.

She wondered if she screamed whether anyone would hear her, or whether it would not only be useless but also incite Steven to

412

even greater bestial behaviour.

With a cry of elation he finally invaded her body and she couldn't hold back the scream of agony that escaped her as she felt her tender flesh being brutally torn.

With a cruel laugh he raised his head in triumph, then as dismay swept over her and darkness began closing in on her, she was afraid that she was about to faint from the pain and mortification.

With a final groan of pleasure, Steven rolled off her and she struggled free, pulling herself to the edge of the bed. For a moment she lay there exhausted as she tried to gather her thoughts. She couldn't believe what had happened to her and although she didn't want to think about it she wondered if this was how he'd treated the girl who had died. She wanted to get out of the room, right away from him before he did anything else to her.

Sobbing because she felt soiled, distraught and on the verge of hysteria, she held her head in her hands, wishing she could treat it all as a bad dream. She knew she mustn't give way to such feelings. She had to remain strong; she had to show him the contempt she felt about the ordeal he had put her through.

Steven had fallen into an exhausted sleep. She had no idea how long she had been in the room with him. It seemed like for ever, but common sense told her it couldn't have been very long because no one had come looking for her.

How could someone create so much devastation in your life in such a short time? She sobbed as she slid off the bed. Her body ached; she felt violated; yet if she didn't want anyone else to know about the way she had been humiliated, she had to try and act in a perfectly normal way.

She picked up the remnants of her torn clothing from the floor, wondering if she could mend her dress or if she'd have to explain the state it was in.

Steven's dark grey trousers were neatly draped over the back of a chair and for one wild moment she was tempted to mutilate them; to ruin his clothes in the same way he had treated her.

The moment passed as she realised the futility of such an action. All she really wanted to do was to get out of the room, away from his presence, and to never see him again.

As she smoothed her hair back into some semblance of order she grabbed the dressing gown hanging behind the bathroom door and hoped she could get back to the staff room without anyone noticing. She was due to go off duty quite soon so she could have a bath and change into her own clothes.

Tears sprang to her eyes as she remembered what a special day she had expected it to be. When she had arrived at work that morning she had been feeling so excited about the treat that lay ahead after she finished work.

Today was her birthday, her eighteenth birthday, and Brian was taking her and Jodie out for a celebration meal. He'd already booked a table for them but he'd refused to tell her which restaurant he had chosen because he wanted even that to be a surprise.

Brian was making such a tremendous fuss about her birthday that she had really been looking forward to it and she knew Jodie was very excited as well. Now, celebrating was the last thing she wanted to do yet she would have to go along with it, otherwise she would disappoint both him and Jodie.

Chapter Thirty-four

Brian could hardly wait for his shift to end so that he could get home, have a wash, shave and get smartened up in his best suit ready to take Molly and Jodie out.

First of all, though, on his way home he wanted to drop in at the restaurant and

415

make sure that everything he'd planned had been taken care of, and that they hadn't overlooked anything.

It was going to be such a special night and he wanted everything to be perfect. Although she had protested that he shouldn't go to so much trouble, when he'd told her about his idea of them going out for a special meal, he was pretty sure from the look on her face that she was delighted by the idea.

'It's the first time since I was a child in Wallasey that I've celebrated my birthday with a party,' she told him, 'so I'll look forward to it.'

Exactly how special she still had no idea, he thought nervously. If everything went as he planned, then it would be an occasion that neither of them would ever forget.

He'd taken such care in selecting the sort of ring he thought was right for her. It was a diamond solitaire in a handsome gold setting. It had cost a great deal more than he had anticipated, but she was worth every penny of it.

He was tempted to show it to Jodie. It would have been reassuring to ask her what she thought of it and to have assurance that he had made the right choice.

But he was afraid that, even if she promised not to tell Molly, she might accidentally say something. If that happened, it

416

would no longer be the wonderful surprise he wanted it to be and the whole occasion would be spoiled.

He hadn't even breathed a word at work about what he intended doing because he didn't want anyone to know about it until after he had actually proposed to Molly and, hopefully, she had accepted.

He tried telling himself that the reason he was keeping it secret was because he knew the chaps at work would rib him if they knew, but that wasn't the real reason for his reticence. He knew that, if Molly didn't accept his proposal, he'd be so mortified that he wouldn't want anyone to know of his failure.

He was afraid to contemplate what he would do if she did turn him down. The trouble was that if that happened it might ruin everything for them both since she probably wouldn't want to go on living in the same house as him and would insist on moving away.

Brian refused to let himself think about it. He was sure that they were right for each other and he hoped she'd accept.

He'd been so determined that the evening should start off romantically that he had told Molly and Jodie that he was arranging for a taxicab to collect them from the house and that he would be waiting for them at the restaurant.

Molly had looked astonished, but he had assured her that it was the way he wanted to do things and that it was all part of her birthday celebration. What he didn't tell her was that he was so nervous that, even though he was visiting the restaurant earlier in the day, he still wanted to make a last-minute check to make sure that everything, including the special flowers he had asked them to arrange on the table, was exactly as he wanted it to be.

Molly was extremely upset after her sordid encounter with Steven Parsons and was in a hurry to get away, knowing Steven had booked the room for the night; she was afraid that she might encounter him again. As speedily as she could, scrubbing at her skin in an attempt to remove the repugnant feel of Steven's hands which seemed to linger on her bare flesh, she took a bath in the staff quarters because she felt so dirty.

When she reached Hankin Street she found Jodie was ready for their outing. She was wearing a pretty blue and white cotton frock that they had bought the previous Saturday, and the blue was the same colour as her eyes.

'Hurry up, Molly, or you won't be ready when the taxicab arrives for us; we mustn't keep it waiting,' Jodie greeted her anxiously the moment she walked in.

'We've plenty of time,' Molly assured her. 'You look very nice, that colour really suits you,' she added, forcing herself to be cheerful for Jodie's sake.

'My dress is lovely, isn't it?' Jodie agreed happily. 'I could do with some help with my hair, though, I don't suppose you'll have the time to do it for me.'

'I'll make time,' Molly assured her. 'Give me ten minutes or so to get myself ready and I'll give you a hand with it.'

As she slipped on the turquoise-green dress she had bought for herself when she and Jodie had gone shopping she felt cleaner and fresher. Her head was still thumping, but not as much as it had been earlier on.

As she put the finishing touches to her make-up and hair she peered closely at her reflection in the mirror and was both surprised and relieved to see that there was no trace of the ordeal she had endured.

She just had time to brush and rearrange Jodie's hair when the taxicab arrived.

'I've never ridden in one of these before,' Jodie exclaimed excitedly as she slid along the leather seat to make room for Molly.

'Neither have I, so it's a treat for both of us,' Molly told her.

'Do you know the name of the restaurant where we are meeting Brian?' Jodie asked.

'No.' Molly shook her head. 'Brian seemed determined to keep that as a surprise as well.'

'Supposing the taxicab driver takes us to the wrong one!' Jodie exclaimed. 'We can't even be sure that he is going the right way; he could kidnap us and drive off into the unknown and we would never know until it was too late,' she added dramatically.

Molly shivered. 'Stop being so silly,' she said, and then bit her lip as she saw the tears well up in Jodie's eyes.

'Sorry, luv,' she said quickly, giving her a hug. 'I know you were only joking; I didn't mean to snap at you.'

'Since it's your birthday I'll forgive you,' Jodie said, giving her a watery smile.

As they drew up outside the Adelphi Hotel in the centre of Liverpool, Molly's heart began to thud uneasily. She kept remembering the horror of the afternoon and wondered how she was going to face sitting in a crowded room when she felt that everyone must know what had happened to her.

Her nerves steadied when she saw that Brian, looking incredibly handsome in his best dark suit, crisp white shirt and silk tie, was waiting for them in the foyer. She noticed the look of relief on his face as the uniformed doorman ushered them in.

Brian greeted them with such obvious pleasure that Molly felt a genuine rush of affection for him as he gave her a warm smile, reached out and took her hand and squeezed it. He really was a lovely person, she thought gratefully.

Molly felt overwhelmed by the opulence of the place as he led them towards the restaurant with its glistening chandeliers, mirrored walls, tables with their crisp white linen and sparkling glassware and gleaming cutlery.

As the waiter showed them to their table and she saw the beautiful centrepiece of white roses and noticed that it was much more elaborate than the flowers on any of the other tables, she guessed that Brian had ordered it specially.

He had also chosen the dishes to be served in advance, and again she thought how thoughtful it was of him to make sure that neither she nor Jodie would be embarrassed because they didn't understand the menu which was in French.

The food was beautifully presented and tasted delicious. As she sipped her wine and smiled across at Brian who was listening to Jodie enthusing about what he had selected for each of them for dessert, Molly knew it really was the most wonderful occasion of her life.

As she felt a light pressure on the back of her chair she waited expectantly for the Peach Melba he'd chosen for her to be placed on the table. Instead, a man's voice, one that she'd hoped to never hear again, spoke her name.

'So this is how you are ending your day, is it? I wonder what it is you are celebrating?'

Molly felt the colour drain from her face as she looked up into Steven's face. He was grinning maliciously. He ignored her and spoke directly to Brian.

'So, has Molly told you what she was doing this afternoon?' he demanded softly. As he spoke he let his hand rest proprietorially on her shoulder.

Brian frowned and looked bewildered. He'd thought, from what Molly had told him, that it was all over between her and Steven and that she no longer saw him.

Molly wanted to speak, but her throat was so dry that she couldn't utter a word.

'Molly spent the afternoon in bed with me and I can't begin to tell you how much she enjoyed herself,' he gloated.

Jodie looked from one to the other of them bewildered. 'What's he talking about, Molly?' she asked in a bemused voice.

'We don't want to hear any more,' Brian said stiffly. 'I think you should go,' he added in a threatening voice.

'Not spoiling your little party by telling you all this, am I?' Steven guffawed. 'Can I guess what's next on the menu, or is it supposed to be a surprise?'

Brian pushed back his chair and stood up. He was not quite as tall as Steven, but he was far more squarely built and Steven quickly took a step back.

'I mean it!'

Steven laughed. 'Perhaps, if you're lucky, she will reward you the same way when you take her home.'

'Will you leave now or shall I call the waiter over and have you thrown out?' Brian challenged vehemently.

Their altercation had already drawn the attention of the other diners. The head waiter came hurrying across the room to find out what was going on. Before Brian could say a word, Steven accused him of insulting him by making unpleasant remarks and demanded that he should be asked to leave.

Even though Brian pointed out that it was Steven who had started the fracas by coming over to their table and that he was the one making insulting remarks, it made no difference.

Quietly but very firmly, the head waiter requested that Brian and his guests should leave.

'I would be grateful, sir, if you would vacate your table quietly and not cause an incident,' he said politely. 'I will arrange for someone to call a taxicab immediately, so please make your way to the door where you will find it waiting for you. There will, of course, be no charge at all for your meal,' he added pompously.

Brian reddened with embarrassment since he was well aware that, despite the polite way he was being asked to leave, it was tantamount to being thrown out.

Realising that there was very little he could do without causing a scene, which would obviously upset both Molly and Jodie, he acquiesced.

The waiter who had shown them to their table was hurriedly despatched to fetch their coats. As he helped Molly into hers he politely added his regrets that their evening had ended in such an unfortunate manner.

'Mr Steven Parsons and his family are highly regarded regular clientele,' he explained quietly. 'They frequently dine here, so you can see the management can't afford to upset them,' he added in a conciliatory manner.

Brian nodded grimly. 'Had I known that was the case I most certainly wouldn't have come here,' he stated as he took Molly's arm and indicated to Jodie to move towards the door.

'I have known Parsons for a long time and he and his family are not the sort of company I like to mix with,' he added as a parting shot as they were shown out.

The taxicab was waiting with the engine running. Brian looked angry, but he said nothing as the doorman opened the cab door for them and they piled inside. He could see that both Molly and Jodie were upset.

He felt both mystified by what Steven Parsons had said and extremely annoyed that the evening he'd planned so carefully down to the very last detail had been so completely ruined.

The box containing the engagement ring that he had intended to present to Molly at the very end of their meal was still tucked away in his inside breast pocket. As it pressed uncomfortably against his chest, it reminded him sharply of his missed opportunity.

Molly was very subdued as they travelled home. She tried to console Jodie about her missed dessert by promising to make her a cup of hot chocolate to compensate for her disappointment and to bring it up to her once she was in bed.

While Molly took Jodie's drink upstairs Brian paced backwards and forwards in the living room, smoking furiously and lighting a fresh cigarette from the stub of the first.

His thoughts were in turmoil and he knew he wouldn't rest until he had talked to Molly about the extraordinary happenings that had utterly ruined their evening. He didn't for one moment believe that it could be true that she had been in bed with Steven Parsons that afternoon as Steven had so blatantly claimed. It troubled him that she had made no attempt to deny it in any way. She hadn't said a single word in her own defence.

She'd probably been too embarrassed to do so, he reasoned, but he felt that, under the circumstances, he must insist that she should tell him what Steven Parsons had meant by his remark. She owed him some sort of explanation.

Molly stayed upstairs for such a long time that he began to think she was intending to go straight to bed. He felt he was going to explode with anger because he was afraid that perhaps she was doing so in order to avoid talking to him.

Eventually he heard her coming down the stairs, and when she came into the room he saw with a degree of relief that the reason she had taken so long was because she had changed out of her pretty dress into her dressing gown and had swapped her elegant high-heeled shoes for comfortable but shabby slippers.

He wished he'd had the sense to do likewise, he thought as he loosened his tie and undid the top button of his shirt. If he'd changed out of his suit, or even put on his slippers, he might feel more relaxed.

To give himself time to calm down and readjust his thoughts he went into the kitchen and made a pot of strong coffee. He had a feeling that both he and Molly were going to need it because there was a lot of talking and explaining to be done.

Chapter Thirty-five

'I was intending to go straight to bed,' Molly told Brian as she sat down in the armchair and accepted the cup of coffee he handed to her, 'but I wanted to explain.'

His throat tightened at the resigned tone of Molly's voice, but he hardened his heart. He'd been on tenterhooks ever since they'd left the Adelphi, waiting and hoping that she was going to deny every word that Steven Parsons had said.

When she remained silent on the journey home his doubts had escalated despite the fact that he kept telling himself that it was only because she didn't want to speak out in front of Jodie.

He'd been patient, but he was filled with a terrifying sense of unease and now he was determined that he must have an explanation. It was the only way they would ever straighten out matters between them.

'Well, go on, then!' He took a mouthful of coffee. It was still so hot that he could feel it burning his mouth, but he was glad of the pain because it helped to counteract the agony in his heart over what she might tell him.

Molly took a sip of her own coffee then pulled back sharply as it seared her lips. She sat up straighter in her chair, as if bracing herself for the ordeal that lay ahead.

Compassion overwhelmed him at the realisation of the strain he seemed to be putting her through. 'Look, if you'd rather not talk about it, then let's leave it,' he muttered.

'No...' She ran a hand through her hair, pushing it back behind her ears, making her look so young and vulnerable that his heart ached. 'No, Brian, you have a right to know.'

He sensed how distressed she was and suspected the worst; it seemed that there was indeed some foundation for what Steven Parsons had said.

Anger welled up inside him. If she had spent the afternoon in bed with Steven Parsons, then the sooner he knew the truth the better. If she had, then it could mean only one thing; that she was still in love with Steven and that he had been under an illusion in assuming she'd finished with him.

The thought was abhorrent to him because it meant that all his dreams that she cared for him, and even of ever marrying her, would be at an end. All he'd been doing over the last few months, ever since she had moved into Hankin Street, was deluding himself and building up his hopes in vain.

'Were you lying when you told me it was all over between the two of you?' he demanded, trying to keep the rancour out of his voice.

How on earth had he ever thought he could compete with a man like Steven who had not only money but also a respectable white-collar job? he thought bitterly when she didn't answer.

As the silence lengthened he could stand the strain no longer.

'Were you in bed with him this afternoon?' he blurted out, his voice hoarse with abject misery.

'Yes!' Her voice was little more than a whisper, as if it had been wrenched out of her very soul.

He slammed his coffee cup back into its saucer, splashing the hot liquid over his hand as he did so. 'Well, that's it, then; there's nothing more to be said.'

He tried to ignore the look of utter misery on her face as she looked up at him. 'You must listen to the rest of what I have to tell you before you judge me,' she protested. 'Please, Brian ... please hear what I have to say,' she pleaded as she reached out and placed her hand on his arm.

'What more is there to be said since it seems he was telling the truth?' he muttered tersely, avoiding her eyes as he shook her hand away.

Tears streamed down her face as she gazed back at him. She looked so discomfited, so woebegone, that he wanted to take her into his arms, gently dry her eyes and whisper words of comfort, but he steeled himself to stay aloof.

'It's not what you think!' She suppressed a shudder and clasped her hands together in front of her so tightly that her knuckles gleamed like ivory.

'Go on; I'm listening.'

She wiped away her tears with the back of her hand and took a deep breath.

'This afternoon, one of the maids asked me to deal with a complaint made by a guest. She said he was demanding an apology because she had gone into his room without knocking. I went along to try and put matters right...'

She hesitated, biting her lip as if conscious of the nervous little tic working the side of her mouth.

Brian leaned forward in his chair, staring at the floor, trying not to anticipate what she was about to tell him.

'I didn't know that it was Steven who had booked the room. When ... when I went into the room he grabbed hold of me, held me down on to the bed, tore off my uniform and ... and then ... and then he raped me.'

The words hung on the air like an obscene

banner that floated in and out of Brian's mind. It sounded so incredible that he had to repeat what she had said out loud before he could convince himself that he had heard correctly.

'Didn't you shout out, fight him, or do anything to get away from him?' he asked incredulously.

She shook her head in a desperate gesture. 'Let me tell you the whole story; I need to explain exactly what happened if I am ever to find any peace again.'

Brian sat there in numbed silence, listening in mounting anger, as in a small, toneless voice Molly related all that had taken place that afternoon.

'And you didn't report him?' His voice rose angrily. 'You didn't tell anyone at the hotel about what had happened?' he admonished in an exasperated voice.

'I ... I didn't know what to do... I was so relieved when I managed to get away from him that I wasn't thinking clearly,' she admitted bitterly. 'At that moment the only thing I was concerned about was getting out of the Brunswick and coming home.'

Brian paced the room, running his hands through his short red hair. 'I find it difficult to believe what you're telling me,' he said suspiciously. 'After all you'd been through, the moment you arrived home you got yourself and Jodie ready and when the taxicab got here you came to meet me at the restaurant as if nothing had happened?' he asked in disbelief.

She shrugged despairingly. 'I didn't want to disappoint either you or Jodie because you'd both worked so hard to make it a special day for me.'

Brian shook his head uncomprehendingly. 'What I still can't understand is why on earth you didn't report him to someone in the Brunswick. You needn't have told them the details; you could have asked them to send for the police.'

'What good would that have done?' she asked bitterly. 'He'd already raped me, nothing I said or did could turn the clock back and undo that, or put things right.'

'By saying nothing you are condoning what he did,' he argued angrily.

'It would have been a waste of time; Steven would have denied it or else turned it to his own advantage in some way and only made things look even worse for me.'

'For God's sake, Molly, stop trying to make excuses; it seems like you're defending him.'

'No,' she said spiritedly, 'I'm doing nothing of the sort, Brian, but you saw how the head waiter treated us tonight. Well, it would have been the same if I had reported him; it would have been my word against his.'

'So does that mean that even now you are

not going to do anything about it? It's not too late for you to do so, you know,' Brian persisted.

Molly shook her head. 'All I want to do is to try and put the whole sordid incident behind me.' She shuddered. 'I don't suppose I will ever be able to forget what happened, but going to the police about it and having to tell them everything would be like living through it all over again.'

'Supposing he comes back to the hotel ... he might even try to get you on your own again...'

'I've thought about that,' she interrupted quickly. She gave a sad little smile. 'I intend to give up my job at the Brunswick. I might even move away from Liverpool. I don't suppose you will want me living here any more, not now that you know what happened today,' she added despondently.

'Look, Molly, I'd intended our evening out to be special in more ways than one,' he said grimly. He hesitated for a split second before rushing on. 'I'd intended to propose to you; I'd waited all evening for the right moment and I was on the point of doing so when that fracas happened. I'd even bought the ring! It's still here in my pocket,' he confirmed, tapping his jacket, 'all ready to slip on your finger the moment you said "Yes".'

For a moment Molly stared at him uncomprehendingly, then her face crumpled and tears streamed down her cheeks as his words registered with her.

She couldn't believe what he was saying. To marry Brian would have been her dearest dream come true. He'd always been there for her, a steadfast friend ever since they were children. She loved him so much; a truly deep love that seemed to be growing ever stronger and more intense all the time.

'Oh Brian, I'm so sorry ... so ashamed by what happened,' she sobbed.

Once again she laid her hand on his arm; this time he took it and held it firmly between both his hands so that she couldn't draw back or turn away.

'If none of this sordid business with Steven had ever happened, and I had proposed to you when we were in the restaurant tonight, tell me what your answer would have been, Molly,' he pursued in a strained voice.

She gave him a watery smile. 'I would have said "yes" and I'd have thought that I was the luckiest person in the world,' she told him, her voice shaking.

'And now?'

She withdrew her hand sharply, her eyes filling with tears. 'Now the situation has changed so much that you are hardly likely to ask me, are you?'

'Would you marry me, though, Molly, if I

did ask you?' he persisted.

As she looked up into his face and saw the love shining in his eyes she felt too choked to speak. It didn't matter, words weren't necessary; he knew her answer from the look on her face and the love in her eyes.

As he pulled her into his arms, burying his face in her hair, murmuring her name over and over and telling her how much he loved her and needed her to make his life complete, she felt her anxiety melting away.

There was no doubt in either of their minds as they clung together that, despite all that had happened, their feelings for each other remained as strong as ever.

'Will you give me time to put all this out of my mind and then ask me again?' she whispered hopefully.

'No!' Gently, he took her face between his two hands. 'I already have the answer; it's in your eyes, on your face and in the touch of your hands. You can forget all about moving away from Liverpool, or from this house ... this is your home ... our home.'

'Oh, Brian...' Tears rolled down her cheeks, but her eyes were shining with happiness.

He dried her tears, holding her close in his arms and kissing each eyelid in turn before finally seeking her lips.

'We're both too tired to talk about it any more tonight,' he said gently. 'Tomorrow will be a new day and we can make a fresh start, a whole new life for both of us ... and for Jodie.'

Chapter Thirty-six

Early morning sunshine was filtering in through the window when Molly awoke. She had no idea what time it was, but she knew it must be late as Jodie was obviously already up.

She lay still for a moment, trying to collect her thoughts. She'd had a restless night even though she'd felt so utterly exhausted when she'd come to bed that she'd expected to fall asleep immediately. The moment she put her head on the pillow, however, all the things she and Brian had been talking about late into the evening started to churn around non-stop in her mind.

The long talk with Brian should have put her mind at rest and brought her sweet dreams, especially when he assured her that he still wanted to marry her despite everything that had happened. Instead she'd found that every detail of her encounter with Steven haunted her like some terrible nightmare.

She felt depressed, angry, humiliated and frustrated; would it be fair to marry Brian with such a cloud hanging over her? she asked herself. Ever since they'd moved from Wallasey her life had been a catastrophic muddle. Nothing had gone right for her, so why should it do so now?

She knew that what she felt for Brian was something completely different from the schoolgirl crush she'd had on Steven. She'd been so naïve to ever think that he was serious about her. She should have been warned by all the secretiveness attached to their meetings, or even their speaking to each other, that he had no intention of ever telling his parents about them. The very fact that he had persuaded his mother to give her a cleaning job should have made her realise that he regarded her as socially beneath him.

She loved Brian with every fibre of her being; what had started out as a youthful friendship had grown into a deep, overwhelming love. She didn't want to imagine life without him, but how could she be sure that it was love and not misplaced gallantry on his part that had made him insist that, in spite of everything that had happened, he still wanted to marry her?

She'd been so relieved to be able to tell him every detail of her ordeal and find that he was able to be so understanding that she'd probably let herself be carried away. Now she was wondering whether he had offered to marry her because he understood how traumatic and demeaning it had been for her and he was trying to help her to restore her self-confidence.

Maybe over breakfast she should try and muster up the courage to tell him that he didn't have to marry her, she decided as she dressed ready to go downstairs.

Brian was already preparing his own breakfast, buttering a round of bread, when she went into the kitchen.

'I've just made some tea,' he said. 'Do you want me to do you a fry up? I'm not very hungry myself.'

As he turned to look at her she saw the strained look on his face and the dark shadows under his eyes.

'Didn't you sleep very well either?' she asked wryly as she reached down two cups and saucers, placed them on the table, and poured out their tea.

'It took me a while to get off; it was quite an eventful evening, wasn't it?' he said quietly.

She sat down at the table, her face flushing. 'Come and sit down, there's something I want to say,' she said hesitantly.

He looked uneasy. 'Go on, what's wrong?'

She stirred her tea. 'It's about what you said...'

She saw him stiffen.

'About us getting married...'

'You've changed your mind!' His voice sounded so despondent that she was filled with guilt.

'I wasn't sure,' she gulped. 'You see...' she couldn't go on; she was unable to say the words because they were like a hard lump inside her throat.

Brian said nothing for a few minutes, but sat there looking a picture of abject misery. 'Why? Is it because of him ... that Steven?' he asked bleakly.

'No ... no, of course not. Well, not really ... though I suppose in a way it is...'

'So you realised that you do care about him after all,' he exclaimed bitterly.

'Of course not! I never want to see him ever again,' she shuddered. 'It's just that because of what he did ... how can I expect you to marry me ... not after that!'

He looked bewildered. 'I told you last night that I wanted to!'

'Yes, I know, but ... but I'm afraid that perhaps you were asking me out of kindness...'

'Kindness! What the hell has kindness got to do with it, Molly? I love you! I don't want a life without you, you mean everything to me. For God's sake stop tormenting me like this. I love you and I hoped you felt the same way about me.'

'Oh, but I do, Brian. I love you with all my heart...'

Pushing back his chair he pulled her to her feet and drew her close. 'Stop all this silly nonsense. We're both as daft as each other.

I've lain awake half the night worrying in case you came to your senses and turned me down!'

'And I spent half the night worrying in case you regretted having asked me.'

He laughed. 'Then I think the best thing we can do is get married as soon as we possibly can and put both of us out of our misery, don't you?' Putting a hand under her chin he gently raised her face so that he could kiss her.

'Now is there any other niggling doubt in your mind?' he asked as he released her.

'Well, there is just one other thing.'

'Then let's have it out in the open. What is it that's still bothering you?'

'It's about what is going to happen to Jodie if we get married. She has no one except me and she has been through so much that it wouldn't be right to expect her to move into lodgings, not at her age,' she said hesitantly.

Brian looked puzzled. 'What's wrong with her staying on here with us? I've never raised any objection to her living here, have I?'

'No, that's true, but then at the moment we are only your lodgers,' she pointed out. 'If we get married, then I thought that perhaps you wouldn't want her living here with us.'

'That's utter nonsense,' he told her gravely. 'Of course Jodie can stay here after we are

440

married; she can stay for as long as she likes.'

'Then I think that you should be the one to tell her so, and that we are getting married, otherwise she might feel unsure about whether she was welcome or not.'

'I think it would be better if we did it together; we'll do it as soon as she comes back in; she said she was going out somewhere but didn't say where. It can't be the library because that's not open on a Sunday.'

Jodie looked very pleased, but not in the least surprised, when she came home about an hour later and Brian told her that he and Molly were getting married.

'I thought you were never going to get round to asking her.' She grinned.

'And we both want you to go on living here,' Brian added. 'We want you to think of it as your home.'

'Thanks, but it won't be for very much longer,' she told him. 'As soon as I am old enough I've decided I'm going to train to be a nurse, that's if they'll have me.'

'You, a nurse!' Molly exclaimed in surprise. 'I thought you'd want to be a librarian or something like that since you've always got your head in a book.'

'I'll have plenty of reading and studying to do if I want to become a fully qualified nurse,' Jodie pointed out. 'I quite enjoyed looking after Mum when she was ill and then when I was in hospital myself I got talking to some of the nurses and found out what a very worthwhile job it could be if you are prepared to study.'

Brian and Molly's wedding three weeks later was a simple register office affair. Jodie, wearing a pretty light blue silk dress, was her attendant and Jack Scott, one of Brian's fireman colleagues, was his best man.

Molly looked almost ethereal in a cream silk dress, matching jacket and a cream cloche hat. It wasn't the billowing white dress and long white lace veil that Brian had hoped she would be wearing for the occasion, but under the circumstances they'd both agreed that such an outfit would have been inappropriate.

He and Jack Scott wore smart suits and white shirts. Contrary to the usual tradition when a fireman married there were no fire engines and none of the trappings or traditional send off.

There was one extra guest, however; someone who brought both an exclamation of disbelief and then tears of happiness from Molly.

At first, she couldn't believe her eyes that the tall, broad young man who was waiting by the door was the scrawny brother who had run away from home. 'Peter!' she gasped. 'How did you get here; how did you know?'

'Sailor's intuition,' he told her solemnly.

'Or perhaps it was a little bird,' he teased as he hugged her gently, careful not to ruffle her outfit or dislodge her hat.

Seeing the puzzled look she gave Brian, he grinned and glanced across at Jodie. 'Will you tell her or shall I?'

'Jodie told you? How did she know where to find you?' Molly asked, nonplussed. 'You've never written, not so much as a card the whole time you've been away,' she added reprovingly.

'I know, I'm sorry about that. I really did mean to the first time we put into a port, but by then I thought you'd probably given up on me and put me out of your mind.'

'Why do you think I have been spending so much time at the library lately?' Jodie laughed. 'I've been looking at newspapers and records there and making enquiries at some of the shipping offices because I was determined to trace him. It was sheer luck that his ship was docking here at Liverpool only two days ago.'

Afterwards the five of them went for a meal at the State Restaurant. This was not nearly as glamorous a venue as the posh restaurant at the Adelphi Hotel where they'd dined on Molly's eighteenth birthday, but it was somewhere where Brian assured her there would be no unpleasant intruders or ghastly revelations.

It was a relaxed and enjoyable occasion

and it brought an added glow of happiness to Molly's heart to know that not only was she with the man she loved with every fibre of her being, the man she knew would bring her peace and happiness, but also that Peter and Jodie were there as well.

She felt confident about the future as she looked around the table at the people she loved most dearly. Seeing Peter again after so long was an added bonus and she looked forward to spending some time with him. There was so much to tell him, some of it sad and distressing, but recounting it was necessary to clear the air for all of them.

As she listened to Jodie happily enthusing over what she was planning to do she felt that this momentous occasion really was a new start for all of them.

When it was time for them to leave, her heart thudded with pride as Jack Scott congratulated them both, shook her hand, and wished her every happiness in her new role as Mrs Baldwin.

'I'll add my good wishes as well,' Peter said, holding out his hand to Brian. 'I won't be sailing for about a week, so perhaps I can come and see Molly in a day or two to catch up with all that has happened since I've been away?'

'Come and see her? There won't be any need for that, Peter, you're coming back to Hankin Street with us right now.'

'That's kind of you, but you don't need to put yourselves out for me. I've booked into the Sailors' Mission...'

'You'll stay with us for the rest of your leave, and whenever you come into port again in the future,' Brian told him firmly. 'Molly's home is home to you and Jodie, too, and don't you ever forget it.'

Whatever happened in the years ahead, Molly thought, smiling contentedly as she linked her arm through Brian's, he would always be there at her side to share not only her joys but also any problems. All her dreams of a man who loved her and a loving family were coming true at last. The past was very much behind her; the future stretched out ahead like a warm, welcoming hand.

The publishers hope that this book has given you enjoyable reading. Large Print Books are especially designed to be as easy to see and hold as possible. If you wish a complete list of our books please ask at your local library or write directly to:

Magna Large Print Books
Magna House, Long Preston,
Skipton, North Yorkshire.
BD23 4ND

This Large Print Book, for people
who cannot read normal print,
is published under the auspices of

THE ULVERSCROFT FOUNDATION

... we hope you have enjoyed this book.
Please think for a moment about those
who have worse eyesight than you ...
and are unable to even read or enjoy
Large Print without great difficulty.

You can help them by sending a
donation, large or small, to:

**The Ulverscroft Foundation,
1, The Green, Bradgate Road,
Anstey, Leicestershire, LE7 7FU,
England.**
or request a copy of our brochure for
more details.

The Foundation will use all donations
to assist those people who are visually
impaired and need special attention
with medical research, diagnosis
and treatment.

Thank you very much for your help.

A DREAM OF LOVE

by

Rosie Harris

Magna Large Print Books
Long Preston, North Yorkshire,
BD23 4ND, England.

MAGNA 18/9/08

British Library Cataloguing in Publication Data.

Harris, Rosie
    A dream of love.

    A catalogue record of this book is
    available from the British Library

    ISBN   978-0-7505-2934-1

First published in Great Britain in 2008 by Arrow Books

Copyright © Rosie Harris 2008

Cover illustration © Rod Ashford

Rosie Harris has asserted her right under the Copyright, Designs and Patents Act, 1988 to be identified as the author of this work

Published in Large Print 2008 by arrangement with Arrow, one of the publishers in The Random House Group Ltd.

All Rights reserved. No part of this publication may be reproduced, stored in a retrieval system, or transmitted in any form or by any means, electronic, mechanical, photocopying, recording or otherwise without the prior permission of the Copyright owner.

Magna Large Print is an imprint of Library Magna Books Ltd.

Printed and bound in Great Britain by
T.J. (International) Ltd., Cornwall, PL28 8RW